THE ARMAGEDDON CONSPIRACY

BY

MIKE HOCKNEY

HYPERREALITY BOOKS

Copyright © Mike Hockney 2009

The right of Mike Hockney to be identified as the author of this work has been asserted in accordance with sections 77 and 78 of the Copyright Designs and Patents Act 1988.

All characters in this book are fictitious,
and any resemblance to any actual persons,
living or dead, is purely coincidental.

All rights reserved. No part of this publication may be reproduced, stored in a retrieval system or transmitted in any form or by any means, electronic, mechanical, photocopy, recording, or otherwise, without the prior permission of the author.

Second Edition

ISBN 978-1-4452-0140-5

The Illuminati

'The madman sprang into their midst and pierced them with his glances. "Where has God gone?" he cried. "I shall tell you. *We have killed him* – you and I. We are all his murderers."'

Nietzsche

Foreword

The archive section of MI5's headquarters in Thames House, London, contains a document referred to as *The Cainite Destiny* that to this day has never been explained. On 22 May 1945, shortly after the end of WWII, British soldiers arrested SS-Sturmbannführer Friedrich Veldt, an adjutant to Reichsführer-SS Heinrich Himmler. The soldiers found a document concealed in a compartment in the heel of one of Veldt's shoes. As soon as MI5 officers questioned him about it, Veldt committed suicide by biting down on a cyanide capsule that he'd hidden in a fake tooth.

The document is a single page from Veldt's personal diary. The rest of has never been recovered and is presumed lost or destroyed. The entry describes the moment on 12 March 1938 when Hitler took possession of the Spear of Destiny – the lance thrust into the side of Jesus Christ at the Crucifixion.

Reinhardt Weiss, the German-born Cambridge University History professor employed by MI5 to translate and interpret the page, said its contents defied any conventional version of history, or of Nazism, of which he was aware. He believed it was the most significant document on earth and claimed the world's very future depended on it. When MI5 rejected his conclusions and dismissed *The Cainite Destiny* as the fantastic ramblings of a Nazi madman, Weiss gave up his job and moved to America to prepare for what he was certain was coming.

1

24 April 2012, London

Even before it happened, people knew it was coming. At three a.m. GMT, everyone in the world in every time zone felt the same sudden dread, as though the planet had stepped over its own grave. Not a single person chose to speak about it. Those who'd been woken from their sleep closed their eyes and prayed it was just a nightmare; those who were in their offices went back to their computers; those who were in the middle of conversations tried to continue with what they were saying.

By seven a.m. in London, the city was getting ready for what everyone prayed would be an ordinary Tuesday. Londoners went to work as usual, had the usual conversations with the usual people, made all the usual journeys on trains, buses and the Tube, performed all the usual routines. For the last month, a heat wave had gripped the southeast of England and today followed the same pattern. Most workers wore light summer clothing to try to make the sultry conditions more bearable. The next few hours passed normally.

At one p.m., Senior Analyst James Vernon left MI5's HQ overlooking the River Thames and went for lunch with his assistant Gary Caldwell. As always on these hot days, they went to the nearby open-air Italian café on the riverbank.

Vernon tried to take his mind off the task he and Caldwell were assigned first thing that morning. He'd seen many frightening intelligence reports over the years, but none to compare with the one that had landed on their desks five hours ago.

'I can't stop thinking about it,' Gary Caldwell said. 'That report…it…'

Vernon put his hand on his younger colleague's shoulder, trying to be supportive, but the gesture was half-hearted. He could barely support himself. As he looked around, everything appeared normal, but he knew there had never been a day like this.

He and Caldwell, following their normal routine, ordered identical lunches: penne arrabiata accompanied by mineral water. After a few minutes, Vernon excused himself and went to the toilet. Ever since three a.m., he'd been feeling unwell. Not in any specific way, in the sense that his whole life was somehow wrong.

When he rubbed his hands together, he was disgusted by how clammy they were. At 5'11" and 170 pounds, he was an athletic man – MI5's current squash champion – and people often commented on how rarely he sweated, but now his shirt clung to him. Even though he was only thirty, he liked to portray the image of a tough, unruffled senior member of the secret services. His colleagues nicknamed him Captain Scarlet after the TV puppet character because of his blue eyes and short, neat black hair. Before three a.m., he thought he was as unfazed and indestructible as the good captain, but it was long after three and everything had changed.

Trying to urinate, he couldn't manage a drop. He turned away, went to the basin, washed his hands then stared into the mirror. Just for a second, he thought he caught a glimpse of his own ghost. F. Scott Fitzgerald's line ran through his mind: *In the real dark night of the soul it is always three o'clock in the morning.* Somehow, he'd become that three o'clock man.

He stood there, his hands shaking. Was he having a breakdown? Over and over in his mind, the details of the intelligence report rewound themselves. Vulcanologists all across the world had reported a dramatic increase in volcanic activity. There were approximately 1600 volcanoes in the world and they were producing alarming signs of pre-eruption activity. *All of them.*

Leaving the toilet, Vernon made his way back to his table. As he weaved between tables, several things happened at once, almost blurring into each other so that when he later tried to recall the precise sequence, he couldn't. All the lunchers, including Caldwell, had stopped eating and were staring at the sky. Some were open-mouthed, others reaching for their mobile phones.

All along both banks of the Thames, thousands of Londoners and tourists stood perfectly still, their gaze fixed upwards.

It took Vernon a moment to register that it was no longer sunny. Also, he could now hear the oddest of sounds – an ear-grating screeching coming from directly above. Reflexively, he clamped his hands over his ears.

Caldwell, pushing his chair back, stood up and craned his neck upwards. '*Jesus fucking Christ.*' The young man pointed his picture-phone upwards and started to snap images. 'There must be millions of them. I swear, the sky was empty a few seconds ago.'

When he looked up at the sky, Vernon felt sick. A witch's curse had come to life. There, overhead, was a seething black mass, like a bubbling cauldron. Birds – sparrows, rooks, swallows, jackdaws, seagulls, starlings, pigeons, magpies, buzzards, thrushes – were wheeling and flocking in countless numbers. They were flying in from every direction, huge formations of them, great V-shapes cutting through the air, squawking, squealing, cawing.

The sky, so blue a minute earlier, was now visibly pink in the few places where it could still be glimpsed through the bird formations, and was rapidly getting redder.

'We better get back to HQ.' Vernon slapped a twenty-pound note on the table and he and Caldwell shoved their way through the throng.

As they hurried past a shop on their route back, Vernon stopped, his attention caught by a TV in a shop window, showing the lunchtime news.

'Don't you recognise that?' He pointed at a building on the screen.

Caldwell shook his head.

'We need to hear what they're saying,' Vernon said, leading Caldwell inside.

'Axum is Ethiopia's holiest city,' a sweating reporter declared, 'and the building behind me its most sacred shrine. This small, unspectacular building is known as *The Treasury*, and has been the centre of obsessive curiosity for decades. The Patriarch of Ethiopia's Orthodox Church has refused to make a statement, but rumours are rife. What is certain is that the people of Axum are inconsolable. They're claiming that the odd phenomena being witnessed all across the world in the last few hours are a direct consequence of this sacrilegious act.'

'Are you following any of this?' Caldwell asked.

'Sshhh,' Vernon said. On vacation last year, he'd had his photo taken outside the very building now on the screen. Like every tourist, he'd been dying to see what was inside, but that was something permitted to only the person who permanently lived there.

'Until we hear officially from the authorities,' the reporter went on, 'I can't tell you anything more about the alleged theft of the western world's most potent religious symbol. Ethiopia's claims to possess this holiest of objects have always been controversial, but many experts have insisted there *is* persuasive evidence that this small building in Axum contained the sacred treasure.'

'I don't believe this.' Vernon's three a.m. feeling was back worse than ever.

'However, for the time being,' the reporter concluded, 'we are no closer to discovering if it has indeed been stolen. The whole world now anxiously awaits news of its fate…the fabled Ark of the Covenant.'

2

Three Days Later

Situation Room, MI5 Headquarters, Thames House, London

Some people were in tears, others bowing their heads in prayer. James Vernon stared at the matrix of TV monitors that were showing pictures coming in from across the globe. The Situation Room, with more than a hundred members of staff crammed inside, was a bland, magnolia-painted space. Much of it resembled a call centre filled with dozens of featureless booths and black plastic seats. Enormous screens on the front wall showed virtual reality computer simulations of whatever situation was the present focus of analysis. Currently, several had crashed and IT consultants were trying to resolve the problems. The TVs remained in full working order, though many people in the room wished they hadn't.

'God help us,' Caldwell groaned as a *Breaking News* sign flashed across the *Sky News* feed. A ticker tape message ran along the bottom of the screen saying, 'Vatican confirms death of Pope. Time of world crisis. Election of new Pope to take place immediately. Sacred College of Cardinals already assembling in Sistine Chapel.'

Vernon put his hand to his head. He wasn't a Catholic but somehow this news was more devastating than the rest. Hours earlier, he had watched the Pope giving a speech in front of millions of stunned people packed into St Peter's Square. Unlike the UK's prime minister and the American president, the Pope had managed to capture the world's mood. While the politicians talked of facts and figures and practical steps to be taken, the Pope spoke of his own frailty, his private fears, of how he could hardly bear to think of the suffering being endured by so many.

'This is humanity's night in Gethsemane,' he said. 'Our Golgotha is surely not far away. Only God can save us now.' Then one of his aides handed him a note. As soon as he looked at it, the Pope collapsed, clutching his heart. The Vatican had still refused to divulge the note's contents.

Vernon shuddered. *Only God can save us now.* Days ago he would have laughed but now he felt like getting on his knees to pray like so many others flocking into churches, temples, synagogues and mosques all over the world.

'Our sins have brought this punishment upon us,' religious leaders were saying. According to atheists, it was a freak combination of natural disasters caused by worsening global warming, but even they were running scared. They whispered of tipping points being passed, of possible ELEs: Extinction Level Events. Just a different way of saying what the holy men had already pronounced – maybe the end of the world was really happening.

It now seemed bizarre that people were so slow to respond to that first sign three days earlier. They all experienced the 'three a.m. event', as it was now being called, but everyone ignored it. Then animals everywhere on the planet started behaving oddly, scampering around in every direction, whelping and whining. It wasn't just some animals – it was all of them. Cats, dogs, horses, lions, elephants, rats, reptiles, insects, the whole list: stampeding, running, scurrying, fleeing, desperately trying to find whatever refuge they could. People still tried to pretend there was nothing to worry about. It was only when the swarms of birds appeared over the cities that it became impossible to deny something catastrophic was taking place.

As one of MI5's senior intelligence analysts, James Vernon was seconded onto an emergency team that included his most talented MI6 counterparts, and experts with high security clearance from top universities. For the last three days, he and his colleagues had waded through classified reports from British agents in every part of the world. It was his job to collate all of the data, summarise it and present it to MI5 and MI6's decision makers.

A week earlier, he'd been thinking he was at the top of his game, that fast-track career opportunities to the top of the organisation were lining up for him. Now he doubted he'd see his thirty-first birthday. He felt so exhausted, mentally and physically. There was a security shutdown and no one had been permitted to leave the building for the last thirty-six hours. He'd snatched a few fitful hours of sleep in the rest room, but it wasn't enough. The Director General had sanctioned the use of amphetamines to combat tiredness.

Vernon glanced around at his colleagues. Everyone was as dishevelled as he was. The sour reek of body odour was everywhere. Even the women, normally immaculately turned out, had abandoned their grooming routines.

'Coffee?' Caldwell asked.

Vernon nodded. He was in the habit of stretching his legs every half hour: anything to avoid staring at the data on his computer and the pictures on the TVs.

The two men went to the vending machine and each selected a strong black coffee. In the old days, they would have gone to the window and admired the view over the Thames while they sipped their drinks. Now, the blinds were permanently drawn. No one in their right mind would enjoy looking at what was out there. Without speaking, the two analysts took their drinks and headed in the opposite direction, towards the small lounge adjoining the Situation Room.

'We can't keep running away,' Vernon said, stopping abruptly.

Caldwell peered at him. Only twenty-two-years-old and fresh from Cambridge University, the younger man was already impressing as an analyst. At 6'4'', he was an ungainly figure, notorious for his ill-fitting suits, but no one doubted his ability.

As they made their way back to the window, several of their colleagues watched them. Vernon pulled on the cord to open the blinds.

'What does he think he's doing?' one of the analysts grunted.

Even though it was a spring afternoon, no light came into the room, just a fluttering darkness. The birds were out there, just as they had for the last three days, going round in circles. It was as though they were trying to find some place of safety but always failing. So they just kept flying. Many had dropped dead from the sky, exhausted. All air traffic had to be suspended; no planes could fly through the swarms. The ground was covered with bird droppings. On the first day, the authorities tried to clean it away. On the second day they gave up. The smell was appalling. Thousands of dead birds lay rotting in their own excrement in every street.

Black vultures that had flown north from Spain took a liking to the Gothic buildings along the Thames and settled on the roofs like medieval gargoyles. But it was the crows that unnerved people, looking as though they'd come straight from hell. When they swooped low over people's houses, they stared with dead, black eyes at anyone who dared to look back.

Vernon rapped his knuckles against the triple-glazed windows, relieved they so effectively blocked out the sound of the outside world. Some people claimed they would get used to the noise – the interminable racket of the screeching birds – just as they had to aircraft noise in the past, but he wasn't one of them.

Jesus!

He recoiled as a black object came hurtling towards the window. At the last moment, he ducked. A crow thudded into the centre and disintegrated. Mush oozed down the windowpane. The crow's blood matched the queer new colour of London's sky. In the brief moments when it appeared through the gaps in the bird mass, it threw a sickly, rust-coloured light over the city that had caused headaches, nausea and migraines to reach epidemic proportions. At sunrise and sunset, the light was particularly lurid, forming great impressionistic coloured streaks across the sky as though some mad artist was at work.

'Close the damned blinds,' a woman snapped.

Vernon pulled the cord and turned away, his queasiness worse than ever.

'I bet you're glad your wife and baby are well out of all this,' Caldwell said. 'Sweden, isn't it?'

'That's right.' Vernon was confident there was nowhere on earth safer than the island of Björkö, eighteen miles from Stockholm, where Anna was living on a farm with baby Louise. But it wasn't a recent move: Anna left him six months ago. 'What about you?' he asked. 'No girlfriend waiting for you somewhere?' In all the time he'd spent with Caldwell, Vernon had never once asked his colleague about his private life.

The response was typically terse. 'No one special.'

Talking was difficult for everyone. The whole of Thames House had surrendered to a peculiar quiet. Voices, when they were heard at all, rarely rose above a whisper. The volume controls on the TV monitors were turned down so that people could barely hear what was being said. Everyone preferred it that way.

The two men finished their coffees and returned to their desks. Vernon found it impossible to concentrate. When governments realised they couldn't conceal what was happening then, for good or ill, they let the media floodgates open, and now one grotesque image rapidly followed another.

Vernon stared at the space on his desk where the framed picture of his wife and baby once took pride of place. Now it lay at the back of his top drawer. The future was all he thought about when Louise was born eight months ago. Now he wondered if she had one: if anyone did. At least Louise was too young to understand.

He kept a second photograph, this one in his bottom drawer, as far from his reach as he could manage. It wasn't of his wife or child. A picture of a ghost, maybe – it had haunted his marriage from the beginning.

Reluctantly, he focused on the TV pictures. He'd never get some of these images out of his mind. Two days earlier, a series of apocalyptic earthquakes hit Turkey, destroying forty percent of the country. Istanbul was in ruins. Millions were dead, their mangled bodies lying in open view as overwhelmed emergency services dug trenches to bury the corpses. In some places, the bodies were gathered into mountainous heaps and set on fire.

In Southeast Asia, two Tsunamis, triggered by huge underwater earthquakes, struck one after another. Most people managed to escape the first, but not the second. No one dared estimate the number of dead. Then reports came in from Thailand telling of people being healthy at breakfast time but dead by noon. They'd complained of nothing more than a sudden heavy cold, but virulent avian flu was soon diagnosed, the start of the lethal pandemic the experts had feared for so long. Despite attempts to impose quarantine zones, it was spreading rapidly across Asia. It wouldn't be long until it reached Europe.

Everyone knew it was just the beginning. The most obvious sign was the sky. Across the world, it was changing colour, turning to the blood red now so familiar to Londoners. The history books said there had been nothing like this since Krakatoa in 1883. That volcanic eruption produced the loudest sound ever recorded by humans. The veil of dust it threw into the sky blocked so much sunlight that the global temperature was reduced by 1.2 degrees Celsius. The deflection of the sunlight from the suspended dust particles changed the sky's colour for months. Normal weather was disrupted for years. A sideshow, apparently, compared with what was happening now.

South of the Equator, storms covering hundreds of square miles were raging, lit by flashes of lightning so fierce that the U.S. meteorological planes monitoring them said they resembled atomic bombs detonating. The video images they transmitted to TV stations were extraordinary. It seemed the weather systems of hell had come to earth.

Vernon closed his eyes and gripped the edge of his desk. As a kid, whenever something on the TV frightened him, his parents told him that if he shut his eyes, the 'monsters' would vanish. Not in the adult world: here, they just got bigger and loomed ever closer.

He heard a gasp and hesitantly opened his eyes. Everyone was still looking at the screens, but all the monitors now showed the same image – a yellow screen imprinted with three flashing scarlet letters: **UGT**. It was the first time in history it had happened. Vernon swivelled round on his chair and gazed at the analysts sitting behind him. They were as stunned as he was. UGT was known as the 'Word of God' because no one was sure whether it really existed, and it only appeared if it was time to say your prayers.

'Now it's official,' Gary Caldwell mumbled.

Vernon swallowed hard. It was official all right: **U**nspecified **G**lobal **T**hreat.

3

'James Vernon, please go to the detention cells immediately,' a voice said over the tannoy.

Vernon got up from his seat, grabbed the jacket of his suit from its hanger, and headed for the door. All around him, UGT kept flashing. The UGT protocols could be declared only if every government in the world concurred because they meant that each service had to share its secrets with its rivals to combat the common danger – usually anticipated as an extraterrestrial threat of some sort.

Vernon shook his head. Once you let others see your secrets, that was it. Right now, requests from all over the world would be arriving, asking for access to the highest security files, the 'black' files, forbidden to all but MI5's most senior staff, and MI5 would be doing exactly the same in reverse.

As he walked along one of the endless corridors in Thames House, heading for the central block of lifts, Vernon wished the building wasn't so enormous. Built in 1930, it had two symmetrical wings connected by a linking block, and visitors always fretted about getting lost. The miles of corridors kept the staff fit, that was for sure. With its riverside location and neoclassical architectural style, Thames House was once described as 'the finest office building in the British Empire'. Its elegant façade was made of Portland stone, decorated with several fine sculptures. Not a building you'd normally associate with the secret services, but the perfect stage, Vernon thought, for the grim announcements that would surely be made in the next day or two.

The bulletproof windows in the corridors didn't benefit from blinds. Normally, Vernon hurried past, but now he stopped, morbidly drawn to look at what London had become. The streets were deserted. It was frightening how fast the city had gone from thriving metropolis to ghost town. Although Europe and North America were largely untouched by the natural disasters, normal life had come to a standstill even here.

Most Londoners fled from their workplaces as soon as the birds appeared and never went back, the stock market suffered the greatest crash in history, and the transport system was overwhelmed. For once, the Government responded fast, using an emergency plan drawn up years earlier in anticipation of London suffering a catastrophic terrorist attack. Within 36 hours, military and police control was fully established. Only a skeleton Tube service operated now, and it stopped at 8 p.m. when the curfew began. Army convoys rolled through empty streets. Under the Government's emergency powers, all of the major utilities – gas, electricity, water, telephones, fuel – were brought under central control until further notice, and key personnel were being forced to work whether they liked it or not. Tanks and barricades ringed Parliament, and similar arrangements had been made at all key civic and administrative buildings. Most TV and radio programmes were cancelled, replaced by constant news reports. Newspapers were still being produced, but probably not for much longer.

It was only natural, Vernon thought, that people wanted to be with their families at a time like this, those lucky enough to have them. Most of those still at work had nowhere else to go.

At first, the Director General ordered every member of staff to remain at their posts. Soldiers prevented anyone from leaving, but some people became hysterical, begging to be allowed to go home to their families. For practical reasons, the DG relented; there was simply no point in trying to get productive work from staff no longer mentally fit for duty. The majority of the family types were allowed out. A handful, determined to do their duty, stayed behind. Practically all of the non-attached members of staff volunteered to remain.

Vernon wondered if he ought to have tried to get to Sweden, but he didn't want to spend his last hours with the wife he didn't love, and seeing baby Louise would make him unbearably sad. There was only one person he wanted to be with at a time like this, but there was no chance of that particular reunion happening.

Six crows swooped down and perched on the window ledge, staring at him. He banged on the window to frighten them off, but they didn't move.

Making his way down the corridor once more, he swore as he tripped over piles of litter – mostly crisp packets, chocolate wrappers and Coke cans. Conditions in Thames House had deteriorated fast. Bins hadn't been emptied for days. The toilets were in a foul condition, many blocked and leaking. Everything throughout the building stank.

The corridors were practically deserted. A couple of days earlier, the activity was frantic, with everyone racing backwards and forwards from one emergency meeting to the next. Not now. In a way, Vernon was glad. Several times, he'd bumped into people in tears, and he'd been unsure what to do. Console them? Ignore them? Tell them to get a grip? Tell bad jokes? Nothing seemed right.

It surprised him how many beautiful women were still left. When he was a teenager, he always imagined that if he were told the world were ending, he would find as many gorgeous women as possible for sex. Now, he realised, no one would be having sex as the world ended. Imminent extinction wasn't any kind of turn-on.

As he was about to step into the lift, he got a call on his mobile phone. Caldwell informed him that within seconds of the UGT declaration, identical requests had come in from three completely different sources. They all wanted an obscure document called *The Cainite Destiny*. It was the identities of the three intelligence organisations that was so intriguing – *Mossad*, the Israeli intelligence service, *Bundesrichtendienst*, the German foreign intelligence service, and *Sodalitium Pianum*, the Vatican's ultra-secretive intelligence service.

'The Vatican, the Israelis and the Germans?' Vernon blurted. 'What the hell is this document they all want?'

'I'm looking at our database entry right now,' Caldwell replied. 'It says *The Cainite Destiny* is a single page from a diary. It was written in 1938 and came into our possession at the end of WWII. Only three people have accessed it since then. Two of them were Director Generals, and that was several decades ago. The third was your boss: *twenty-four hours ago*.'

'Are you certain?'

'That's what the database says.'

'What's the high-level description of this document?'

'*The Cainite Destiny* was handwritten in German by one of Heinrich Himmler's senior adjutants. The British army arrested him after the German surrender in 1945. According to our database, this document gives some inexplicable version of the Nazis' ideology, based on the occult. A professor analysed the document and said its implications were terrifying. His interpretation was rejected out of hand. Nevertheless, the document was given the highest possible security classification because it was feared it was a coded reference to a Nazi plot that might be resurrected by neo-Nazis at some future date.'

There was a long pause. Vernon wondered why Caldwell had stopped speaking. 'What is it?'

'Listen to this. The reason the document is called *The Cainite Destiny* is that it suggests a direct link between the Nazis and the Biblical figure Cain.' He hesitated again. 'And there's one more thing.'

The Nazis and Cain? Vernon shook his head. Hokum. Why would three of the world's best intelligence services be giving something like this even the slightest credence? And why had his boss looked at it so recently? 'Come on,' he said. 'I don't have time to mess around. What's the final thing?'

'Sir, it predicts the end of the world.'

Vernon swallowed hard. Once, those words seemed so abstract. One day, they were certain to come true. He just hadn't expected it to be in his own lifetime.

He pushed the button to call the lift. As he waited, he studied the MI5 crest above the lift doors, showing a combination of a golden, winged sea-lion on a blue background; six red roses; three five-pointed green cinquefoil heraldic flowers, and three portcullises. The crest also displayed MI5's motto: *Regnum Defende* – Defend the Realm. Right now, Vernon didn't know from what he was defending it. Hitler reaching out from the grave?

When the lift doors opened, Vernon was startled to see Old Harry, the veteran lift operator. Still in his pristine bottle-green uniform, Old Harry hadn't abandoned any of his normal habits.

'Good afternoon, sir.' Old Harry squinted at Vernon's badge.

Vernon couldn't believe he was still having his ID checked. Perhaps it was reassuring: the world hadn't completely gone to pieces if Old Harry was still following the rules. He'd even taken the trouble to spray the lift with air freshener – a welcome relief from the sour smell that permeated the building.

Vernon stepped inside and the doors swooshed shut.

'Which floor?' Old Harry asked.

'Basement.'

'Right you are, sir.'

Vernon couldn't avoid seeing himself in the lift's mirror. An exhausted man gazed back, with black rings round his eyes, a gaunt face, a crumpled suit and crooked tie. He took out a comb and tried to tidy himself up.

The lift stopped and the doors opened again. A girl came in, dabbing her eyes. Vernon looked away. They'd had a casual fling on a training course in Cardiff six months earlier. Another ghost of the past.

'Well, don't acknowledge me,' she snapped.

That's all I need, Vernon thought as he awkwardly stepped past her into the detention block's reception area.

'Good luck,' Old Harry said as the lift doors closed.

Vernon nodded half-heartedly then watched as the changing lights on the panel above the lift doors showed the lift making its way to the top floor. It wouldn't be long before the lifts were shut down; too much of a drain on the building's limited electricity. MI5 and MI6 had already taken themselves off the National Grid and were using their own generators to ensure they didn't suffer power cuts. Soon, everyone would be tramping up and down stairs.

He placed his security smartcard against the electronic reader and pushed through the turnstile. Glancing at the security guard, he noticed that the man was clutching a set of Catholic Rosary beads. He tried to think of something to say, but nothing came. Normally, he would make a comment about football, but every game had been cancelled and it seemed meaningless now.

'*Sir*,' the guard said once he'd gone past.

Vernon stopped and turned. 'Yes?'

The guard fidgeted. 'Sorry, nothing. It's just that...'

'What?'

'Can't you feel it? Ever since they brought that man in...'

'What man?'

'Isn't that why you're here?' The guard lowered his head and went back to counting his Rosary beads.

Vernon shrugged and headed for the coffee machine. The world was full of riddles these days. He needed something to wake him up before the next shock arrived. It wouldn't be long judging from what the guard had said. The cells definitely weren't a place for innocent meetings.

He'd rather have stayed in the Situation Room. There was so much new work to be done now that UGT had been called. Strange times required the strangest procedures. Computer programs would be searching databases for any documents that mentioned words like Armageddon, Apocalypse, End of the World, Doomsday, Extinction, End Times, Judgment Day. Analysts would be scrutinising prophecies by every nut and mystic. Even an old favourite like Nostradamus, debunked or not, would be back in the frame. It was the moment when the secret services gave credence to the supernatural. Not because they believed any of it, but because there was nothing else to go on. And those programs would no doubt soon locate *The Cainite Destiny*. He hoped he'd get an opportunity to study it.

He vaguely recalled something about *Godwin's Law* having a habit of cropping up everywhere. The precise wording, if he remembered right, was, 'As an online discussion grows longer, the probability of a comparison involving Nazis or Hitler approaches one – certainty.' The same was obviously true of apocalyptic predictions.

Maybe it wasn't so odd that the supernatural was being taken seriously. Right from New Year's Day, newspapers were reminding their readers that the Mayans long ago predicted that the world would end on 21 December 2012. It started as a bit of a joke, one of the 'things to look out for this year', but no one was laughing now. On top of that, the only notable thing that happened immediately before the chaos descended was the series of spectacular thefts that had grabbed worldwide attention, seemingly taking place at precisely that three a.m. moment when the whole planet shivered.

The Treasury in Axum was just one of seven high-profile locations raided by expert thieves. It soon became obvious they were looking for very particular, highly prized artefacts, all of a religious nature. Religious leaders were openly saying that these thefts were the cause of the natural catastrophes. They were the ultimate insult to God, they claimed, forcing him to decide that humanity must be purged, just as in the original End Days of Noah's Flood.

Hysterical nonsense, Vernon thought, but always there lurked that one flicker of doubt. After all, not only had the thieves apparently stolen the Ark of the Covenant, they were also said to have found perhaps the most elusive treasure of them all.

The Holy Grail.

4

Vernon wasn't sure what he'd been expecting when he arrived in the detention area, but it wasn't this. These cells hadn't been used in anger for years; prisoners nowadays were taken to the high-security police facility at Paddington Green.

Soldiers in camouflage uniforms were everywhere. There was an odd atmosphere: the soldiers silent and visibly agitated. Normally, soldiers could be relied on for their black humour. Not these ones. Whoever the mystery prisoner was, his presence had spooked them.

Vernon was starting to feel the same way. He guessed that a terrorist had been apprehended, someone who needed to be interrogated immediately. His boss probably wanted him to provide detailed background intelligence on the prisoner, to try to work out his movements over the last twenty-four hours, discover who was helping him and so forth. Maybe the terrorist had tried to take advantage of the current chaos to stage a 'spectacular'.

When he reached the battleship-grey block that contained the detention cells and interview rooms, a soldier inspected his ID badge.

'Commander Harrington is waiting for you in Room One,' the soldier said. He was jumpy, his eyes darting around.

'Why all the extra security?' Vernon asked.

'You'll soon find out.' The soldier knocked on the iron door. A second soldier looked through a viewing slit then opened the door.

Vernon stepped into the main detention block with its austere walls and worn-out black and white floor tiles, his unease accelerating fast. He loosened his tie.

The soldier who greeted him was nervous and on edge. He escorted Vernon to the main interview room, knocked, then punched in a security code to open the door.

The first thing Vernon noticed as he entered the room was the polished black table in the centre, at which two men were sitting. One was his pin-stripe-suited, fifty-year-old boss Charles Harrington; the other a black man wearing the uniform of a colonel in the U.S. Marine Corps, and with a typically severe military crew cut.

The American stood up and held out his hand. 'I'm Colonel Brad Gresnick of the Defence Intelligence Agency. I've just flown in from the Pentagon.'

Vernon peered at him. A clean-cut type, probably in his early thirties, the colonel was over six feet tall and about 190 pounds, with a muscular build. Vernon didn't like to acknowledge it, but Gresnick was a dead ringer for Hollywood's top black heart-throb actor Jez Easton. Immediately, he felt a desire to put Gresnick down. A by-the-numbers soldier, he decided, a yes man who'd do anything to climb the greasy pole.

Vernon was no fan of the DIA, having worked with them a couple of times before. They were the military counterparts of the CIA, responsible for gathering foreign military intelligence, analysing military threats to America, making sure the American armed services were ready for any eventuality. They provided the Secretary of Defence and Joint Chiefs of Staff with all the information they needed to make decisions. Vernon found them pedantic, lacking the flair of the CIA. What was one of their men doing over here at a time like this?

'I thought all flights were suspended because of the birds,' Vernon said.

'Military flights have special equipment for dispersing them.' Gresnick resumed his seat.

'Sit down, Mr Vernon,' Commander Harrington said. 'We have a lot to get through.'

Putting down his coffee, Vernon took a seat opposite the others. Numerous documents were laid out on the table, all bearing 'Classified: Eyes Only' stamps. Next to the paperwork, sitting on a black cloth, was a translucent globe, emerald green in colour, the size of a tennis ball. A paperweight of some kind, Vernon thought. Finally, there was a small microphone.

'Why don't you bring Mr Vernon up to speed, colonel?' Harrington said.

Gresnick nodded. 'Four days ago, the thirty men of our top Delta Force unit went awol from their base at Fort Bragg. Within twenty-four hours, one of our analysts discovered an extraordinary and hitherto unknown connection between all of them. Without exception, they were grandchildren of members of *Section 5*, a military intelligence unit from World War Two. In April and May of 1945, Section 5 interrogated Nazi officials responsible for part of the vast treasure hoard the Nazis looted from all over Europe. The treasures these particular Nazis looked after were of an esoteric, religious nature, and were stored in deep bunkers beneath Nuremberg Castle.'

'That's quite a story.' Vernon realised he was going to have trouble avoiding the Nazis today.

'All these Delta Force guys were single and childless,' Gresnick said. 'Before they deserted, they sold their homes and withdrew all of their money from their bank accounts.'

Vernon had no idea what any of this had to do with MI5. Intriguing for sure, but it seemed like an internal American Army issue, of trivial importance given world events.

'You're probably wondering what the punchline is,' Gresnick said. 'No doubt you're aware of the recent thefts of religious artefacts from various sites around the world.'

Vernon nodded. Three of the seven sites were in the British Isles.

'The DIA has concluded that all of the thefts bore the hallmarks of operations by U.S. Special Forces – unauthorised, I must emphasise. We're certain these deserters were responsible.'

Vernon sat upright. 'Why would American Special Forces go renegade and start stealing religious relics?'

Gresnick slid a folder towards Vernon.

'Finish your coffee and take a few minutes to read that file. I think I can safely say it's the strangest document you'll ever read.'

5

Defense Intelligence Agency
Classified: Eyes Only
For circulation amongst Sigma Access Group only

Alpha Summary – supposed theft of iconic religious artefacts as hypothetical cause of current global environmental instability.

Beta Summary: On 24 April 2012, at 3 a.m. GMT, seven locations said to be associated with three famous religious relics were raided. All of the raids were synchronised and took place under cover of darkness. Within hours of the raids, reports came in from across the globe of cataclysmic earthquakes, an alarming increase in volcanic activity, formation of multiple category-5 hurricanes, and acute weather conditions in almost every country. The colour of the sky across the earth was observed to start changing to blood red.

Religious leaders declared that the thefts were a blasphemy and the direct cause of the natural disasters. They demanded the safe return of the treasures and stated that, otherwise, the world would suffer the 'Wrath of God.'

All governments agreed that the severity of the natural disasters posed an unprecedented threat to the future of life on earth. The United Nations met in emergency session to coordinate a global response. It was decided a twin-track approach should be adopted. While scientific solutions were urgently sought, governments would, at the least, pay lip service to the possibility of the current crisis having a supernatural origin. To prevent possible religious hysteria breaking out amongst billions of believers, governments of all major powers agreed to use their intelligence services to apprehend the thieves and retrieve the stolen artefacts.

At present, scientists have been unable to account for the pattern of extreme environmental events. Investigations, analysis and data gathering are ongoing. Emergency conferences involving the world's leading scientific experts have been organised and will be given the full support of all governments. Religious leaders will also be consulted about ways forward. For the sake of public morale, it's critical for governments to be seen to be taking all possible courses of action at this time.

****

(His Eminence Thomas Cardinal Lenihan of the Archdiocese of New York and Rabbi Dr. Menachem Grien, Professor of Theology at Columbia University, were consulted in the preparation of the following.)

The three holy relics said to be connected with the seven raids are the most famous in Western religious history:
1) The Ark of the Covenant
2) The Holy Grail.
3) The Spear of Destiny.

The seven locations raided are:
1) Temple Mount, Jerusalem.
2) The Church of Saint Mary of Zion, Axum, Ethiopia.
3) Chalice Well, Glastonbury, England.
4) Schatzkammer (Imperial Treasury), Hofburg Palace, Vienna, Austria.
5) Oak Island, Nova Scotia, Canada.
6) Rosslyn Chapel, Edinburgh, Scotland.
7) Hill of Tara, Republic of Ireland.

Brief descriptions of the three artefacts are provided below:

1) The Ark of the Covenant
A portable wooden vessel, the size of a large chest and overlaid inside and out with gold. According to the Book of Exodus, God commanded Moses to

make the Ark and furnished him with a precise set of instructions. The Ark was the container for the two stone tablets inscribed with the Ten Commandments. The Ark was mentioned many times in the Old Testament before abruptly vanishing. Many conflicting theories have been proposed concerning its fate and current whereabouts.

In the present context, it is important to highlight that the Ark was considered to have many dangerous properties, including the characteristics of an early Weapon of Mass Destruction.

The following is a list of powers attributed to the Ark:

1) Levitation: it could raise itself and other nearby objects off the ground.
2) It emitted light and sparks.
3) It had a flamethrower capability, which it allegedly used to kill two sons of Aaron, the Ark's first High Priest.
4) It was associated with a fiery cloud that materialised above it and from which a voice spoke to Moses and Aaron.
5) It could induce leprosy and tumours in people.
6) Those who touched it without permission, even accidentally, usually died. Ordinary people could not safely approach within half a mile of it.
7) During battles, it rose into the air, emitted a terrifying sound and sped into the heart of the enemy army. In one battle, it allegedly killed 50,000 enemy soldiers.
8) During the siege of Jericho, Jewish priests circled the city on seven separate days. Some priests blew trumpets as they went round the city walls while others carried the Ark in procession using special poles so that they did not come into direct contact with it. It has been speculated that the Ark may have amplified and directed the sound waves like a sonic cannon, eventually bringing down the walls of Jericho.
9) The High Priest had to wear special protective clothing whenever he approached the Ark.
10) When the Ark killed Hebrews, Moses insisted that their bodies be taken far from the Israelites' camp to be buried, contrary to normal religious practice. No explanation was ever offered as to why Moses took these extraordinary precautions.
11) The Ark was said to give off a dazzling supernatural radiance.

2) The Holy Grail

Usually defined as the cup used by Christ at the Last Supper. This event supposedly took place in the house of Joseph of Arimathea who may have been Jesus' uncle. Reputedly, Joseph used the cup to catch a few drops of the blood shed by Jesus at the Crucifixion, and the blood was said to be miraculously preserved in the cup. Another legend said that the cup was originally made for Abraham, the great patriarch of the Hebrew People. Like the Ark of the Covenant, the Grail was said to emit an unearthly radiance.

Other theories say that the Grail is a dish, a stone, a person (Mary Magdalene), the head of Jesus, the skeleton of Jesus, or even Jesus' bloodline following his alleged marriage to Mary Magdalene and birth of a daughter. As with the Ark, many conflicting theories have been proposed concerning its fate and current whereabouts.

3) The Spear of Destiny
A Roman Centurion thrust this spear into Christ's side as he hung on the cross. The spear was highly prized, and many powerful figures throughout history went out of their way to possess it, including several emperors of the Holy Roman Empire and Adolf Hitler.

It became a museum piece and was put on display in a prestigious palace in Vienna as part of the Imperial Regalia of the Holy Roman Empire. Note that the Holy Roman Empire is sometimes referred to as the *First Reich*. Bismarck created the *Second Reich* and Hitler ruled over the *Third Reich*.

****

Brief descriptions of the seven locations that were raided are provided below:

1) Temple Mount, Jerusalem
Temple Mount contains secret underground passageways that belonged to the original Temple of Solomon and survived the temple's destruction by the Babylonians in 586 BCE.

The raiders on 24 April blasted open one of the sealed tunnels using plastic explosives. There is evidence that the explosives were detonated using timers. However, no indication has been found that anyone entered the tunnel or that anything was removed. The Israeli Defence Force has sealed off the area, and no one is currently being granted access. No further investigations are possible at this time.

Rioting broke out in Jerusalem within minutes of the explosions, with Muslims accusing Jews of attempting to blow up the Dome of the Rock – one of Islam's holiest sites. The gold-domed mosque is built above the ruins of the Temple of Solomon and the later Temple of Herod.

2) Treasury of the Church of Saint Mary of Zion, Axum, Ethiopia
Axum is Ethiopia's holiest city, and the Church of Saint Mary of Zion its holiest church. *The Treasury*, a separate building located just behind the church, was said to house the Ark of the Covenant, supposedly brought there by Menelik I, the son of King Solomon and the Queen of Sheba. (Menelik means 'son of the wise man', and the ancient kingdom of Sheba is believed to have incorporated Ethiopia.) A monk known as the Keeper of the Ark

protected the Ark at all times. He was shot dead during the raid. The Ethiopian authorities did not allow investigators to enter *The Treasury*. They refused to confirm that the object they claimed was the Ark of the Covenant was taken.

3) Chalice Well, Glastonbury, England
Legend says that Joseph of Arimathea was imprisoned after Jesus' death. When he was released, he fled from the Holy Land and took the Holy Grail to the safe haven of Glastonbury in England. He hid the Grail at the bottom of Chalice Well at the foot of Glastonbury Tor, a sacred mound overlooking the town of Glastonbury. The well's water is allegedly tinged red and reputed to have healing powers. The April 24 raiders climbed into the well and removed a section of the well's wall, revealing a small, rust-free iron chamber, previously unknown. There is no indication of what, if anything, they discovered.

4) Schatzkammer (Imperial Treasury), Hofburg Palace, Vienna, Austria
The Schatzkammer houses the Imperial Regalia of the Holy Roman Empire: the European empire created by Charlemagne and dissolved centuries later by Napoleon Bonaparte. The only item stolen from the collection of treasures was the so-called Spear of Destiny. All alarm systems and CCTV cameras at the Hofburg Palace were disabled during the raid. A top-secret tranquillising gas knocked out security guards. Only U.S. and U.K. Special Forces are known to have access to this gas.

5) Oak Island, Nova Scotia, Canada
A small, remote island off the east coast of Canada, practically uninhabited, and reputed to be the site of a vast, inaccessible buried treasure located at the bottom of a booby-trapped, intricately constructed 200-feet-deep vertical shaft known as the *Money Pit*. Originally, pirates were thought to have buried the treasure; Captain Kidd and Blackbeard being the most likely candidates. However, some experts have said pirates lacked the engineering skills to construct such a complex structure. Leonardo Da Vinci has been mentioned as a possible designer of the pit. Other theories claim that Freemasons or the Knights Templar created it. Following the forcible arrest of the Knights Templar in 1307, those leaders of the Order who managed to evade capture gave instructions for their treasure to be hidden from their enemies. It was removed by the ships of the Templar Fleet and vanished from history. Some accounts say it included the Holy Grail and the Ark of the Covenant. Several experts believe the Templars discovered the Americas before Columbus, and that the Templar Fleet possibly went to North America to bury the treasure.

The raiders at Oak Island appeared to know exactly how to access the Money Pit. A previously unknown route through the booby-traps was cleared, leading to a large subterranean, waterproofed chamber, the walls of which were carved with swastikas, many hundreds of years old. A couple of Roman coins were discovered near the mouth of the pit. The coins were from ancient Judea, with one side showing the head of the Emperor Tiberius and the reverse the Roman Governor Pontius Pilate.

On a tombstone near the Money Pit is a Latin inscription: *I tego arcana Dei* meaning *Begone! I conceal the secrets of God.*

6) Rosslyn Chapel, Edinburgh, Scotland

Rosslyn chapel was built between 1446 and 1486 and is often described as the most mysterious Christian chapel in the world. Like Oak Island, Rosslyn is linked with the lost treasure of the Knights Templar, including the Holy Grail and the Ark of the Covenant. Many Templars fled to Scotland in the years after 1307 because the Scottish king, Robert the Bruce, having been excommunicated for killing a rival in a church, wasn't bound by the Papal edict to suppress the Templars. Several experts believe the Templars regrouped in Scotland and eventually emerged in a new guise – the Freemasons. Informed speculation says that Freemasonry originated specifically at Rosslyn.

The Rosslyn raiders disabled all of the chapel's alarm systems and CCTV monitors. As at the Schatzkammer, security guards were rendered unconscious by tranquillising gas. The raiders removed a section of wall from the crypt, revealing a sizeable stone chamber. There is no indication of what, if anything, they discovered.

7) Hill of Tara, Republic of Ireland

Ancient Ireland's most sacred site where the High Kings of Ireland were crowned. Legend says that the Hebrew prophet Jeremiah brought the Ark of the Covenant to Ireland for safekeeping after the destruction of King Solomon's Temple, burying it somewhere on the Hill of Tara.

The raiders used an excavator stolen from a nearby building site to dig a trench several yards away from a feature known as the *Mound of Hostages*. A large bronze chamber was exposed. It is unknown whether the raiders found anything.

Conclusions

The raiders at each location used similar methods. The top-secret tranquillising gas used in two of the locations indicates the involvement of U.S. or U.K. Special Forces. Thirty U.S. Special Forces' personnel went absent without leave on 23 April. It appears probable that these individuals were responsible for the raids.

The raiders clearly had access to secret information concerning each site. However, the only object that has definitely gone missing is the Spear of Destiny from Vienna's Hofburg Palace.

It is speculation whether the raiders also retrieved anything that might be described as the Holy Grail or the Ark of the Covenant, or any other religious treasures. It is unknown whether the raiders found a particular religious relic at each of the seven locations, or if they were looking for the same objects at different locations. However, given their detailed knowledge, it is likely the raiders knew precisely what they would find at each site. On the other hand, it's possible they carried out some fake thefts to create confusion and mask their true intentions (the raid at Temple Mount may be one example). Were they seeking publicity by targeting high profile sites? By their actions at the Temple Mount, were they seeking to generate unrest between Jews and Muslims? No claims of responsibility have been issued.

The blood of Jesus Christ is an obvious connection between the Holy Grail and the Spear of Destiny, and these two items are historically regarded as two of the four so-called *Grail Hallows*. These four objects appear in the legends of King Arthur and the Holy Grail and are said to have enormous power, particularly when brought together. The other two Grail Hallows are a sword and dish. There is no known link between the Grail Hallows and the Ark of the Covenant. The Hallows are associated with the Christian New Testament while the latter is an Old Testament, and specifically Jewish, sacred artefact.

The Ark, by reputation, is a potential WMD. The Spear of Destiny allegedly confers great power on its owner. The Holy Grail is said to be the goal of the ultimate spiritual quest of humanity. The Grail Hallows, as a collection, supposedly possess unprecedented power.

Do these fabled religious relics have the capacity to be the centrepieces of some hitherto unsuspected Armageddon conspiracy? Cardinal Lenihan and Rabbi Grien concur that they do. Prominent scientists have ridiculed this notion, but have at this time been unable to explain the current global crisis, and have provided no suggestions as to what ought to be done.

REPORT ENDS

6

Vernon laid the document back on the table. Well, Gresnick wasn't exaggerating. Days ago, he would have considered that everyone involved in compiling this report was nuts. Now he didn't know what to think. Crazy things were happening everywhere and no one had any answers. It was the duty of the intelligence services to follow all possible leads. In an odd way, Sherlock Holmes' formula was the right one: 'When you have eliminated all which is impossible, then whatever remains, however improbable, must be the truth.' If there were no credible leads, you had to look at the far-fetched ones, and they didn't come much more far-fetched than the theory outlined in Gresnick's document.

'Let me get this straight, colonel,' Vernon said. 'The DIA are claiming that a few days ago an elite Special Forces unit deserted en masse and became – how shall I put it – Tomb Raiders, or Raiders of the Lost Ark? And now their activities may have brought down, um, God's fury on us.'

'That's as good a way of putting it as any other. We think all of the deserters are now in the UK…in the southwest of England, to be precise.'

Vernon turned to Harrington but his boss's blank expression signalled that he too wasn't sure what the hell he was listening to.

Vernon couldn't figure it. Why would Delta Force deserters steal holy relics? And what were they doing in the southwest of England? It was a part of the country he was more than familiar with, and it certainly wasn't where you'd expect to find renegade U.S. Special Forces.

'I'm sorry,' he said, wondering why Gresnick was now, in his turn, exchanging a meaningful glance with Harrington. 'This is a lot to take in.'

'There are some other things I need to throw into the mix,' Gresnick said. 'Two of the deserters were apprehended in London last night by your armed police group CO19. They had detailed maps of southwest England in their possession. They were picked up in one of the reading rooms of the British Library after breaking in very amateurishly, almost as though they wanted to be discovered. When CO19 found them, they were studying microfiche of rare manuscripts. They're being held in the cells next door.'

'The British Library?' Vernon queried. 'Microfiche of what?'

Gresnick and Harrington again interchanged glances, but neither replied.

'Beyond what it says in the document you've just read,' Gresnick said, 'what else do you know about the Holy Grail?'

'Nothing,' Vernon snorted. 'Absolutely nothing.' He folded his arms.

Gresnick raised his eyebrows. 'That's not quite right though, is it?'

Vernon dug his fingers into his arms. He'd had his fill of hearing about the Grail. For three years, his former girlfriend talked of little else. Girlfriend? *Ghost*. How else would you describe the person who haunted you day and night? The last thing he wanted was to be dragged back into that circus of horrors.

'Mr Vernon,' Commander Harrington said, 'the reason we've brought you down here is that one of the prisoners had certain information in his possession.'

Vernon felt the room growing cold.

'It appears the prisoners were planning to kidnap or assassinate someone,' Harrington went on.

Vernon jerked his hand forward, almost knocking over his coffee. 'The Prime Minister?' he ventured. 'The Queen?'

'Actually, it's your ex-girlfriend. We have no idea why, particularly given her condition.'

Vernon's hands trembled and he thrust them against his thighs to steady them. *This is impossible.* He stared hard at Harrington. 'Lucy?' The name, as it emerged, scraped his mouth like sandpaper. 'Condition?'

Harrington looked away. 'I'm sorry, James, I thought you knew.'

7

'Time for your medication. One blue and one red. Take a sip of water.' The nurse leaned over and placed the tray with its pills, glass of water and half an orange on the table next to the patient.

Lucy Galahan let the nurse see her taking her pills then sat back in her rocking chair, pulling her blue blanket up to her neck. It didn't take long for her to feel the usual drowsiness creeping over her: the dull march of numbed senses, of everything fading into the distance. Occasionally she resented how her life retreated from her at pill-time, but usually she simply felt less bad. That was all she wanted, for the hurt to stop.

Sometimes she fantasised about gathering all of her pain together, every jagged fragment she had collected in her life, and fashioning it into some misshapen snowman. She'd place it next to a radiator and watch it melt, taking all her hurt with it.

As she drifted off, Lucy remembered that as a kid the thing she'd most looked forward to was when her mum put her to bed, kissed her good night and said, 'Sleep tight, don't let the bed bugs bite.' Nothing had hurt in those days, not even the bed bugs. Every time mum switched off the light, she felt warm and safe. There were never any bad dreams. Now, that's all there were.

When her eyes opened again, she was in her bed and two nuns and a nurse were staring down at her. The only light in the room came from a couple of candles, the flickering light drawn to the silver crucifixes hanging from the nuns' necks.

'Leave us,' a voice said – a man's voice.

Lucy was startled. It was months since she last encountered a man. The six-hundred-year-old convent of Our Lady of Perpetual Succour was strictly women-only.

'Are you certain, your Excellency?' one of the nuns said. 'Mother Superior didn't…'

'There's no mistake,' the voice said. 'She's the one.'

Lucy didn't understand. *Excellency?* Who was this person? She tried to prop herself up on her elbows to see him, but she was exhausted and her head flopped back onto the pillow.

The nuns and the nurse closed the door behind them as they departed. They'd left a single candle on Lucy's dressing table. She could hear the sound of breathing – her own and the man's. Where was he? The foot of her bed, she decided. It didn't leave him much room. It was a narrow hospital bed with broken springs. Not much else could be fitted into the room. In the days when this was an ordinary convent, it would have been called a cell rather than a room.

'Let me apologise for disturbing you like this,' the man said.

Lucy thought she detected traces of an Irish or Scottish accent.

'I know this must be uncomfortable for you,' the man went on.

'Who are you?' Lucy's eyes followed the direction of the candle flame up to the ceiling. The candlelight danced over the paintings she'd stuck up there so that when she awoke each morning they would be the first things she saw. She sensed the man was as intent on her paintings as she was. They covered most surfaces of her cell. She'd even doubled up in some places. It would be a lie to describe her as a skilful painter, but it was the one activity that relaxed her. She transmitted her pain through the brush and onto the canvas. It comforted her to see the pain becoming something separate from her, in the distance, anywhere other than lodged in her heart.

Maybe the signs had always been there. As a teenager, she engaged in mild self-harm – a few shallow cuts on her legs and arms with razor blades. She read Sylvia Plath's *The Bell Jar*, entranced by expressions like 'breathing sour air.'

The man's voice interrupted her thoughts. 'So, it's true,' he said. 'I hardly dared believe it.'

'You still haven't said who you are.' Lucy wasn't certain she was having this conversation. Dr Levis, her psychiatrist, told her she'd been delusional on a few occasions. The delusions were only part of it. Severe trauma can lead to Dissociative Identity Disorder, Levis said. The new name for old-fashioned Multiple Personality Syndrome. Voices in the head; several of them. But that was in the past, wasn't it? Getting better now, Levis said, much better.

'I'm from the Vatican,' the man stated. 'My name is Cardinal Joseph Sinclair. I'm the Prefect of the Congregatio pro Doctrina Fidei.'

Lucy concentrated hard. Was this a new voice in her head, or the genuine voice of a real person? All the time, she had to check for clues to separate the real from the imagined. In the ancient world, she wouldn't have had a problem. 'Reality' was much more fluid then. People knew there was an afterlife because they'd seen it. *Dreams* – how wondrous they must have seemed to those who had no idea what they were. Another world, where the dead were alive again. The ancients believed the dream world was the *real* world, that when we went to sleep we were afforded glimpses of the world we would inhabit when our sleep became permanent. When her parents died, Lucy lost the ability to know where the dream ended and reality began.

'Sorry, I should have said the Congregation for the Doctrine of the Faith,' the cardinal said. 'It's my job to protect the teachings of the Roman Catholic Church from those who seek to subvert them.'

Congregation for the Doctrine of the Faith? A fragment of Lucy's old life came back to her. At Oxford University, she was an expert in non-standard belief systems and she was well aware of whom the unorthodox – the heretics – feared the most.

'Why don't you say who you really are?' She felt she was talking to the past, to all the normal things she'd lost. Maybe she had conjured this urbane man as a substitute for her father. She longed to be hugged by her dad again. It seemed impossible that he would never hold her anymore, nor ask how she was feeling, never make clumsy inquiries about her love life or how her career was going.

'So, you've heard of us,' the man said. There was something different about his voice. A sudden harshness.

Lucy felt a shiver running through her. 'When did you people stop calling yourselves the Inquisition?' she asked.

8

Vernon couldn't concentrate. In a world that might be dying, his personal ghost had resurfaced. Lucy Galahan was the love of his life, the one who for three years treated him to every bizarre theory about the great holy relics – real and fabled – that littered human history. A lecturer in Comparative Mythology and Esoteric Studies at Oxford University, she was dazzlingly clever. It helped that she had great looks too, and an athletic body honed by her obsession with scuba diving. Put it all together and she was Vernon's ideal woman...until she dumped him.

'This is a file found in the possession of one of the prisoners,' Gresnick said, sliding a folder to Vernon. 'It's a surveillance log. It's all there: a detailed diary of Lucy Galahan's movements in the last week, her daily schedule, who are carers are, long-lens photographs, background reports and so on.'

Vernon, shifting uneasily in his chair, glanced at one of the pictures: a close-up of Lucy in a wheelchair in a garden, accompanied by a nun. It shocked him to see the face that had tormented him for so long. Even worse was to see Lucy so helpless. Often enough, he'd tried to pretend she meant nothing to him, but that just made things worse. Her raven hair entangled his thoughts. He'd spent so much time running his fingers through it, playing with it and smelling it. Her eyes did the most damage, though. They were big and tender, almost childlike. The shade of blue was remarkable, practically violet.

Swallowing hard, Vernon flicked through the rest of the material. The file stated that Lucy was in a care home, on the outskirts of Glastonbury, for the recuperation of Catholics who'd suffered from mental breakdowns. Care home? Judging by the photos, it was some spooky old convent. *Our Lady of*

Perpetual Succour it was called. You'd know you were in big trouble if you ever ended up in a place with a name like that.

With Glastonbury being one of the most famous locations in southwest England, frequently linked to mystical forces, Vernon wondered if Lucy was the true reason the Delta Force deserters were in that part of the country, or if Glastonbury itself was the key. It seemed a bizarre proposition that soldiers would have any interest in Lucy, especially given her mental state.

It was eighteen months since they broke up. When her mother died from breast cancer, Lucy hadn't coped. She threw herself into her work. The more he tried to comfort her, she more she pushed him away. Finally, she sent him a letter saying she didn't want to see him again. No reasons given. It was the coldest thing he'd ever read, and inconceivable that Lucy had written it. She never answered his calls, and didn't reply to any of his e-mails and letters.

On the rebound, Vernon met the Swedish nurse who became his wife, and he tried to put Lucy out of his mind for good. Deep down, he never stopped thinking about her. It was such a struggle to pretend that his wife was the great love of his life when she could never hope to displace Lucy.

Anna was blonde and not in the least cerebral; the opposite of Lucy. That was why he chose her, of course. He couldn't blame her for going back to Sweden. Their relationship began sliding from the moment she announced she was pregnant, weeks after they started seeing each other. He did the honourable thing and married her, but now he wondered where the honour was in making two people miserable. What would be the effect on baby Louise? Nothing healthy, that was for sure. She was a gorgeous little thing and he loved every moment he spent with her, but she was better off with her mum. Out of sight out of mind, he thought. But that wasn't the case with Lucy. It still hadn't sunk in. Lucy in a loony bin?

Gresnick passed over another folder. 'The DIA have produced a detailed file on Lucy,' he said. 'We're trying to find some reason why Delta Force deserters would be targeting her. During our researches, your name cropped up, which is why I've asked to see you. So far, the best we've been able to come up with is connected with the fact that the two deserters we caught last night were studying old manuscripts concerning the Holy Grail.'

Vernon nodded. A couple of years ago, Lucy published *The Unholy Grail: The Secret Heresy*, a controversial analysis of the Grail legend, claiming it was a coded reference to heretical rituals. Initiates would understand what the Grail story was really saying, she argued, while non-initiates would think it was simply an exciting tale. Because the story was dressed up to make it look superficially consistent with orthodox Christianity, the Catholic Church never banned it, though they were always uncomfortable with it. So, the Grail legend allowed heretical beliefs to be safely distributed across Europe.

A book published in 1920 inspired many of Lucy's ideas. *From Ritual to Romance* by Jessie Weston was, in its day, both highly influential and much derided. Lucy's book suffered the derision part of the equation, but, unlike Weston who'd enjoyed admirers of the calibre of T.S. Eliot, Lucy didn't have any supporters.

'I know it's a lot to take in,' Gresnick said, 'but I'm afraid there's more. I think we ought to let you see the two prisoners now.'

Vernon stood up, expecting to leave the room.

'Oh, we're not going anywhere,' Gresnick said. 'I want to show you the video footage we took when the prisoners were brought in.'

'Why can't I see them in the flesh?'

'Just watch the video.' Gresnick turned to the large LCD TV at the side of the room, currently showing a screensaver of mathematical symbols. He pressed a button on a remote control and the screensaver disappeared, replaced by video images of soldiers bringing in, at gunpoint, two handcuffed men in dark suits.

One of the prisoners glanced at the camera.

God Almighty. Vernon looked away in revulsion.

Gresnick froze the picture. 'What age would you say that man is?'

'Seventy? Eighty?' Vernon was baffled by how an old man could be serving in Delta Force, and even more perplexed by how an elderly man arrested in a library ended up in such a horrific state. Surely he should have been taken straight to hospital. Much of his flesh was charred; third degree burns by the looks of it. Strips were flaking off.

'He's thirty-one,' Gresnick replied. 'A doctor said he's been exposed to incredible levels of radiation.'

'Thirty-one? *Impossible.*'

Gresnick pressed the *play* button again.

The soldiers took both prisoners to the detention block and put them in separate cells. Dr Hugh Wells, a friend of Vernon's, laid the burned man on a prison bed and attended to his wounds. Another doctor started to cut away the prisoner's clothes.

Gresnick fast-forwarded the pictures until they showed Dr Wells alone in one of the interview rooms, talking quietly to an overhead camera.

'The man's body is covered from head to foot with blisters and sores,' Wells said. The doctor then mentioned that, as a young trainee, he was part of an international team of doctors sent to the Soviet Union to treat victims of the Chernobyl disaster. This prisoner's condition, Wells said, reminded him of the nuclear engineers who'd been nearest to the site of the partial meltdown. Many died in agony within days. This man, according to Wells, was much worse off and unlikely to survive hours never mind days. All they were trying to do now was ease his pain.

As for the second prisoner, Wells said that although he seemed healthy, he was being kept in isolation as a precaution. No one would be allowed to approach either prisoner directly without protective clothing. Any interrogation of the prisoners would have to take place remotely.

Gresnick stopped the video and the screensaver reappeared.

'I just don't get this.' Vernon shook his head. 'I mean, what happened to that man? A radiation source? Where? How?'

'We have no idea.' Gresnick reached forward and raised the emerald paperweight. 'Something very odd happened when the armed police arrested the two men. They told them to raise their hands and stay where they were. Instead, one of the men put his hand in his pocket and snatched this out. A policeman thought he was reaching for a weapon and opened fire. The bullet hit this ball. It didn't leave a mark.'

'It's just a paperweight,' Vernon blurted.

Gresnick shrugged. 'Well, the prisoner seemed to think it was valuable. The police had to prise it away from him. There's another curious thing – before he touched this object, the prisoner was uninjured, and looked like a normal thirty-one-year-old. The burns and rapid ageing appeared while he was being brought over here, but he wasn't exposed to any radiation en route. The ball was seemingly the last thing he touched.'

'What are you saying? That the radiation came from that ball?'

Gresnick tapped the back of the orb with a pencil. 'As far as I can make out, it's just a coloured glass ball. Several of us have touched it without mishap, but we're sending it to a lab to have it analysed in depth.'

Vernon imagined he was looking at the scattered pieces of some giant jigsaw, but he couldn't form any idea of what the big picture might be.

'The burned man is Captain Lucius Ferris,' Gresnick said. 'His colleague is Sergeant Samuel Morson. Both are highly decorated veterans. These were the Special Forces men chosen for the most dangerous operations. In terms of our elite soldiers, they were the cream of the cream.'

Vernon couldn't think of a single plausible idea why America's top soldiers would go AWOL.

'It's time to see if these guys want to talk.' Gresnick picked up the remote control again and pressed a button.

On the LCD TV, a live feed appeared of the prisoners in their adjoining cells. The cell walls were made of reinforced glass to allow unobstructed 24/7 observation. It was possible to see both men from one camera. Sergeant Morson had been made to sit in a position giving him a clear view of his superior in the adjacent cell; a tactic, Vernon assumed, designed to make the sergeant anxious and more talkative, but Morson wasn't showing any signs of distress. His expression mixed arrogance with satisfaction. Vernon was nonplussed. Why did Morson seem so pleased with himself when his captain was likely to die at any moment?

Gresnick drew his microphone towards him and coughed a couple of times.

Vernon noticed how neatly Gresnick's cufflinks were arranged, how straight and pristine his tie was. He was obviously the sort who spent a lot of time getting everything just so.

'What is this object, Sergeant Morson?' Gresnick held up the emerald globe, pointing it towards the overhead camera.

Morson peered at it on the monitor that had been set up in his cell to allow easy, two-way communication. 'Isn't it a paperweight?'

'So, you wouldn't mind if I smashed it on the floor?'

'Do whatever you like.'

If Gresnick believed the object held some great significance for Morson and his colleague, he'd received no encouragement. 'Why did you and your men carry out seven raids?' he asked. 'What did you want with religious relics?'

Morson didn't answer.

'Why were you examining microfiche of ancient manuscripts in the British Library?'

This time, Morson smiled, but still didn't speak.

'Why did the natural disasters start straight after your seven raids?'

'You have no idea, do you? The kingdom of the blind, and no one-eyed man in sight,' Morson said without warning.

'What do you want with this woman?' Gresnick lifted up Lucy's picture.

'*He* knows.' Morson pointed at Vernon.

Vernon shrugged. He'd had to read the DIA file to find out what had happened to Lucy since their break-up. After her mother died, her father committed suicide several months later. At the same time, Lucy's professional reputation was ruined when her theories about the Grail were ridiculed as speculative, unacademic nonsense. 'This poor woman is clearly losing her mind,' one of her critics said, before literally being proved right. The whole world was going nuts, Vernon thought, but Lucy got there before everyone else.

'You've gone to a lot of trouble,' Gresnick said to Morson. 'She must be very special.'

Morson grinned.

'Why her? She can't possibly help you, or be a threat to you. She's been diagnosed as suffering from acute post-traumatic stress disorder, leading to Dissociative Identity Disorder. If she were going to harm anyone, it would be herself.'

'You know nothing,' Morson snapped. 'That woman...'

'Yes?'

'She's the most important person in the world.'

9

Cardinal Sinclair was tall, probably in his early fifties, with silver hair, a weather-beaten face and grey eyes.

'I'm not here to harm you,' he said. 'Our enemies always exaggerated our reputation for torture.'

Lucy, sitting up in her bed, was amazed by the cardinal's physical likeness to her father. Maybe her brain was deceiving her again, projecting her own desires. In her black pyjamas, she was a good match for the cardinal.

Dressed in black with a white dog collar, like an ordinary priest, Sinclair wore nothing to suggest he was the second most powerful man in the Catholic Church, the Vatican's doctrinal enforcer, their ultimate authority on heresy. Taking the candle from the dressing table, he held it up to examine Lucy's paintings.

She watched him closely. For the last few minutes, she'd been silent, trying to absorb his news. No TVs, radios, newspapers or computers were permitted to the patients in the convent and none of the nurses or nuns had chosen to pass on word of the outside world. From what the cardinal said, hell itself had materialised out there in the last few days. Her own life was a wasteland, and now it seemed the rest of the world was joining her. Sinclair claimed that seven so-called supervolcanoes were on the verge of eruption. America, with three, including one in Yellowstone National Park, was particularly vulnerable. If, as now seemed likely, they all erupted in the next day or two, civilisation, if not all life on earth, would vanish.

'Why would you come here?' Lucy asked. 'I mean, at a time like this you must have so many more important things to do.'

The cardinal didn't take his eyes off the walls of her room. 'These paintings,' he said. 'What I haven't told you is that I've seen one of them before.'

Lucy stared at him. He had never been to the convent before, so how could he possibly have seen one of her paintings? Was he playing a game? She looked towards her medicine cabinet. Got to calm down. She reached towards the cabinet where she kept her tranquillisers, but the man took her hand and held it firmly.

'You're not having delusions, Lucy. I read your latest medical report. It says you're getting much better. They were about to put you on day release into the community. Dr Levis is delighted with your progress.'

Getting better? Lucy wanted so much to be well again, but every time she imagined it, it ended with her falling over.

'How can you say you've seen my paintings? It's impossible.'

'I scarcely believed it myself until now.'

Lucy was startled when the cardinal sat down beside her. Her father used to sit beside her in that exact same way. *Not dead*. Still here, still able to comfort her. She'd give anything for that to be true.

The cardinal pointed at the painting in the middle of the wall behind the headboard of Lucy's bed. It was the first she ever worked on, the template for the others.

'I don't know how,' Sinclair said, 'but that painting right there is also in Rome. It's part of a huge mural found in a secret vault in the tomb of Pope Julius II. The artist who painted it died the day after its completion. The mural was his final, greatest masterpiece.'

Lucy closed her eyes. A name leapt into her mind. It was as though thousands of locked doors were opening in her mind and light was bursting through, banishing the darkness that had gripped her for so long. All manner of weird facts were pouring into her, things she couldn't possibly know. She started to tremble. *My God, what's happening to me?* 'Raphael,' she said hesitantly, hoping Sinclair would tell her she was wrong. The expression on his face proved there was no mistake.

'Only three living people have seen Raphael's mural,' Sinclair said slowly.

'Raphael died almost five hundred years ago.' Lucy was mystified. Ideas were flashing in her mind, things she didn't have time to process, almost overwhelming her.

'Raphael died in 1520 at just thirty-seven years of age,' Sinclair replied. 'He painted your picture five hundred years before you did.'

Lucy clutched her knees, shaking her head from side to side.

'Come with me.' Sinclair got up and walked towards the door. 'You can see for yourself.'

10

Vernon peered at the TV screen, searching Sergeant Morson's face for clues. How could Lucy be so important? While Harrington had a whispered conversation with Gresnick, he again flicked through her DIA file. It said she spent most of her time working on a series of depressing paintings, covering every inch of her room with them. Each canvas had a blue background and featured a female figure with long black hair, wearing a black wedding dress. The female's face was always blank; just a white, featureless oval.

A psychiatrist's report said Lucy was terrified of being 'in the blue' – Lucy's own description of her condition, apparently. Vernon didn't need any translation. Lucy and her father were both keen divers and they'd taken him out with them on several expeditions. 'In the blue' was a diving term for the place in a deep dive in clear water where the diver could see neither the surface of the sea nor the seabed: all he had around him was the colour blue in every direction. Many divers found it an inspirational, exhilarating place, but for a few it was disorienting and filled them with panic. Vernon was one of the latter. He once heard a diver who'd suffered a mental collapse describing the experience as being 'in the blue'. The diver had subtly changed the meaning from a specific point in a dive where it becomes difficult to know up from down, backwards from forwards, to the perfect label for acute depression – the loss of a person's bearings, their very identity. Lucy was now using it in that context too, it seemed.

Vernon had been in the blue just once – on a summer's dive in amazingly clear water off the Cornish coast near Penzance – and never wanted to be there again. Lucy and her dad accompanied him at the start but were anxious to explore an old shipwreck. He stupidly said he'd like to be on his own for a while, and they swam off. After a couple of minutes, he couldn't see anything except blue. He was in a blue world extending in all directions, a place where he had no anchors, no bearings, no pointers. He quite simply lost himself. He began to think he might actually have drowned and was now in some blue hell, but Lucy swam up from below and dragged him back to the surface.

'What's happening to your captain?' Gresnick's voice jerked Vernon back to the present. 'What caused those injuries? You must know he'll be dead within hours.'

'The captain isn't dying.' Morson smirked. 'He's being reborn.'

'What?'

'You'll see by morning.'

'Some people are saying the world is about to end. What's your opinion, sergeant?'

'Something astonishing is coming. The very earth will tremble beneath your feet.'

'Are you referring to the Turkish earthquakes?'

Morson continued to smirk. '**He** knows we're coming for him. He stopped us before, but this time there's nothing He can do.'

'What are you talking about?' Commander Harrington spoke for the first time in the interrogation. 'Who is *He*?'

'Are you a religious man?' Morson asked.

Harrington nodded.

'Then you know exactly who I mean.'

Vernon leaned forward, curious to see Harrington's reaction. His boss had never concealed the fact that he was a fully paid up God squadder – a Methodist, Baptist or Quaker; Vernon couldn't remember which. He wasn't interested enough to find out the difference between the three, and always got them mixed up. Harrington, to Vernon's irritation, kept a Bible prominently displayed on the desk in his office. Vernon felt it was inappropriate for religion to make such a brazen appearance in MI5's HQ.

Harrington's expression barely changed. He gazed at a wall-calendar showing Ferrari supercars. 'Are there any significant days coming up, Mr Vernon?' he asked. 'Anniversaries, religious festivals, that sort of thing?'

Vernon knew the drill. Spectacular acts of terror, protest, revolt, rebellion were often scheduled for memorable dates, as if they could draw legitimacy, power perhaps, from the previous incidents. Swinging round to a computer on a side-table, he used the internet to search for imminent big dates. The first one up was 30 April, the eve of May Day.

'The Germans call April 30 Walpurgis Nacht.' Vernon read from the first entry that appeared onscreen. 'It's supposedly the night when witches emerge into the open to wreak revenge on God-fearing people.' He quickly scanned the second entry. 'It's also an ancient Celtic festival called Beltane, involving a sacrificial fire.' He noticed a third possibility, unconnected with the supernatural, but quite as chilling. 'And it's the day Hitler committed suicide.'

Gresnick sat up straight when he heard that. 'What do you think of Hitler, sergeant?'

'He *knew*.'

'Knew what?'

'The dead have always outnumbered the living. They call the living *monsters*. They'll call us monsters too, perhaps the worst monsters of them all.'

'This is getting us nowhere.' Harrington cut off the link to Morson.

The mathematical screensaver reappeared on the TV monitor. Ancient Greek letters, large and small, in every colour, flooded the LCD screen, rotating, inverting, shrinking and expanding. An insoluble equation, Vernon thought, just like this whole situation. Distracted, it took him a moment to register that Dr Wells had entered the room.

'I thought you ought to be told right away,' Wells said to Harrington. 'The tests we've done on Captain Ferris don't make any sense. We haven't made any progress in identifying what type of radiation he's been exposed to, but it seems to be causing a metabolic transformation.' He rubbed his face nervously. 'I mean he's changing at a molecular level.'

'I'm not following.'

'Commander, I've never seen anything like it. The things that are happening to that man – nothing in medical science can explain it.'

'What are you saying?' Harrington got up from his seat and stood face to face with Wells.

'Do you believe in God?' Wells asked.

'I'm sure my religious beliefs are quite irrelevant. Get to the point, doctor.'

'The prisoner's burns aren't getting any worse. In fact, they're healing. He's becoming younger again.' Wells dabbed his forehead with a tissue. 'All the charred flesh has flaked off. The skin beneath is – how shall I say it – *translucent*. You can practically see through him. But there's something else. Symmetrical growths have appeared on each of his shoulders, almost like – Jesus, I know how this must sound.' He pronounced his next words very slowly. '...*budding wings*.' He shook his head. 'I know it's impossible, but...Christ, this can't be happening.'

'Get a grip on yourself,' Harrington barked.

'I'm not a believer. If I were – no, it's insane.'

Harrington folded his arms and turned away from the doctor.

Wells stared at the floor. 'Commander, I think the prisoner is turning into…' The pause was painfully long. '…*an angel.*'

11

It was some kind of trick. There was no other explanation. Lucy wanted to get up from her seat and run. When Cardinal Sinclair brought her to the chapel, switched on the slide projector and inserted the slide he'd brought with him from Rome, she expected to see a conventional Renaissance painting, but what was in front of her was a miracle: it simply couldn't be. As she stared at the huge image projected onto the back wall, she trembled.

'In five hundred years, only a handful of people have seen this,' Sinclair said. 'No one's allowed into the vault where it's kept without the Pope's express permission. Raphael worked so feverishly on it that it killed him. It was the strain and exhaustion that led to his death at just thirty-seven.'

Lucy made a fist and pushed her knuckles against her forehead. She got up and stepped, almost staggered, backwards, trying to absorb everything in the mural. Twenty-four small panels were arranged around a large central panel that was split in half, the upper portion showing a traditional celestial scene of angels bathed in divine light; the lower an image of the end of the world, focusing on the terrified faces of masses of ordinary people as they fled from fire raining down on them from a black, burning sky.

Of the surrounding panels, one showed the Temple of Solomon, another the Ark of the Covenant. There was a picture of the moment when a Roman centurion pierced Christ's side with a spear; another showing the beheading of John the Baptist. The Tree of Knowledge and the Garden of Eden were featured, and Cain killing Abel. One showed Jesus drinking from a chalice at the Last Supper.

Lucy's eyes darted from panel to panel. There were several other conventional religious scenes, but then things turned weird. One panel showed King Arthur at Camelot, another the procession of the Grail Hallows in front of the old Fisher King in the hall of the Grail Castle, another King Arthur's final apocalyptic battle at Camlann. There were a few other Arthurian images and then several panels depicting scenes whose significance was entirely lost on Lucy.

Arthurian Art, she knew, never took off seriously until the Pre-Raphaelites became obsessed with it in the 19th century. No art historian had ever suggested that Raphael painted Arthurian scenes. If these images were authentic, they could revolutionise art history, maybe history itself.

But it wasn't those panels that kept drawing Lucy's gaze back to the mural. They were improbable but not impossible. The mural also contained one feature for which no explanation was conceivable. That was the panel in the centre of the bottom row, a panel that had nothing at all in common with Raphael's sublime style.

Lucy urged herself to wake up. This simply couldn't be real. What was in front of her wasn't just familiar, it was her *own* work. The panel was an exact copy of that first painting she made in her cell.

'I know it's difficult to accept,' Sinclair said, 'but there it is.'

Lucy, standing in her black pyjamas and slippers, rubbed her arms. The chapel was so cold. She kept rubbing, the motion growing more frantic. Maybe she could rub away what she was seeing, erase it from her mind.

'If you study the panels,' Sinclair remarked, 'you'll see that they form a narrative as you move clockwise. Pope Julius II died seven years before Raphael. We have no idea if he left Raphael with specific instructions to create these images, or if he permitted Raphael to use his artistic imagination. Raphael didn't leave any explanation as to what the images meant.

'The Vatican showed the mural to trusted experts, and not one could account for all of the images. Many are unlike any Julius was known to favour. Only one person offered any clues to what was going on.'

Lucy had taken a seat in one of the pews. With a jolt, she sat upright. One second there was nothing in her head, the next a name sprang at her, just as it had earlier with Raphael, as though it had been waiting there for years. It was so bright, so vivid, it might as well have been lit in neon. '*Nostradamus,*' she said. Why was she so certain? It made no sense. She bowed her head.

The cardinal sat down beside her, giving her a little nod of confirmation.

'What's happening to me?' Lucy closed her eyes. Words were bubbling up in her mind, things she didn't comprehend. 'Decision...' she said, '...Decision Point. Salvation. Damnation. Choose. Destroyer or Redeemer.'

Sinclair gazed at her. 'Why are you saying those things, Lucy?'

'I have no idea.'

'Are you afraid?'

'I don't understand any of this. What's going on?'

'It's all there, in your subconscious, Lucy. You know what you have to do.'

'I don't know anything.'

'Lucy, the Vatican has never revealed that it once consulted Nostradamus regarding this mural. They warned him under pain of death not to divulge a word. The things he wrote down were locked away. Only Popes and the holders of my office have ever been granted access to his writings. Yet, without prompting, you mentioned his name. Every word you just told me was used by Nostradamus.'

Lucy cradled her head.

'Nostradamus said the Decision Point was when the world would be saved or destroyed by a Chosen One.'

Lucy stood up then walked towards the wall where the mural was being projected. She stretched her hand towards the panel that, somehow, belonged to her. The projection played over the back of her hand, rippling and twisting as she moved her hand through it. 'Either I reproduced an unknown work by Raphael,' she said, 'or he reproduced an unknown painting by me, five hundred years before I was born.'

'The Pope died a few hours ago,' Sinclair replied. 'I'm supposed to be with the other cardinals in the Sistine Chapel to elect the new Pope. Now you can understand why I came here instead.'

The Pope dead? Lucy snatched her hand back to her side and turned to face the altar. She'd once gone to see the Pope in the days when she was still a good Catholic, when she still believed in all the things that now seemed so ridiculous to her. She'd stood in St Peter's Square with tens of thousands of the faithful, waiting for the papal blessing on Easter Sunday. Now he'd gone, just like her parents. They all went, sooner or later.

She again gazed at the faceless woman floating in blue. Why would Raphael deface his stunning work of art with that guileless piece of work? It couldn't have meant anything to him. It had significance purely for her. In the days when she went scuba diving, the part of the dive she most eagerly anticipated was being in the blue. She used to hang there, in that strange watery limbo, that blue world, feeling weightless, freed from the pressures of life. Nothing could touch her. No one could demand anything from her. It was as if she'd found the perfect place to hide.

'I don't know who that faceless woman is,' she said quietly. 'A figure looking for an identity, that's all. It's no one in particular.'

'But it couldn't be more obvious,' Sinclair replied. 'It's *you*.'

Lucy couldn't blame him for thinking that. He needed it to be her. After coming all this way, he had no room for mistakes.

'Nostradamus said Raphael's mural was a prophecy about the end of the world,' Sinclair said. 'The individual pictures are a code. If it's solved, the world will be saved. If not, everything ends.'

'I can't help,' Lucy said. 'Look at me: I'm in an asylum.'

Without warning, an unfamiliar noise interrupted them and they went quiet.

Lucy was first to speak. 'Firecrackers?'

The sounds were distant, but clear enough. Staccato bursts, loud bangs. But why would anyone be celebrating at a time like this?

Sinclair stood up then hurried to the door, bolting it shut.

'What are you doing?' Lucy felt panic rising through her.

'Those sounds,' Sinclair said. '*It's gunfire.*'

12

Vernon was struggling to take it in. An angel? Of all his colleagues, Hugh Wells was the most rational, but now he watched in astonishment as the doctor's hands trembled.

'There must be another explanation.' Wells flopped into a seat, clutching his head.

Vernon glanced around the room and, for a moment, imagined that the walls were closing in on every side.

Commander Harrington shook his head. Wearing his pinstriped suit like a City financier, he seemed to Vernon to be in the wrong place and the wrong job. Colonel Gresnick was the only one maintaining any calm. Wasn't he rattled by the thought that there might be an angel in the cell next door?

'What do you think, colonel?' Vernon asked.

'I haven't filled you in on everything I know about Section 5.' Gresnick rolled his pen back and forth between his fingers. 'Originally, it had twenty members. By 1945, they'd been together for two years and hadn't suffered a single casualty. Within a month of starting the interrogations of the Nazi officials, nine were dead.'

'But wasn't the war practically over?'

Gresnick nodded. He explained that shortly before the death of the ninth man, that same man made an astonishing accusation to General Patton. He claimed his eight colleagues were murdered, and his most incredible claim concerned the identity of the murderers: the other members of Section 5.

The next day he was discovered hanged in his room. The official verdict was suicide. An inquiry found that he had been depressed for some time. Unfiled interrogation notes discovered amongst his possessions related a crazy story involving a conspiracy going back ten thousand years, of which the Nazis were supposedly the current inheritors. The other interrogators denied that any such questioning ever took place and said the claims were preposterous. The victim's notes were taken as firm evidence that he'd lost his mind. There was no reason to question the inquiry's findings.

'But now things are different, huh?' Vernon interrupted.

'It's my job not to rule anything out. All we can do is go on facts. Something unexplained is happening to Captain Ferris. Of that, there's no doubt. Anything else is speculation.'

'That's right,' Harrington said, 'pure speculation.' He turned back to Dr Wells. 'Doctor, I want you to continue to monitor Ferris's condition and let us know immediately if there are any significant changes. In the meantime, I'll post extra guards. And Colonel Gresnick, I want to know exactly what Section 5's task was in 1945. What were they trying to discover?'

'Section 5 reported directly to General Patton,' Gresnick said. 'Patton was obsessed with knowing what Hitler did with the Spear of Destiny.'

'We're talking about *the* General Patton?' Vernon said.

'The man himself.'

'Why would a brilliant soldier like Patton care about an old spear?' Even as he asked the question, Vernon felt sweat running down his back. He already knew something about the Spear of Destiny. It featured prominently in Lucy's book, but in a peculiar way. It was her belief that it, and not crucifixion, killed Jesus Christ.

'Mr Vernon, Patton wasn't a conventional general. He believed he was the reincarnation of Hannibal. Also, he had highly unorthodox ideas about the post-war situation in Europe.'

'Like what?'

'He wanted to re-arm two Waffen SS divisions, incorporate them in his army and attack the Soviet Union. He believed Communism was the biggest threat imaginable.'

'He was a Nazi sympathiser?'

'Many people thought so. He died from injuries sustained in a car crash in Germany at the end of 1945. On an empty road in foggy conditions, his chauffeur-driven car collided with a U.S. military truck coming in the opposite direction. For no apparent reason, it swerved right into the path of his car. Some people didn't think it was an accident.'

'What about the Spear of Destiny?' Once, Vernon asked Lucy questions like that. He remembered how excited she became whenever she found a new piece of evidence to fit into her jigsaw. She was so full of life and energy. It was horrific to think of her now as a lunatic being pushed around in a wheelchair.

'Patton supposedly wanted to take it to America,' Gresnick said. 'He declared that if the Americans owned it they would rule the world.'

'So why did he give it back to the Austrians?'

'He didn't. Rumour has it that Patton arranged for a convincing replica to be made. That was the one sent to Vienna.'

'In that case, what happened to the real one?'

'From what we can make out, it was shipped back to America and hidden in a safe location in North Carolina.' Gresnick put down his pen. 'Fort Bragg, to be exact.'

Vernon turned to Harrington, expecting his boss to be as amazed by that revelation as he was. Instead, Harrington's face had blanched.

'Is something wrong, sir?'

'I never thought I'd see the day,' Harrington said slowly. 'I assumed it was the purest madness. It can't be true.'

'I don't understand, sir.'

'Don't you see? All of this; it's all linked. Somehow, Hitler is reaching out from the grave.'

'I beg your pardon?'

'Mr Vernon, I want you go to the archive section immediately.' Harrington took out a handkerchief and cleaned his spectacles. 'I need you to bring back one of the black files, together with its official translation. When you get there, ask the archivist to phone me for the authorisation code.'

'Which black file?' Vernon asked.

It was Gresnick who answered. *'The Cainite Destiny.'*

13

The gunfire had stopped. Cardinal Sinclair stood at the chapel's main door, listening for sounds in the corridor outside.

Lucy sat in the pews, facing the altar. She had briefly looked at the cardinal to see what he was doing, but now she just focused on her knees, wishing she could curl up into a tiny ball. She was the one in the asylum, wearing just pyjamas and slippers, but there were people out in the corridors with guns and grenades who were much crazier than she could ever be.

According to Sinclair, a squad of soldiers had come for her. He said others knew how significant she was. Significant? She couldn't imagine anyone less important. If she took her medication, would it all go away? Maybe she'd taken the wrong pills that morning. One time she took too many and they pumped her stomach. Sometimes she pretended it was just an accident. More usually, she painted new pictures, bluer than ever, trying to find the shade that captured her feelings that day, but she never got close. What colour is suicide?

'What soldiers?' she asked.

'If I know about you, Lucy, then so do others.'

'Everything was secret. You said so.'

'What we know, the other side knows too. That's always been the way. God must test us. What would be the point otherwise?' Sinclair glanced at the door again. 'I have to get you out of here.'

'The other side?' Lucy repeated. 'What are you talking about?' She knew this was a good time to move, but she stayed where she was. 'I'm not going anywhere.' She hadn't left the convent for six months. The idea of being out *there*. It was bad before but now it was unthinkable.

'Good and evil,' Sinclair said. 'The other side is always just a step behind.'

When the cardinal gripped her arms, Lucy screamed. 'I didn't ask for any of this. Get away from me.'

There was a flash of emotion in the cardinal's eyes: *hate*. Startled, Lucy tried to get to her feet but Sinclair held her down.

'God Almighty.' Lucy recoiled. 'You detest me.'

'Come on now, Lucy, you're frightened. You don't know what you're saying.'

'*Fuck off!*' Lucy's mouth fell open. She couldn't believe what she'd just said. In her whole time in the convent, no one had sworn, not once. To swear in a chapel...what kind of punishment was reserved for that? The words reverberated. They sounded strange, as if the convent had heard them, failed to understand them, and was now spitting them out. So obscene, so nasty. Lucy was ashamed.

The cardinal, clearly shocked, released her, took a few steps then knelt in front of the altar. He began to pray. For a second, Lucy thought she'd never seen anything so absurd. Then she felt idiotic. How can you accuse a cardinal of being ridiculous for praying?

Shooting began again, this time much closer. Sinclair prayed more loudly, in Latin. The words were beguiling, somehow much more potent than English. They were imbued with holiness, with *magic*. Once, Lucy had prayed like that too. She prayed until her knees were red and raw, until her hands were almost bleeding. She wanted God to cure her mother's cancer. Within days, her mum was dead.

He's not there, she said to herself, looking at the figure of Christ. *He never was.* It was so obvious to her now. Sure, she had a Creator. In fact, she had two, but they were both dead. First her mother, ravaged by the tumours that spread everywhere inside her, then her father, ravaged just as lethally by despair. He left a suicide note. **In the blue** was scrawled all down the page in increasingly desperate writing, until the last three words: *Forgive me, Lucy*.

What do you do when your creators are dead? They gave you life, but they couldn't save their own. And they certainly can't save yours. They'd abandoned her. Nothing made sense any longer. First, you're created – and the thing about that is that no created thing ever *asks* to be created – then you're stuck with it. You're forced into existence whether you like it or not. The very last thing you're offered is a choice. And you soon learn there's only one exit: death. The creators made you knowing how the story must end. And creation is meant to be *good*?

She closed her eyes. All she could think of was an old nursery rhyme. *London Bridge is falling down*. Over and over again, she said the words. They comforted her somehow. *Falling down, falling down.*

14

'What do you mean?' The veins on Commander Harrington's forehead were bulging. 'It can't be gone.'

Vernon explained again, and surprised himself by reporting the facts so calmly. He hadn't been calm a little earlier when he stepped into the archive section, normally the most well-ordered part of Thames House, and discovered the archivist dead, his face stricken with terror, and the archive room looking as though it had been bombed. Top-secret documents, many of them charred, lay strewn everywhere. All the filing cabinets were smashed open, bookcases pushed over, as if some intruder in a mad rage had frantically been searching for something.

'The black files,' Harrington said. 'They must be OK. They were in our top-security vault.'

Thames House's vault was modelled on America's Fort Knox. Constructed from steel and concrete, it was divided into several secure compartments. The vault door weighed more than 20 tons and no one person knew the precise combination for opening it. Now, somehow, it no longer existed.

'The vault door has gone,' Vernon said. 'Vaporised. All the files inside were taken or incinerated. There's nothing left.'

'But that vault was impregnable.'

'Commander, I saw it with my own eyes. It was completely destroyed, and *The Cainite Destiny* has gone.'

Harrington slumped into his seat. 'But that was the key to this.'

'A forensic team is sifting the wreckage,' Vernon said. 'The CCTV pictures show a white light and nothing else. It's a mystery.'

Colonel Gresnick, who had been quietly drinking coffee in the corner, put his cup down. 'Have you considered that we've been set up? Maybe Ferris and Morson's real plan was to get in here to steal *The Cainite Destiny*.'

Vernon glanced at the colonel in surprise. 'Christ, a Trojan Horse: the oldest trick in the book.'

Harrington switched to the TV picture showing the prisoners' cells. Sergeant Morson was sitting exactly as before while Captain Ferris was lying under his sheets, writhing and moaning.

'Poor bastard,' Vernon said. 'I guess that's the end of that theory.' He turned to Gresnick. 'Why did you think the prisoners might be interested in *The Cainite Destiny*? You make it sound as if it's something special.'

'*The Cainite Destiny* is the most valuable document in the world.'

'What do you mean?' Harrington shifted uneasily. 'I'm one of only three people who have seen it in the last sixty-seven years. No one else has been anywhere near it. You couldn't possibly know anything about it.'

'That's where you're wrong,' Gresnick answered. 'My grandfather...*he was the man who translated it.*'

15

Lucy's eyes opened, reluctantly. Sinclair was still on his knees, praying.

'De profundis clamavi ad te, Domine,' he said in Latin.

Lucy knew those words too well. *Out of the depths I have cried to thee, O Lord* – the opening words of Psalm 129. Sometimes, she thought they'd been branded on her heart. They were the cry of everyone annihilated by grief.

As more gunshots sounded, Sinclair's voice grew more desperate. 'Vanitas vanitatum,' he said, 'et omnia vanitas.'

Lucy bowed her head. *Vanity of vanities, and all things are vanity.* How often had she thought that since her parents died? Life had no point now. How could it when the Creators were dead, when love had been ripped from her forever?

She left the pews and tiptoed to a side-door hidden behind red velvet curtains. As quietly as possible, she eased the door open and slipped into the corridor outside. A shot rang out in the next corridor, the one leading to the refectory. A soldier in a black uniform staggered into view and slumped forward into the middle of the intersection of corridors.

Lucy stared at the man's head. Blood was pouring from a gaping hole in his lower jaw and spreading over the floor. His eyes were wide open, but there was no life there. She tried to move, but couldn't. *All is vanity.* She wanted to curl up, lie on the floor, and hope no one would hurt her.

In due course, the soldier's poor parents would learn of their son's death. His brothers and sisters would be devastated. His girlfriend, maybe pregnant, would never recover: love destroyed just when it was needed most. A whole tree of suffering, branches sprouting in scores of places, pain squeezing through the roots and spreading. Broken hearts falling like autumn leaves.

Out of the depths.

Feeling sick, she crept into one of the toilets. A bucket of dirty water had been pushed into the corner, with an old mop sticking out. She poured some of the water over the floor in front of one of the cubicles then stuck an 'Out of Order' sign from the cleaner's cupboard on the cubicle door, and locked herself in. Perching on top of the toilet seat, she pulled her knees up to her chin and tried not to make a sound. She shut her eyes. Minutes passed. No noise. *Nothing.*

Her mind flitted back to Raphael's painting. Everything about it was wrong, or too right – and maybe those amounted to the same thing. When she tried to mentally reconstruct the mural, she found all the details were somehow imprinted in her memory, as though they had been with her forever. More and more, she was convinced she'd seen this mural before...but she had no idea how that could be.

God, the delusions were coming back; how else could she explain it? The more she concentrated, the more vivid the painting became. It turned into a 3-D representation that she could rotate and flip, see from every angle. Why did she feel she knew it so well? In many ways, it was like a smaller-scale version of Michelangelo's Sistine Chapel ceiling fresco. It had much of the same religious iconography and told a similar story of Creation. Except there was something subtly different, some ambiguity. Perhaps it was a mirror image, or not quite in focus. What she didn't doubt was that buried in these images was a radically different history of mankind from the one she'd been taught at school.

She brought the top left-hand panel to the forefront of her mind and studied it as though she were back at Oxford University. Rusty thought processes cranked into gear.

The panel showed a dazzling lightshow, full of rainbow lights swirling like the wind, but in one corner was darkness; a thick, ominous murk. This must be a depiction of the separation of light from darkness described in the Book of Genesis.

Moving clockwise to the next panel, Lucy felt uneasy, but wasn't sure why. God was shown sitting on a throne made of diamonds, surrounded by a host of glowing, translucent angels. But again there was an unsettling ingredient – a dark angel about to throw a spear at God. Lucy assumed this was a depiction of Lucifer's rebellion against God.

Next, the same dark angel was falling to the earth clutching the spear, surrounded by a torrent of black raindrops. The expulsion of Lucifer from Heaven, presumably.

Next came the Garden of Eden, featuring a Tree of Knowledge shaped like a human being with a huge brain. A naked Adam and Eve stood in front of it. Near them, a serpent slithered over an odd emerald globe.

Then Cain, a surprisingly handsome figure, was depicted killing a swarthy Abel with a spear. Next up was Cain bearing a strange double S mark, like two serpents, on his forehead. The Mark of Cain, Lucy assumed. Behind Cain stood a city with a high, gleaming tower. Lucy guessed this was the Tower of Babel.

Panel 7 on the top right corner showed God in a mystical cloud above the Ark of Covenant in a tent – the Tabernacle – with a Moses-like figure looking on. The next panel showed the gold Temple of Solomon with a High Priest praying in front of the Ark.

Panel 9 was Jesus being baptised by John the Baptist in the river Jordan. Another Jesus-like figure waited in the background. Lucy had no idea who this other person was but, for some reason, she thought this figure had immense significance.

Panel 10 showed Salome doing the dance of seven veils for King Herod. In the next panel, John the Baptist's severed head rested on a gold, jewel-encrusted dish. The eyes and mouth were wide open, and something about it reminded Lucy of Munch's *The Scream*. Another man was being beheaded in the background. Lucy wondered if this was the same person who was shown earlier waiting to be baptised by John the Baptist. Who was he?

In Panel 12, The Last Supper was depicted with 30 pieces of silver lying between Jesus and Judas. Prominently displayed were a gold, jewel-encrusted dish containing bread and a beautiful chalice full of wine – the Holy Grail.

Panel 13 on the bottom right corner showed a Roman soldier thrusting a spear into Christ's side at the Crucifixion, with a man, presumably Joseph of Arimathea, collecting blood in the Holy Grail.

Panel 14 presented the Resurrection. A crowd were witnessing the event, half of them cheering, the other half with deeply gloomy faces. Lucy couldn't understand why Raphael had painted some people looking so unhappy at this joyous event.

Panel 15 showed a siege of a castle on a mountaintop. Men were climbing down the mountainside in the dark, while on the other side of the mountain, men and women were being burnt at the stake in the dawn light.

Panel 16 was the most baffling of all the images: Lucy's own painting. How could it possibly have ended up in this collection of unknown masterpieces by one of the world's greatest artists?

Panel 17 showed, apparently, King Arthur's Camelot – a castle overlooking a raging sea. Panel 18 depicted the battle of Camlann where Arthur, clutching Excalibur, was killed by the lance of his nephew Mordred. In the background was a round chapel and a castle on a high mound surrounded by trees. A cloud of dark ravens hovered above the chapel.

The next panel presented a desolate land, full of beggars in rags. In one corner was a dark cave, with a pool at its centre, full of stalactites and stalagmites. In the other was a forest with a ruined abbey in the middle.

Panel 20 showed a mountain castle overlooking a lake in a wooded valley. Painted directly onto the surface of the lake was the Holy Grail.

The next panel depicted the procession of the Grail Hallows: Spear, Sword, Chalice and Dish in front of the Fisher King, the guardian of the Grail Castle.

Panel 22 showed the Fisher King with a spear sticking out of his inner thigh.

As for Panel 23, it was simply bizarre. It was divided into four quarters, one of which showed a blue swastika on a white flag, the next a rising sun, the third a black and white flag, and the last a skull and crossbones. In the middle of the four flags was a circle containing a pyramid incorporating a staring eye, with a Phoenix hovering over the whole structure.

The final side-panel was the most striking of all. It showed the city of Rome in a mirror. The Vatican was displayed upside-down in an egg timer. In the upper section of the timer was a miniature universe of dazzling lights.

Lucy's eyes opened wide. She could hear voices directly outside her cubicle, speaking in German. *What's happening*? The language changed. Cardinal Sinclair was with them, talking in Italian. He was evidently angry.

Without warning, someone kicked the cubicle door open. A soldier stared down at Lucy, a machine gun slung over his shoulder. 'If you want to live, you must come with me immediately,' he said in good English.

'I don't want to.'

The soldier gripped his machine gun and pointed it at her. 'Then I'll kill you.'

16

'Your grandfather was Professor Reinhardt Weiss of Cambridge University?' Harrington asked, seemingly dumbfounded.

Gresnick nodded. 'He moved to Harvard at the end of 1945 because of the way MI5 treated him. They agreed his translation of *The Cainite Destiny* was accurate, but said the document was patently meaningless.'

Vernon remembered what Caldwell had told him about *The Cainite Destiny*. Now Gresnick was confirming it. He wondered if he should confront Harris about his accessing *The Cainite Destiny* within the last twenty-four hours. He decided to wait.

'Reinhardt Weiss signed the Official Secrets Act,' Harrington said. 'He agreed he wouldn't discuss this matter with anyone.'

'My grandfather said you were all blind. If you weren't willing to help, he was prepared to go it alone. He made it his life's work to discover the truth behind *The Cainite Destiny*. Before he died, he passed on all of his work to his daughter, my mother. She's now a History professor at Harvard. When my mum married, she made sure it was to a leading authority in Esoteric Studies. My father, at Yale, was her perfect match.'

Vernon felt queasy. Esoteric Studies was what Lucy taught at Oxford. Would Lucy – the old Lucy rather than the shadow she'd become – be attracted to Gresnick with his Hollywood good looks and his expertise in all the same stuff she loved?

'Your grandfather made an unauthorised copy of *The Cainite Destiny*?' Harrington was irate. 'He bequeathed it to his daughter and she to you, is that it?'

Gresnick nodded.

'Commander,' Vernon interrupted, 'I know for a fact that you accessed *The Cainite Destiny* yesterday.'

Gresnick stared at Harrington with sudden curiosity.

'How...?' Harrington shook his head. 'No matter.' He stared into space. 'When I joined MI5 from Oxford, I was appointed special assistant to the then Director General. One night, just before he was fired, he got drunk in his office. He was in an odd mood. I think he knew he was about to be kicked out. "If the world ever looks like it's going to end," he told me, "seek out a document in our archives. It's called *The Cainite Destiny*. I swear to you, Harrington, it brings me out in a sweat whenever I think about it."

'The DG then made one of the strangest comments I've ever heard. "If any of it is true," he said, "we're kidding ourselves that we know anything. It means there are people out there who are party to an incredible secret that the rest of us can only guess at – a secret history of the world, a world stranger than we could ever imagine.'"

Harrington shrugged. 'I had a quick glance at the document out of simple curiosity, but it didn't make any sense. I agreed with the official assessment that it was nonsense. I honestly can't remember much of it. The Spear of Destiny was significant – that's all that made an impression on me.'

Gresnick gave a half-smile then slid out a paper from one of his folders. 'My grandfather knew the document would be buried and forgotten. He couldn't let that happen. Although *The Cainite Destiny* was baffling, my grandfather recognised it as a key to something astounding: a re-interpretation of history based on ideas we in the West have never dared to take seriously.' He placed the paper in the centre of the table. 'This is my grandfather's translation of *The Cainite Destiny*.'

****

March 12 1938

Schatzkammer, Hofburg Palace, Vienna

How to begin? I'm shaking as I write these words. Himmler made us swear to record nothing of what happened today. I've never disobeyed him in my life, and my only excuse now is that these are private words that only I shall ever read. I want to be able to relive today for the rest of what, I pray, will be my brief future in this world.

We arrived at the Imperial Treasury at noon. Himmler ordered the Austrian staff to leave and then twelve of us stepped inside, one from each of the twelve families of the original priesthood. It made me shiver to think that we must have looked just like Cain's original twelve priests. Just as they wore black robes and carried the mark of the Death's Head on their silver rings, all of us were in our black SS uniforms, with the gleaming Totenkopf badge on our caps.

The Führer, in his brown leather coat, followed us in. Cain himself couldn't have looked more majestic. If anyone was marked out by destiny as our deliverer, it was the Führer. We formed two lines, gave the Roman salute and shouted, 'Heil Hitler!' as he strode past us.

Following him, we walked through the Imperial Regalia of the Holy Roman Empire, ignoring the glittering trinkets. Already, we felt the Spear's presence. I imagined that the legions of martyrs who struggled for so long to avenge our Lord, to bring us back to the true light, marched behind us.

For thousands of years, the Enemy's persecution of us never faltered. They hanged us, beheaded us, drowned us, burned us alive, disembowelled us, did everything in their power to exterminate us. Always there were traitors, infiltrators, spies, deserters, turncoats, the weak and the fainthearted, but the *Secret Doctrine* survived every attempt to destroy it. And now the Spear of Destiny was about to be ours.

It lay in an ordinary glass cabinet – the world's most sacred relic, the most powerful object ever created, resting on a red velvet cushion. It was under their noses all the time and they never saw the truth. Born in ignorance, mired in error, damned by their stupidity. They deserve every horror we'll soon unleash upon them.

Sunshine caught the Spearhead and it glinted as though it were bathed in the light of the one, true God. I could practically reach out and touch the weapon that would free us forever. The words of the legend came back to me: *The man who wields the Spear of Destiny will control the fate of the world.* We knew the legend better than anyone: it was *our* legend. We alone knew where the Spear originated, the identity of its true owner and the reason it was made.

The Führer gave a signal to SS-Hauptsturmführer Neumann. He unlocked the cabinet and the Führer stepped past him and gripped the Spear. When he raised it in his right hand, the spearhead glowed, just as the legend said it would. We all clicked our heels and yelled, 'Sieg Heil!'

'Our quest is nearing its end,' the Führer said. 'Cain's destiny is almost fulfilled.'

I wanted to weep when I heard those words. I stared at the two sig runes that made up my SS insignia. Sig for victory. Sig for vengeance. Sig Sig – the mark the Enemy once branded on us to humiliate us, but which we now wore with pride. It reminded us every day of what we had to do.

'The creature's *box* is in Chartres Cathedral,' the Führer continued, 'and it will be ours as soon as we conquer France.'

When he lifted the spear above his head, we all knelt.

'After France falls, England will be helpless,' he said. 'Then we'll locate the remaining two Grail Hallows and finish this once and for all.'

He ordered us to leave then remained alone with the Spear for over an hour. When he emerged, he didn't speak, but it was obvious something had changed. I can't begin to describe the odd expression in his eyes.

'Our Enemy hasn't begun to suspect our true nature,' he said. 'They call us warmongers, fascists, totalitarians. Not for one second have they conceived who we really are. Soon we'll bring humanity its greatest and most unexpected gift.'

He smiled in a way I'd never seen before, as though he knew that the great burden he carried would soon be lifted.

'Don't you feel it?' he remarked, and I could swear he trembled. 'It's almost here.' Then he said the words we had all waited so long to hear.

'*The end of the world.*'

17

Harrington pushed away the translation as though he found everything about it distasteful. 'You know no one has ever satisfactorily explained it. Your grandfather offered plenty of speculation, but no facts. We didn't think we'd ever find out what it meant. I suppose you're going to say now that you understand it completely.'

'I wasn't chosen for this mission by accident,' Gresnick replied. 'When I was at West Point I wrote a dissertation on the influence of mysticism and the occult on the Nazi war effort in WWII. As soon as the DIA established a Nazi link to the Delta Force deserters, I was called in.'

'So, what do you think *The Cainite Destiny* means, colonel?'

'I have no more hard facts than my grandfather did, but I'm as certain as he was that the mystery can be solved. You have to realise that the Nazis were very strange.'

'That's hardly news.'

'I assure you, Commander Harrington, you have no idea of just how weird they were. When I wrote my dissertation, I had to tone it down because I didn't want the DIA to think I'd gone crazy. I said that a few senior Nazis – Himmler in particular – were interested in mysticism, but that it was little more than a sideshow. What I really thought was that mysticism was at the core of Nazism. The Nazis were anything but an ordinary political party, and the war they waged was unlike anything that had gone before. They were more like religious fanatics fighting a Crusade, but it was no conventional God they believed in.'

Vernon flicked his thumb against his index finger as Gresnick gave an account of the Nazis' secret beliefs. It was hard to credit his story. Apparently, many of those who helped to set up the Nazi party were members of the *Thule-Gesellschaft* – the Thule Society. They believed that a mythical land known in ancient times as Thule was the home of a blue-eyed, blond, Aryan master race – the original Germans – who later populated the famous Atlantis. Thule was said to be Iceland, Greenland or somewhere close to the North Pole. A central part of the Nazi dream was to recreate Thule/Atlantis on a global scale, with Aryans restored to their godlike status and everyone else enslaved. It was a member of the Thule Society who chose the swastika, an ancient Aryan symbol, as the Nazi emblem. In addition, the members of the Thule Society were well known for their virulent anti-Semitism. The SS had a special division called the *Ahnenerbe Forschungs und Lehrgemeinschaft* – the Ancestral Heritage Research and Teaching Society, nicknamed the *Nazi Occult Bureau* by their enemies. Their task was to find scientific, anthropological and archaeological evidence to support the theories of the Thule Society. They went on an expedition to Tibet because there was a legend that descendants of the original master race of Thule settled there. The legend said there were huge underground caves in Tibet where descendants of the first master race still lived in hi-tech cities in a subterranean paradise. These hidden Aryans were masters of an astonishing occult power known as *vril*. It was one of the tasks of the Ahnenerbe to make contact with the people in these cities and learn the secrets of vril.

Right up to the end of the Second World War, the Nazis believed a secret weapon would save them. The weapon they had in mind was vril. When Russian troops entered Berlin in 1945, they made one of the most extraordinary discoveries of the war. They found a thousand Tibetan monks dressed in SS uniforms in a bomb-wrecked barracks, all of whom had committed ritual suicide. These monks were the Third Reich's last, futile attempt to harness vril as a WMD to repel the Red Army.

'I can see why you kept that quiet,' Vernon said.

'Hold on.' Harrington was fiddling with his cufflinks. 'Do you think it's possible vril is real? One could imagine that a release of unusual energy was behind all the disturbances we've seen lately.'

Gresnick shrugged. 'I can't rule it out. But why all the raids on holy relics. That doesn't fit, does it?'

'Well, we know the Ark of the Covenant was treated by the ancient Hebrews as a kind of WMD. Perhaps holy objects can channel vril in some way.' Harrington's face reddened. 'Jesus, am I really saying this?'

'I've heard of vril before,' Vernon said. 'It's the stuff they put in Bovril.' He smiled awkwardly.

'That's precisely where Bovril gets its name from,' Gresnick said. 'Bovine vril.'

'What?'

'Forget Bovril,' Harrington snapped. 'If, for argument's sake, we accept the Nazis were occultists, where does the Spear of Destiny come in?'

Gresnick frowned. 'It crops up in Arthurian mythology, and that was something else the Nazis were obsessed with. In Himmler's castle of Wewelsburg, the central banqueting hall contained a round table. Years before the outbreak of WWII, Himmler sent an SS officer called Otto Rahn to the south of France to look for the Holy Grail. Rahn was convinced the last owners of the Grail were a heretical sect called the Cathars, exterminated by the Catholic Church in the Middle Ages. They were the first people to face the Inquisition – in fact, it was invented specifically for dealing with them. Rahn thought the Cathars were descended from Celtic Druids and that they were steeped in the legends surrounding King Arthur.'

'We're coming back to Lucy's book, aren't we?' Vernon said. 'She used Otto Rahn's work as one of her primary sources, and the Cathars featured heavily in her writings.'

'Actually, I know very little about Lucy's book,' Gresnick remarked. 'It was never published in the States.'

'The world wasn't ready for Lucy,' Vernon said flatly.

'I hope you have a good memory, Mr Vernon. I need to know exactly what Lucy's theory was. She may have inadvertently stumbled on the key to this whole thing.'

18

'What the...' Vernon was just about to reply when all the lights flickered and went out. The temperature plummeted.

'Christ, what's going on?' Gresnick blurted.

'Must be a generator failure,' Harrington said. 'The backup should kick in soon.'

Vernon gazed into the blackness. 'That wasn't a generator fault...'

'What do you mean?'

'Didn't you feel it? When the lights went out...some sort of...*presence*.'

'Get a grip of yourself,' Harrington said. 'You can't be falling for that hokum about angels.'

The lights came on again, and the room heated up. 'You see – simple technical fault.'

'I felt something too,' Gresnick said. 'It was the weirdest thing. Like some huge power source being activated.'

'Well, it's gone now,' Harrington said. 'We're all a little on edge. Our imaginations getting a bit overactive, I dare say.'

Vernon called Gary Caldwell and asked if anything unusual was going on. Caldwell said security teams were sweeping the building, trying to find whoever was responsible for the attack on the archive department. The badly damaged electrics amongst the wreckage had shorted out and crashed the primary generator.

'Satisfied?' Harrington said. 'Nothing mysterious. Now, let's get on with this. You were about to tell us about Lucy's book.'

****

Vernon poured a glass of water and took a long drink. He was rattled and felt embarrassed. He urged himself to focus. 'Yes, Lucy's book.' He'd proofread it before she submitted it to her publisher. It wasn't exactly his field, but he still remembered most of it – one of the benefits of being a research analyst. Ever since he was a kid, he'd been able to rapidly absorb a lot of complex material, and was often able to recall chunks of it years later. It helped that he was genuinely fascinated by Lucy's work.

'Lucy's starting point was an old book by an English folklorist called Jessie Weston,' he began. 'Weston claimed that the Grail legends were a recasting of old fertility rituals from ancient Egypt, Babylonia and Greece. She went through each of the main aspects of the Grail stories and showed how similar they were to features of myths concerning the ancient gods Osiris, Tammuz, Adonis and Attis.

'Lucy agreed with Weston about the Grail legends being a representation of something else, but she disagreed that fertility rites were involved. Her idea was that a particular group of people produced the Grail stories to preserve their beliefs from an enemy they could never defeat.'

'The Cathars, right?' Gresnick interrupted.

Vernon nodded.

'Well,' Harrington intervened, 'both of you may be experts, but all I know about the Cathars is that they came from Languedoc in the southwest of France, and I only know that because I once went on a weekend trip to Carcassonne to see the walled city, and it turned out to be the capital of Cathar country.'

'OK, I'll give you my one-minute introduction to the Cathars,' Vernon said. 'They were one of the strangest sects in history. Their name comes from the ancient Greek word katharoi meaning *the pure*. The Cathars, the pure ones, were renowned for living good, simple lives. They had few possessions, were peace-loving, vegetarian, and frowned on sex.

'Lots of ordinary Catholics looked at the ascetic lives of the Cathars and thought they seemed much holier, much more Christ-like than most Catholics, especially the priests and monks who were notoriously sleazy at that time. Before long, many Catholics started converting to Catharism.

'The Catholic Church wasn't slow to see the danger. Realising war was coming, perhaps a war of extermination, and that their beliefs might be lost forever, the Cathars desperately thought of how they might pass on their religion to future generations. They had to come up with something that communicated their beliefs without attracting the suspicions of the Catholic Church. The legend of the Holy Grail was their solution. On one level, it seemed like an orthodox Catholic story, but it was the opposite – pure heresy. It's a simple fact that before the Grail romances appeared, there wasn't a single mention of anything called the Holy Grail, and no legend saying that Joseph of Arimathea was its original keeper. Even as far back as 1260, the legend of the Holy Grail was known not to be an authentic Christian story.

'Following Otto Rahn's line of thought, Lucy argued that the Grail legends described in coded form the initiation ceremonies and religious rites of the Cathars, but now transformed into chivalrous stories. Everything was symbolic, all of the characters in the stories carefully chosen. Many of the troubadours, the great romantic poets of the Middle Ages, were Cathars and they brought all their art to bear on the creation of the legends. These were the greatest romances ever devised, inspiring everyone who read them, and unwittingly feeding them incredibly powerful heretical ideas.

'Meanwhile, relations with the Catholic Church continued to deteriorate. Pope Innocent III decided on drastic action. He ordered a Crusade against the Cathars and on 24 June 1209, the feast day of John the Baptist – one of the Cathars' most sacred days – the Crusader army set out from Lyon.

'Although the Cathars didn't approve of violence, they fought back, mostly using mercenaries, and the war dragged on for decades. In 1231, the next Pope, Gregory IX, set up an institution for stamping out heresy once and for all – the Inquisition. In 1243, the Cathars made what was effectively their last stand at their mountain stronghold of Montségur. The Catholic army besieged it for months before the garrison finally surrendered in 1244. Those in the garrison who refused to recant their heresy were burnt at the stake en masse at the foot of the mountain.'

'OK, I get the picture,' Harrington said. 'An unorthodox religion gets wiped out by a much bigger religion and tries to survive in some way by hiding its beliefs in the form of a story that lives on after the religion has died, providing hope that the religion can be reborn some day.'

Vernon nodded again.

'So, what was Lucy's theory about these hidden meanings? Why was her work controversial? I mean, what did she say that Rahn didn't?'

'According to the basic legend, the Grail is in the keeping of a man called the Fisher King who lives in the Grail Castle, surrounded by warrior monks. He has a mysterious wound on his upper thigh, or even in his genitals, which never heals. Lucy was curious about the use of the title *Fisher King*. The symbol of the fish was known from antiquity to represent divine life. Only one person can offer divine life, and so Lucy argued that the Fisher King must be another name for God. The worthy – the Cathars – would be caught in his fishing nets while the unworthy – the Catholics – would swim right through. It saddened God that so many fish in the sea couldn't be saved. They were his metaphorical wound that never healed. Only when all of humanity returned to him would his wound vanish.

'The Fisher King's Grail Castle, hidden from the unworthy, was heaven; the Wasteland outside, hell. The Wasteland would disappear only when the Fisher King was cured, and that would happen only when Catharism triumphed.

'Lucy wanted to know how those in the Wasteland could find the hidden Grail castle. Only those who rejected their old, false beliefs and started seeking the truth – Catharism – would succeed, she claimed. In the castle, they would be shown a solemn ceremony where the Grail Hallows – a spear, cup, sword and dish – would be presented to them.

'If they understood the meaning of the ceremony – which would signify that they'd been fully initiated into Catharism – the Grail seekers would know to ask the Fisher King a particular question. If they failed to ask the right question, because they were still clinging to the false doctrines of other religions, they'd leave the castle and never find it again.

'Lucy thought the Grail Hallows should be separated into two pairs: the spear and the cup, the sword and the dish. The first pair represented Christianity. The spear was the Roman lance thrust into Christ's side at the Crucifixion, and Christ used the cup at the Last Supper.'

'What about the sword and dish?' Harrington asked.

'That's the radical part of Lucy's theory. She said the sword was the one used to behead John the Baptist. His head was placed on a dish to be presented to Salome as her reward for dancing for King Herod. So, the sword and dish stood for John the Baptist rather than Christ. Grail seekers had to choose between the two pairs. If you chose correctly, you were a true believer; otherwise you were damned.'

'I don't understand,' Gresnick said. 'Are you saying Lucy thought there was some kind of opposition between John the Baptist and Jesus?'

'Exactly, colonel. People forget that John the Baptist was only six months older than Jesus, and that they were related by blood. Their mothers were cousins. Some people thought John was more important than Jesus. Lucy believed the Cathars were descended from an early Gnostic sect called the Johannites who considered John the Baptist the true Messiah. Jesus, so the story goes, was merely one of John's disciples. Jesus openly said, 'None is greater than John. He is *more* than a prophet.' In other words, Jesus himself acknowledged that John was the real Messiah. But things changed and Jesus decided to betray John, and one of his fellow conspirators was Salome. That's why she asked for John's head. There's supposedly a gospel called *The Gospel According to Salome*, suppressed by the early Christian leaders, that relates the whole sordid tale.

'In the book, Salome claims that Caiaphas, the High Priest of the Temple was a secret follower of John the Baptist, as were Pontius Pilate, Judas Iscariot, and the Roman soldier who thrust a spear into Jesus. All of them had vowed to avenge John, and the Johannites subsequently revered all of them. Pilate in particular was an extraordinary individual. Very little was officially recorded about his life, but it's likely that he was born in Fortingall in Scotland, son of a Druid and related to a Scottish tribal chief called Metallanus. Metallanus wanted to establish good relations with Rome, so he sent the sons of several prominent families to Rome to be brought up as Romans, with Roman names. Pilate was one of those. The Royal Scots, the oldest regiment in the British Army, claim to be descended from Pontius Pilate's bodyguard. With his Druidic family background, Pilate was highly receptive to the Gnostic message.

'The Knights Templar were also believed to be Johannites. Every Grand Master of the Knights Templar took the name John. The Catholic Church accused the Templars of worshipping a severed head called Baphomet. Lucy said this was none other than John the Baptist's preserved head. At their trial by the Inquisition, the Templars were accused of trampling and spitting on the Christian Cross. Again, this made perfect sense according to Lucy's theory. Even the Templars' famous red cross was far from conventional. It wasn't a Latin cross with unequal arms of the type that Jesus was crucified on, but a Cross pattée with equal arms. This allowed them to masquerade as Christians while actually showing they weren't Christian at all to those who understood the symbolism.'

'That's some theory,' Gresnick said.

'Why are Delta Force so interested in Lucy's ideas?' Harrington asked.

'My guess is that Lucy rediscovered or elaborated on something the Nazis knew about the Holy Grail,' Gresnick said. 'Otto Rahn, in two books *Kreuzzug gegen den Gral* – Crusade Against the Grail, and *Luzifers Hofgesinf* – Lucifer's Court, had already put forward the case that the Grail Romances were a coded reference to Catharism. Like her, he said the Quest for the Holy Grail was a symbolic representation of the Cathars' search for God. The Procession of the Grail Hallows was a reconstruction of the Cathars' most sacred initiation ceremony.'

Harrington tapped the table with his fingers. 'Is there any hard evidence that the Cathars wrote the Grail stories?'

Gresnick spun his pen between his fingers. 'The evidence is circumstantial, but persuasive.'

'And what about the theory that the Cathars and the Knights Templar were closely related?'

'Again, circumstantial but convincing. The Templars' main powerbase was in the Languedoc, exactly where the Cathars lived. Many Templars came from Cathar families. The Templars refused to join in with the Catholic Church's persecution of the Cathars even though, as elite Catholic Crusaders, they ought to have led the attack. In fact, they were suspected of giving safe haven to many prominent Cathars.

'The Cathars were subjected to a savage Crusade by knights from northern France, had to endure all the rigours of the Inquisition and were eventually wiped out. A few decades later, the Templars were arrested by knights from the northern France, accused of heresy, brought in front of the Inquisition and stamped out. History repeats itself, don't you think?

'My grandfather was convinced the Cathars and the Templars were created by the same people, and, like Lucy, he thought they both traced their roots back to the Johannite followers of John the Baptist. The Cathars were an overt challenge to the Catholic Church while the Templars were more like a fifth column, pretending to be orthodox but in fact completely heretical. The secrecy demanded of every member of the Templars was the perfect way to guarantee no one discovered the truth about them. New members were warned of the appalling retribution that would be taken against them if they ever revealed any of the Order's secrets. They'd have their tongues removed, their eyes poked out, and their hearts taken from their chests while still beating.'

'That sounds like the oaths Freemasons take,' Vernon said.

'That's no coincidence,' Gresnick said. 'The Freemasons were probably founded by the Templars. They were the next step of the revolt against Catholicism.'

'So, you're saying the Cathars, the Templars and the Freemasons are all really the same?'

'I believe so. The papacy forbade Catholics from becoming Freemasons and accused the Masons of worshipping a false god. The Freemasons' ceremonies and rites are all connected with the Temple of Solomon, and the proper name of the Knights Templar is *The Order of the Poor Knights of the Temple of Solomon.*'

Harrington leaned forward. 'OK, for argument's sake, let's say you're right. How do the Nazis fit in? Are you implying that they're linked to the Cathars and the Templars too?'

Gresnick gave a sardonic smile. 'I don't have any conclusive proof, but it's well known that Himmler thought of the SS as an order of knights: as the modern successors of the Knights Templar and their Germanic counterparts, the Teutonic Knights. He was obsessed with the Spear of Destiny and the Holy Grail, both of which are strongly linked to the Templars. The Holy Grail was rumoured to be the Cathars' most sacred treasure. Otto Rahn, an expert on the Cathars, was personally appointed to the SS by Himmler and was sent on expeditions to the Languedoc to look for it. There's no doubt Himmler was fascinated by the Cathars and the Templars, but I think it goes further than that. *The Cainite Destiny* suggests that the Nazis thought they could trace their lineage back to Cain and I think that two of the stopping-off points in the Nazis' ancestry are the Cathars and the Knights Templar. When Otto Rahn was exploring caves in the Sabarthès Mountains in the Languedoc, he found hidden chambers where the walls were inscribed with Templar and Cathar symbols, side by side. There were also depictions of the Spear of Destiny, the Holy Grail, and the Ark of the Covenant.'

'You know what you've done?' Vernon said. 'You've linked just about every conspiracy theory imaginable: Atlantis, Cathars, Druids, Freemasons, Nazis, the Knights Templar, the Ark of the Covenant, the Spear of Destiny, the Holy Grail – they're all in there.'

'What if all the conspiracies we're familiar with are subsets of a much bigger conspiracy?' Gresnick replied. 'A *superconspiracy*, if you will. Each minor conspiracy theory gives us a tantalizing glimpse of the superconspiracy – a taste of the truth but no more than that. So, we're always left with unanswered questions and room for new conspiracy theories. But, with the superconspiracy, every smaller conspiracy is explained, every answer given, every loose end tied up. All along, there weren't separate conspiracies, just one huge, misunderstood conspiracy.'

'What would your superconspiracy be about then?' Vernon asked. 'Who's doing the conspiring and who or what are they conspiring against?'

'Don't you see? – every conspiracy is connected with religion. What were the Knights Templar really up to, what did the Cathars really believe in, why did the Catholic Church hate and fear them so much, what was the ultimate Nazi objective, what was the quest for the Holy Grail really about, what power does the Spear of Destiny really have, what was the Ark of the Covenant really used for, and so on.'

'What are you saying, colonel?' Harrington asked.

'It's simple. Every conspiracy comes back to just one thing – the identity of the True God.' Gresnick started making a chopping gesture with his hand, as though he were cutting the problem into pieces. 'Imagine you were in a world where you knew the truth but were forced on pain of death to embrace a lie. Openly expressing your opinions would get you killed, so you were forced to create secrets and codes that your enemies wouldn't notice or understand. But your enemies weren't stupid. They cracked your codes, exposed your secrets and killed you in huge numbers. The survivors had to create ever more complex codes and pass on the keys to unlock them. What if the keys were lost? What then? Without the keys, the codes would eventually become incomprehensible; their true meaning lost. Unless, of course, there was one group that never lost the key, that maintained the secret perfectly intact right from the beginning and through everything thrown at them by their enemies.'

'You're saying such a group exists?'

Gresnick nodded, but didn't elaborate.

'Well, are you going to tell us?'

'I think that when Section 5 interrogated the Nazi officials in 1945, they were told what the conspiracy was. I think half of Section 5 went along with it and the other half didn't. The half that bought it killed the others to stop them revealing the secret.'

'That's unlikely, don't you think?' Vernon commented. 'Why would some be persuaded and the others not, and why would the former be willing to kill the latter? Surely the evidence would have to be irrefutable, in which case everyone would have believed it.'

Gresnick rattled his pen against a jug of water. 'But what if the half that believed had a particular reason to believe, and the others didn't?'

'I don't follow.'

'Well, imagine the Nazis provided physical proof of their claims. In fact, imagine the only reason they revealed the conspiracy in the first place was that they knew some of the Americans were sure to believe them because of that proof.'

Vernon had to intervene. 'Some of the Americans had a mark on them, is that what you're telling us? A mark which meant that they and the Nazis were somehow on the same side.'

'That's exactly what I'm saying.'

'What kind of mark?' Harrington asked.

'The most famous mark of all, sir.' Gresnick pointed at his forehead. *The Mark of Cain.*'

19

Think about it. Half of Section 5 murder their colleagues and preserve the Nazis' secret. They go home to America and involve their children, and later their grandchildren, in a conspiracy. It would have to be something dramatic that would make them do that, something that removed any possibility of doubt. My grandfather's theory was that there was more than just a historical link between the elite members of the Cathars, the Knights Templar, the Freemasons and the Nazis. There was a physical connection too – they were related by blood, and all of them bore the Mark of Cain.'

'But the Mark of Cain, if I remember right, was a crescent-shaped red mark that appeared on Cain's forehead,' Vernon said. 'It would have been obvious if every surviving member of Section 5 had a distinctive mark on their forehead.'

'The truth is no one knows what the Mark of Cain looked like. It wasn't explicitly described in the Bible. My grandfather speculated that the mark appeared only when it was activated by the presence of a specific holy object. He had in mind the Spear of Destiny.'

'Why that in particular?' Harrington asked.

'My grandfather was convinced it wasn't a Roman spear at all. It was much older. In fact, he thought it was actually the weapon Cain used to kill Abel. It practically says as much in *The Cainite Destiny*. That's why it was so revered by the Nazis. It seemed to have special powers. Perhaps it revealed hidden marks.'

'This is just speculation.'

'Conventional approaches haven't got us anywhere, commander. Scientists don't have a clue what's going on in the world right now. They haven't a single theory between them.'

'But this is so far fetched.'

'And when Dr Wells says one of our prisoners is becoming an angel, that isn't? To use a cliché, it's time to think outside the box.'

'Well, tell me this much. I remember reading somewhere that the Holy Grail wasn't an object at all – it was the bloodline of Jesus or some such thing. What do *you* think it is?'

'Listen, the reason the Holy Grail is so mysterious is that no one has ever been clear what it is. That was deliberate, of course. The best way to camouflage something is to give it multiple identities, or no identity at all.'

'Well, how much do we know about it? It must have a beginning. It must be *something* even if it's a coded something.'

'OK, here's the quick history of the Holy Grail. The three main Grail Romances all appeared at the end of the twelfth and beginning of the thirteenth centuries, exactly when the Cathars realised they were living on borrowed time. The first person to mention the Grail was a man called Chrétien de Troyes who lived in the second half of the twelfth century. It's not known when and where he was born and when and where he died. His life was shrouded in mystery – exactly what you'd expect from someone with secrets to hide, someone who didn't want to be too conspicuous. In fact, it's not even clear what his name really was. Chrétien is the French for Christian, and Troyes is simply a French town, so Chrétien de Troyes is literally, 'Christian from Troyes.' In fact, maybe it's just *a* Christian from Troyes. It's not telling us much, is it?

'Robert de Boron was the next person to write about the Grail. De Boron was a French knight who fought in the Holy Land as a Crusader. He was the first of the Grail writers to introduce an unmistakable Christian theme into the Grail story, identifying it with the cup used by Christ at the Last Supper, which Joseph of Arimathea later used to collect the last drops of Christ's blood. It was Robert de Boron who said Joseph brought the Grail to Glastonbury in England.'

'So, no doubt, you don't think it's any coincidence that Lucy is in Glastonbury,' Harrington said.

'No coincidence at all. Anyway, the third main player in the Grail stories was Wolfram von Eschenbach. As with the others, few facts are known about him. Many suspected he was one of the Knights Templar, and he explicitly claimed the Templars were the guardians of the Grail. This was long before the Templars were suspected of heresy. Interestingly, he claimed to have been told the story of the Grail by a man called Kyot from the southwest of France. Even less is known about Kyot than about Wolfram von Eschenbach, but some experts think Kyot was both a troubadour and a Cathar.

'My grandfather believed all three Grail authors knew each other and were writing different versions of the Grail legend to sow confusion, and make it impossible for any outsiders to make sense of the story. I mean, these three writers produced three different Grails, one of which was highly Christian, and the other two scarcely Christian at all. So, it meant that no one could be sure what you were talking about when you spoke of the Grail. If the Inquisition asked, you could say the Grail was Jesus' cup. If someone else asked, you could say it was one of the non-Christian objects.'

'And what were the *other* objects?'

'The word 'Grail' comes from the old French word *graal*, which comes from the Medieval Latin word *gradalis*, meaning dish. So, when Chrétien de Troyes first mentioned the Grail, he was talking about a dish. He described it as made of gold and encrusted with jewels. Robert de Boron, the second

Grail writer, then said it was Jesus' cup. Arguably, a deep, small dish might not be too unlike a cup, so this isn't such a great leap, but Wolfram von Eschenbach denied it was either a cup or a dish. He said it was a stone of a very pure kind, and he gave it another name – *lapsit exillas*.

'A dying human who held the stone would not die, he said, and anyone who possessed the stone would never age. *Lapsit exillas* was poor Latin and posed yet another mystery. Some scholars thought he intended to say *lapis lapsus ex caelis* meaning *the stone fallen from heaven*. Alternatively, he might have meant *lapis philosophorum – the philosopher's stone*. That was the miraculous object sought by alchemists that could turn base metals into gold, provide an elixir of life, and cure all diseases. Later, Wolfram said the stone was an emerald jewel from the crown of Lucifer that fell to the earth when Lucifer's army fought God's host and lost. So, take your pick.'

Vernon peered at the green globe the prisoner had brought in. 'You don't think...' He pointed at the object.

'You think this is an emerald from Lucifer's crown?' Gresnick smiled.

'Well, look what it supposedly did to the prisoner.'

'It's not doing anything to me, is it?' Gresnick held it up to the light and squinted at it. 'I told you we'd have it checked out, but it seems like a cheap glass ball to me.'

'Give it to me.' Vernon took the ball from Gresnick, held it for a moment then, without warning, let it drop to the floor.

'What the hell do you think you're doing?' Harrington yelled.

Vernon picked up the ball. 'Whatever it is, it isn't glass.'

'You can't be suggesting we have the Holy Grail here with us right now.'

Vernon shrugged. 'I'm not sure what I'm saying.'

There was a knock on the door. A soldier opened it and Caldwell came in, looking flushed.

'You had better look at the TV.'

'Why?' Harrington asked. 'What's happened?'

'The Ark of the Covenant has just been found.'

'What!?'

'It's in the middle of the south lawn of the White House.'

20

The men switched on the BBC's *News 24*. A reporter was talking excitedly, only just managing to stop garbling his words. He was framed against a long shot of the White House, lit up in the dark.

'I've just come from a press conference,' he said. 'The Press Secretary announced that an hour ago a security incident occurred outside the White House perimeter. A military truck drove up to the front gates. The driver got out, was picked up by a motorbike and rode off. No trace of him has been found.

'The Secret Service suspected that the truck contained a fertiliser bomb and ordered an evacuation of the White House. An anonymous caller then contacted the White House press office, claiming that the Ark of the Covenant stolen from Ethiopia was in a crate in the back of the truck. The call was recorded and played back to us.

'The caller, British and well-spoken, said that the world had become Godless and that the coordinated thefts of religious icons three days ago were intended to jolt the world into re-engaging with the divine, or to suffer the consequences. The Spear of Destiny and The Holy Grail would also be returned if the crate were unloaded in the centre of the White House lawn in full view of the world.

'"What better demonstration of divine power versus earthly vanity could there be," the caller said, "than to have the ultimate symbol of God placed on the lawn of the centre of worldly power. It's time for the people of the world to choose once and for all where their real allegiances lie."

'The Press Secretary announced that the Secret Service were convinced that, in the unlikely event that the Ark was actually inside the crate, it was probably accompanied by a WMD – a dirty bomb more than likely – and strongly advised against unloading it. They wanted to drive the truck to a military base, or do a controlled detonation.

'However, we were told that President Adams, renowned for his born-again Christianity, overruled the Secret Service. "A God-fearing nation has nothing to fear from God," he apparently declared. "He will never harm us."

'So, in the last fifteen minutes, the truck, driven by a Secret Service volunteer, was admitted into the grounds of the White House. We are now waiting for the crate to be removed from the back and placed on the floodlit South Lawn, in front of the world's TV cameras.'

The anchorman in the BBC studio appeared. 'We're interrupting Tim's report to bring live pictures of the crate being unloaded by U.S. Marines. This is an extraordinary development. For thousands of years, people have believed the Ark of the Covenant was irretrievably lost. If this is indeed the Ark then we're looking at a miraculous time machine, taking us right back to the time of Moses. Some claim that God himself resides within the Ark. In the next few minutes, we'll discover the truth for ourselves.'

The camera shot showed the Marines manoeuvring the heavy crate onto the lawn and carefully dismantling it, eventually revealing an object under a red velvet cover. One of the Marines went forward and removed the cover.

Vernon, Harrington, Gresnick and Caldwell all gasped at once. They didn't doubt that everyone watching across the globe was reacting in exactly the same way.

The Ark was beautiful beyond imagining. The camera zoomed in on the glistening gold chest bearing engravings of Biblical scenes. It seemed literally made in heaven. Its lid had a crown of gold, and on each side were two gold rings, in which two gold poles were placed. On top of the lid were two winged-creatures, the famous cherubim, made of solid gold, with their faces turned towards each other and their outstretched wings almost touching. The wings formed a seat – a throne for God, according to the Bible.

'It's all true,' Harrington said, 'everything they said about it.'

Vernon shook his head and glanced at Gresnick. 'You can't be buying this.'

The colonel seemed even more awestruck than Harrington. 'My grandfather's theories don't sound so crazy now, do they?'

'This is as suspicious as hell,' Vernon muttered.

'Look,' Caldwell blurted, 'President Adams is walking towards it.'

The camera tracked the President as he moved towards the Ark, his hands clasped in prayer. He circled it for a few seconds, tears streaking his cheeks. He closed his eyes, as though he couldn't believe that the world of Moses had come to life in the twenty-first century.

He knelt in front of it, with the two cherubim directly in front of him. He held out his hands and began to recite the Lord's Prayer. *'Our Father, which art in heaven, Hallowed be thy name, Thy kingdom come...'*

And then the Ark exploded.

21

Lucy wanted them to slow down. The roads near the convent were too narrow, too twisting, for vehicles travelling at high speed. Above all, there was the darkness. It was one o'clock in the morning, so it ought to be dark, but not *this* dark. It had a special quality, as if extra layers of black had been added. It was thicker, murkier, more resistant to light. The beams from the vehicles' headlights were swallowed almost before they'd lit the way.

To Lucy it seemed that her life had become full of lights like these, ones that failed to reach as far as those in other peoples' lives. Everyone else had their bright, wide, beams illuminating everything they did. They were all so certain of the direction in which they were going. She'd been like that once. *Once.*

She was in a convoy of five black Land Rovers: 4-door *Defender 110*s. The soldiers, twenty or so of them, had smuggled her out of the rear door of the chapel and made her run to the Land Rovers, parked on an old sports field. Cardinal Sinclair was pushed into the front vehicle, she into the second while a wounded soldier was helped into the rear Land Rover. From what Lucy could make out, two dead soldiers were left behind.

It was hard to accept that people were actually dying and somehow it was her fault: they wouldn't be here if it wasn't for her. That soldier really would have shot her, wouldn't he? Captain Jurgen Kruger, he said he was. He had *that* look in his eye. For an instant, she'd wondered if that was the best way out for everyone, but when she saw the barrel of that gun pointing at her, her nerve failed her.

Now, staring out of the window as the countryside, illuminated by the underpowered headlights of the convoy, raced past, she repeated her mantra: *Out of the depths*. She feared she was about to descend deeper than ever.

The headlights picked out dark hedges and low stone walls lining the roads. There were never any people or houses, and no signs of other vehicles. Was there some sort of curfew in force? From what she could figure out, two groups of soldiers had arrived at the convent at almost the same time from opposite directions. Captain Kruger led the group that found her. A tall, wiry man with short dark hair, he had blue eyes that always seemed to be scanning around him. She didn't know what army he belonged to, or who his men were shooting at. His black uniform didn't bear any insignia.

She suspected Cardinal Sinclair knew exactly who Kruger and his men were, but she had no opportunity to ask him before they were separated. Had she been kidnapped? If they knew Sinclair then surely she was safe. But in that case why did the captain threaten to kill her? It was impossible to work out if these were the good guys or bad. As for what they expected from her, she was clueless.

She was in the rear of the Land Rover, wedged in beside an armed guard. Breathing against the window, she waited for the condensation to form a surface then traced *Help Me*. The Land Rover made a sharp turn and her stomach lurched. When she was young, she always got carsick but, reaching her teens, she vowed not to let it bother her. If she concentrated hard enough, she could isolate the sick feeling and pretend it existed outside her. After that, she'd been able to go on rollercoasters and all the fairground attractions that had been off-limits to her. She'd lost that gift now: the childhood nausea was firmly back.

'Who were you shooting at?' Lucy wasn't sure her guard spoke English, but she was determined to get something from him.

The soldier glanced at her but didn't answer. He seemed uneasy, as if he found her presence objectionable, even disturbing. She'd been given a large black parka jacket to keep her warm and she pulled the hood over her head. Her feet were freezing. When she'd left the convent, she'd had to run across the damp grass in her slippers. She had no socks on. It was crazy, given the situation she was in, but she really longed just to have warm feet.

Got to distract myself, she thought – to avoid thinking about dead soldiers and where the living soldiers were taking her. Her mind went back to Raphael's mural. As soon as she saw it, she thought it might be the proof she'd pursued for years. The experts had sneered at her interpretation of the search for the Holy Grail. 'Embarrassing,' they said, 'lacking any credible evidence.' That mural could change everything.

Her fingers reached for the zip of her parka and she started pulling it up and down. Why couldn't these critics *see*? It was so obvious that the Grail Quest was a quest for a very different God from the one worshipped by Christians. Now, with Raphael's masterpiece, she had proof either that her theory was wrong and the Catholic Church had no problems with the Arthurian romances, or that something was going on that could shake Catholicism to its foundations. But if the mural were perfectly orthodox, why was it shut away in a secret vault of the tomb of one of the most controversial popes of all? There was a much likelier explanation. An infiltrator once led the Catholic Church: *Pope Julius II was a heretic.*

22

Vernon was still trying to take it in. First the flash – the searing light – followed by the thunderous boom, then silence. Smoke obscured everything in the TV picture. The picture started to break up.

The BBC's studio anchorman reappeared. 'I'm sorry, we've, uh, lost sound and vision from Washington. I...as you saw, there was an explosion...we're trying to reconnect to our reporter at the scene. We...President Adams hasn't...we have received no confirmation...the bomb was hidden inside the Ark, it seems.'

'Jesus Christ, Adams is dead.' Harrington, ashen, stood up. 'It was a trap all along.'

'I told you,' Vernon blurted. 'The whole thing was a set-up. Adams couldn't resist playing the Saviour. The easiest fucking target imaginable.' He looked at Gresnick then felt guilty.

The American had a film of tears over his eyes.

'I'm sorry,' Vernon said. 'That was insensitive.'

'I don't give a damn what you thought of him,' Gresnick snapped. 'He was my commander in chief.'

'First the Pope, now the President,' Harrington said quietly. 'Who's next?'

'The Vice President's an old man with a bad heart,' Gresnick mumbled. 'He won't last long.' He slammed his fist on the table. 'Goddamn it.'

'What about the Ark?' Vernon spoke softly to avoid aggravating Gresnick. 'Do you think they blew up the real thing or a fake?'

'We'll have to wait for the FBI's forensic reports,' Harrington answered.

Gresnick and Harrington amazed Vernon. They had wanted so much to believe the Ark was real, to believe that God himself would appear on his throne above the Ark and announce that the world was saved.

'I need to clear my head,' Gresnick said, looking like he was on the verge of throwing up.

'I'm sorry, colonel,' Harrington said. 'It must have been a nightmare to see your President dying like that. I can't say I liked the man, but...'

'This ends right now.'

'We'll take a half hour time-out.' Harrington picked up the green orb. 'I'll, uh, take this to the lab.'

****

Vernon gazed at the phone in his private office, wondering if he should contact his wife, but there probably wouldn't be a working connection to Sweden. Besides, he would probably hear his baby gurgling in the background and he couldn't cope with that. Deep down, he was convinced he'd never see little Louise again. Anyway, what would he say to his wife? The right words, any words, had long since dried up.

Caldwell had given him the latest situation report. Each passing hour brought grimmer news. Seismologists across the world were saying their equipment was going haywire. The Governor of California ordered the evacuation of San Francisco after being informed the San Andreas Fault might rupture catastrophically at any moment.

An unprecedented number of Category-5 hurricanes were forming off the east coast of America, from Boston to Key West. Twelve had been counted so far. Each one released in a day the same energy as one million Nagasaki atomic bombs. An expert said that if all the hurricanes merged into one superhurricane they'd annihilate everything in their path.

Vernon still couldn't believe Lucy had any role in what was happening. What would he do if he met her again? Those old feelings, they would overwhelm him, wouldn't they? He dreaded that the last images in his mind, the last feelings in his heart, might not be for his family but for the woman who rejected him. How many had suffered that same fate, thinking of the *wrong* person at the end?

Someone hammered on his door: Gresnick. The colonel tried to speak, but couldn't get his words out.

Vernon smelt whisky on the American's breath. 'Are you all right, colonel? Come in and take a seat.'

'I don't want a goddamn seat,' Gresnick snapped. 'Both prisoners have vanished. The green ball has gone from the lab too. What kind of ship are you people running?'

'What are you talking about?'

'Are you hard of hearing, mister? The prisoners have disappeared.' He waved his hand. '*Into thin air.*'

23

Vernon, still bristling at Gresnick's outburst, checked the CCTV tapes for the third time. Engineers had confirmed there was no malfunction. He sat in the guardhouse studying the pictures on two monitors, one showing the footage from Sergeant Morson's cell and the other the footage from Captain Ferris's. He froze both tapes at the same frame. It was impossible to concentrate with the alarm blaring out. The corridors were full of people scurrying around, pistols in hand. Every exit had been sealed. Somehow, he knew it wouldn't make any difference.

He scrutinised Ferris's tape. The captain was alternately lying still in his bed, with the sheets pulled over his head, or writhing underneath. The odd thing was he had stopped making any sounds. On Morson's tape, the sergeant stared straight at Ferris through the special glass wall separating their adjoining cells. Far from showing any concern, he was smiling.

Vernon moved both tapes forward, frame by frame. He studied Ferris's tape in particular. At one point, everything was normal then a point of intense light appeared beneath the sheets just where Ferris's head was. On Morson's tape, the sergeant was getting to his feet at that instant. In the background, one of the soldiers shouted something and started to raise his Heckler & Koch machine pistol.

Vernon cursed. Just when he needed to see exactly what was happening, the tape showed nothing but a dazzling light, so bright he had to turn the monitor's brightness down to minimum. At the same time, the sound cut out. Apparently, the same thing had happened to the CCTV pictures in the archive section just before it was destroyed. He was certain it was a technical problem but now he'd been assured the equipment was in perfect working order. That meant...what *did* it mean? All he knew for certain was that neither prisoner could be found. Their guards were dead though there wasn't a mark on their bodies. It appeared they'd suffered heart attacks. Whatever they saw, it left their faces disfigured with – only one word fitted – *terror*; the same terror visible earlier on the face of the dead archivist. The two incidents had to be related, but how? The prisoners were unquestionably in their cells during the attack on the archive.

The bars of Ferris's cell weren't damaged. As for Morson's, it looked as though the door-lock had melted, allowing the door to swing open. There were no signs that the prisoners had left the building, and none that they were still inside. So, where? A digital keypad was used to open and close the cell doors. The keypad for Morson's cell was destroyed but Ferris's was intact. Vernon checked the logs to see if anyone had opened the door since 6 p.m. when Dr Wells last inspected the prisoner. There was no unauthorised access. In fact, no access of any type.

Maybe I've missed something. Vernon rewound the tapes to the time of the attack on the archive. He'd assumed that because the two prisoners were in their cells *after* the attack they must have been in there *during* the attack.

Nothing strange happened on Sergeant Morson's tape, but Captain Ferris's was a different matter. Shortly before the attack on the archive, a wisp of what looked like black smoke emanated from under the sheets where Ferris lay. It was visible for only a moment then vanished. It had either dispersed or moved away exceptionally rapidly, too fast to be recorded on the video. He couldn't make any sense of it.

'They've gone, haven't they?' a voice said.

Vernon turned to see who'd entered the guardhouse. Hugh Wells was standing there, his face chalk-white.

'I'm just checking the tapes,' Vernon said.

'You won't find anything.' Wells gripped a piece of paper. 'These things can't be true. They're myths, legends, primitive superstitions.'

'What have you got there, Hugh?' It looked like something Wells had printed from the Internet. Vernon took it then started swallowing hard, hardly believing what he was reading.

And after some days my son, Methuselah, took a wife for his son Lamech, and she became pregnant by him and bore him a son. And his baby was white as snow and red as rose; the hair of his head as white as wool and his long curly hair beautiful; and as for his eyes, when he opened them the whole house glowed like the sun...And his father, Lamech, was afraid of him and fled and went to Methuselah his father; and he said to him, 'I have begotten a strange son. He is not like a human being, but he looks like the children of angels of heaven to me, his form is different, and he is not like us...It does not seem to me that he is of me, but of angels...'

The Book of Noah

'What is this?' Vernon had never heard of the Book of Noah. At a guess, he thought it might be one of the books of the Apocrypha in the Old Testament.

'There's so much we're ignorant of,' Wells said. 'The Book of Noah was one of the holiest texts ever written. It described Noah's life before and after the Flood. The original was lost and only fragments survived, like this extract.'

'You can't be taking this seriously, Hugh. It's mumbo jumbo.'

'That prisoner should have died,' Wells retorted. 'No one could have withstood the changes happening to his body.' His hands were shaking. 'There's another part to that quotation from the Book of Noah. It finishes by saying that "angels" is perhaps the wrong word. It ought to be...'

'Let me guess.' Vernon closed his eyes. '*Demons.*'

24

It couldn't happen, but it had: two prisoners gone without trace. Worse, it seemed one of them wasn't exactly human anymore. It was a relief when Commander Harrington gave Vernon something else to focus on. Hunched over the computer in his office, he was now trying to put together a PowerPoint presentation. In half an hour, he, Harrington and Gresnick would have to take their preliminary findings concerning the two prisoners and their possible connection to world events to the Director General. With no answers, the prisoners no longer in custody, Dr Wells possibly having a breakdown, an ex-girlfriend in a lunatic asylum, and no end of fantastical speculations, Vernon feared they'd be sacked on the spot.

Where to begin? Not with the angel, that was for sure. Dr Wells was speculating that maybe there had always been some humans unlike any others, capable of supernatural feats. Vernon thought his friend was losing it, but there was no denying something spectacularly odd was happening. As for Lucy, every time Vernon thought of her, he felt nauseous.

He peered at the computer screen. The bullet points he'd put into his presentation were taunting him. Again, he tried to fit the facts together into some coherent hypothesis. Facts? *Christ.*

Fact 1. The world's weather had turned apocalyptic; animals everywhere were spooked. Global disasters were happening on an unprecedented scale.

Fact 2. A unit of American Special Forces had deserted and raided sacred sites linked with the Western world's three most famous religious artefacts.

Fact 3. The Ark of the Covenant, real or fake, had found its way to the White House where it was used to conceal a bomb that killed the President. No one had claimed responsibility. No demands were made, no explanations offered.

Fact 4. The Delta Force deserters were all grandchildren of U.S. intelligence officers who interrogated senior Nazi officials at the end of WWII. These Nazis had specific responsibility for looted religious treasures. Half of the intelligence officers then died in mysterious circumstances, perhaps murdered by their own colleagues.

Fact 5. The top-secret document *The Cainite Destiny* was stolen from MI5's archive, but Colonel Gresnick had a copy of his grandfather's original translation. The document said Hitler had a peculiar fascination for the Spear of Destiny and spoke of a ten-thousand-year-old mission somehow revolving around the Spear.

Fact 6. Two members of the Delta Force unit had been apprehended. They broke into the British Library and were caught looking at microfiche of old documents about the Holy Grail. They had returned from a surveillance mission in the southwest of England and their target was someone very familiar.

Fuck. Vernon still couldn't accept that Lucy was part of all this, yet one of the prisoners had actually described her as the most special person in the world. He had thought that himself at one time, of course. Maybe he still did, but that was because of love. Sergeant Morson didn't love Lucy, so why did *he* think she was so significant?

Fact 7. *Fact 7.* **Fact 7**. Vernon groaned. It was preposterous, no kind of fact at all. One prisoner turned into an angel then vanished with his colleague after breaking out of high-security cells and killing several guards without leaving a mark on their bodies. The angel also apparently attacked the MI5 archive and stole *The Cainite Destiny*.

It needed occultists, not MI5 staff, to make any sense of all this.

****

Vernon had been in the Director General's penthouse office only once before. He'd never forgotten how spectacular the view of the Thames was from up here. Located in the top corner of the building, the penthouse had a grand balcony with fluted Greek columns, and commanded a prime location near the Houses of Parliament.

While the DG read his report, Vernon opened the balcony doors and stepped outside. From up here, on bright days, the Thames sparkled like a vein of silver. Last summer, he stood on this same spot and marvelled at how beautiful London was. Several of Vernon's friends fantasised about having sex in their offices: if that were his game too, he would have chosen to have sex right here. But all he could see now was the strange darkness that had clung to London for the last three days, scarcely penetrated by the streetlights that were now switched on 24/7. Even during the day, with that sickly red sky, everything was dark. Sometimes Vernon wondered if it were psychological – a manifestation of the spiritual malaise that had afflicted everyone.

The newspapers he'd seen in the last couple of days used expressions like 'peculiar haze', 'impenetrable mist', 'smoky fog.' Every few hours, fierce lightning storms broke out, but there was never any thunder, and no rain, at least not over London. On the other hand, in the north of the country, there was nothing but rain. Flash floods were reported in scores of locations. Hailstorms in Scotland went on for hours rather than minutes, with ice pellets the size of tennis balls that maimed anyone caught in the open.

Not long ago, London had enjoyed a mini heat wave. The sun blazed down every day, a huge yellow disc in a perfect blue sky. Now Vernon scarcely remembered what it looked like. The thing that stood in its place cast nothing but that eerie, unsettling, rust-coloured light. London, full of energy days earlier, was old and worn now, like a sepia photograph of a scene of long ago.

He breathed in the strange air. It seemed to smell differently now, to have a different texture. Gazing out over the Thames, he wondered if the *thing* were out there somewhere – a dark angel, circling in the blackness, the noise of its wings hidden by the birds' incessant squawking.

He returned to the main room and took a seat in front of Director General Eva Barnes. A small, fierce woman with short, neatly parted grey hair, she never showed any signs of feeling threatened by the select group of ambitious managers, all male, who reported directly to her. Commander Harrington was one of them. He'd made it clear more than once that he didn't like Barnes, but he respected her. As for Colonel Gresnick, he sat quietly on a sofa, with a folder in his hand.

Vernon wondered what Barnes thought about his presentation. The rings round her eyes showed she was sleeping as badly as everyone else. No doubt the Prime Minister was phoning her constantly. Vernon was glad he wasn't in Barnes's position of having to answer the PM's questions, to have to admit there were no leads. It was hard even to define the problem. Was it an intelligence matter or something for scientists? For priests?

According to the latest reports, fuel shortages were rife across Britain. Emergency reserves had dwindled rapidly. Power cuts had commenced in central England, and were likely to get longer and more frequent. The rest of the country wouldn't be far behind.

In America, CNN disclosed that the new President had ordered key White House staff to relocate to an underground bunker beneath the Blue Ridge Mountains of Virginia. Did they know something everyone else didn't?

But no one could hide the news regarding the world's volcanoes. Dense, choking black clouds were spewing out from all of them. With an exploding volcano releasing the same energy as five hundred atomic bombs, if they all erupted at once it would be like the simultaneous detonation of 800,000 A-bombs. If it happened, all the smoke and dust in the sky would block out the sun and bring a permanent winter, a new and irreversible ice age. At the least, the blast was likely to destabilise all the major fault lines across the world, triggering massive earthquakes.

Was there any way out? Newspapers, now reduced to little more than a sheet, were still speculating about the theft of the three world-famous religious artefacts and promoting the claims of religious leaders that God was showing his just wrath. Could there really be a connection between stolen relics and natural disasters? At one level, it was absurd, but with the world's scientists squabbling amongst themselves, superstition had filled the vacuum. The assassination of the American President, with its religious overtones, had only served to massively heighten the frenzy.

On BBC *News 24*, bulletins reported that COBRA meetings were taking place continuously, with the Prime Minister chairing most of them personally. What everyone knew about COBRA was that it was activated only in times of national emergency.

COBRA had always fascinated Vernon. The acronym was far more interesting than what it stood for: *Cabinet Office Briefing Room A*. COBRA held its meetings in an undisclosed location in Whitehall, although everyone in MI5 knew it was a secure suite of offices within the Cabinet Office building itself, adjacent to Downing Street. It had everything an advanced communications centre required – banks of computers, fibre-optic cabling, fax machines, telephone lines, video conferencing facilities, its own generators. Everything was state of the art, with all communications encrypted. All so that the PM, senior ministers and key government officials could obtain information about critical incidents and have reliable, secure lines of communication to the police, the fire service, the army, hospitals, and all branches of government.

No one involved with COBRA would be impressed if Barnes were forced to explain what MI5 thought might be going on. It would be embarrassing to admit the nature of what they were contemplating. But with TV pictures coming in from all over the world showing people flocking to places of worship, maybe it was hard not to be caught up in the religious hysteria.

'We have no other lines of enquiry,' Barnes said. 'The contents of your report are bizarre, Mr Vernon, but we don't have anything else. From a political perspective, we have to be seen to be doing something. I'll tell the PM that we're pursuing leads concerning the stolen religious artefacts. If we recover them, we'll be able to demonstrate that they have no connection with the natural disasters. You and Colonel Gresnick will be supplied with whatever resources you need.'

To achieve what? Vernon wondered. He didn't have a clue what to do with the information he already had.

'I'm not going to comment on some of the remarks about the escaped prisoners,' Barnes said. 'I want them recaptured as soon as possible, and a detailed explanation of how they got out in the first place. Commander Harrington can look after that.'

She placed her hands on the table as though she were trying to find something solid to hang on to. Vernon knew how she felt. Everything was crumbling, every certainty disappearing.

'I want you to know,' Barnes said, 'that I've been in touch with the heads of every major intelligence service in the world. None of them is any better off than we are. Most are saying that global warming is responsible for everything that's happening, and they're focusing their efforts on helping the scientific community.'

Vernon glanced at Gresnick. Before the American's arrival, he would have agreed with that. Now, after everything Gresnick had revealed, maybe there was a chance something else was at the root of this.

'There's a helicopter waiting for you on the roof-pad,' Barnes said.

'Where are you sending us?' Vernon grimaced, hating the idea of venturing outside. 'Anyway, nothing can fly. The birds out there – a helicopter could never get through them.'

'The Chinook has been fitted with a device that emits an ultrasound frequency. I'm assured it drives the birds crazy and clears them get out of the way, at least temporarily. I believe Mr Gresnick's flight to England used the same technology.'

'We had no problems at all,' Gresnick said.

Vernon wasn't convinced. He thought the birds were unlikely to be scared off by any gizmo.

'An SAS unit has been mobilised to accompany you,' Barnes added. 'Commander Harrington will stay here to coordinate things at this end.'

'Where are we going?' Vernon repeated.

'Your mission is to find your ex-girlfriend.'

Vernon tried to hide his shock. So, it was actually going to happen. Whatever you feared most was bound to happen – you attracted it in some crazy way.

'We're going to Glastonbury?' He hated that place. It was a New Age circus, full of every religious nut imaginable. They had more religions there than people.

'Yes and no,' Barnes said. 'You'll be picking up the trail there.'

'Trail?'

'We received a report half an hour ago that a firefight broke out at the asylum where Lucy Galahan was being kept. Four soldiers are dead. The police scanned their fingerprints and we ran them through our database of Special Forces' personnel. We've now had positive IDs. Two belonged to the Delta Force deserters. The other two...'

'The deserters have got Lucy?'

'She's with the others,' Barnes answered.

'*Others*?'

'I was about to tell you that the other two dead men have also been identified. They're Swiss Guards.'

Vernon shook his head. 'You mean the people who guard the Pope?'

25

Lucy peered out of the window and tried to see what was going on. The convoy had halted five minutes earlier, with Captain Kruger and a colleague in the front vehicle getting out, their torchlights cutting the darkness. What were they doing? Kruger, clutching a pair of night-vision binoculars by the looks of it, scrambled up a rocky hill overlooking the road. His colleague was busy studying a map, his face lit by torchlight. Lucy wondered if they were checking to see if they were being followed, looking for the best route to avoid pursuit.

She turned to the soldier sitting beside her. He hadn't said a word during the journey. Every time his long legs threatened to brush against hers, he pulled them away. Did he think she had something contagious? Now and again, she caught him staring at her, the same way people stared at modern art exhibits they didn't comprehend.

'Can I get some fresh air?' she asked.

'I'll give you a few minutes to stretch your legs.' His English was impeccable, tinged with only the slightest foreign accent. He twisted round, leaned into the back of the vehicle and grabbed something. 'We have a spare uniform for you.'

Lucy took off her parka and slipped the black uniform over her pyjamas. The soldier handed her a pair of army boots and socks. The boots were a bit big, but she tied the laces tight, and the thick socks helped.

Before she opened the door, she put her parka back on and zipped it up to the top until only her eyes were exposed. As she was about to get out of the car, the soldier tapped her arm.

'Wait,' he said. 'You'll need this.' He handed her a black rubber torch.

Once more, she reached for the handle to open the door.

The soldier patted his machine pistol. 'I'm watching.'

Lucy took a few steps away from the Land Rover. Did the soldier really think she'd try to escape? It was pitch black apart from the lights of car headlamps and a few torches, and the temperature was below freezing. She had no idea where she was, and she was sure to die of exposure if she stumbled off into the dark.

At the convent, she'd begun to think of the outside world as a forbidden zone: it would kill her if she ever went out there. Yet here she was. *Still alive*, actually feeling quite strong. She knew it wouldn't last.

Shining her torch around her, she discovered that the convoy had stopped next to a picturesque stone bridge over a brook. She *knew* this place. It was called *Guinevere's Sigh* because this was supposedly where Queen Guinevere realised her love for Lancelot was too strong to be resisted. James Vernon brought her here once, keen to show her an old, stone water well with a wooden canopy bearing carved angels at its corners. Legend said this was the wishing well where Guinevere made her fateful choice to sleep with Lancelot, sealing Camelot's fate. After their illicit affair, Camelot was plunged into civil war and ultimate collapse, taking all the dreams of a golden world with it.

Lucy shuddered as she pointed her torch at the well, but it wasn't the cold making her shiver. This was where she came the night she decided to end her relationship with James. Was it perverse to have come here of all places to make that decision? Did she need to commune with the ghost of her former self before she could go ahead with it?

James made no secret of what he wished for when he threw his coin into the well that first time.

'I wish that we'll be married before the year's end,' he said gleefully.

She didn't say yes to him. She didn't say anything. She closed her eyes and tried to wish too. But nothing came. No desires, no dreams. What she wanted was for things to stay exactly as they were. She told James she was scared and couldn't give him an answer right now. Yet he really was the ideal boyfriend. He had a job in MI5 that he never spoke about, but she liked that. It made her feel safe, and she knew any secret could be safely entrusted to him. They'd been getting on so well. It amazed her how lovingly he looked at her, as if she were some rare beauty. He once said he wasn't sure whether she was his idol or ideal. At first, it scared her – how could she ever live up to his expectations? But, whatever she did, James was never disappointed with her, even when she disappointed herself.

He didn't complain when she made him join her for scuba diving, and he said he loved listening to her theories about the Arthurian legends. He seemed to mean it. When her book was rubbished, he quoted Jonathan Swift to console her: 'When a true genius appears in the world, you may know him by this sign, that the dunces are all in confederacy against him.' She loved him for that.

It was the day after their trip to *Guinevere's Sigh* that the phone call came. Her dad had sounded like an automaton. 'Your mother has breast cancer,' he said. 'It's aggressive. Stage four. She has less than six months.' That was it. Her dad put the phone down. From that moment, she started to unravel. She had friends who had been in the same position. They'd been distraught, of course, but somehow it was all superficial. They brushed it off like dust. They had a funeral and got on with their lives, and people said how brave they were and how their parents would be so proud that they'd kept the show on the road.

'The last thing your parents would want would be for you to be miserable,' they'd say. Did these people not *feel*? How can you go on when the people who made you aren't there anymore? The sun has been stolen from the sky. The heat has gone. Nothing can continue, nothing at all.

'Lucy, can I have a word?' Cardinal Sinclair wandered over from the lead Land Rover. Several soldiers were watching him. One pointed a torch at his face, forcing him to raise his hand to block the beam.

The night had a weird thickness, as though it were made of cloth. Lucy wondered how long the nights had been like this. Her convent cell was windowless. She saw the outside only when she went into the convent garden for her daily exercise. Not so long ago, she hadn't even managed that much, and had to be pushed around in a wheelchair. Then, lately, just as she'd started to feel stronger, they'd stopped anyone from going outside at all, and given no reasons – now she knew why.

Watching Sinclair approaching, Lucy was still unsure whether she trusted him. She was convinced she was a captive, but what about him?

'What do you want?' Her tone was much sharper than she'd intended. 'I hope you're going to explain what's going on.'

She wondered if he were in the same mould as Grand Inquisitors like Torquemada. They didn't get the chance to torture anyone nowadays, but maybe in their hearts it was still there, that desire to make everything clean, to root out all dissent, incinerate every impurity.

'I assure you,' he said, 'I didn't expect any of this.'

'You know who these men are, don't you?'

'They're Swiss Guards from Rome.'

'Swiss Guards?' Lucy was taken aback. 'I thought their job was to guard the Pope.' Another question occurred to her, but she didn't say it: if they were from the Vatican, why didn't Sinclair know they were coming? But he seemed to anticipate her concern.

'Kruger said they were a special unit, reporting only to the Pope,' he said. 'No one else in the Vatican knows about them. They were formed a year ago and have been training with the French Foreign Legion ever since.'

Lucy groaned inwardly. A secret Vatican military unit? This was getting worse. 'But didn't you say the Pope was dead?'

'That's the thing.' Sinclair lowered his voice. 'The captain said the Pope ordered them to carry out this mission no matter what. Even if he died, they were to keep going.'

'I don't get it, cardinal. Why wouldn't the Pope tell you about Kruger's team?'

Sinclair looked away.

Lucy had almost forgotten how to interpret body language like that. In the convent, no one hid things. She felt painfully rusty analysing Sinclair. Why was he so uncomfortable talking about the dead Pope? Something else bothered her. Why had these Swiss Guards shown up now, when things were so dire? Why didn't they come weeks ago?

'Are we prisoners?' she asked.

'No, but we can't come and go as we please. We must do everything Captain Kruger says.'

'So, we *are* prisoners.'

'They're protecting us.'

'From what?'

'Lucy, other soldiers are chasing us. Kruger knows who they are.'

Lucy stared at Sinclair then started to turn away. She hated this.

'American Special Forces, Lucy, that's who's after us. Kruger reckons they're only a few miles behind.'

'What?' Lucy hadn't formed any idea of who might want to harm her, but Americans were at the bottom of the list.

'Deserters,' Sinclair said.

Deserters? Did that make it any easier to understand? Had they deserted just so that they could come to England to murder her?

'Get back in the vehicles,' Kruger shouted, coming down the hill. 'We're leaving.'

'Where are they taking us?' Lucy asked Sinclair.

The cardinal shook his head. 'Kruger wouldn't say.' His breath condensed in the freezing air. 'I haven't told you the codename for Kruger's mission.'

Lucy watched Kruger climbing back into his Land Rover. She sensed he was one of those men who didn't give up. Once he had his orders, he would go on relentlessly until they were carried out. The late Pope chose him precisely for that reason, didn't he?

She closed her eyes and stood there for a moment. The wind was seeded with tiny ice particles, biting into her flesh. One word came into her mind, just as had happened back in the convent. She knew it was the same word Cardinal Sinclair was about to use. She had no idea why she was so certain, and it frightened her.

'I already know,' she said, opening her eyes. 'Their mission is codenamed *Armageddon*.'

26

The helipad on the roof of Thames House was a recent innovation, only three months old. To make room for the helicopters, the building contractors had no choice but to vandalise the beautiful gold-coloured sloping roof. The whole aesthetic look of Thames House was destroyed in one swoop, Vernon thought. Everyone else loved the convenience but, then, they were all keen flyers.

He stood outside the small air control office, slapping his hands together to keep warm. Although he was in a warm uniform – he'd managed to borrow spare kit from one of the soldiers in the basement – he didn't have gloves. It was 1 o'clock in the morning. Most sensible men were at home with their wives and children instead of getting ready to head out into this darkness, the sort of murk that made you think you wouldn't be coming back.

As for his own wife and baby, Vernon was convinced they couldn't be in a safer place. A sparsely populated island near Stockholm, with plenty of food and water, was as good as it got. Besides, he had other ghosts to haunt him. Or just one. All of his emotional energy now swirled around Lucy. She had discarded him, so it was perverse to still be holding a torch for her, but you don't have control over that type of thing, do you? That sort of torch is sure to scorch you one day. Unless the miraculous moment arrives when you realise you've stopped loving. But what's so great about that?

The Chinook, painted in camouflage colours, looked brand new. It had two toughened glass-fibre rotor blades, one at the front and one at the rear. The SAS – Britain's elite Special Forces unit – used it on their missions because of its reputation for ruggedness. Its fuselage was watertight, so it could make amphibious landings. Vernon prayed it didn't come to that. The last thing he wanted was to go swimming in the dark. The two M60 machineguns were more to his liking. He suspected they might see a lot of use.

He was also worried about the noise: last time he was in a helicopter, he couldn't hear a thing over the sound of the rotor blades and engine. For the whole of the following day, he was partially deaf. NASA had apparently recently helped helicopter manufacturers to make the cabins much quieter environments where you could actually hold a civilised conversation, but Vernon remained to be convinced.

One by one, SAS troopers climbed into the Chinook. Vernon was startled by how short they were, not one taller than about 5'6''. They were tough, muscular little men, mostly with shaved heads. Four of them had broken with convention and sported long, straggly hair and almost comical drooping moustaches. As he listened to their conversations, he realised that nearly all of them were Scottish, Welsh and Northern Irish. There were only two English: a Geordie and a Scouser.

The troopers wore camouflage uniforms and helmets, bulky packs on their backs, and black gloves. If anyone looked like they were going to war, they did. Armed with Colt Commando assault rifles, Heckler & Koch MP5K submachine guns and Browning High Power handguns, they were bristling with weaponry.

Vernon made a point of shaking hands with the unit leader, Captain Kerr, a gruff Glaswegian. The captain deliberately used one of those ridiculously macho grips, designed to show who was the boss. Vernon hurriedly pulled his hand away.

He was the last to climb into the helicopter. On vacation in San Francisco three years ago, he and Lucy took a sightseeing trip in a small chopper. It was the scariest journey of his life. When the helicopter flew under the Golden Gate Bridge, he thought he was going to lose control of his bowels, but Lucy simply laughed all the way through. She once told him she suffered from motion sickness. Not anymore, it seemed. It frightened him how exhilarated she was, almost as if she were revelling in overcoming her natural limitations. When she chose, she could be incredibly determined. More than once, he'd decided she was the most obstinate person he'd ever met. Mostly, he admired her for it. At other times...

Gazing up at the sky as he clambered inside, he was convinced the birds would be an insurmountable problem. Thousands of them were wheeling above Thames House, making that interminable screeching noise. It drove him crazy. He'd heard reports that, for some unexplained reason, the birds were congregating only over cities, and whole stretches of the country were now entirely devoid of bird life.

He took his seat beside Colonel Gresnick, just behind the cockpit, and strapped himself in. Several SAS troopers joined him on the same side of the Chinook, while the others sat opposite, about ten men on either side.

'What did the Vatican say about the Swiss Guards?' Vernon asked Gresnick as the Chinook prepared for takeoff.

'They said the matter was a religious one and they didn't wish to involve secular authorities,' Gresnick said as he casually flicked through a file of intelligence reports. 'When Commander Harrington pointed out they were kidnapping a British citizen they told him not to interfere in matters that were God's concern.'

Vernon couldn't help grunting with amusement. 'I wish I could use a line like that to get people off my back.' He stared at the SAS men as they smeared their faces with black paint. 'Did the Vatican say anything about the Delta Force deserters?'

'The Vatican said, and I quote, "The deserters are working for Satan."'

'I hear he pays better,' Vernon muttered, squinting at Gresnick's fashionable sheepskin flying jacket and fur cap. *Who does he think he is*, he thought – some ace fighter pilot?

He grabbed the armrests of his seat as the helicopter's rotor blades whirred into action, and prayed the pilot would have time to abort the flight if the birds didn't clear out of the way. Seconds later, the Chinook was airborne. As it rose fast, Vernon listened for the sound of shrieking birds, but the rotor blades drowned out everything. Seconds later, something smashed into the cockpit. Vernon's heart jumped.

'Just a stray,' the pilot said over the intercom. 'The flight path is clear.'

Within seconds, they were racing over the deserted streets of London. Vernon glanced at Gresnick and breathed out hard. He'd been doubtful this mission was ever going to happen. Now, he could no longer avoid thinking about the mission's objective. It was really going to happen – he was going to see Lucy again, and discover why she was at the centre of world events.

The American deserters were stealing religious artefacts; the Catholic Church was the most powerful religious organisation on earth. Put those two facts together and what did you get? Maybe the Americans had stolen something of special significance to the Catholic Church. Whatever it was, Lucy must have expert knowledge of it. Maybe she was the world authority. Given the book she'd written, the identity of the artefact seemed all too obvious – *the Holy Grail*.

When he mentioned his idea to Gresnick, the American nodded and grinned. 'Could be.' Gresnick had one of those dazzling Hollywood smiles, with the sort of perfect teeth that seemed impossible to an Englishman. Vernon hated smiles like that. He didn't have bad teeth exactly, but nor did he have a smile worth mentioning. It wouldn't seduce women, that was for sure. But Lucy had a beautiful smile. He wondered how she'd managed it.

'Our number one priority is to find her,' Gresnick said. 'Then we'll learn one way or another why she's causing so much fuss.'

As the Chinook cleared London, Vernon felt motion sickness kicking in, but he didn't want to show signs of weakness in front of the others. Something else was contributing to his sick feeling. He hated the idea, didn't want it to be true, but every time he thought of Lucy, he found himself replaying the old emotions he hoped he'd killed. It was horrifying to realise that all he'd done was bury them. Things like that couldn't be relied upon to stay buried – like the Holy Grail itself maybe. Would Lucy enjoy the irony?

Perhaps there was a bigger irony. Lucy might be more than just depressed or traumatised. If it turned out she was hopelessly insane, what then? The deserters would have no use for her, so they might as well kill her.

Would Lucy understand what was happening to her? Surely that brain of hers could fire up one last time. She was so impressive when she was in full flow, seeing connections where others saw chaos, cutting through pomposity and illogic. She didn't care about hurting feelings when others were wrong, which was why they treated her so viciously when they got the chance to retaliate. If she refused to help the deserters, they'd threaten her, maybe torture her. Out of sheer cussedness, she might not cooperate. She would have no idea how much danger she was in. These people wouldn't stop. They were ruthless killers, veterans of many lethal missions.

And there was something particularly odd about them. Vernon could hardly believe it when Gresnick revealed this singular fact, but the American assured him it was true. The deserters' grandparents only wanted male children and had handed over any daughters for adoption, while the deserters' parents had taken active steps to ensure that they only had male offspring: any female embryos were aborted. They seemed to belong to some cult of misogynists. The lives of women, it seemed, didn't hold any value for them whatever. Would Lucy's?

27

Project Armageddon, Lucy mouthed as she stared out from the Land Rover. Many people imagined the end coming in shades of black. For her, the world could end in only one way – a blue flood. In Orwell's *Room 101*, she would be standing at the edge of a blue lake, being pushed into the water. Blue, and only blue, was Armageddon's colour.

'Where are you taking me?' she asked, thinking the guard would ignore her, but the reply was instant.

'Tintagel.'

At first, the name passed through Lucy as though it was never said. She tried to pretend it was just another name, a place on the map like any other. The Land Rover went over some bumps and Lucy's head banged against the window. Blue rushed into her mind, a tidal wave. For a second, the wave froze and she saw thousands of people trapped inside, their bodies sticking out at odd angles. Then it moved again, so fast it became a blur, shaking out the drowned bodies like salt and pepper. *Tintagel.* She'd spent so long blocking it out of her mind, persuading herself there was no such word, no such place.

'My medication,' she said. 'I have to take my medicine.' Still that torrent of blue swirling in her mind. The Land Rover accelerated and her stomach lurched.

The soldier didn't respond and just stared out of the other window. Earlier, he'd forbidden her from taking anything without his permission.

Lucy pictured herself as a tiny, remote dot in the centre of a blue ocean. Helpless, hopeless, a speck of dust in eternity. If she didn't get her medicine, she was finished. 'I'm going to die,' she yelled, grabbing the soldier's arm. The ocean in her mind had turned to blood, a red sea under a yellow sun, lapping onto a white beach.

The soldier glared at her then pushed her away. 'OK, OK, take them.'

In a flash, Lucy's hand was inside her pocket, snatching for her bottle of pills. She stuffed two into her mouth and swallowed, praying they'd kick in right away. Within seconds, she was feeling that familiar drowsiness. Her mind started to drift. Yellows and oranges, no blues.

There was a time when Tintagel didn't have the same meaning for her that it did now. Then it was just an academic curiosity, another of the sites in southwest England that claimed a connection with King Arthur to hook the tourists.

Tintagel Castle, in its time, was an island stronghold built high above the crashing Atlantic breakers, and connected to the mainland by a natural causeway. Some said it was Camelot itself. Other stories claimed Arthur was conceived here, or that Merlin the Magician was born in a cave beneath the castle. A legend said that the cave was still walked by Merlin, whose voice could be heard on stormy nights. Merlin's ghost supposedly stood on the beach outside the cave's entrance with the infant Arthur raised high in his arms, holding him up to the moon.

Nearby, at Slaughter Bridge, Arthur may have fought his final cataclysmic battle of Camlann, the last of his brave knights dying that brutal day in the thick mud.

Lucy felt her arm being shaken and sleepily lifted her eyes. The Land Rover had stopped and the door was wide open, letting in freezing air.

Captain Kruger peered down at her, his face flushed. 'Don't you understand anything? You can't take drugs anymore. You need to be alert at all times.' He tried to reach into her pockets.

'Get away from me,' Lucy shouted. 'I've finished all the pills. I threw the bottle away.' She tried to push him away, but he brushed her flailing hands aside. Grabbing her, he dragged her out of the car, lifted her off her feet and slammed her against the front door. He frisked her, but didn't find anything. The bottle was in the breast pocket of her pyjamas. She almost smiled. She knew he'd never touch her *there*. Not Captain Kruger. Not the saint, the Vatican's superhero.

'I'll never help you. You're crazy.'

Kruger's eyes bulged. He brought his head down to hers, until their noses were almost touching.

'You can't lay a finger on me.' Lucy felt an urge to goad him. Hard rain was pelting down now, driving into her face. 'You can't do anything to me.'

A stinging blow exploded against her left cheek, and her body lurched involuntarily to one side, her legs giving way beneath her. Lying in mud near the front wheel, with blood in her mouth, it took her a moment to comprehend what had happened. 'You hit me,' she mumbled in disbelief.

'I don't have times for stupid games,' Kruger barked. 'We know the precise moment when the world will end. Only you can stop it.'

28

Vernon was irritated when he glanced at Gresnick and found the American calmly reading his files. 'Doesn't it get to you?'

'What's that?'

'We're flying in pitch darkness. Aren't you worried?'

The helicopter was vibrating so much that Vernon's teeth were chattering and he felt like he was inside a washing machine.

'I know the pilot,' Gresnick said. 'He's one of your guys now, but he used to be a Night Stalker.'

'What?' Vernon struggled to hear over the *thwup thwup* of the rotor blades and the helicopter's powerful engines. So much for the new NASA noise-reduction technology. To be fair, it had made a bit of a difference. A year ago, he wouldn't have been able to hear anything at all in a helicopter. Now, with a suitably raised voice, it was possible to communicate. Better than being in a nightclub, that was for sure. He turned and faced Gresnick straight on.

'Come on, you must have heard of Night Stalkers,' Gresnick said. 'Black Hawk down and all that – elite pilots, the helicopter equivalent of Delta Force, specialising in night operations. Some of these guys actually prefer flying in the dark. Their navigation systems are state of the art. When they look at the LCD monitors on their control panels, the images are so clear it might as well be noon in Vegas rather than the middle of the night in London. They can see everything that's happening outside.' He patted

Vernon on the back. 'Besides, they have those lightweight holographic night vision goggles – stereoscopic, total depth perception, can see in the dark. Much cooler than the coolest shades.'

Vernon wasn't convinced and questioningly raised his eyebrows.

'Don't sweat it,' Gresnick said. 'Even at night in bad weather this bird can do 150 mph. We'll be there in no time.'

Vernon sat back, trying to persuade himself he was safe. He couldn't wait to get out of this helicopter and feel solid ground under his feet again. 'That superconspiracy you were talking about back in Thames House,' he said. 'Do you really believe there's a group out there that's existed for thousands of years? Puppetmasters controlling everyone else.'

'There's a superconspiracy all right, Mr Vernon, but these are no puppetmasters. They are shadow-people, operating in the darkness, trying to achieve their aims against overwhelming odds. That's why they're the masters of codes, and steeped in secrets. The early Christians used all sorts of signs to recognise each other, such as drawing a fish in the sand, but when they became the majority, there was no further need for secret signs. Those who control the superconspiracy have never been in the majority. In fact, they've always been persecuted. But they endured, and passed their secrets down the generations, waiting for the day when their schemes could come to fruition.'

'If the Christians had the fish, what do these superconspirators use?'

'My grandfather was sure there was one quick way to identify them: the Skull and Crossbones.'

'Why that?'

'Do you know where the Skull and Bones originates?'

'Pirates?' Vernon replied, with an unsure smile. 'The Jolly Roger?'

Gresnick nodded. '*Jolly Roger* is a corruption of the French term *jolie rouge*, which means *pretty red* in English. It was the nickname the Knights Templar gave to the flag flown by their fleet. The flag was a white Skull and Crossbones on a blood-red background. When the Templars buried their dead comrades, they removed the head and the legs and placed them in a Skull and Crossbones arrangement.

'Freemasonry is also full of Skull and Crossbones symbols. And the SS chose the Totenkopf, the Death's Head – a skull on crossbones – as their cap badge. My grandfather was convinced that the Cathars also used that symbol, though he only found circumstantial evidence.'

'OK, maybe they all used the Skull and Crossbones,' Vernon said. 'But it doesn't prove they belonged to the same conspiracy. Maybe they just like the symbol. I mean, pirates used it too, and they're not part of your conspiracy.'

'Aren't they?'

'Come on, you can't be suggesting pirates were in on it.'

'Listen, the Knights Templar were officially dissolved by the papacy. After that, anyone who still dared to call himself a Templar was excommunicated. It's a fact that the Templar fleet vanished before the authorities got the opportunity to seize their ships. The Templars' treasure vanished with their ships. Most people assumed the treasure was loaded onto the fleet and taken to an unknown destination. Maybe Scotland, maybe Oak Island in Nova Scotia. If they buried it in a remote location, they were sure to have made a map.'

Vernon could see where this was leading. 'Treasure maps and Jolly Rogers – it sounds like pirates but you're telling me it was the Knights Templar all along.'

Gresnick leaned back in his seat. 'The Templars were the first pirates. They were excellent sailors, and they were outlaws under a death sentence if they should ever be caught. What else would you expect them to do? Over time, the last of the official Templars died out, but no doubt they had children and passed on their traditions.'

Vernon couldn't deny it was a plausible theory. 'But the pirates used a black Jolly Roger and the Templars red. Why the difference?'

'Pirates used two Jolly Rogers. The usual one was the black Jolly Roger, but it was the other one, the red, that seafarers dreaded most. When pirates flew the red Jolly Roger it signified *No Quarter*. They would slaughter everyone they found onboard an enemy vessel. The red Jolly Roger – the Templar flag – was the most terrifying sight on the high seas. Ships belonging to Catholic powers – Spain, Portugal and France, in particular – were almost exclusively the pirates' targets, as revenge for what the papacy did to the Templars.'

'And you think the Skull and Crossbones flutters across the world even now?'

'One of the most powerful secret societies in the world is based at Yale University and comprises current and past students. Many of the former students have gone on to be amongst the richest and most influential people on earth, assisted at every step by the guiding hand of their secret society. President Adams was a member, and so is the new President. In fact many presidents, CEOs, and Directors of the FBI and CIA have been members.'

'What's it called?'

'Skull and Bones.'

Vernon's stomach turned as the helicopter climbed sharply. The weird acoustics were freaking him out too. He hated the combination of whirring blades, thrumming engines, and shouting voices inside the passenger cabin.

'But isn't there one big problem with your theory?' he said. 'I mean, that the Cathars, the Knights Templar, the Freemasons and the Nazis are all different guises of an ancient secret society?'

'A problem?'

'Well, didn't Hitler hate the Freemasons? He persecuted them. Many of them ended up in concentration camps.'

Gresnick smirked. 'To a true Freemason there's nothing more embarrassing than toy-town Freemasons. Ninety-nine percent of modern Freemasons don't have a clue what Freemasonry is about, or what true Freemasons actually believe. Most Freemasons nowadays just want to be part of an *I'll scratch your back if you scratch mine* group of social climbers. Throw in a few spooky ceremonies, some titillating ancient oaths and curses, a bit of ceremonial dressing up, declarations of undying loyalty to "the brotherhood" and you have yourself an irresistible package for shallow, greedy capitalists.

'Hitler, as a Freemason of the highest possible order, despised them. They were a mockery of the true principles of Freemasonry. It's no wonder he wanted rid of them.

'To be fair, these amateur Freemasons once served a purpose. They were an effective weapon against the Catholic Church. Freemasons were forever agitating against priests and popes. The Catholic Church responded by forbidding any Catholic from joining the Freemasons. If they could have managed it, they would have subjected the Freemasons to all the rigours of the Inquisition, but Freemasons only came out into the open in Protestant countries.

'With the Inquisition consigned to history, and the Vatican just a colourful historical pageant, there's no need for ersatz Freemasons. They're an embarrassment.'

'How do you know all this?' Vernon asked.

'I told you, my grandfather researched this stuff for decades and passed on his work to my parents. This is my family's life's work. We've given everything to make sense of this conspiracy. Not only out of academic curiosity. We genuinely believe these people pose a threat to the world.'

'But if they communicate in code all the time, how can you find out what's going on?'

'Codes can be broken. Many times in history, members of the conspiracy have been captured and tortured until they revealed their secrets. We've gained huge insights into how they operate. One of their main techniques was to use elaborate, ambiguous metaphors.'

'Like the Holy Grail?'

'Exactly. That's their ultimate metaphor, but there have been many others.'

'Such as?'

'Take Alchemy. The very last thing Alchemists were seeking was something that literally turned base metals into gold. They were highly religious people seeking true knowledge of the universe, hence their obsession with obscure experiments. The "base metals" they were talking about were ordinary people. The "gold" was what people became when they discovered the True God. When they talked about an elixir of life, the Alchemists meant the promise of eternal life offered by the True God.

Similarly, when they spoke about finding a cure for all human diseases, they meant heaven, where no one suffers any illness.'

'You make them sound like priests.'

'That's exactly what they were. Their predecessors were the Druids.'

'So, the Alchemists were part of the superconspiracy too?'

'Any time you come across an unusual group of people attracting the hostility of the Catholic Church, you can be sure they're part of it.'

'And they will all be using metaphorical ways of speaking?'

'I think you're finding it hard to take this in, but it's simple stuff. All you have to bear in mind is that whenever Christians are faced with a choice between a literal and a metaphorical interpretation of something, they'll invariably accept the literal interpretation even when it's absurd. *Especially* when it's absurd.'

'I don't understand.'

'I'll give you a few examples. The Johannite sect in ancient Judea referred to John the Baptist as the *Word of God*. So, an expression like "The Word of God could be heard by all" merely meant that John the Baptist was speaking loudly enough for the people at the back of the crowd to hear him. It certainly didn't mean that God was talking to the human race. Nor did it mean that they thought John the Baptist was God; simply that he was God's chosen mouthpiece. He spoke *for* God, not *as* God.

'Similarly, the Johannites referred to non-Johannites as "blind" because they couldn't *see* the light of the True God. When John the Baptist converted someone, he was "making the blind see" i.e. introducing them to the true religion. He wasn't curing actual blind people of physical blindness. "Lepers" were Johannites who had lapsed from the true religion, making them "untouchable" as far as practising Johannites were concerned. "Curing a leper" meant bringing such a person back to the fold; it had nothing to do with a diseased person being cured of leprosy.

'The "dead" were those who were excommunicated from the religion for grave offences. To be "raised from the dead" meant to be released from excommunication. Any Johannite would have regarded the idea that it signified a man coming back from actual death as ridiculous. And, think about it, if Jesus really raised Lazarus from the dead, it would be one of the most well known events in history, talked about by everyone. Lazarus would be famous, invited to Rome to see the Emperor to describe his experience. As it was, no further mention was ever made of Lazarus. How could a man who came back from the dead be forgotten so easily? Obviously, he never died in the first place, and no one who was there at the time said he did.

'The "poor" were those who'd newly joined the Johannite sect and still had much to learn; the "sick" were those who had heard the message and rejected it. New Johannites were only allowed to drink water for the first year; afterwards they were permitted to have wine. So, turning "water into wine" simply meant helping new Johannites through their initiation period.

"Walking on water" described the final part of the initiation ceremony. Johannites threw themselves in a line in front of their religious master to prove their devotion and subservience. Barefooted, he walked over them. Christians, of course, took this all too literally, as ever. Those "with ears to hear" understood the coded language perfectly; outsiders had no idea of what was being discussed. Christians, entirely on the outside, never tired of getting it spectacularly, almost comically, wrong.'

Vernon shifted uneasily in his seat. He had little doubt Gresnick was right. It was easy to think of a modern example. A teenage girl might write in her diary that her new dress was *wicked*, her new boyfriend *hot*, and the new song by her favourite group *bad*. Someone discovering her diary two thousand years later might conclude that she believed her dress was possessed by evil spirits, her boyfriend had a fever, and she didn't think her favourite band's latest tune was any good. All of a sudden, it seemed mad to Vernon that anyone could ever have believed that Jesus cured lepers, restored sight to the blind, turned water into wine, walked on water, raised Lazarus from the dead and all the rest of it.

Vernon looked at the SAS troopers. Most of them had closed their eyes, but clearly weren't sleeping. A couple of Welshmen in the corner were talking about rugby. Vernon breathed out hard. At least his conversation with Gresnick had taken his mind off the flight, but now he was feeling sick again.

'A lot to think about, huh?' Gresnick raised his voice as the weather outside began to worsen. The wind was getting louder, heavy rain driving against the helicopter.

Vernon nodded. 'With all the commotion going on in Thames House, we didn't get time to pin anything down. There are so many loose ends.'

'Brain feels like jelly, right? I felt the same way when I first came across all this stuff.' Gresnick pulled his cap down, until it was almost concealing his eyes. 'We need to have a good idea of what we're going up against or we won't stand a chance. Those Delta Force guys out there hold all the cards. They know exactly what's going on, and we're just taking shots in the dark.'

It was only occurring to Vernon now how out of his depth he was. Going on active service wasn't his thing. His job was to provide agents in the field with the information they needed. Now, he was the person needing the hard information, and there wasn't any.

He noticed the pilot whispering to one of the crew and strained to hear what they were saying. It was hard to make out over the sound of the engines and rotor blades, but he thought the pilot said something about a 'strange shape' appearing above the Chinook. A flock of birds, maybe?

'Are you all right?' Gresnick asked.

'Just thought I heard the pilot mentioning a problem.'

'Night Stalker, remember? If he can't handle it, no one can.'

Vernon smiled half-heartedly.

'*The Cainite Destiny* says the Nazis can trace their lineage back to Cain,' Gresnick said. 'What do you know about Cain?'

'He killed Abel. He was the first murderer in history. God branded him and made him an outcast. He lived in the Land of Nod, East of Eden. I seem to remember he was a bit of a scientist and built a city.'

'An early Alchemist, perhaps?'

'I suppose so.'

'How do you think Cain felt about God?'

'He hated him, I guess.'

'Did he want revenge?'

'Probably.'

'What do people who want revenge normally do?'

Vernon tried to leap ahead to see where this was leading. An odd childhood memory came back to him. He remembered standing outside his parents' room one night, with his ear pressed against the door. Moaning noises were coming from inside. No humans, he thought, could make such sounds. Behind that locked door, his parents must have transformed themselves into their true shape – aliens of some kind. He didn't speak to them for days afterwards.

He hesitated, not wanting to seem stupid in front of Gresnick, but the words pounding in his mind were pressing against his lips. They insisted on forcing their way out. 'Perhaps Cain wanted to...' He shook his head. This was insane. But Gresnick was staring at him, encouraging him to finish his sentence. Vernon had never been particularly religious, but nor was he attracted to atheism. The words now in his mind seemed like the ultimate sacrilege.

'Perhaps he wanted to what?' Gresnick said. '*To strike back?*'

Vernon bowed his head. Beads of sweat were erupting on his forehead. His parents weren't aliens, he discovered all those years ago, just ordinary humans doing ordinary human things. But no ordinary humans could accomplish the extraordinary thought that had now seized his mind and was refusing to let go.

'Go on,' Gresnick said. 'You know exactly what this is all about.'

Vernon rushed out the words, as though to say them quickly enough was to render them harmless. 'I think Cain might have wanted to kill God.'

Gresnick sat back.

'*Precisely.*'

29

The convoy was at a halt again. They had passed through a village a little earlier, but no lights were on. Maybe there was a blackout.

Lucy watched as Captain Kruger held a conference with three of his soldiers, each taking a turn to use the night vision binoculars. It would be a miracle, she thought, if they could see anything in this darkness even with the newest technology. There was no moon, no starlight. Even though the headlights of the Land Rovers were on, the beams seemed to break into pieces and fall to the ground. It was as though light itself were beginning to die, its brightness fading, like everything else in this dimming world. No one would be able to follow them in these conditions. Their convoy would appear as nothing more than a faint afterimage of something that passed here long ago. These days it was difficult to separate people from spectres.

Each time any of the soldiers got out of a vehicle, they had to take a torch with them. They seemed like shadow-figures, ghosts stepping through a half-world where things couldn't take on full form. Their flesh was unnaturally pale, almost blue.

Kruger turned and pointed his torch at Lucy. He had one of those faces that seemed incapable of smiling. God, she loathed him. She thrust her hand inside her jacket and traced the outline of her medicine bottle with her fingers. Her lips formed a sly smile. It was so easy to fool Kruger – he didn't dare touch any sexual part of her body. She wouldn't stop taking her medication just because he said so. Without it, she would never have survived the last few months. Even now, her pills were the only things keeping her calm. It amazed her that everything that had happened tonight hadn't made her crack. A few months ago, after anything remotely as weird as this, she would have slumped into a zombie state. There, nothing could touch her. She'd be beyond caring, always the best place to be. Her psychiatrist said she deliberately put herself in that condition, that she was fleeing from life. Who in their right mind wouldn't? Life equalled pain. It was the only equation anyone needed to learn.

'I need to go to the, uh...' She waved her hand.

Her guard turned away in disgust. 'Don't go far,' he said.

As Lucy opened the Land Rover's door, the freezing wind stung her skin. She reached inside the vehicle, grabbed a plastic water bottle and stuffed it into one of her pockets. Stumbling a few feet into the dark, she fumbled for her torch's on-switch then scanned around, looking for a private spot.

Crouching down behind a broken-down wall at the side of the road, she switched off her torch so no one could see what she was doing. She was relieved by how noisy the wind was, drowning out the sound she was making. When she finished, she poured some bottled water over her hands to rinse them. While she zipped up her combats, she wondered if she should try to get away after all. But where would she go? She didn't have a map, had no clear idea of where she was, and the weather was out of Siberia. She screwed the cap back on the bottle of water and stuffed it into her pocket. Whether she liked it or not, she was stuck with Kruger. She still had no clear sense of what his plans were for her other than that they were taking her to *that* place. Beyond that, zilch.

For a moment, she wished she could check her appearance in a mirror. She never bothered in the convent. There were virtually no mirrors there anyway. Would she recognise herself? They told her in the convent that she was getting better. She had such a long path to retrace. Just weeks ago, she was being pushed around the convent's garden in a wheelchair, dribbling, understanding nothing of who or where she was. The only reason she even knew about it was that she'd sneaked a look at her doctor's report. Now, not only was she getting back to her old self, but, in a strange way, accelerating past. It was as though there were someone else inside her, much more together than she ever was. She imagined herself like some human snake, sloughing off its old skin. Was there such a thing as a recovery that left you healthier than you were before you fell ill?

Sinclair called her name. For a moment, it freaked her out. *Lucy*. Somehow, that simple label made her concrete again; proved that she truly existed in this world outside the walls of the convent.

Clambering over the small wall, she flashed her torch at Sinclair.

'There you are,' he said. 'You shouldn't wander off like that.'

'What do these soldiers want with me? You have to tell me.' It was so cold that she imagined icicles were growing inside her nose. She stuffed her left hand deep into one of her pockets, and wished she had thick gloves. Every few seconds, she had to switch the torch from one hand to the other to stop her hands freezing.

Sinclair scanned around. His face dipped in and out of shadows. He was wearing a large parka too and slapping his hands together to keep warm.

'Don't trust these men.' He glanced at the soldiers sitting inside the Land Rovers.

'Are they going to kill me?'

Sinclair bowed his head. In the torchlight, his features were harsh and angular. His grey eyes caught the light in a way that made them look unearthly.

Lucy gazed at the ground and saw smears of blood. A wheel of one of the Land Rovers had crushed a rabbit. Its entrails were hanging out and one of its eyes was mangled.

'I didn't want to tell you,' Sinclair said. 'The late Pope…I confess I had concerns. Julius IV was…'

'You think he was a heretic, don't you?'

Sinclair squinted at her. 'How could you possibly know that?'

Lucy turned towards the soldiers. She wanted to be warm and comfortable inside a vehicle just as they were, but she knew this was the only chance she'd get to talk to Sinclair in private.

'Pope Julius IV gave himself that name in honour of Julius II, didn't he? Yet it was Julius II who commissioned that mural hidden in his tomb. It's utterly unorthodox. Those images from Arthurian legends were unacceptable to the Catholic Church. I wrote about papal hostility to the Arthurian romances in my book.'

She reeled off the reasons. Arthur's Knights of the Round Table – military knights with religious leanings – were an obvious echo of the Knights Templar whom the Church had outlawed. Arthur himself died in mysterious circumstances and legend had it that he and his army were asleep in a great cave, waiting to be resurrected and ride out to save the world from destruction. That sounded like an alternative Messiah. The legend of the Holy Grail revolved around the figure of Joseph of Arimathea, not St Peter. That suggested a Secret Church of the Grail and a potential rival priesthood, taking their legitimacy from Joseph rather than Peter. That was a direct challenge to the authority of the popes. As for Merlin, the Catholic Church would unquestionably have burned him at the stake as a sorcerer. Then there was the cult of 'courtly love'. Young knights were supposed to declare their love to 'unattainable' married women, just as Lancelot did to Guinevere. That was tantamount to advocating adultery. So, the papacy gave no encouragement to Arthur's legends. No Arthurian art was commissioned – no paintings, no sculptures, nothing.

Sinclair nodded. 'Those are just the most obvious reasons. You're aware of others, of course.'

'What do you mean?'

'I have to confess you weren't unknown to me before I came to the convent tonight. I read your book last year. It was brought to my attention because it was about heresy and it's my job to know everything about the latest theories on heretical ideas. Most things you wrote were correct.'

'Well, thanks for your support.' Some of Lucy's old rage fired up again. It infuriated her how her book was dismissed so easily by a bunch of old men. Sinclair's endorsement would have been priceless.

'You know it's not the Vatican's policy to fuel controversies,' Sinclair said. 'Anyway, we'd always known that the Arthurian stories were rife with heresy. Julius II was posthumously regarded with suspicion because of his mural. He's not actually buried in that tomb – he's in St Peter's – but that doesn't change anything. The mural was paid for by him, was worked on secretly and without explanation, and no senior Churchmen were allowed to see it. When the mural was uncovered several years after the death of a later Pope, Julius III, no Popes ever again took the name Julius. So, you can imagine the consternation when the last Pope chose Julius as his papal name.

'You just need to look at the centrepiece of the sculpture over Julius II's tomb to see how suspect he was. He commissioned Michelangelo to produce a statue of Moses. Nothing so surprising about that, except for one thing – Moses was given horns like the Devil. Anyone can go along there and see it for themselves. We have no reason to believe it was Michelangelo's idea. Even the name of the church containing the tomb is curious. It's called *San*

Pietro in Vincoli – St Peter in Chains. Perhaps Julius was acknowledging that the successors of St Peter ought to be chained like criminals because the line of Joseph of Arimathea were the true leaders of Christianity.'

Now Lucy understood why there was so much tension between the cardinal and Kruger. One was the loyal defender of the late Pope, while the other suspected he was a heretic. They didn't trust each other, and she, in her turn, saw no reason to trust either of them. Ernest Hemingway once said that the best way to find out if you could trust somebody was to trust them. It was also the best way to get yourself in a lot of trouble, she thought.

'How did Julius IV die?' she asked.

'His aide handed him a note moments after he'd completed a speech to the world from the balcony of St Peter's. He collapsed on the spot. Within minutes, he was pronounced dead. A massive heart attack, apparently.'

'What did the note say?'

'No one understood it.'

'Well, what?'

'The precise words were: *Not one of us.*'

'Who wasn't?'

'No one knew.'

'Who sent it? They must know that much, surely.'

'The aide said the Pope had asked to be notified immediately if an anonymous message arrived from Israel. It concerned a matter the Pope believed was critically important. The aide didn't divulge any other details. We think a Mossad agent sent the message, but Mossad later denied they knew anything about it.'

'But why did the aide give the Pope the note at a moment like that?'

The cardinal shrugged. 'As I said, the Pope wanted to hear immediately.'

'Why would the Pope have any dealings with Mossad?'

'The whole thing was odd. I guess we'll never discover the truth now.'

Lucy's guard knocked on the window of the Land Rover and gestured at her to get back in. When Lucy didn't move, the soldier got out of the vehicle.

Sinclair grabbed Lucy by the hand and pulled her towards him.

She recoiled, hating his rough grip. His breath was all over her.

'Listen to me, Lucy,' he whispered as the soldier came closer. 'I didn't want to tell you this, but I can't lie. If it looks like you're about to be captured by the deserters, Kruger has orders to kill you.'

30

Can't bear the sound. Vernon pressed his hands against his ears to shut out the din. For ten minutes, hailstones had battered against the helicopter's fuselage like machine-gun fire. The pilot climbed steeply to get above the weather, but it hadn't worked. It amazed Vernon that the hailstones weren't smashing through the cockpit's windscreen. How could the pilot fly through this? The Chinook kept plunging downwards into air pockets. Vernon scanned around for something to vomit into. The wind was gaining strength, howling. He was terrified one of the rotor blades would shear off, sending the helicopter into a death spin.

He stared at Colonel Gresnick. *That bastard's inhuman*, he thought. The colonel was calmly reading his reports, acting as if this were a routine flight. How could the American be so relaxed after what they discussed earlier?

Vernon repeatedly clenched and unclenched his hands, trying to channel his nervous tension into a single action. The helicopter was vibrating so much he imagined he was in a tin suspended in a wind tunnel. Everything not firmly locked down shook and rattled, threatening to fly loose. Normally, the thought that the helicopter could drop out of the sky would have absorbed all of his concentration, but now his mind flitted back to Gresnick's theory.

Even if the Biblical Cain really existed and had the most murderous hatred of God imaginable, he surely didn't think he could kill his Creator. It was impossible by definition. God was immortal, deathless, the first and last. How would you even begin to plan his murder? There was no starting point because there was no possibility of an end.

Lucy, in her book, hadn't mentioned anything as absurd as a cabal of fanatics conspiring to assassinate God, but what she *had* said was that some religious believers – the Gnostics – had a very odd idea of whom the Creator of the earth was. According to them, he wasn't the benevolent, loving God everyone else imagined, but an evil monster: the Devil, in fact. The Gnostics maintained that the earth, as the Devil's finest creation, was an abomination, a prison camp for souls. The more extreme Gnostics believed that the Last Judgment had already taken place and this planet was where the damned were sent. Earth was quite literally hell.

Sometimes, when he saw how vile people were, Vernon thought the Gnostics had a case. Glancing to his right, he noticed an SAS soldier in the far corner reading a book. He squinted to see what it was. When he recognised it, he suppressed an instinctive snigger. He'd never imagined that an SAS trooper would read the Bible, but why not? Maybe the SAS were more in need of divine reassurance than anyone else. He didn't doubt which chapter the trooper was studying so intently – St John's Revelation, the *Book of Apocalypse*.

As a God-fearing Christian, the trooper would no doubt be horrified by the Gnostics. As for Vernon, he'd never got round to either embracing or rejecting Christianity. Raised as an Anglican, he found that religion never impinged too much on his life. Weddings, christenings, funerals and midnight Mass at Christmas – those were his only contact with the Church.

He first read about Gnosticism as a teenager for a school A-level history project. One Gnostic text claimed that Jesus was married to Mary Magdalene and that they had a daughter, Sarah. He'd found that notion deliciously subversive. Many commentators, he discovered, had a soft spot for the Gnostics and often portrayed them as early hippies – tolerant, non-violent, vegetarian, non-sexist, unmaterialistic – pretty much the nicest people in the world. So, it was a shock when he dug deeper and discovered that their core beliefs were about as disturbing as you could get.

He'd never heard of any other religion openly proclaiming that this world, its Creator and everything in it were wicked to the core. He admired its perversity. If you went along with it, it opened up a new way of thinking about the world. It meant the forces of darkness had cunningly deceived the human race. We were the unknowing damned.

Apart from the Gnostics, that is. They weren't fooled. For them, being 'good' was meaningless. What counted was knowing the truth, and the Gnostic truth was the astounding one that the material world was malignant. The stuff that comprised the world – what we nowadays labelled as protons, electrons, neutrons, and all the atoms and molecules born from them – was imbued with evil. At the most fundamental level of material existence, evil was ingrained. Vernon remembered enough of his Oxford PPE degree to know that philosophers of antiquity often referred to the *animus mundi* – the world soul. To the Gnostics, this soul was irredeemably wicked.

From that belief, everything flowed with inexorable logic. The Creator of the material world was evil, everyone who worshipped him was evil, everything his prophets and priests proclaimed as true was false. On the other hand, everyone who opposed those prophets and priests was righteous. The task of the human soul was not to be good, but to be clever enough to escape this hell.

When they described the Creator of the world, the Gnostics used an ancient Greek word *demiourgos*, a term used by Plato that meant *craftsman*. Because Creation was intrinsically evil, the Demiourgos – Demiurge in English – was identified with Satan. Sometimes the Gnostics used another term, *Rex Mundi*, meaning the *King of the World*, but that was just one more epithet for Satan, the Devil.

The True God existed in a universe of pure, incorruptible light, the opposite of the violent world of matter, this cruel circus. Sometimes, angels from the divinely illuminated universe fell in perverse love with the physical world. Sex, inevitably, was what tempted them; Satan's perfect bait. Crazed with desire for carnal knowledge, the angels came down to earth and inhabited human bodies to find out what sex was like. Too late, they discovered they were trapped.

When their physical bodies died, their souls were reincarnated in new bodies. There was no way out, unless they acquired enough wisdom, enough true knowledge, to fathom how to get back to the kingdom of the True God. Gnosis – the ancient Greek word for knowledge – was all about gaining that special knowledge. Faith didn't matter in the slightest, only knowledge.

Gnosis was a religion for the intelligent, not for blind believers brainwashed from birth.

According to *The Cainite Destiny*, the Nazis were well acquainted with these ideas. Were the Nazis Gnostics? That would explain so much, such as their pathological hatred of the Jews. After all, according to the Jews' own account, they were the Chosen People of the Creator. To the Jews, that Creator was Jehovah, but, to the Gnostics, Jehovah was Satan.

It would also account for why Hitler was fascinated by religious relics, why the Nazis chose an ancient religious symbol as their emblem, why they sent expeditions round the world looking for proof that they were unlike ordinary human beings. Was the Aryan Race some ancient Gnostic cult tracing its origins back to Cain, the first human to have violently opposed the will of Jehovah?

Vernon gripped his armrest and closed his eyes. It all fitted together. These things couldn't be coincidence. *The Cainite Destiny* was no mad fantasy of a deranged soldier. The Nazi leaders actually thought it was true, didn't they? They genuinely believed they were the descendants of Cain and that they had found the means to kill Jehovah. When Hitler took possession of the Spear of Destiny, he was convinced that gave him the power to do it. But how? Was the Spear really *that* special?

He turned to Gresnick. The American had shown he was smart and unusually well informed about esoteric matters. How much did he know about the Spear? A lot more than was in the DIA report, no doubt. Just as Vernon was about to ask, he stopped himself. There was something about the colonel he disliked. Too confident? Too much the perfect soldier? He didn't trust him, and he wasn't sure why. Or maybe he knew too well.

He closed his eyes. The hailstones were louder than ever, threatening to blast through the Chinook's metal shell. It seemed that the material world was coming alive, its soul burning. It was enraged by something, and determined to destroy it.

It might be impossible for the Gnostics to kill God, but destroying a planet was a different matter. Across the universe, planets were dying. Earth itself was dying. Billions of years in the future, it would no longer exist. It was, to use the oldest of clichés, simply a question of time. Had a group of scientists, infected with extreme Gnostic beliefs, worked out how to accelerate the process? Perhaps they'd invented devices to manipulate the weather, to activate fault lines, boost volcanic activity. Maybe the 'angel' that escaped from Thames House was the product of some top-secret genetic engineering experiment to make people resemble the angels the Gnostics claimed we'd all once been, and might be again. Maybe everything had a 'rational' explanation, if that word still had meaning.

Vernon opened his eyes again and gazed at the SAS troopers. Most of them were cleaning their assault rifles or staring into space, as if in meditation. Could he rely on them? They were elite soldiers, but they had no idea of what they were up against.

The wind was growing fiercer. The helicopter no longer seemed to be moving forward but was caught at the centre of a violent lightning storm. Thunderclaps boomed like artillery fire. It was easy to imagine that something was whipping up this storm, an elemental force tapping the vast energy locked in the world and focussing it on a single spot with catastrophic fury. The Chinook shook so much that even Gresnick looked up from his file.

In the cockpit, the pilot was struggling with the controls and yelling at the co-pilot. The words vanished in the noise of the wind, hail, rotor blades and engines. Everyone in the cabin was fully strapped into their seats, but loose kit bags that had fallen from the overhead storage lockers were sliding around on the floor.

In the distance, a few faint lights appeared. *Thank God*, Vernon thought, *almost there*. He heard two of the SAS troopers shouting that they could see a shape heading for the side of the helicopter at high speed.

'Look out!' the pilot cried.

Inside the Chinook, every light flickered.

'God, did you see that?' Gresnick shouted.

Vernon turned and stared out through the cockpit window. Something had appeared in front of the helicopter. *Something*. For a second, he thought a rip had appeared in space. The shape was so dark it was sucking light into it. It was more than an absence of light, it was as if the thing were actually killing light. Vernon was certain he knew what it was, but his mind refused to accept it. He felt exactly as he had when all the lights went out back at Thames House.

'Jesus, what the fuck is that?' The navigator threw his hands in front of his face.

The soldier who had been reading the Bible made the sign of the cross and got to his feet, gripping his assault rifle. 'You don't understand, do you?' he said, attracting hostile looks from his colleagues. 'It's here, it's come, just as the Bible said it would.'

'What are you on about, McGregor?' his neighbour snarled.

'Don't you get it – none of us is coming back from this alive.' McGregor was wild-eyed.

'Shut up, trooper,' his captain yelled.

None of us is coming back. McGregor's words burned into Vernon's mind. He was right, wasn't he? This was a one-way mission. And maybe the end was coming this very second.

Vernon's saliva tasted foul. Was that what fear did to you? All of his muscles were flexing, getting ready for combat. He blinked rapidly – shit, he wasn't seeing in colour any longer, just black and white. Colour vision took up too much brainpower, he remembered. It simply wasn't needed in survival situations. Just the essentials: tunnel vision, monochromatic, everything stripped down. Even time was becoming distorted, seconds expanding, elongating. He was able to notice so much more, all the details that might help to save his life.

'I'll pray for your souls,' McGregor yelled before receiving a punch in the abdomen from his neighbour.

Vernon braced for a collision. With what, he wasn't sure.

'Fire the machine guns,' Gresnick yelled at the pilot, but his voice turned back on itself. The din inside the helicopter was distorting every sound, turning human voices into nothing but weird sound effects. The 'whup whup' of the twin rotor blades had reached a deafening level.

An SAS soldier unbelted himself and tried to make his way to the front of the cabin. Vernon thought the trooper planned to slide open the side-door and shoot at the shape with his assault rifle.

The pilot slammed the Chinook into an emergency dive and the helicopter plunged towards the ground, throwing the SAS man onto the floor.

Vernon unstrapped himself and tried to reach out to the soldier to help him back to his seat. The Chinook lurched again and Vernon toppled onto the floor. He found his face inches from the trooper's black boots, so close he could smell the polish. It made him gag, and he had to fight not to vomit over the trooper's feet.

Jerking his head away, he took in a sharp breath. His face ended up next to Gresnick's folder: the American must have dropped it in the confusion. A picture of Lucy had slipped out. Staring at that face, he couldn't stop a splutter of vomit escaping from his mouth.

When, all those months ago, Lucy sent him her letter telling him that she never wanted to see him again, she might as well have shot him. Before that letter, he'd never thought of himself as anything other than a whole, happy person. After, he imagined he had a gaping hole in his chest, as though he'd been shot at point-blank range by a double-barrelled shotgun. A wound, he knew, that would never heal. Metaphysical injuries were much worse than the physical type. No medicine, no surgery, could treat them.

The noise around the helicopter died for a second. The Chinook had found the eye of the storm.

'We're OK,' Gresnick said, breathing out hard. His forehead gleamed with sweat. 'We've levelled out.'

Vernon, unentangling himself from the SAS trooper, started patting his chest. There was no physical wound, but the old hole was still there, radiating raw pain. He dreaded seeing Lucy again. Would he hate her for what she did to him? Even worse, would he still love her? He couldn't go through all that again.

'Making our approach for landing,' the pilot announced over the intercom. 'I don't know what happened up there, but we're OK.'

The SAS soldiers were clutching their guns and grimly staring out of the porthole windows.

Gresnick went forward, whispered to the pilot and came back seconds later, pale.

'What did the pilot think it was?' Vernon asked as Gresnick got back into his seat. He avoided Lucy's picture, gazing up at him from the floor.

Gresnick hesitated. 'He didn't get a clear view.'

'But he did see *something*?'

Gresnick leaned down, retrieving his folder and Lucy's photo. 'He said the thing had wings.'

31

The small cluster of picturesque cottages stood in darkness, their neat stone walls picked out by the headlights of the Land Rovers. No streetlights were on anywhere in Tintagel village. Lucy had never been here in the dark before, and never since *it* happened.

As the convoy manoeuvred through the few narrow streets, she sensed an eerie atmosphere. *Abandonment.* She was convinced the villagers weren't asleep in their houses; they weren't here at all. The Government had probably cut off gas and electricity supplies to isolated communities like this. The villagers must have fled to the cities.

As the convoy headed down a long slope towards the castle and the sea, Lucy tried to summon the good feelings she once had for this place. She'd made this journey ten times previously. Each time, the weather was perfect, and she thought she'd discovered a backdoor to paradise. Those days didn't belong to the routines of ordinary life. They were tinged with a unique glow. *Numinous* was the word she liked to use. Tintagel was that kind of place, touched by the Otherworldly. But now all that awaited her here was horror.

They parked outside the English Heritage ticket-office, the lights of the lead vehicle shining onto the gloss-painted blue door. A sign, scrappily handwritten with a black marker pen, was pinned to the door saying: *Temporarily closed. Apologies for any inconvenience.*

Lucy's guard told her to get out of the Land Rover and she stiffly clambered out, her right foot squelching into a puddle. Frost covered the grass around her. It was cold enough for snow. Thrusting her hand into her pocket, she took out her rubber torch, wishing again that she had gloves.

One of the Swiss Guards used his pistol to shoot away the padlock on the gate sealing off the Heritage office from the ruins of Tintagel Castle. Kruger screamed at him in German. Lucy assumed he was angry that the gunshot might have given away their position.

They climbed up a narrow path, avoiding the iced-over puddles scattered all around. Kruger led the way with a torch set to a narrow beam. He'd told everyone not to wave their torches for fear of attracting attention. As they walked, they cast weird shadows. Lucy remembered once coming across an old sundial in Brick Lane in London. On it was an inscription: Umbra Sumus – *We are shadows*. That was what she thought they'd become.

Kruger took them across a narrow bridge separating the mainland from the small island where the most intact sections of the castle's ruins were situated. Even now, with its walls reduced to stumps, it was possible to imagine how the castle once was, as if its ghost were here, every now and again shimmering into full view with its high turrets and fluttering pennants, its knights in shining breastplates riding out over the drawbridge.

Kruger stopped in the middle of the ruined castle and told his men they could rest. They sat down on the walls and started to eat army rations from their backpacks. Lucy sat down too, but Kruger kicked her foot.

'You're coming with me.' He pointed towards the surviving shell of the island's small chapel. It was to the rear of the castle, on the summit of the rock outcrop, close to *there*.

'I'm not going.' Lucy turned her head away.

Grabbing her hand, Kruger hauled her to her feet. 'I don't have time for this.' He started pulling her towards the gate leading to the chapel.

Lucy grasped the gatepost and tried to hold on, but Kruger was too strong. He dragged her along behind him, almost crushing her hand in his. All the time, the sea hissed. They were only feet from sheer cliff-faces, and there were no protective barriers. Inside, Lucy was churning up. She was so close to where it happened. Please God, anywhere else on earth but here. Tintagel was a tomb where the dead kept watch.

When they reached the chapel – little more than an outline on the ground after centuries of decay – Kruger stopped and shone his torch into Lucy's eyes. The light stung, and she raised her hands to block the beam.

'Don't trust Cardinal Sinclair,' he said. 'He's an ambitious man.'

Lucy didn't know how to respond. Should she shout at Kruger, or be cooperative, sympathetic, to try to win him round? 'What do you mean?' She spoke softly, as non-confrontationally as possible, hoping she could persuade him to turn back.

'Last year, the Pope had a health scare,' Kruger said. 'There was speculation about who might succeed him. The Pope told me what was likely to happen. Sinclair would initially claim to have no interest in becoming the new Pope, but, using his influence, he would ensure that the Sacred College of Cardinals was unable to reach a decision. When the cardinals were deadlocked, he'd step forward and say, for the good of the Church, that he was prepared to accept the burden. Julius believed Sinclair would then be elected unanimously.'

Lucy nodded, but she was scarcely listening. She wanted to go back to the others. Why had they come here? This place had nothing to offer. It was long past time to leave. Besides, she'd recalled a disturbing fact. The founder of the Swiss Guard was…Pope Julius II. If, as she now believed, he was a heretic, what did that mean about his private army?

'I've heard the Sacred College of Cardinals is now deadlocked.' Kruger pointed his torch beam at the frost-covered grass, glittering like a lake of ice.

'And you think Sinclair will go back to Rome and be proclaimed Pope?' Lucy maintained her pretence of calm. *Please get me away from here.*

'Everything is exactly as Pope Julius predicted.'

'But what's wrong with Sinclair having ambition? Why does that make him suspect?' Lucy's ambition was to get as far from Tintagel as possible.

'Popes are supposed to be humble.'

'I see.' It was a ridiculously idealistic remark, Lucy thought. She pointed her torch at Kruger. 'Please, let's go back now.' Staring at his blue eyes, she hoped to see some sign of...she didn't know exactly. An answer? Sympathy? Kruger was so cold, a real soldier, his face lacking any trace of compassion. She couldn't imagine him loving anyone or anything. Except duty. That sort of abstract love would appeal to him, but what was certain was that he'd never whisper things of love to a woman.

Kruger frowned. 'You have no idea, do you? You're still in denial.'

'I didn't ask for this. I don't know why you brought me here.'

'You know exactly.'

Lucy stood there in the darkness with the wind swirling around her. She'd never felt more alone in her life. Kruger *knew*, didn't he? For some twisted reason he'd brought her right here to where it happened. A sadist.

'I'm here to make you face reality.' Kruger grabbed the hood of Lucy's parka and pulled it back. 'I'm going to make you break through all the garbage in your head.'

Lucy swallowed air as the wind blasted into her face. She stared at Kruger, at his face slipping in and out of her torchbeam. Maybe she should hit him with the torch, try to knock him out, then run away. If she didn't, he'd take her to *that* place.

'Please let me go.' Her voice was pathetic, taken by the wind. Why was Kruger doing this? Did he want to torture her, make her crazy again?

Another look flashed across Kruger's face. *Disgust*?

'You can't stand me, can you?' she blurted. Maybe it was more than that. He might kill her, just as Sinclair predicted. Throw her off the cliff.

'We're going for a little walk.' Kruger gripped her again.

She tried to dig her heels into the ground, to resist the overwhelming force he was exerting on her. For a second, she thought he was going to lift her off her feet.

'I'm not going,' she yelled. 'You can't make me.'

Kruger spun her round like a child's toy then wrapped her in his huge arms. Slowly, he manoeuvred her forward, as though he were moving a coal sack. She kicked her heels against his shins.

'Don't, I beg you.'

Kruger kept pushing her forward, closer to the edge of the cliff. The moon broke through clouds and threw a sickly light over the frothing sea.

Lucy closed her eyes, trying to avoid thinking about what was happening. Agonising pains were in her stomach, spreading through her bloodstream to every part of her body.

'Open your eyes,' Kruger barked.

Thick, driving rain was descending now. Drops spattered Lucy's face.

'I told you to look.' Kruger's voice was a harsh snarl in Lucy's ear.

Slowly, she let her eyes open. At first, the blinding rain stopped her from seeing anything. Then her vision cleared. She was inches from the edge of the cliff, confronted by the wild sea, tossing waves up at her like the tentacles of a giant squid. She was terrified that they'd take her feet and she'd plunge over the edge. Jagged rocks were down there.

Kruger held her tight, his body pressed against hers, his hot breath on her neck. He was panting.

As she stared at the sea, Lucy thought she saw tiny lights in the water, making the water glow with an eerie blue luminescence.

'You have to move on, Lucy.' Kruger's voice was almost tender. 'You can't let the past destroy you.'

Lucy was afraid she'd hyperventilate. Was this how *he* felt? She was certain she was standing at the exact spot, staring into the same sea. It was about 2 a.m. The coroner said her father committed suicide some time between 1 and 4 a.m. Seven months ago. A lifetime. Did he count to ten before he jumped or do it straight away? He'd kept it so bottled up. When she found his diary after his funeral, she discovered that his meticulous entries stopped the day mum died.

'In the blue,' was all he wrote that day. Every day afterwards, he wrote the same three words, the writing growing progressively more jagged.

Those words were burned into Lucy now. Her whole life was in the blue. The sea glowed blue in front of her. The nightmare, living and breathing.

'He loved you, Lucy,' Kruger said. 'Do you think he wanted you to end up in a care home?'

Tears filled Lucy's eyes. People had always remarked on how close she was to her parents, even for an only child. Sometimes she thought love was the worst thing in the world. What no one told you was that it was simply a seductive wrapping for pain – the worst pain of all because you never expected to find it beneath something so beautiful.

'Why?' she said, talking to the blue sea. 'Why did you leave me?' She longed to hear her dad's voice again. Cancer had taken her mum, but it was love that took her dad, and love that put her in an asylum. Now she wanted her heart to freeze.

'You must learn to love life again,' her psychiatrist told her. 'There's so much beauty out there, so many wonders. You just to need to reach out and take them.'

Did some people really believe that? They made it sound so easy. In time, they'd learn. In the end, they'd be flattened. They didn't have the bitter taste in their mouth, the nausea in their bellies, that came when love showed its true colours. But, one day, they would, and it would be much worse for them because they'd denied it for so long.

Transfixed by the increasing glow of the sea, Lucy wondered if her father's heart had choked with love. When love is everything and then it's snatched away, what can fill that aching void?

Her dad's body was found down there in the icy water, by a tourist in a rowing boat, taking pictures of Tintagel from the sea. It was shameful, she thought, that a stranger should know about her father's death before she did. What did the tourist think when he fished the bloated body out of the water? He would have known nothing of who this body once was, the love he enjoyed. The sea took all that human warmth away. All that remained was an anonymous body in the water with no one to speak for it, to make anyone care. A complete stranger finding a corpse and wondering what to do with it so often marks the end of a life. *Some life.*

Sometimes, back at the convent, Lucy imagined her father calling to her from the sea, inviting her to join him and her mum in death. The family would be whole again. Love restored, the Wasteland redeemed. Now she had the chance to be with him, but she couldn't jump into the blue. As long as she lived, she didn't want to go into the water ever again.

It still stunned her that her dad killed himself here of all places. The Arthurian romances never interested him. As a Professor of Classics at Bristol University, he was obsessed with Ancient Rome. He liked to tell her that so much of what we knew of Rome was mistaken. His favourite example was the thumbs-up sign used at the end of gladiatorial fights.

'We have it completely the wrong way around,' he said. 'When the crowd raised their thumbs, it didn't mean they wanted the loser to be saved. It was the opposite: they were demanding he be despatched to the afterlife. The thumbs-down signified they wanted the defeated fighter to stay on this earth, to live. Something that would have been blindingly obvious to any Roman ended up being perfectly misunderstood by us.

That had left a big impression on Lucy. How many of the greatest certainties were false, just like the thumbs-up sign? It was impossible to trust anything. Which one should she trust between Kruger and Sinclair? Her life might depend on it, but she had no idea. Thumbs up or thumbs down?

Was it because of her that her dad came here to end his life? He knew how much the story of Arthur meant to her. This was where Arthur was supposedly conceived. It might even be Camelot. Each time she visited Tintagel, she phoned her dad and told him how enchanting it was. She described its spectacular setting, talked about how powerful the sea was, about the imposing cliffs, how exquisite he'd find it if he ever came. Did he finally make the trip because it was as close as he could get to her without physically being with her? No one, on the day they planed to kill themselves, would want to see their loved ones, but maybe they'd choose a place that reminded them of those closest to them.

How much she wanted to see him again. To say all those things she never had the chance to tell him, to *love* again. Why had he done it? It was so unjust. They shouldn't do these things, these irrevocable things. Why didn't he speak to her? Together, they might have coped. On their own, there was no hope. She remembered something Kafka said: *There's an infinite amount of hope, but not for us.* Those words might as well be engraved on her heart.

When her dad jumped, did he hear anything other than the raging of the sea? More and more, she longed for silence; it allowed her to imagine she was alone in the world. Sometimes that was all she wanted. Other people brought pain. If they didn't exist, she wouldn't suffer. Above all, she'd be protected from love. Sometimes, she was certain love was the proof there was no God. No benevolent deity could inflict something so cruel.

She had loved only one other person – James Vernon. It was a dark, freezing night just like this when she decided to tell him it was over between them. She wasn't brave enough to say it to his face so she took the coward's way out and wrote a letter. Love made her do it. She couldn't go through with losing the last of the people who meant something to her. Better to end it and save them both from the suffering. It didn't work out, though. Just another reason to be depressed.

'You know about my father, don't you?' she said.

Kruger pressed his face against hers. For a second it felt lovely and warm.

'It was critical that we know as much about the...'

'The what?'

Kruger didn't answer.

'I can't help you,' Lucy said. 'It's all a mistake. Can't you see?'

Kruger's hand pressed against the small of her back.

'Shall I push you now?' Kruger's mouth was right against her ear. '*Into the blue.*'

Lucy tried to cry out, but the wind whipped into her face again.

'Two of my men died for you tonight,' Kruger said. 'Another is badly wounded. And why? To save a lunatic? So, perhaps we should forget our mission. Perhaps we should end it right here. Maybe it's best for everyone.'

Lucy stood there, rooted. She couldn't think of any words. The whole sea was shining now, as if every marine creature, no matter how small, was luminescent.

'You see that glow?' Kruger said. 'I know what's causing it. Something is very near. It will change everything. If you're not ready to fight it, you might as well be dead. We'll all be dead soon enough unless you get your wits about you.'

Lucy wanted to say, 'I don't understand,' but that would be lying. Something had changed. Every part of her sensed it. An odd electricity was in the air. She felt a presence nearby, a creature of some kind, yet so much more. Something had come to the earth, ancient and unspeakable. It was here right now, watching. Everything in the sea was glowing because of this creature. She knew its name, but refused to say it.

Soon, everyone would be dead. She would join her dad. She leaned back against the hand. *Do it* she felt like saying. Maybe it was what love demanded. But she couldn't face that blue sea. Any death except that.

Kruger pulled her back from the cliff edge and twisted her round until they were face to face, his arms wrapped securely around her back. It took a second for her to realise he was shaking. Overwhelmed by emotion? He wasn't the type. But he was trying to compose himself, wasn't he?

'You've seen Raphael's mural,' he said. 'Don't you think we've examined every part of it? Don't you think we've done everything in our power to understand it? You're the key, Lucy. We're certain several of the panels on Raphael's mural form a map of where you're going to be over the next seventy-two hours. One of the panels shows King Arthur at Camelot, and there's no doubt Raphael thought Camelot was here at Tintagel. He painted this place *exactly*. I didn't bring you here, Raphael did.'

He put his hand into his pocket, pulled out a scrap of paper and read out a bizarre sentence: **Arthur's conception. Only the chosen one can do what no other can. The suffering place. The death plunge. Death of one, or death of all.**'

Lucy swallowed hard. 'What is that?'

'Nostradamus wrote a note for each panel. They're all cryptic, but this one is clear enough, don't you agree? Arthur was conceived at Tintagel. Your father leapt to his death here. This place makes you suffer unbearably, doesn't it? You're trembling like a little girl, but it's time to grow up. Somehow, you'll do something here that will remove any doubt about who you are. If you fail, we'll all die.'

Lucy shook her head. Kruger kept saying these things to her and still they made no sense. She had no great talents. There was nothing special about her. Anything that depended on her was already doomed. Anyway, how could Raphael be responsible for her presence here? Kruger was the reason. He was twisted. Why did he insist on telling her how important she was? Could there be a sicker joke?

'You've been in a mental prison, Lucy.' Kruger's expression was a strange mixture of desperation and kindness. He seemed confused, as if he didn't know whether to despise or love her. 'I'm trying to release you. You need to confront your demons before you can move on. This is the place that will destroy you or set you free.'

'Set me free?' Lucy echoed. There was only one thing that could do that. She needed her medication. Needed to close her eyes. Drift away into tranquillity.

'Snap out of it,' Kruger barked. 'The world needs you. I don't care whether or not you believe it, I do.' He yanked down the front zip of her parka and thrust his hand inside her uniform, gripping first her left breast and then her right. She was too shocked to scream. Snatching out her medicine bottle from her right breast pocket, he held it in front of her like a trophy.

'Give me that you sick bastard.' Her hands flailed in front of Kruger, but he hurled the bottle past her into the sea.

Her mouth fell open as she tried to conceive of a world without the oblivion, the chemical mercy, her medication brought.

Kruger gripped her arms and shook her...so hard she thought she'd snap. His expression was fanatical. Then he let her go. She collapsed, sobbing, dropping her torch. She lay on the damp grass near the edge of the cliff.

'I can't bear any of this. I can't go on.'

Kruger stood over her in the wind. 'Do you believe in Jesus Christ, our Lord and Saviour?'

Lucy raised her head. *Believe*? Once, it all made sense to her. She went to Mass every Sunday, confessed her sins every six weeks, prayed for absolution and believed it when it was granted. She believed in good deeds, justice, divine grace, the intercession of saints. When she took Holy Communion, she didn't doubt that's exactly what it was – by swallowing the host the priest offered, she was in direct, sacred communion with the body of Christ, the divine essence, the holiest of holies.

But now she believed nothing. According to the Church, her father was a suicide, guilty of a mortal sin that could never be forgiven, a man damned for eternity. So, there was no justice, no heavenly grace, no mercy of Jesus Christ. There was nothing at all.

'Your life is a wasteland, Lucy Galahan.' Kruger pointed his torch down at her as she lay sprawled on the grass. 'That's what happens to those who turn their backs on God. The whole world is becoming a wasteland. When humanity rejected God, it was just a question of time before God rejected them.'

She thought he was about to kick her as she lay there looking up at him. Bizarrely, she pitied him. He placed such store in absurd things.

'Do you think I'm happy *you* were chosen? Why not me? But God always works in mysterious ways. So, we're stuck with you. Now get up.'

Lucy didn't move. She wasn't going anywhere with this man. The world could take care of itself. Closing her eyes, she lay flat, pressing her face against the wet grass. She didn't want to look at Kruger, to hear that scolding voice any longer. The ground beneath her was frozen hard. She felt her body heat draining into the rocks and soil. Maybe Kruger would realise she was a hopeless case and leave her alone.

She was amazed when Kruger dropped down and lay beside her on the grass. He'd tossed his torch away. What was he going to do? It was as if he'd been broken by everything that had happened tonight, by all his efforts that would be so futile if she refused to help him.

'I can't save anyone,' she whispered. 'Leave me alone, I beg you.'

Kruger's head was turned away from hers and he was prostrate, lying in an awkward position. She assumed he couldn't hear her because of the wind.

'Why won't you listen to me?' She strained to raise her voice. As she stared at him, she realised how much she wanted to hear his voice: to be forgiven, pardoned, told that all of this could happen without her. Kruger was so unlike James. Whenever James hugged her, he made her feel safe and loved. Not Kruger. Where was the kindness, the humanity? He was the one in need of help.

Stretching out her hand, she tried to touch him. There was something dreamlike about the way her hand moved, as though it didn't belong to her. Was she hallucinating? She wanted to stroke Kruger's hair. He was such a strong man; that rugged, silent type that sometimes seemed so attractive. If she touched his hair, maybe she could draw on his power, feel his strength running through the strands and into her body. She'd been so weak these past months.

Why was he so still? Was he weeping? Maybe that's why he wouldn't turn his face towards her. She knelt up. Her knees were soaking wet. The wind was whipping around her, much more ferociously than before. Kruger continued to lie there, as if he'd simply given up and just wanted to rest. He was vulnerable, fragile, just like everyone else. Would he let her touch him? No, not Kruger. He was so tough, so brittle, he'd detest it if she put her hand on him.

But her hand kept stretching forward. Moving in the beam of Kruger's abandoned torch, it cast a long shadow, much larger than her own hand, so much more definite. *Umbra Sumus.* She and Kruger had become shadow people, their silhouettes more real than they were. Her hand suddenly made contact with the back of Kruger's head, pressing against his hair. He didn't speak, not a word.

Why was his hair so sticky? Sweat? Rain continued to lash down on them. Her hand grew wetter as she moved it through his hair. This was all wrong. None of this was happening. It couldn't be.

She snatched her hand back and squinted hard at the captain. It took her several seconds to make sense of the thick, dark liquid spreading out over his head…to properly register its colour.

And then she began screaming.

32

Vernon, standing at the front entrance of Lucy's convent, watched the Chinook's pilot pacing up and down in front of the cockpit, and wondered what he was thinking. Without him, they'd all be dead. What the hell had they encountered up there?

It was odd, he thought, that he hadn't heard a single soldier mentioning what happened in the air less than an hour earlier. Everyone was getting on with their jobs, pretending everything was normal, pretending no winged creature attacked them. But he'd seen it with his own eyes. They all had. At the time, most of the SAS troopers were content to dismiss it as a freakish bird, or some kind of giant bat. Even the bible thumper McGregor kept his mouth shut. The co-pilot had unconvincingly written it off as a mirage, caused by the odd atmospheric conditions, but the pilot said nothing. Vernon knew it was none of those things, yet the alternative was preposterous.

The shape had frozen for an instant outside the cockpit, its wings extended, as though it were being crucified. It was man-shaped. No light came from it and no light reflected from it. Vernon shivered. Did he really believe a dark angel had trailed them from London?

At university, he was mystified by George Orwell's concept of *doublethink*. It was idiotic, he thought, for Orwell to argue that people could simultaneously hold two contradictory beliefs and accept both completely. Now he understood it perfectly. It was the only way to stay sane in a situation like this.

The helicopter, sitting in the middle of the deserted car park, resembled a huge bug. It was bathed in the glow of three floodlights that the nuns had used to illuminate a bronze sculpture of Jesus Christ overlooking the iron gates of the chapel. As SAS troopers drifted past, heading towards the loading ramp at the rear of the helicopter, Vernon wondered how much longer the nuns would insist on lighting up their Saviour. They had their own generator, but it wouldn't be able to supply them indefinitely. Sooner or later, they'd have to switch off Jesus.

The first SAS troopers back from the sweep confirmed that the convent was clear. The bodies of four soldiers – two Americans and two Swiss – were lying in a temporary mortuary in the convent's small gymnasium. There was no sign of Lucy, and none of the remaining Swiss Guards or Delta Force deserters. Tyre tracks in the grass behind the convent's chapel showed that five vehicles left at high speed on a southbound road. There were other tracks on the opposite side of the convent, indicating two trucks. Vernon had already alerted local police, telling them to get in touch immediately if they sighted any unexpected convoys.

As for the nuns and nursing staff, none was hurt. The Mother Superior said they hid in their rooms as soon as the shooting began. She was keen to get information from Vernon about what was going on, but he said he couldn't reveal anything because of the Official Secrets Act. As it turned out, she was better informed than he was. Not only did she know he had come for Lucy, she was able to tell him that Cardinal Sinclair, the Vatican's No. 2, was here a few hours earlier, specifically to see Lucy. It seemed he left with her and the soldiers. Presumably, he was in charge of the Swiss Guards. Did that mean Lucy was safe? But perhaps the deserters arrived first and took Lucy and the cardinal with them. There wasn't enough evidence to say either way.

The Mother Superior kept saying how sweet Lucy was, and how she was praying she'd come to no harm. Vernon had made his excuses and left.

As one of the last SAS troopers trudged past him, Vernon noticed that the soldier was carrying a slide projector. Just as he was about to ask him what he was doing with it, his mobile rang. He glanced at the display: *Commander Harrington.* Their conversation was brief. Harrington said a policeman based in Tintagel village in Cornwall had reported a gunshot. Several Land Rovers were parked near the castle. When Vernon asked if there was any news of the two escaped prisoners, Harrington cut off the call.

'Let's get going,' Vernon shouted at Gresnick. The colonel was sitting on a wall several feet away. He hadn't bothered helping with the search of the convent, preferring to spend his time studying his files. Vernon disliked the way Gresnick had taken a few troopers to one side before the sweep began and whispered conspiratorially to them.

Earlier, Vernon had noticed the American continually staring at Lucy's photograph. It annoyed him that Gresnick was so interested in looking at her. Didn't he have something better to do with his time?

Lucy was perhaps pretty rather than beautiful, but that didn't make her less striking. There was something beguiling in her expression, a sad, soulful look. She had those big blue eyes and that raven hair that sometimes formed a curl under her jaw, sometimes fell as a fringe over her face.

Again, he thought of Sergeant Morson's comment that she was the most important person in the world. Did Morson believe she was some kind of Messiah? Lucy would have found the idea so funny. What did Messiahs look like anyway? He once read a book claiming that Jesus Christ was a five-feet-tall woman with a genetic disease that made her resemble a man. The book made the valid point that anyone who wanted to help the weak, the meek, the poor, and the rejected was hardly likely to be a six-feet-tall, hunky, blue-eyed, blond Aryan with an enviable six-pack, particularly since perfect Aryans were rather thin on the ground in ancient Judea. Why not a repulsive, freakish, diseased woman? Who better to champion the downtrodden?

Gresnick closed his file, climbed off the stone wall and walked towards Vernon. 'We don't know for sure why the deserters want Lucy,' he said as they both returned to the Chinook. 'It's critical we find out.'

'Why?'

'If the deserters need Lucy alive at any cost, you know what that means.'

'I'm not sure I do.'

'Come off it, you know exactly what I'm getting at.'

'Why don't you say it?'

'Very well. To guarantee the enemy can't use Lucy, we may have to kill her.'

33

They were running towards Lucy, shouting something, but she couldn't make it out because of the noise of the wind. The light from Kruger's torch shone onto her hands. Blood was everywhere, even under her fingernails, dripping from her.

The soldier who'd guarded her in the Land Rover was first to reach her. She thought he was going to scream at her, but instead he bent down to look at Kruger. Two soldiers grabbed her and dragged her back the way they'd come. Other soldiers took cover behind the castle's ruined walls and fired machine gun bursts into the darkness. Some of the bullets formed glowing arcs across the sky. Lucy tried to remember what name was given to bullets like that. Tracer? They were incredibly beautiful, like speeding fireflies. The night glowed.

The soldiers pushed her down the rough path towards the little beach that lay beneath the cliffs, adjacent to 'Merlin's Cave', the great hollow under Tintagel Castle where legend said Merlin was born.

Cardinal Sinclair was already there on the beach with several soldiers. Waving torches, they were standing beside five motorised dinghies that had been dragged onto the beach. Kruger must have arranged for them to be picked up here so that they could continue their journey by sea. There was probably a ship waiting for them off the coast. Lucy shook her head. If they thought she was getting on a ship, they were crazy. The sea was a forbidden zone, a graveyard with waves for headstones.

Staring at her bloody hands, she wanted to throw up. Kruger would still be alive if it weren't for her. She had to get the blood off, but she didn't want to go near the sea. Turning with her torch, she spotted a pool amongst the rocks. Something glinted in the water. The soldiers shouted at her as she hurried towards it, but she ignored them.

Kneeling down at the edge of the pool, she dipped her hands in. The water was freezing cold and she let out a gasp. After rinsing off the blood, she scooped up the water and splashed it over face.

'Get into the dinghy,' one of the soldiers yelled at her. 'Stay low, for Christ's sake. There's a sniper out there.'

Again, she ignored him. Shining her torch into the water, she looked for the glinting object. She had an inkling of what it was, but it seemed impossible. Her heart was pounding.

There.

It had got itself tangled amongst some pebbles. She breathed in hard. Frantically at first, then more slowly, she cleared away the pebbles until the object lay in clear view. *Mother of Mercy.* First Kruger, now this. She didn't want to look at the object, to be reminded of everything it represented. Tears welled in her eyes, stinging and burning. A single word was engraved on the silver medallion gleaming up at her from the pool – *Lucy*.

Could she bear to touch it? Maybe it would take some of her pain away. Closing her eyes, she pulled it out. Perhaps she should hurl it into the sea where it belonged. It needed all the water in the world to dilute the emotions it contained. She still remembered how amazed she was when her father's body was found without his medallion on its chain. She never saw him without it. Even when he went diving, he wore it. Now, clasping it against her heart, she bowed her head. All over again, she was in the blue, being dragged down to oblivion.

Her eyes flashed open. The water in the pool was rippling. She felt something strange in the air, just as she had on the clifftop. *Something* was here, *watching*.

She glanced back at the dinghies. She needed to get out of here, but the sea was out of the question. Even if she had the nerve to go near the water, the conditions were getting wilder. The soldiers in the dinghies screamed at her to get in. All around, bullets slammed into the sand and sea from machine-gun fire from the clifftops.

A flare exploded high over the beach, throwing a pink glow over Tintagel Castle. The front of Merlin's Cave lit up.

Someone gripped one of Lucy's arms: her guard from the Land Rover. His face, caught in her torchbeam as she twisted round, was raging.

'What do you think you're doing? We can't let you be captured.'

He had the same intensity as Kruger. Were all the Swiss Guards like this?

'I'm not going with you. 'The water…I can't do it.'

The soldier stood there, seemingly unsure what to do. 'Only one person believed in you,' he said. 'The rest of us thought the whole thing was crazy, but the captain said that the moment he saw you he knew there was no mistake – you were *the one*.'

'What?'

'What really gets me is that he admired you. You had an inner strength, he said. Now he's given his life for you.'

Captain Kruger admired her? Lucy shook her head. As for inner strength, she couldn't imagine anyone weaker.

The soldier stared up at the cliff where Kruger died. 'I wish the sniper had got you instead.' Grabbing her hand, he tried to pull away.

Lucy dug her heels into the damp sand. Got to get away. Kicking the soldier in the leg, she broke free and ran towards Merlin's Cave. She heard a shout from above and all the shooting stopped, but all of her attention was focused on the cave. There, she would be safe, away from the hissing sea, from all of the soldiers, from whatever monstrous thing was out there. Several Swiss Guards leapt out of the dinghies and sprinted after her.

She reached the cave just ahead of them. She only had a second or two to sweep her torchbeam round the stone walls to find a hiding place. Spotting a small recess in the cave wall, she threw herself into it, forming herself into a tight ball. But the Swiss Guards saw her immediately, grabbed her legs and tried to haul her out. Ferociously, she kicked back. Her hands reached for anything to grab onto. As her fingers stretched out, they made contact with something. It was hard and regular, man-made, jammed into the wall of the recess. The very moment she touched it, an electric current surged through her.

She closed her eyes, trying to shut out the images that now flooded her mind: arid landscapes, Roman soldiers, ancient palaces, bearded prophets. What was happening to her? This object was concealed here many centuries ago, she thought. Someone had created a perfect hiding place for it using a natural fault in the cave wall. She kept pulling, and more and more of the object slid out with practically no resistance. She scarcely knew what she was doing, but she couldn't stop herself. The object was getting heavier, and she guessed it was several feet long. As the Swiss Guards dragged her out, her hands fully locked round the object and she pulled it with her, freeing it from its hiding place.

When her eyes opened, the Swiss Guards were staring down at her. Their mouths had fallen open. No one moved. They just stood there. Cardinal Sinclair was with them. Without warning, he lowered himself onto one knee and made the sign of the cross. All the others did the same. They had a reverential look in their eyes.

Had they gone mad? Lucy was still holding whatever it was she'd pulled from the recess. Several torches pointed down at it, and it glinted in their light. She wanted to rub her eyes. In her hand was a sword in mint condition. She knew the Arthurian legend better than anyone. Arthur was the rightful king because he drew a sword from a stone. Now she'd done that exact same thing. But this sword didn't belong to any English knight. It wasn't even European. The grip was made of gold plates engraved with ornate designs. There was no crossguard characteristic of medieval European swords. The gleaming blade had Latin writing down one edge, and Aramaic down the other. Lucy suspected it was from ancient Judea when the Romans ruled there...from about two thousand years ago.

'There's no doubt now,' the cardinal said. 'She's the one.'

'It's not what you think. I found it, that's all.' Lucy was terrified of that look in their eyes.

'No one but you could have found that sword,' her guard said. 'Right in front of us, you pulled it from the stone.'

'Stop resisting, Lucy,' Sinclair said. 'There's no mistake.' He leaned down and gently released her fingers from the hilt of the sword. Raising the sword, he kissed the blade. It was such an odd gesture for a cardinal, a man of peace. 'The *One*,' he said again.

The One? Lucy Galahan – the Messiah, the saviour of the world, the Redeemer? *Insane*. She'd come from a mental asylum, but that didn't make her any crazier than these people. The world needed a saint, a genius, a leader of men. It didn't need her.

'Get back to the dinghies,' her guard shouted. 'We're leaving.'

The others got to their feet and ran out of Merlin's Cave. Sinclair trailed behind, clutching the three-feet-long sword.

Lucy was left alone with her guard. His eyes were filling with tears.

'Captain Kruger said that once we reached Tintagel you'd answer every doubt,' he said.

Lucy trembled. Captain Kruger's words came back to her: *Only the chosen one can do what no other can.*

'Oh my God,' she said.

The guard seemed transfixed. 'My brother didn't die in vain.'

Brother? Lucy gazed at the soldier's face and only now did she see the resemblance. She felt herself choking. Taking the soldier's free hand, she whispered, 'I'm sorry. Your brother...'

'Come on.' He helped her to her feet.

She was dazed as they emerged from the cave. The din was incredible. Bullets were again peppering the sand and water. Tracer fire lit up the night. *Trapped*. It was impossible to escape from here.

When they tried to reach the others, Lucy's boots sunk into the boggy sand and she slumped forward onto her face. The shooting from the cliffs immediately stopped.

All she wanted to do was lie there. She was soaked through and the wind was freezing her to the bone, but anything was preferable to going near those dinghies. What sort of Messiah was she? Scared of the sea, scared of going back and even more scared of going forward.

Kruger's brother hauled her to her feet. 'If you're afraid of the sea, don't look.' He grabbed the hood of her parka and pulled it over the front of her head. Manhandling her, he bundled her into the nearest dinghy.

Lucy closed her eyes and tried to shut out every sensation. A second later she heard Sinclair screaming that the sword had been shot out of his hand. He was desperate to retrieve it.

'Leave it,' Kruger shouted. 'There's no time left. Lucy's all that matters.'

All of the dinghies moved out to sea, their outboard engines roaring, trying to force a way through the choppy sea. Lucy sat near the engine, shivering. Soldiers were talking excitedly, but she was concentrating only on her fear. The wind had risen again and waves were lashing over the sides. Her parka was saturated with water. She imagined that the sea was deliberately forcing them back to the beach. They'd capsize before they got near any ship out there at sea.

They had travelled only about twenty metres from the beach when a huge wave crashed over the dinghy. With her hood covering her face, Lucy didn't see a thing. The wave smashed into her and she toppled backwards into the icy waves.

Instantly, choking water engulfed her. *In the blue.* It had actually happened. She kicked frantically with her legs, but the motion soon began to slow. *Drowning.* Need air. Desperately, she tried to remember how she used to swim. Did she once cut through the water with efficient, powerful strokes? It seemed impossible. Her arms flapped ineffectually. Can't swim. Can't live. Can't do anything. She just hung in the water, incapable of resisting. Soon what little breath she had left would run out, and it would all end. All she could see was blue, an infinity of it. *I'm dying.*

Someone gripped her collar and began pulling her to the surface. Her father? Can a ghost save you? The blue in her mind started to fragment, breaking into a trillion tiny dots, then blew away like dust.

When her eyes opened again, she was lying on the beach on her back, gasping, water dribbling from the corners of her mouth. Her parka had been washed away. She gazed at the sky. Was death as black as that? Was that what greeted mum and dad? Turning her head, she saw the cardinal beside her. It astonished her that he was such a strong swimmer. And he'd managed to find the sword he was forced to leave behind. He was clutching it as if he'd never let go, as though it were the most precious object on earth.

She tried to raise her head to see what had happened to the dinghies, but pains shot through her neck and her head flopped back. She hoped Kruger's brother and his men would forget about her. Go back to where they came from, out of danger.

'Don't shoot,' Sinclair shouted, getting to his feet and wildly waving his arms at the dinghies. 'You can't kill her. She's innocent.'

Lucy tried to process the words. What did they mean? *Christ.* Her heart thudded. Kruger had orders to kill her if she was captured, didn't he? His brother was bound to follow through. She tried to move, but couldn't.

'Mortars!' someone barked in an American accent.

Several torchlights shone into Lucy's face. Rifles were pointing at her. The sea began to explode as mortar shells rained down on the dinghies.

'Get up,' the American voice said.

He was quickly drowned out. A helicopter had appeared overhead, its searchlight pointing straight down on the beach.

34

The Chinook's spotlight had picked out a group of soldiers in a tight cluster heading away from the beach, but Vernon couldn't see any sign of Lucy. Maybe she was in their midst, but he couldn't be sure. Some soldiers were shooting up at the helicopter, but he didn't want to return fire for fear of hitting Lucy. They had to get an exact fix on her.

'Take us down,' Vernon ordered the pilot. The SAS squad were checking their weapons and getting ready to disembark from the rear ramp. For them it was just a standard hostage rescue operation with a few complicating factors – they'd be up against elite forces, either Delta Force or Swiss Guards, the precise location of the hostage was unknown and the success of the mission was entirely dependent on extracting her alive.

Vernon was appalled when Gresnick said earlier that Lucy might have to be killed. He couldn't believe how callous the American was. Lucy was an innocent victim in all of this. She might not even be in a fit state to understand what was happening to her. He'd given the colonel strict instructions that Lucy mustn't be harmed under any circumstances.

As the helicopter searched for a landing spot, Vernon glanced at Gresnick. The American was fitting a magazine into his Ruger P85 pistol.

'No stray shots, colonel.'

Gresnick stared at him. 'I'm a crack shot.'

Vernon wondered if he should ask Gresnick for his firearm. It was hard to believe how things had changed. One moment he thought Gresnick was attracted to Lucy. Next thing, the American was talking about killing her. Was it just an act, all front? He feared Gresnick was for real.

The helicopter started to vibrate, gently at first, then with increasing force. The pilot struggled with the controls, while the co-pilot shouted information at him. The Chinook swung backwards and forwards then plunged up and down. Something was wrong, *catastrophically* wrong.

Vernon stared at the pilot, willing him to say that everything was OK. Instead, the pilot removed his hands from the controls and sat back. *Jesus.*

'Fly the goddamn thing,' Gresnick barked.

For a second, Vernon thought the American was about to point his pistol, but the pilot just sat there, doing nothing.

'Brace for crash landing,' the co-pilot yelled.

Everyone sat, belted up and bent over, protecting their heads.

Vernon couldn't figure out what was wrong with the pilot. This was the famous former Night Stalker. Nerves of steel, ability to remain calm in the tightest situations and so on. Not now. He'd totally lost it.

The shell of the helicopter started to fold in on itself, like a tin can crumpling. Vernon realised why the pilot was doing nothing – the helicopter wasn't in his control. *Something else was moving it.*

The helicopter lurched forward. The pilot sprang back to the controls and tried to pull it out of freefall, but it was too late.

'We're going down!' he shouted.

****

Vernon opened his eyes. He tried to move, but couldn't. Something was pressing down on his chest. Everything was dark. He wondered if he'd gone blind, but then he saw scores of burning fragments around him. When he pushed against the thing on his chest, he realised it was a body. By the light of the blazing cockpit, he saw who it was...McGregor, the religious nut, his Bible still clasped in one hand. Nauseated, he pushed the corpse off, then collapsed back, exhausted. All his energy was gone. He closed his eyes again. Gunfire? He was sure he could hear automatic fire, not far away. Then he heard breathing. Someone was crouching over him.

'James?'

That voice. It couldn't be. Must be hallucinating. His eyes flicked open once more.

Lucy.

Exactly as he remembered her. That dark hair falling over her face. Her eyes, so tender, so full of compassion.

Someone else was looking down at him. Startled, he tried to turn away. It was a man with a dog collar – a priest. God, last rites. A third face appeared, one he recognised immediately: Sergeant Morson, one of the missing prisoners from Thames House. How could he have got *here*?

'So, who's the prisoner now?' Morson said then turned to a soldier standing at his side. 'Finish him off.'

Vernon heard the soldier pulling back the slide of his pistol and releasing it. Bullet loaded. Any second now.

He wanted to say something to Lucy. To ask for forgiveness? To forgive her? To ask her *why*? To...

Then he heard the shot.

35

Lucy felt sick. The Americans had made her change out of her wet clothes and given her a padded white winter uniform. It was much too big for her. She kept putting her hands in the pockets, trying to find her medicine. Kruger had thrown the bottle into the sea, but she was convinced it would come back if she concentrated hard enough. That ought to be how things worked. The dead should return to life if you miss them enough.

She needed her medication more than ever. In Greek mythology, the dead souls drank from the Lethe, one of the rivers of the underworld. It made them forget their previous lives and prepared them for being born again. She longed to have medicine made from the Lethe's water. If she forgot everything, she might be able to start again too.

They had taken her away from the helicopter wreckage and put her in the back of a military truck full of American soldiers. Now they were travelling along a dark, deserted road. At some point, she hoped, she would wake up and be back in her convent room, staring up at her paintings. *Safe.* This nightmare had become much worse. Somehow, she'd managed to keep James out of her dreams. Not anymore.

It appalled her to see him lying there in all that burning debris. When the American sergeant told his colleague to shoot James, she screamed at him to stop. If she could, she would have hurled herself in front of the bullet. But someone else started firing. The Swiss Guards, she thought. She was dragged away, but when she looked back, the soldier assigned to kill James was dead.

James Vernon. When she saw his face, the love she thought she'd destroyed flared again, almost overpowering her. She prayed he had survived. There was so much she wanted to say to him.

She bowed her head. The soldier sitting opposite had never once taken his eyes off her. It was freaking her out. He wore a different uniform from the others, he was the only black man amongst them…and he was clearly under guard. Had he come with James in the helicopter? What in God's name happened to that aircraft? She'd never seen anything like it; that thing that had enveloped it, gripping it as though it were a toy. It tossed it around then hurled it to the ground. When nightmares become real, it means either you've gone mad, or the things you fear most are truly out there.

No one had told her where they were going. In fact, all of the Americans, apart from their sergeant, hung back from her, scarcely looking at her. They'd put Cardinal Sinclair in the other truck, so she didn't have anyone to speak to. She wanted to thank him for saving her life. Lying on the beach, staring up into the night, she had realised how glad she was to still be alive. Yet part of her insisted that the best thing for her was to be dead. She could hear the old whispers, telling her to seize any opportunity to kill herself. But there was no denying the relief she felt when the cardinal hauled her to safety. Left to herself, maybe she would have let the water rush into her lungs. How can you want life and death simultaneously?

She'd once read about Schrodinger's cat, a hypothetical cat in a locked black box containing a poison capsule that might, or might not, release its lethal contents. Scientists pondered whether at any particular moment the cat was alive or dead. Their conclusion was that, in some sense, it was both alive *and* dead, at least until the lid was lifted and its fate discovered. She felt she was in the same ghostly, indeterminate state as the cat.

She should never have doubted the cardinal. No one risks their life for you if they wish you ill. When she watched him bending over James, starting to give him the last rites, she wondered if he could perform another miracle and prevent him from dying. It seemed ridiculous that people were telling her how special she was. If she had any powers, she would have used them to save James.

The truck went over a bump, and the man opposite her tumbled forwards onto her.

'Get back.' One of the others pushed the man back to his seat at riflepoint.

During the confusion, the man slipped something into Lucy's hand. She looked across at him and he gave her an odd stare. Discreetly, she picked up the towel the sergeant had given her earlier to dry herself, and covered the note with it. That gave her a chance to glance at it when no one was looking.

'I am Colonel Brad Gresnick,' it said. 'I came with James Vernon. I'm a friend.'

She scrunched up the note and put it in her pocket. A friend? She didn't even know this man, yet he was telling her he was her friend. He said he knew James, but there was no proof. Maybe he was a plant with a mission to gain her confidence.

Too much paranoia, or not enough? She was so confused. She didn't want to look at the man. Instead, she stared out of the opening in the back of the truck. She could understand why some people were saying the Apocalypse was at hand. The light was abnormal light and the taste of everything was indefinably strange. There was an odd quality in the air, a peculiar acrid smell. People seemed to crackle as they moved, showering the world with tiny blue sparks. It was as though everyone had grown faint halos. A world of saints...of angels?

Then she heard an unearthly scream. None of the soldiers reacted, except the man opposite her. He looked every bit as startled as she was. There was no question he shared her thoughts about the piercing howl.

Nothing human could have made it.

36

Vernon could hear engines. Strong vibrations passed through him. *On the move.* Where was he? He opened his eyes again, but this time there was no burning wreckage, no trooper's body, no priest giving him the last rites, no Sergeant Morson. Above all, no Lucy. How wondrous it was to see her again, just that glimpse; but so much disappointment to know it must have been a dream. Now here he was in a white room, in bed. He moved his head. Someone was beside him, a soldier in a black uniform.

'I'm Sergeant Ernst Kruger,' the man said.

Vernon tried to understand the accent. Definitely not American: European English.

'Do you remember what happened?' Kruger asked.

Fragments, dreams: Vernon wasn't sure what he remembered.

Kruger explained patiently. A helicopter crash. Crew wiped out. Half of an SAS unit killed too. The others somehow managed to fight their way out. They drove back an attack, but lost another two men. One of the SAS troopers killed a soldier who was about to shoot Vernon. The SAS managed to withdraw, dragging Vernon with them down to the beach. The only person unaccounted for was Colonel Gresnick. He was presumed dead or captured.

I did see her, Vernon thought. Lucy in the flesh. Not a dream. She seemed normal, healthy, just like she used to be.

The Swiss Guards must have picked up the survivors of the crash on the beach. Now, if his guess was right, he was on a ship.

'You're with friends,' Kruger said. 'You're badly bruised and have a number of cuts, but we've bandaged you up and you'll be OK.'

Kruger started talking about how much he admired the SAS troopers – to be able to put up a ferocious firefight after being involved in a crash like that. Remarkable, he said, especially after what they'd seen seconds earlier.

'What *did* they see?' Vernon asked. He groaned as a pain tore through his ribs when he tried to adjust his position.

'Later,' Kruger said. 'Right now, I need you to think very carefully about something. I'm sure you know that my men and I work for the Vatican. Lucy Galahan was under our protection. The Delta Force unit…were you pursuing them?'

'How did you know about them?'

Kruger smiled. 'The Vatican has the most efficient intelligence network in the world.'

'Where are we going?' Vernon started panicking. They might be heading away from Lucy. That was no good. They had to find her, save her.

'We're on a ship on our way to Bristol. I don't know how much you know about all of this, so it may sound strange, but we're certain the deserters will take Lucy to sites linked with King Arthur, just as we were planning to do. Tintagel was our starting point, but we weren't certain what came next. We were expecting Lucy to work it out for us, but now we have you instead.'

'We need to go back,' Vernon groaned. 'Follow the trail of the deserters.'

'We can't go after them. We were lucky to escape alive from Tintagel.' Kruger turned away. 'Most of us, that is. We had to leave our captain behind.' He got up, walked to one of the portholes, and stared out. 'I detest snipers,' he said. 'Snakes.'

'We can't leave Lucy behind.' Vernon was practically shouting.

'We have no choice but to regroup. We need to work out their next move, to be a step ahead and surprise them.'

'How?'

'We have something to show you. We think we can use it to work out where they'll take Lucy.'

Vernon hated being in this bed, feeling so weak. 'It had better be good.'

Kruger gestured to him to get up. 'Come and see for yourself.'

Vernon pulled the sheets away and hauled himself out of bed. It only now occurred to him how fortunate he'd been. No serious wounds, no limbs missing, practically unscathed. 'What happened to the helicopter?' he asked as he followed Kruger down a narrow corridor.

Kruger halted. 'If I hadn't seen it with my own eyes...'

'Was it...' Vernon hesitated. It seemed so ridiculous. 'An angel?'

Kruger spun round and stared at him.

'Where *he* came from, he was the brightest of all.'

'What?'

'He was the only one who could rival God himself. The most beloved, like a son.'

Vernon shook his head. 'I don't understand.'

'In this world, he's the opposite. No light, just darkness, the most terrible darkness of all.'

'You're not making any sense.' Yet Vernon understood perfectly. He'd never seen darkness like the one that wrapped itself around the helicopter. A black hole. A perfect absence of light.

'You understand that these are the End Times, don't you? That's why *he* appeared.'

'For God's sake, tell me what you saw. What was it that attacked our helicopter?'

Kruger made the sign of the cross. When he answered, a shiver swept through every cell of Vernon's body.

'*Lucifer.*'

37

Half of the soldiers in the truck were asleep, while the others looked around drowsily. They probably took it in shifts to sleep. Lucy realised something had changed – the noise of the engines had vanished. That's why she'd woken. She gazed out of the small, uncovered section at the back. It was no longer night time, but it wasn't clear what type of day had arrived. Mist covered everything.

The black soldier sitting opposite her had his eyes closed, but she didn't think he was sleeping. His nametag said he was Colonel Gresnick. Perhaps he'd come with James just as he said. It was certainly remarkable that he was the only black. These days, every American army unit had many black soldiers, but not this one. Each soldier here, apart from Gresnick, was blue-eyed and blond. Were they some sort of racist unit, a pure white 'elite'?

'Everyone out,' a man barked, and all of the soldiers began climbing out.

A soldier stepped past Lucy and looked down at Gresnick.

'Wake up, sleeping beauty.' He kicked the colonel's feet.

Gresnick opened his eyes and glowered at the soldier. When the colonel stood up, the soldier grabbed him, turned him round and forced handcuffs on him. He was pushed out of the truck at gunpoint.

Lucy followed and climbed down to the ground. For a second she felt invisible: no one was paying any attention to her. Some Messiah. One of the soldiers started handing out food and drink from a large holdall – cartons of orange juice and nondescript energy bars.

She munched on her bar and, with each bite, felt more alone. She wanted to talk to someone. What was that weird noise last night? Had anyone else sensed the strange presence out there? Was it following her? The mist wasn't like any she had seen before. It had an odd orange tint and a surreal quality. But that was true of everything these days.

As they breakfasted, the mist gradually lifted. Someone muttered something about how beautiful the new dawns were now. *New dawns*? She gasped when she saw the sky. It didn't contain even a trace of April blue. It was red, like blood. Now she understood the strange comments she'd heard the nuns making lately, why they'd stopped taking her outside, why they'd boarded up the windows throughout the convent. They spoke of the world suffering from stigmata, of bleeding wounds across the earth, of natural catastrophes reflecting the corrupt state of humanity's soul. Lucy had imagined the sky bleeding. If it had started to rain, would blood have fallen? If the whole world were like this, no wonder people thought the end was coming.

It was only when she studied the countryside around her that she realised she knew where they were. Everything had initially seemed unfamiliar because of the strange light from the sky, but now it all fell into place. The big giveaway was the mound a few hundred yards away, rising several hundred feet above the plain – Cadbury Castle in Somerset. Like Tintagel, this was considered a possible site for Camelot. In fact, it had the stronger claim. If King Arthur existed, he was likely to have been a warrior chief living in the years after the Romans left Britain. He would have been a leader of the native Celts, fighting off the barbarian tribes invading from the Continent – the Angles, the Saxons and the Jutes. Ultimately, he failed. That's why England was named after the Angles.

What was certain was that Arthur wasn't a medieval king living in a great stone castle. All of England's monarchs were known in detail, and Arthur wasn't one of them. He lived before the time of kings, before the age of stone castles. That meant that Camelot, if there ever was such a place, was wooden. Archaeological studies at Cadbury Castle revealed there was a wooden hill fort on top of the flat-topped mound. The stone castle at Tintagel could never have been Camelot, but the long-vanished wooden fortress that once stood here fitted the historical profile perfectly.

Lucy took in the red-tinged scenery and let out a deep breath. Cadbury Castle, surrounded by picturesque farming land, was breathtaking. Last time she was here, the fields were full of grazing cows and sheep. There were no animals now. A circle of trees surrounded the mound, while the plateau was empty apart from a small chapel in one corner. Despite the name, there was no visible castle at Cadbury Castle. Cadbury Hill would have been a better name. There were elaborate earthworks round the top level of the mound, the remnants of the defences its Celtic inhabitants once constructed. There was little doubt thousands of people once lived here. In its day, it must have been a glorious sight, a huge fortified hill dominating its surroundings.

Near Cadbury was the River Cam. Lucy always believed this was the most likely location of Arthur's final battle. Why had the soldiers brought her to such a place? Her mind searched for possible connections with other mythical battlefields. The Jews spoke of an ancient, terrible battle at a place called Megiddo. They believed the same site would one day host the final Doomsday battle between good and evil. It was more familiar to people under its Westernised name – *Armageddon*.

Camlann was like an echo of Megiddo. It was the battle that marked the end of old Britain, the end of a way of a life. Was that why they were here? Was this the place where everything would end under a blood-red sky? She sipped her orange juice, and tried to stay calm.

Sergeant Morson emerged from amongst the other soldiers. He was wearing a scabbard, containing the sword Lucy had found at Tintagel. He must have seized it from Sinclair. 'Everything OK?' he asked.

Lucy, tuning into his accent, realised how well spoken he was. *Ivy League*, she thought. She'd encountered that accent often enough at Oxford and at international conferences. But there was something even more odd. It wasn't just the sergeant who was Ivy League; all of his men were too. This had to be the most unusual Special Forces unit ever – a group of Ivy League graduates, and not a single black man amongst them, assuming Gresnick was telling the truth and wasn't one of *them*.

Morson looked at her in a peculiar way, almost as if he were gazing at a famous statue in a museum, weighing up if it lived up to expectations.

'I don't suppose you're going to tell me what you want with me?' Lucy surprised herself by how unafraid she was. When Captain Kruger made her look down into the sea at Tintagel, she'd never known fear like it. She doubted she could ever be that afraid again.

'Later,' Morson replied. 'We can't get our trucks any closer to where we're heading, so we're going on foot.'

'Where?'

Morson turned and walked away, barking orders at his men. They formed into a column, with Lucy and Gresnick wedged in the middle, and set off along a narrow track edged by hedgerows. Lucy wondered where Cardinal Sinclair was and looked up and down the line of soldiers. She spotted him near the back, looking grim, his hands cuffed behind his back.

Lucy breathed in hard. There was a delightful smell of lavender. It took her by surprise; it was too early for lavender, and she didn't think it grew here anyway. Was everything changing somehow? She'd always loved the Somerset countryside. Even now, in the sickly light, it still looked like an idyllic rural setting, full of meadows and orchards.

After making their way past several fields, they found the track petering out and were confronted by a vast field of dandelion clocks. When she was a child, Lucy loved blowing the hairs off them and making wishes. Now there were so many of them they were frightening. It was as if nature had started to overproduce. Growing cycles were becoming shorter. A more fertile world in its final hours?

A gust of wind blasted past them. All the dandelion seeds lifted into the air, creating a flurry that resembled a snowstorm in one of those shake-em-about children's toys. She gazed at the swirling white clouds. They had a mesmeric quality. Was the whole world like this? People could become addicted to dying worlds, to last things, couldn't they?

'Let's go,' Morson yelled and they plodded over the field until they reached the bottom of the slope.

The last time Lucy was here, she took James for a picnic in a small clearing in the woods on the hillside. She told him about the history of this hill fort, about how the Romans came here in the first century CE, destroyed the fort and slaughtered its entire Celtic population – men, women and children. Arthur supposedly rebuilt the fortifications four centuries later and created a beautiful palace in the centre of the hill's flat top. Even now, the plateau was known as King Arthur's Palace.

They followed a winding mud track through the woods, with steep banks on either side. The trees seemed much darker than she remembered. Almost sinister. The forest was named Ravenswood. After the destruction of the fort, thousands of ravens came to live in the trees. For centuries afterwards, people were scared to come here.

Lucy felt something nudging her elbow. She turned and found Gresnick looking at her. He gestured upwards with his eyes. She tilted her head up. On the upper branches of the trees were thousands of ravens, neither moving nor making any sound. They simply stared. She'd never seen so many together before. *The birds of death.* She always found them terrifying. She recalled stories of ravens darkening the sky as they descended on battlefields to eat the rotting flesh of the fallen. It was the surest sign of disasters to come.

The whole group moved quietly, as if terrified of making any sound that might disturb the birds. Even though it was spring, all the leaves had fallen from the trees. The soldiers' boots scrunched on the decomposing leaves.

Lucy breathed out hard when they emerged from the trees. She prayed she'd never see ravens again. They went past several large ditches and earthworks and finally reached the plateau. It was empty apart from the picturesque chapel in the far corner. Its name was most unusual – *St Gaius*. Lucy had researched it several years earlier and discovered it was named after a Roman Centurion, Gaius Cassius Longinus, the soldier who thrust his spear into Jesus' side as he hung on the cross, to prove he was dead. Some of the Saviour's redemptive blood fell on him and miraculously cured him of his failing eyesight. Soon after, Longinus left the army, became a Christian and was martyred. One legend claimed he came to Britain in the same party as Joseph of Arimathea, meeting his death at this very location. The legend claimed he had all of his teeth pulled out, and his tongue cut off, yet he was able to go on speaking clearly, praising Jesus right up to the moment of his death.

The story of Longinus and his spear fascinated Lucy for an odd reason – she thought it proved that Jesus wasn't dead before the spear pierced his side. Jabbing bodies with a spear was the standard Roman custom for checking who was dead on a battlefield. Dead people have no heartbeat, no blood pressure, and so no blood flows. Yet, in the Bible, it clearly stated that blood and water spurted out of the wound in Jesus' side: impossible for a dead man. She wondered why no one had pointed this out before, but when she checked it on the internet, she discovered that a debate had raged for years over this precise point. Some people agreed with her that the spear and not the crucifixion killed Jesus. Others said that Jesus was indeed dead but the spear thrust pierced his pericardium – the sac containing watery fluid that surrounds the heart – and then entered the heart itself, from which blood might conceivably spurt even after death. Others produced even more elaborate medical explanations. Nonetheless, the possibility remained that Longinus was Jesus' true killer.

It would be a hard trick to turn Christ's killer into a saint, but that's exactly what Longinus became. He was the man who ensured that the scriptures were fulfilled. Jesus was crucified on Friday and the Jewish Sabbath is on Saturday. It was profane for executions to take place on the Sabbath, so the traditional remedy was to make sure that any crucified men died on the Friday. The usual method was to break their legs so they'd be unable to support their weight, their lungs would collapse under the pressure, and they'd die of asphyxiation. The High Priest Caiaphas intended this fate for Jesus. But the scriptures made two unambiguous statements about the Messiah: *"Not one bone of his will be broken"* and *"They will look to the one whom they have pierced"*.

If Jesus' legs were broken, it would prove he wasn't the prophesied Messiah. Equally, if he wasn't pierced, he was no Messiah. Longinus solved both problems. Some people claimed that as he held the spear, Longinus controlled the fate of the world, and that all those who wielded it after him also held destiny in their hands.

Lucy and the soldiers trudged across the grassy plateau towards the old chapel. The view was spectacular, somehow enhanced by the gaudy red light. Lucy wondered if the sky had been red like this when the battle of Camlann took place, if King Arthur gazed up and saw a scarlet sun.

It was obvious that they were heading for the chapel, but why? Were they on some sort of pilgrimage? What possible significance could St Gaius Longinus have for these Delta Force deserters? Something clicked. Lucy realised it wasn't St Gaius they were interested in. *It was his spear.*

38

'Lucifer? – you can't possibly believe that.' The ship was being tossed about as it ploughed through rough water. Vernon thrust his hands against the walls to steady himself.

'So many people are in denial,' Kruger retorted. 'When will they realise this is *really* happening? Only miracles can save us now.'

Vernon stared at Kruger. The signs that the world was ending were indeed everywhere. At some level, he was convinced it was true, yet still he refused to acknowledge it as an absolute fact. There had to be rational explanations for all of this, scientific solutions that could be implemented in a short time by smart people to save the day. It couldn't be all over, it just couldn't. And the world crisis couldn't, *mustn't*, have supernatural origins. The idea of the Devil being behind it was unthinkable.

'The helicopter got caught in turbulence.' Vernon feebly waved his hand. 'A swarm of birds hit the rotor blades.' Desperately, he tried to construct explanations, but each died as it came out of his mouth.

Lucifer. Was it possible that the prisoner in the detention cells had transformed not into an angel but the ultimate demon? Then the Lord of the Flies, Beelzebub, the Prince of Darkness had tracked them all the way from London. All the old, terrifying names flooded Vernon's mind. Nothing was darker than that thing which had appeared in the sky in front of the helicopter. Maybe the creature had carried Sergeant Morson with him, outpacing a helicopter. What rational rules can you apply to the irrational world of the supernatural?

'You *know* it's true,' Kruger said. 'You saw it as clearly as I did.'

'I don't know what you're talking about.' Vernon turned away. 'I didn't see anything. It was too dark.'

'Come with me.' Kruger took a few steps along the narrow corridor and pushed open a door. He disappeared into a room.

Just as Vernon was about to follow him, the lights in the corridor flickered. He stopped and listened. Over the thrumming sounds of the engines, he heard the wind howling. The sound was terrifying, like thousands of creatures baying. Orchestrated by Lucifer? The ship was creaking and shaking.

'What state is your soul in?' Kruger said as Vernon joined him in a large, wood-panelled dining room.

Vernon didn't respond. How could he answer a question like that? He stared instead at a projector sitting on a table, pointing at the far wall. He guessed it was the same projector he'd noticed the SAS soldier carrying at Lucy's convent.

'What's that doing here?' he asked.

Kruger went to one of the small portholes and gazed out. 'God works in mysterious ways, his wonders to perform.' He explained that one of the SAS survivors had insisted on saving the projector from the helicopter wreckage, despite the fighting going on all around him. 'The trooper said he was given specific instructions from someone called Colonel Gresnick.'

I knew it, I *knew*. It was obvious to Vernon that Gresnick was following his own agenda. 'What did Gresnick say?' he asked.

'He told all of the SAS men to look for anything unusual in the convent. He said he was particularly interested in strange paintings, parchments and books. Above all, antique objects such as swords, cups, dishes and spears.'

The Grail Hallows! Did Gresnick seriously think they had somehow found their way into Lucy's convent? Why hadn't he discussed it with him? As for pictures, did Gresnick mean Lucy's? There were dozens of them.

Kruger turned and pointed at the back of the room. A collection of amateurish paintings was pinned to the wall, all showing a female figure against a blue background. *Lucy's paintings.*

'The trooper said he grabbed a few from behind the headboard of Lucy's bed,' Kruger explained.

They had large crease marks on them. The trooper must have simply folded them and stuffed them inside his jacket.

The ship was struggling in the heavy sea, and Vernon again had to hold on to prevent himself toppling forward. The engines seemed much louder, working overtime.

Kruger gestured at a chair and invited Vernon to sit down.

'It's not Lucy's paintings I wanted you to see, Mr Vernon, but the slide that was inside this projector. My guess is that Cardinal Sinclair brought it from the Vatican to show Lucy.' He paused. 'I assume you knew the cardinal was in England.'

Vernon nodded, but it still astonished him that such a prominent figure was mixed up in this given what was happening back in Rome. Sinclair, as the Vatican's Number Two, was a strong favourite to become the new Pope. Why would he jeopardise his chance, probably lose it completely, to be with Lucy? Was she *that* important?

'We found the cardinal in the convent with Lucy,' Kruger went on. 'He said he was on a special mission from Rome, just as we were.'

'But you didn't know he was there, did you? And nor did he know about you.'

Kruger didn't reply, but motioned at Vernon to face forward.

Hours earlier, Vernon imagined, Lucy must have sat just like this, waiting for Cardinal Sinclair to show her his slide. It felt comforting somehow, as if he were physically connected to her again.

'Lucy…she's all right, isn't she?' Vernon tapped the side of his head. 'I mean up here.'

'We weren't sure what to expect when we arrived at the convent. It was hard to imagine that Lucy could be of any use to us if she were mentally ill, but it was obvious right away that she'd made a good recovery.'

Good recovery, Vernon mouthed. He'd begun to form a convenient theory that when Lucy dumped him it was the first sign of her breakdown. If she were back to anything like her old self – God, what would he do if she wanted to take him back? He'd throw his wife aside and even his beautiful baby to be with Lucy again. No point in denying it. What sort of person did that make him? Selfish? Callous? Disloyal? A fraud? Those were the least of it. A terrible husband, a terrible father, a man who broke the most sacred of vows. No kind of hero. But to spend a few hours – maybe his last – with Lucy, he was prepared to become the vilest of men. Love's price, he supposed. Nothing is more guaranteed to debase a man than love.

In his schooldays, he had a particular dislike of poetry. Only one poem ever made an impression on him. *La Belle Dame Sans Merci* by Keats: *The beautiful lady without mercy*. An unidentified passer-by asks a distraught knight what's wrong. The broken knight tells his woeful tale. He loved a beautiful lady who abandoned him. Now, in the darkness of a great forest, he's fading away, the will to live stolen from him by the mysterious beauty. All the birds in the trees have stopped singing.

Even as a school kid, even though he knew nothing of love, Vernon felt that knight's pain. Maybe that was the way poetry worked – it predicted your future. When Lucy dumped him, he stepped into that tragic knight's armour. He was in the same iron prison, locked in the same strange, twilight forest, vainly waiting like the knight for the birds to sing.

Kruger switched on the projector and an image of a stunning Renaissance painting appeared on the far wall.

Vernon gazed at it in amazement. He twisted round to look at Lucy's pictures on the wall behind then stared again at the masterpiece in front of him. Almost involuntarily, he raised his hand and pointed at the central panel on the bottom of the projected image. '*How?*' he said then fell silent.

39

'It's a miracle, isn't it?' Kruger's voice was full of wonder. 'What you're looking at is a five-hundred-year-old mural by Raphael, hidden in a secret vault in the tomb of Pope Julius II.'

'But...' Vernon still couldn't take it in. He closed his eyes and shook his head. This couldn't be.

'I can't even begin to guess how this is possible,' Kruger said. 'Lucy couldn't have known anything about Raphael's mural. But just look at that panel. It's the first thing you look at because it's so out of place. It certainly isn't in Raphael's style. It's inconceivable that he painted anything so amateurish. Yet there it is. The *impossible* panel.'

Vernon opened his eyes again, his gaze switching to the small portholes at the side of the room. The sea was smashing against the ship as if it were trying to break in.

'Even Cardinal Sinclair wasn't supposed to know about this mural,' Kruger said.

'What do you mean?'

'We were told the Pope forbade him from looking at it.'

'I don't understand.' Vernon was shocked. If the Pope didn't trust the enforcer of Catholic doctrine, how could anyone be trusted? But maybe there was more to it. Had Sinclair trusted the Pope? These Swiss Guards were on an exceptionally unusual mission. It stank, frankly. The Swiss Guard never left the Vatican. Could *they* be trusted?

'Wasn't Sinclair the Pope's right-hand man?' Vernon asked. 'Everyone said he was a shoe-in to become the next Pope.'

'The Pope only allowed one other man to see the mural. My brother – Captain Jurgen Kruger.'

'Is he here too?'

'My brother's dead.' Kruger's face blanched. 'He was the leader of this mission. A sniper shot him while he was with Lucy on the cliffs at Tintagel. You arrived in your helicopter soon afterwards.'

'I'm sorry. It must be hard for you.'

'It will be hard for all of us. My brother was an exceptional man. He always knew what to do. The rest of us are lost without him.'

'What did your brother think about Sinclair?'

'He didn't trust him. My brother found the Pope's death highly suspicious.'

'You can't be suggesting Sinclair had anything to do with it. The Pope was handed a note with bad news and he suffered a heart attack. It's not mysterious.'

'These are the strangest of times. Soon all of our loyalties will be tested. This is when we will find out who we really are, what we truly believe in.'

Vernon shuddered. He was already finding out who he was, and he didn't much like what he saw.

'My brother believed in Lucy,' Kruger said. 'He gave us a detailed briefing on her before we arrived in England. We know that you were her only serious boyfriend. From what my brother could make out, Lucy never stopped loving you, despite what you may think. You're invaluable to us, Mr Vernon. You can help us get Lucy back.'

Get Lucy back. That was everything, wasn't it? Sergeant Morson said Lucy was the most special person in the world. When he first heard those words, Vernon thought they were absurd. Now it was obvious how true they were. He remembered one of the best days he spent with her. They sat on a bench gazing out towards one of Cornwall's most famous sights – St Michael's Mount. It was a wondrous castle on a high mound, a couple of hundred yards out to sea, and could only be reached at low tide. It was such a lovely day. They sat for hours holding hands, hardly speaking. Then Lucy kissed him and told him how much she loved him. Was that the kiss of a Messiah?

She was his very own Holy Grail. It was odd that she spent so much time thinking about it, writing about it, discussing it. When you became obsessed with something, did you become *it*?

But everyone wanted to get their hands on the Grail. Lucy was now the most precious commodity of all. That was why Colonel Gresnick was so interested in her. He was another who couldn't be trusted – the man who looked like a Hollywood star, and too well versed in myths and legends. He and Lucy could no doubt talk for months on end. He would fascinate Lucy. Would she find him attractive? The answer was obvious.

Vernon's face flushed with anger. In his mind, he had an image of Gresnick kissing Lucy. Yet the colonel had threatened to kill her. There was no way those two could get together. Anyway, maybe Gresnick died in the helicopter crash. For a second, Vernon felt a thrill of relief. Then he was appalled by himself. He felt himself becoming capable of the worst things.

'What do you think of the painting?' Kruger asked. 'What does it tell you?'

Vernon shook his head. 'I'm no art expert.' He had to raise his voice because the whole ship was vibrating. 'It's some sort of narrative. A lot of it looks quite conventional. You know, traditional Biblical scenes and the like. I don't know how King Arthur and the Grail fit in, though.'

Kruger nodded. 'My brother said the Vatican had no idea how to interpret the mural until the Pope read Lucy's book. At once, he realised that what Lucy said about the Arthurian legends applied to the mural. It was a coded reference to the claims of two competing religions. The Pope said that a moment would come when the rival religions would clash head on, with the fate of the world at stake. If the wrong choice were made, the world would perish.

'That's what the painting was showing – the human raced damned to hell for eternity, or saved and admitted to paradise. The Pope believed that Julius II intended the mural as a warning for what would happen if the Catholic Church should ever allow heresy to spread. By putting it inside his own tomb, Julius II intended that other popes, coming to pray for his soul, should see it. As they considered their own mortality, they would see that the world itself was mortal. Everyone and everything was endangered by heresy. It was the greatest danger of all because if mankind placed its faith in the wrong God, the True God would have no option but to eliminate his own creation.'

'Didn't you say it was a secret vault?'

'Secret to everyone but other popes. They alone were given access. We don't know what Julius II's immediate successors thought of it, but we know Pope Marcellus II was shocked when he saw it in 1555. He died just twenty-two days after becoming Pope, and some said the cause was his horror at seeing the mural.'

'And what about Lucy?' Vernon asked.

'The late Pope made enquiries about her. When he discovered she was a Catholic, he held a special Mass in St Peter's to give thanks.'

Vernon was unsure how to react to that. It was true Lucy was once quite a devout Catholic, but she lapsed after her mother died, and made it obvious she was heading rapidly towards atheism. On top of that, she was always fascinated by the Gnostics, and once said their ideas made more sense than Christianity. If anything, she was in a religious no-man's land. The late Pope had made a horrendous error if he believed Lucy was automatically on the Catholic side.

'He was certain God chose her to save humanity,' Kruger continued. 'When he heard from the Mother Superior at the convent that Lucy was painting pictures, he asked for photos of them. When he discovered she had painted a picture identical to the one in Raphael's mural, he took it as proof that she was the Chosen One.'

Vernon stared at the floor. More and more, it seemed to be true. Even the late Pope thought so. Was it possible that a struggle was raging for Lucy's soul and the outcome would determine the fate of earth?

'What are the two competing religions?' he asked, but he already knew the answer – Christianity versus Gnosticism, two religions that couldn't be more different. A believer in one was the automatic enemy of a believer in the other.

Kruger gave a half-smile. 'You've read Lucy's book. You know the answer.'

The answer? Vernon had nothing but questions in his mind right now. Despite everything he knew about the Gnostics, it was still hard to accept just how radical their beliefs were. To replace the Christian struggle between good and evil with the Gnostic struggle between spirit and matter involved a whole new mind-set. Sins and crimes didn't matter at all. What mattered for Gnostics was gaining the spiritual knowledge that allowed the soul to escape from the material hell they were trapped in.

Strangely, some Gnostics claimed to revere Jesus Christ and even called themselves Christians, but *their* Christ was nothing like the Christian one. They didn't believe he was ever physically incarnated since that would mean he had become part of the evil material world. So, they denied the reality of the Crucifixion. It was impossible to crucify Jesus because he didn't have a physical body, so the Crucifixion scene was a phantasm. Oddly enough, the Muslims believed exactly the same thing. His death, they said, was nothing but an illusion to deceive his enemies. Not so much the Crucifixion as the Cruci*fiction*.

Since Jesus didn't die, nor was he resurrected. Since he didn't have a body, he couldn't be part man part god. The Gnostics denied the Catholic belief of transubstantiation. This was impossible, they said, because Jesus would never become part of the malignant physical world in any way. For them, Jesus was a divine messenger from the kingdom of true light, his task to preach love, peace, compassion, and forgiveness – all the things that Jehovah, the creator of the material world, despised.

The Gnostics venerated everyone who opposed Jehovah. Lucifer, as Jehovah's great enemy, was their hero. For them, the identification of Lucifer with Satan was ridiculous. Satan, patently, was Jehovah.

If the Gnostics were right, everyone else was wrong. The human race, by worshipping the creator of the material world had committed the gravest error conceivable. Humanity had spectacularly misunderstood the nature of life, of the world, of reality. And was thereby condemned to eternal hell.

If, as Kruger insisted, Lucifer really existed and had come to the earth, did that prove that the Gnostics were right, or the Christians? Was that the reason why the weather was so turbulent, why so many disasters were happening? – the planet was gearing up for the final apocalyptic struggle between Lucifer and Jehovah. Although Vernon was desperate to be on the side of good, he was no longer sure which side that was, and he suspected Lucy was equally uncertain.

40

As he stared at one of the panels on the left of the mural, Vernon recognised something. When Sergeant Morson stared down at him after the helicopter crash, he noticed that the sergeant was wearing strange insignia on his uniform. In a line, above his breast pocket, were four different badges. One showed a blue swastika on a white background, one a red rising sun on a white background, one a silver skull and crossbones on a black background, and the final badge was black and white, divided into two halves, black above white.

These exact badges were displayed on the panel in front of Vernon. When he pointed it out to Kruger, the Swiss soldier wasn't surprised.

'Those badges are Gnostic symbols. The blue swastika on a white background was the flag of the Gnostic sect, the Cathars. The Rising Sun symbolises that the Gnostics believe in the True God's universe of light. The skull and crossbones is a symbol that the physical world is a place of darkness, decay and death.'

'And it's one of the flags used by Knights Templar,' Vernon said, recalling what Gresnick told him.

Kruger nodded. 'You're well informed. In that case you probably know what the fourth is.'

Vernon gazed at the black strip over white. He had no idea.

Kruger squinted at him. 'No?' Vernon shrugged. 'That's called the *Beauseant*,' Kruger said. 'It's the most sacred banner of the Knights Templar. It shows that in the hellish world we live in, darkness triumphs over light. The Templars' task, as they saw it, was to fight their way through the darkness to the light.'

'So, you think the Templars were Gnostics?'

'That's why the Pope dissolved the Order. The Templars were planning to overthrow the Catholic Church. Their preparations were well advanced.'

Preparations? The word reverberated in Vernon's head. What preparations had Kruger made for Lucy? 'Where did you plan to take Lucy?' he asked. 'Rome?'

Kruger turned away. 'It's no accident that the deserters are Americans,' he said after a moment.

'What do you mean?'

'You're not a Catholic, are you Mr Vernon?'

'What has that got to do with anything?'

'If you were a Catholic, you'd know that the Vatican has always opposed Freemasonry. If you knew American history, you'd know Freemasons founded America. Practically everyone who signed the Declaration of Independence was a Freemason. Paul Revere, the man who rode to warn the Boston colonists that the British army was coming, was a Freemason. The general the Americans chose to lead their army against the British was George Washington, a Freemason. He was their first president, of course, and nearly every subsequent president was overtly or covertly a Freemason.

'In fact, the first confirmed non-Masonic president was JFK, a Catholic, and he won by only a handful of votes. The Freemasons tried everything to stop him, but Kennedy's father knew how to fight back and he mobilised a huge political machine to harness the votes of all the immigrant Catholics – Irish, Italians, Poles, Hispanics, and so on – to get his son into the White House. It wasn't the Cubans or the CIA or a lone nut who killed JFK, it was the Freemasons. Who replaced JFK? LBJ – a high-ranking Freemason. When anything terrible happens on the world stage you ought to ask *cui bono?* – to whose benefit. The Freemasons were the ones who profited from Kennedy's death. They killed RFK too, and Martin Luther King.'

'That's ridiculous. You don't have any evidence.'

'Mr Vernon, the Catholic Church has long expected America to wage a war of aggression against the world. When the War on Terror began, it was no surprise to the Vatican. It was only a question of time before the Freemasons made their move. When you hear the word "neocon", you ought to translate it as Freemason. Their plan is world domination, and to make their Freemason God the universal God of the earth.'

'You can't be serious. This is mad conspiracy stuff.'

'But there *is* a conspiracy. There always has been.' Kruger turned and pointed at the panel showing a pyramid with an eye above it. 'Haven't you seen that before?'

Vernon did think it looked familiar, but he couldn't place it.

'It's one of the most powerful symbols in the world. You see it everywhere, all the time.'

Vernon shook his head. 'I'm certain I've seen it somewhere, but I just can't...it's so familiar.'

'It's familiar because it's on the back of the U.S. dollar. And on the back of the official Great Seal of the United States of America. It's the symbol of the secret society the *Illuminati* whose sworn mission is to topple the Catholic Church. You'll hear all sorts of weird theories about the Illuminati – that they began as a group of disgruntled scientists in Rome in the 1500s, that they were formed from the last few survivors of the Cathars and the Knights Templar, that they were black magicians and worshippers of Lucifer. I've even heard a theory that the Illuminati are alien reptiles wearing human disguises.

'But the Catholic Church believes they're the most ancient and sinister secret society on earth and came into existence long before the advent of Christianity. They're at the root of all the attempts to subvert Catholicism, which, for them, was the institution created by their Satanic enemy to crush them. The Illuminati created the Cathars, the Knights Templars, the Alchemists and the Freemasons. The Protestant leaders Luther and Calvin were Illuminati, and the whole Reformation was engineered by the Illuminati. The Illuminati eventually decided that they wanted to create an entire country, far from the reach of the Vatican, that would become the most powerful nation on earth, capable of challenging the Catholic Church once and for all.'

'America,' Vernon muttered.

'Exactly. America is the Masonic heart of the world, every part of it created by Freemasons, all of its laws designed by Freemasons, nearly all of its leaders Freemasons. The Declaration of Independence is a Masonic document par excellence. Without the knowledge or consent of the vast majority of its people, the American Freemasons have been pursuing a relentless Masonic agenda since the country's inception. America's top politicians, lawyers, businessmen, soldiers, spy chiefs, policemen, medics are all Masons. It's almost impossible to rise to any position of real power in America if you're not a Mason. And behind the Masons stand that even more shadowy organisation, the ultimate puppet masters – the Illuminati.

'If you look at the pyramid on the Great Seal of America you'll see that it contains two Latin inscriptions. *Annuit Coeptis* means: God has favoured our undertakings, and *Novus Ordo Seclorum* means: A new order of the ages.'

'The new world order,' Vernon muttered.

Kruger nodded. 'They want to sweep away the old world where the Catholic Church holds sway and replace the Catholic God with their Masonic God.' He again pointed at the pyramid painted by Raphael. 'You see that the capstone hasn't yet come down on the pyramid. That symbolises that their plan isn't complete, and will be finished only when the Catholic Church is destroyed. The eye in the centre of the capstone is that of the Illuminati's God. Some call it the *All Seeing Eye*, others refer to it as the *Eye of Horus*. To those who oppose the occult, it is simply the *Evil Eye*.'

James shuddered as he gazed at it. MI5's old crest was a pyramid capstone, and the symbol at the top was unquestionably an All Seeing Eye, there for the improbable reason of representing the 'I' in MI5. Was there a more sinister reason? Even the modern MI5 crest was dubious – containing five-leafed red roses and five-pointed green cinquefoils that, if you looked closely, appeared suspiciously like black-magic pentagrams.

'On the back of the dollar, on the other side from the pyramid,' Kruger went on, 'is the national bird of America, the bald-headed eagle. But, in fact, it's a disguised version of another of the Illuminati's most sacred symbols – the Phoenix. The Illuminati believe that they are like the Phoenix because no matter how many times the Catholic Church tries to eliminate them, they always rise from the ashes.

'If you scrutinise the so-called eagle, you'll see that the right wing has thirty-two feathers – the number of ordinary degrees in Scottish Rite Freemasonry, the origin of modern Freemasonry. As for the left wing, it has thirty-three feathers to represent the Thirty-Third Degree of the Scottish Rite that's conferred on individuals for outstanding services to Freemasonry. The stars above the eagle's head form a hexagram. That is one of the most potent symbols of the occult. The Illuminati were the power behind witches and warlocks, just as they were behind alchemy, black magic and all the occult arts. Their mission, at all times, was to find ways to attack Catholicism, to undermine it, and pave the way for the Illuminati to replace it.'

Kruger grabbed a book from a shelf and thrust it into Vernon's hand. Pointing at a highlighted passage, he said, 'Read that.'

Vernon turned the book towards the light and read out the passage: 'Not only were many of the founders of the United States government Masons, but they received aid from a secret and august body existing in Europe which helped them to establish this country for a peculiar and particular purpose known only to the initiated few. (Manly P. Hall, *The Secret Teachings of All Ages*, pp. XC and XCI.)'

'Manly Hall was one of the twentieth century's greatest experts on Freemasonry,' Kruger said. 'The European "secret and august body" was the Illuminati. Only the highest-ranking Freemasons knew this. The "peculiar and particular purpose" was the final overthrow of Catholicism.'

'For over two centuries, the Vatican anticipated an attack from the Illuminati of America, but the Illuminati stunned them by taking advantage of the economic chaos in a powerful European state to seize that nation and use it to begin their assault on the world. Then something astounding happened. Instead of attacking Catholicism, they launched the most savage attack on their other ancient enemy – the Jews.'

'You're talking about Nazi Germany, aren't you?'

Kruger nodded. 'Hitler and all his top henchmen were leading adepts of the Illuminati. Some have said Hitler was the supreme Grand Master, having complete authority over the American branch of the Illuminati.'

'If that were the case, why did Hitler declare war on America?'

'The American Illuminati were crippled by the Wall Street Crash, temporarily losing a vast amount of their wealth and influence. It took them decades to recover. Hitler believed that the Jews stepped in and seized most of the levers of power in America.'

'Well, if America is again under the influence of the Illuminati and they despise Jews, why is the USA such a slavish supporter of Israel?'

Kruger laughed. 'Adolf Hitler detested the Soviet Union and firmly believed Bolshevism was a Jewish conspiracy to destabilise the West. After all, Marx, Lenin, Trotsky, Kamenev, and Zinoviev were all Jews. Yet Hitler signed a non-aggression pact with Stalin before WWII began.

'The Israeli-American link-up is another unholy alliance. Anti-Semitism was rife in America before WWII and, under the surface, it's still there. There was simply no good reason for the USA to support the new state of Israel in 1948. Many leading American politicians, including the Secretary of State George Marshall and most of the State Department, were appalled, for reasons of simple logic, that America ever recognised Israel. Marshall, one of America's most distinguished politicians and soldiers, and the man credited with reshaping post-war Europe, resigned the following year.

'What has America ever got from that relationship other than endless trouble, and the hostility of every Muslim country on earth? In foreign policy terms, it's the most incomprehensible decision ever reached. No rational person would deliberately antagonise 1.5 billion Muslims to support a few million implanted settlers in a small country far away. Hitler would certainly have claimed that it was precisely because of the power of Jews in America that this decision was taken. Afterwards, as the Illuminati regained their strength, it suited them to maintain the status quo and it served to throw the rest of the world off the scent of the Illuminati's grand conspiracy. Besides, the Illuminati are no friends of Islam. The Pope wasn't fooled for a second, though. The Vatican saw through it all from the beginning.'

Vernon was no conspiracy theorist. Trouble was, Kruger was worryingly convincing. It was impossible to think of a single way in which America had benefited from its relationship with Israel, and easy to list a whole hornets' nest of problems. So, if there was no rational foreign policy justification for it, there had to be a hidden agenda.

'Let's get back to Hitler,' Kruger said. 'Only he and twelve of his companions knew the complete history of the Illuminati. It was rumoured that there was a *Secret Doctrine* that involved a clandestine mission whose nature was so diabolical that it was revealed only to a handful at the highest level of the Illuminati. The late Pope said the Nazis tried to carry out the mission in the early years of WWII, but failed for some unknown reason. The Illuminati then spent the subsequent decades trying to work out what went wrong. Now, the Pope believed, the Illuminati had solved their problems and were about to try again. This time, he feared their plan was flawless.'

'And he turned to his Swiss Guard to stop them?'

'That's right.'

'He placed immense trust in you, didn't he?'

'We swore we'd give our lives to ensure the success of this mission.'

'I want to know exactly what your mission is.'

'The Pope told us he knew the precise day when the Illuminati would make their final strike. He said it was written in the centre of Raphael's painting.'

Vernon saw several small Roman numerals: XXX – IV – MMXII. He did a rapid conversion: 30 – 4 – 2012. 'God Almighty. 30 April 2012.'

Kruger nodded. 'Two days away.'

Vernon stood there, frozen, trying to take it in.

'The Pope was convinced he knew what the Secret Doctrine was,' Kruger said. 'He believed the Illuminati were the founders of Gnosticism and that the Gnostics' central belief – that the material world is evil – was the key to the Secret Doctrine. He thought it went far beyond a mission to destroy the Catholic Church. He reached the conclusion that it was nothing less than a plan to destroy the world itself. He believed the Illuminati had found a weapon of mass destruction so powerful it could blow up the planet.'

Vernon thought back to *The Cainite Destiny*. Everything Kruger said fitted. This was becoming terrifying.

'You must understand that my soldiers and I are men of faith,' Kruger said. 'Like the Pope, we don't believe any normal man-made weapon can destroy the planet, but we know from the Bible that there's a weapon described there that has awesome destructive power, perhaps unlimited.'

'The Ark of the Covenant.'

'Exactly. We believe the Illuminati have spent millennia looking for the lost Ark and now they have found it. We think they know how to activate it and make it unleash maximum destruction.'

'But it was blown up a few hours ago, outside the White House. Someone used it to assassinate the President.'

'What are you talking about?'

'I saw it live on TV.'

Kruger shook his head. 'I don't know anything about that, but whatever you saw, it wasn't the real Ark. Solomon created a replica Ark and hid the true Ark beneath the Temple to safeguard it. The fake Ark was stolen from the Temple by Solomon's son, thinking it was real, and taken to Sheba – modern-day Ethiopia.'

'Let's say you're right. Where does Lucy fit in?'

'Lucy is a unique person, Mr Vernon.'

'You don't need to tell me that.'

'You don't understand. We carried out the most detailed trace of Lucy's ancestry. We discovered something astonishing about her. Whatever you may think you know about her, you have no inkling of who Lucy Galahan really is.'

41

Lucy had always considered the chapel of *St Gaius* a peculiar place. It looked hundreds of years old but in fact only the altar and its surroundings were ancient, dating back to 1150 CE when the Knights Templar constructed the chapel in their traditional circular style. When the Templars fell from grace, so did the chapel. Local farmers carted away much of the stone for building walls and outhouses in their fields.

According to the tourist brochure available in the chapel's entrance hall, an anonymous benefactor, with a particular interest in old Templar churches, rebuilt it after WWII. He reconstructed it in the original style, and provided funds for a long-term caretaker, who was nowhere to be seen today. The brochure paid particular tribute to the beautiful stained glass windows showing the Stations of the Cross, the most iconic incidents in Christ's last hours on earth. The chapel was never actually used for religious services because the Catholic Church refused to consecrate it because of its Templar connotations, and there weren't enough locals in this rural location to provide a congregation anyway. The whole thing was a vanity project, a pointless folly in the wilderness. Tourists were the only people who ever visited, and they were mostly only interested in the toilet facilities.

Sergeant Morson ordered two men to stand guard then everyone else filed inside. The soldiers spread out into the wooden pews, some lying down and stretching out. It was obvious to Lucy they'd be staying for some time.

Cardinal Sinclair and Colonel Gresnick, with their hands in cuffs behind their backs, were placed in the front pew on the left of the altar, with Lucy in the right-hand pew. No attempt was made to restrict her movements. In fact, Sergeant Morson couldn't have been nicer to her. Quaintly, he offered to make her a cup of tea, but she declined. He showed no friendliness towards Sinclair, staring at him with cold eyes.

'How's our holy fool?' he said. 'All the prayers in the world won't save you now.'

Sinclair didn't answer. He just gazed at the altar.

Morson glowered at Gresnick, but didn't speak to him. Lucy sensed there was something going on between the two men. Because they were both American and both in the military? Or some racist thing? If her original suspicion was correct and Gresnick was a double agent, he was doing his job well. She was rapidly feeling she could trust him.

She was permitted to go to the toilet and, on her return, she found everyone sitting or lying around, trying to relax. She went back to her pew, wondering why no one was showing any signs of urgency. Wasn't the world supposed to be ending at any moment?

As she gazed around the ornate chapel with its peculiar carvings of mythical creatures, reminiscent of those in Rosslyn Chapel in Scotland, she tried to figure out the significance of this place. The answer, she was still convinced, must lie with Longinus's Spear.

In her book *The Unholy Grail: The Secret Heresy*, one of the central themes was the significance placed on the Grail Hallows by the Cathars and the Knights Templar. She argued that these were essential elements in the heretics' most sacred ceremonies. In the past, she believed, the heretics had all the Grail Hallows in their possession, but lost them one by one as Catholic persecution intensified and they ran out of safe hiding places for their treasures.

What if the mission of these Delta Force soldiers was to rediscover the lost Hallows? Maybe they thought she had expert knowledge of where to find them. Was that the real reason they'd kidnapped her? Maybe it was something else. Perhaps it was more than knowledge they wanted. Her intuition? Somehow, she'd managed to retrieve the hidden sword at Tintagel, literally pulling it from a stone and demonstrating, if old legends were true, that she was a rightful leader. But a leader of what?

Kruger predicted she would do something to remove all doubts about who she was. Had he been proved right? Was it all preordained? In her blood somehow, her *holy* blood? Somehow, she was connected to these Hallows in a way she couldn't fathom. The sword she found in Merlin's Cave was no ordinary sword. As soon as she touched it, she knew it was one of the Hallows, probably hidden there by Templars trying to conceal their most precious treasures from the reach of the Inquisition.

The Spear of Destiny was even more special than the sword. Some people claimed it had existed on earth since the beginning of time, passing from one powerful dynasty to the next. Another story said it was forged by the Ancient Hebrew Prophet Phineas to embody the power of God's Chosen People. It came into Moses' possession and he gave it to his brother Aaron. It was then passed down the line of Jewish High Priests, right up to the time of Caiaphas. On the Friday of Jesus' Crucifixion, the Temple Guard, led by their captain holding the Spear of Destiny, went to the mount of Golgotha to break Christ's legs as he hung on the cross.

The legend said that Longinus thwarted their plan by grabbing the Spear from the captain and thrusting it into Jesus' side. The Spear then passed into Roman hands and was used by Plautius, the general commanding the army of Emperor Claudius that conquered Britain. Centuries later, Emperor Constantine carried the Spear in his victory over a pagan army at Milvian Bridge, the battle that established Christianity as the official religion of the Roman Empire. When Alaric the Visigoth sacked Rome in 410 CE, he took possession of the Spear, and it was then passed onto his illegitimate son Theodoric I. The Visigoths and the Romans combined their armies in 451 CE to fight Attila the Hun at the Battle of Chalons. Theodoric led a heroic cavalry charge, but after losing his grip on the Spear, fell from his horse and was trampled to death. Despite his death, the allies were victorious, the battle proving to be the final major military operation ever undertaken by the Western Roman Empire.

The Spear next resurfaced at the decisive Battle of Poitiers in 732 CE when the Frankish commander Charles Martel stopped the Muslim hordes and saved Europe from succumbing to Islam. Decades later it became one of the most potent symbols of the Holy Roman Empire, being wielded by great emperors such as Charlemagne, Otto the Great and Frederick Barbarossa. Napoleon, a high-ranking Freemason and the man who ended the Holy Roman Empire, tried to take ownership of the Spear after his spectacular success at the Battle of Austerlitz, but it was deliberately hidden from him, and some said that was why he was eventually defeated at the Battle of Waterloo. Later, Hitler and General Patton were both obsessed with it, each being familiar with the legend that whoever possessed the Spear of Destiny would be master of the world.

The legend said that if the Spear's owner or his minions should ever lose it, it would prove fatal. Charlemagne, successful in forty-seven battles with the Spear, died soon after he accidentally dropped it. The Emperor Barbarossa died seconds after the Spear slipped out of his hands when he was crossing a river with his army. Two ravens that had accompanied him everywhere for years flew off just before he began the crossing, and he apparently knew at that moment that he'd never get across the river alive. Minutes after American soldiers found the Spear in Nuremberg near the end of WWII, Hitler committed suicide in his bunker in Berlin. He couldn't have known anything about the Spear's fate, but that wasn't how the Spear operated. *It knew.*

Lucy always thought the stories were complete baloney. Now, she wasn't so certain. Maybe it was true, maybe the Grail Hallows contained a power that could start and end empires, that controlled the personal fate of those who dared to possess them. She'd never heard of any legend describing what would happen if all the Grail Hallows were brought together. Perhaps they generated a power unprecedented in human experience. Enough to destroy the world?

Was the Spear of Longinus the most potent Grail Hallow of them all? Some called it the *Heilige Lance* – the Holy Lance – because of its religious connotations. Others said it was the *Reich Lance* because the rulers of the Holy Roman Empire, the First Reich, revered it. Hitler had wanted to make it the most sacred relic of the Third Reich. He believed it was the guarantor of his historic destiny, the ultimate talisman of world conquest. If Lucy remembered right, the spear Hitler coveted so much was now in a museum in Vienna, back in exactly the same place from where he took it in 1938.

Then another thought occurred to her. What if that spear were fake? What if someone had substituted it at some point in its long history? Perhaps the true lance of the Grail Hallows disappeared from history and a replica took centre stage. Was that why they'd brought her here? Were they expecting her to find something they'd lost long ago? The genuine Spear of Destiny?

42

Whatever it was Kruger knew about Lucy, Vernon wasn't sure he wanted to hear. He was already struggling to take in that the woman he loved was at the centre of world events. He'd always found her exceptional, of course, yet she was ordinary too. Outside her academic life, she liked smalltalk and gossip, watched junk TV, read trashy novels, enjoyed getting drunk.

'Lucy is the only living descendent of Seriah,' Kruger said.

'Who?'

'Seriah was the last High Priest of King Solomon's Temple before the Babylonians destroyed it in 586 BCE.'

Vernon stared straight ahead. High Priests and King Solomon's Temple? Crazy talk.

'The Book of Exodus makes it clear that the Ark of the Covenant only functions properly in the presence of a High Priest,' Kruger stated. 'The High Priests always came from a particular bloodline – the descendants of Aaron, brother of Moses. When her mother died, Lucy was left as the last of that holy bloodline.'

'I had no idea, and I'm certain Lucy didn't either.'

'There was no reason for her to know. Things like that get buried over the centuries. Some secrets are just too dangerous.'

'Weren't High Priests always male?'

'The Vatican has documentary evidence that Aaron said that the High Priest could be male or female, as long as they belonged to his bloodline. Moses was the one who insisted on a male-only succession.'

'Am I understanding this? The Delta Force deserters think Lucy can operate the Ark of the Covenant for them?'

Kruger nodded. 'And by unlocking the power of the Ark, they believe they can destroy the planet.'

'She'll never help them.'

'The Pope agreed with you. He was sure Lucy would turn the tables and harness the Ark for the good of humanity, heralding a golden age, a new Garden of Eden.'

'Isn't there a simpler way to guarantee the Delta Force deserters never succeed?' Vernon detested saying these words, but there was no avoiding them. 'Why isn't your mission to kill Lucy?'

'*It is.*'

'What? I thought...'

Kruger turned towards Lucy's paintings. 'The Pope believed disaster was certain if we carried out an immoral action, even if the object was to save the planet. We shouldn't do evil that good may come, he always insisted. He was powerfully affected by Dostoyevsky's novel *The Brothers Karamazov*. Dostoyevsky poses the question that if a single creature has to suffer, especially an innocent child, is Creation justified? The Pope was tormented by that question. He thought, in the end, that suffering was an inescapable aspect of the human experience, but we must avoid needless suffering, the deliberate inflicting of pain. That was Christ's message. That's what the Ten Commandments were all about. Above all, unnecessary killing is never justified. Our mission was to find Lucy and protect her from the Illuminati. If we failed, her death would no longer be unnecessary, it would be essential.'

'But why didn't you take her straight back to the Vatican? She'd be out of all this trouble now.'

'It's not that simple. If, as we believe, the Illuminati have the true Ark of the Covenant, there's no telling what will occur if they try to make it work for them. The Bible is full of terrifying stories about what happened when people interfered with the Ark.'

'But didn't you just say the Ark was useless if someone of the right bloodline wasn't there when it was used?'

'I didn't say it wouldn't do anything. I said it wouldn't work properly. If the Illuminati tamper with the Ark, they could trigger exactly the catastrophe we're trying to avoid.' The sea was lashing furiously against the portholes and Kruger glanced nervously across the room. 'The Pope was certain the Illuminati had already tried to interfere with the Ark. He said it was no coincidence that the natural disasters began across the world within minutes of the first reports coming in that the Ark may have been found and taken. The Ethiopian Ark was a fake, but that doesn't mean the real one hasn't been discovered.'

'You seriously think everything happening to the world is caused by the Ark?'

'What else could cause disturbances like that?'

'Global warming? Sunspots? Cosmic radiation?'

'Don't be fooled by the atheist scientists. They have no idea what's happening. All of this is far beyond their tiny realm of facts and logic. We're in the time of faith now.'

'Is Lucy some kind of bait? Is that why you didn't take her back to Rome?'

'I wouldn't say bait, but I don't deny we want to use Lucy. To be precise, we want her to lead us to the Ark. If we can retrieve it, the Illuminati will be finished forever.'

'I don't care about any of that. I just want to find Lucy and get her out of this.'

'With your help, we can achieve both objectives.'

'You really believe in all of this, don't you?'

'This is the Final Conflict, Mr Vernon, the fight that was always destined to come: the Catholics and the Jews versus the Illuminati. Lucy is a Catholic, but in terms of her bloodline, she's Jewish. Her mother, and all her ancestors on her mother's side were Jews. If she had lived in Nazi Germany, she would have been sent to the gas chambers. I must confess that the Pope was horrified when he learned that Lucy might be connected to Jewish High Priests. Caiaphas, the High Priest in Jesus' time and the instigator of Christ's death, denied that Jesus was the Messiah, rejected Christianity and persecuted the early Christians. The Pope was so disturbed that Lucy might have any link to the likes of Caiaphas that he sent one of us to Israel to check all the genealogical records of the High Priests. He prayed we wouldn't find a connection, but we did.'

'So, the note he received just before he died was the confirmation?'

Kruger nodded.

'But it makes sense, doesn't it? The Ark has always been linked to the Jews, not Catholicism.'

'Even so, I can appreciate the Pope's concerns. It's God's will that Christianity replaced Judaism. The Christians are the new Chosen People. Why revert to Jews who rejected Christ? Nevertheless, we are where we are. The Illuminati are our mortal enemies, not the Jews.'

'If these Illuminati are so evil, why doesn't God destroy them? I mean, he didn't hesitate to wipe out Sodom and Gomorrah. He practically drowned the whole human race in the Flood.'

'This is our third and ultimate test, Mr Vernon.'

'I don't follow.'

'The first test was in the Garden of Eden when Adam and Eve were told not to eat the forbidden fruit. They did, of course – the Original Sin. Later, humanity became so corrupt that God almost wiped them out, sparing only Noah and his family. Now this. The third strike. Why shouldn't God destroy mankind? The Illuminati worship Lucifer. If they take over, why would God stay his hand? He would surely end this farce once and for all. God will spare us only if we stop the Illuminati. Otherwise, we all die, Illuminati and non-Illuminati alike.'

'But you've told me Lucifer is here on earth. Doesn't that mean the Illuminati have won?' Vernon pointed at Raphael's mural. 'It's so obvious. That painting tells us that the world ends in a couple of days and we should prepare ourselves for heaven or hell. We might as well give up now.'

'There's always hope,' Kruger said. 'It's possible we're on the verge of something wonderful.'

'What do you mean?'

'Think about it. We can use this situation to do something to redeem humanity forever, to permanently erase Original Sin.'

'I'm not getting you.'

'We can use the Ark to kill Lucifer.'

43

Lucy raised her head and found Gresnick staring down at her. She twisted round to see what the soldiers were doing. None of them was paying any attention.

'May I sit here?' he asked.

She shrugged, moved to one side and let Gresnick join her on the wooden pew. His hands were still in cuffs behind his back.

'I thought you were one of them,' she said. 'I mean you're in uniform and you're American.'

'I told you, I came with James.'

Lucy bowed her head. 'I saw him back at the helicopter crash. I couldn't believe it. James and I...'

'Was he injured? I didn't see what happened back there. I have no idea who survived. It was a mess.'

'I didn't get a proper look. It was so dark.'

'Did you see what attacked us? Did an RPG hit us? Everything went crazy. It was as if the night came alive.'

Lucy shifted uneasily. 'A dark shape enveloped your helicopter. There was a bizarre fluttering sound. I'm certain nothing was fired at you.'

'I didn't think so.' Gresnick tapped the floor with his foot. 'I can't make sense of what happened.'

'What were you and James doing?'

'Our mission was to find you and take you back to London. To safety.'

Safety? That seemed such an odd concept to Lucy now. 'I presume you went to the convent at Glastonbury first.'

'Yes.' Gresnick started fidgeting. 'If you don't mind me saying so, you're a lot more lucid than I was expecting.'

Lucy twisted round to face him. She was surprised by just how good-looking Gresnick was, and even more surprised she was thinking that. It was inappropriate in just about every way. 'So, you thought I'd be a nutcase?' She almost managed a smile. 'Given what's happened in the last few hours, I ought to be crazier now than ever. The odd thing is I feel sharper than at any time in my life. Sometimes I'm not sure I'm really myself. It's as if someone else is inside me, much stronger than I ever was, someone who knows things I never did.'

Gresnick raised his eyebrows.

'Mad, huh? It sounds bizarre, I know, but it's true.'

'I'm not doubting you, Lucy. We came to find you because we heard things about you, incredible things.' He lowered his voice. 'Yesterday, Sergeant Morson was in our custody in London. He told us you were the most special person in the world.'

Inwardly, Lucy groaned. From every angle, she kept hearing this stuff. Didn't Chosen Ones have to believe it themselves? If she wasn't convinced she was special, why should anyone else believe it? She had no intention of getting on a donkey and riding into Jerusalem. No one would be placing palms in her path. Whatever anyone said, she was no Messiah.

Something Gresnick said didn't make sense. 'So, did you bring Sergeant Morson with you from London? Did he escape from your helicopter?'

'Sergeant Morson broke out of our cells in London. I can't explain how he did it. He had a colleague who was suffering from horrific radiation wounds. That man escaped too. Something freakish was happening to him, some sort of transformation.'

'What do you mean?'

'Truthfully, I don't know. Whatever it was, it wasn't normal.'

Lucy nodded. That was true of just about everything that had happened lately.

'Listen,' Gresnick said, 'I'm sure you've found out lots of vital stuff in the last few hours. I have too. We need to compare notes, try to get the big picture. Whether you like it or not, you're the key to everything that's happening. We need to figure out exactly how and why. Everything may depend on it.'

'What were your orders if you couldn't rescue me?'

Gresnick couldn't hold her gaze. 'I guess there's something I should let you know,' he said after a long pause. 'James Vernon told me that if he had to, he was prepared to kill you.'

44

*K*ill *Lucifer*? Vernon shook his head. That was as absurd as trying to kill God. 'I just want to find Lucy, that's all.' He tried not to sound too dismissive. He got up from his seat and wandered to the back of the room to look at Lucy's paintings. 'You didn't give me a straight answer before. You had no intention of taking Lucy out of the country, did you?'

'One way or another, everything will be settled here in England,' Kruger replied. 'My brother believed Glastonbury was the key, where Joseph of Arimathea hid the Holy Grail in the first place. He said it was no accident Lucy was living in a convent in Glastonbury.'

'We're going back to Glastonbury?'

'This ship is taking us to Bristol. My brother always thought we were likely to be pursued. His plan was to make a sea journey to take our enemies by surprise, guaranteeing no one could follow us. Fresh transport is waiting for us in Bristol, and it's only a short drive from there to Glastonbury. Unless you have any other ideas, that's where we're going.'

Vernon turned away. *I've been so stupid.* If Lucy was everything people claimed she was then her life was inextricably linked with the Holy Grail. Maybe Gresnick was right and the Holy Grail was actually hidden in Lucy's convent. It ought to have occurred to him straight away that Lucy didn't end up in Glastonbury by accident. She was obsessed with that place, dragging him there far more times than was healthy. It was a beautiful little town, but suffered from severe TOD – tourist overload disease.

Every new-age believer was convinced Glastonbury was the legendary Isle of Avalon, the Apple Island where the fatally wounded King Arthur was taken after his final battle. It was known that the land around Glastonbury was inundated centuries ago by the floodwaters of the Bristol Channel, meaning that the high ground may well have stood as an island in a great lake in those ancient times.

He turned and peered at Raphael's mural. Something was wrong.

'We can't go to Glastonbury. That's not where the Americans are taking Lucy.' He went over to the image and pointed at the panels showing the Arthurian scenes. 'Look, we've just been to Tintagel where King Arthur was conceived. The next panel shows the battle of Camlann where Mordred fatally wounded Arthur.

'Didn't Lucy think Camlann was near Tintagel?' Kruger asked. 'I think she said that in her book.'

'No, Slaughter Bridge was one of the possible sites for Camlann, but Lucy was convinced the real site was somewhere else.'

'Where?'

Vernon pointed at the painting, but then his hand dropped.

'I'm sorry, I can't remember.'

45

Lucy stood up. 'I want to be on my own.' She walked away from Gresnick, appalled by his suggestion. It was impossible that James was ready to kill her. There was no one on earth less likely to harm her than James. Why had Gresnick lied?

She went to the toilet and splashed water over her face. Gazing at herself in the small mirror, she found it hard to recognise herself. In the convent, she encountered few mirrors. She hated her reflection. To see her face was to see what life had done to her.

When she left the toilet, Sergeant Morson was waiting for her.

'Come with me.' He led her out of the chapel, and took her on a short walk to a viewing point on the edge of the mound. It offered a clear view of the nearby River Cam, tinged red by the sky.

'All things pass away,' he said. 'Can you imagine King Arthur fighting down there on the mud-banks of the river, Excalibur in his hand? The river that day must have run red with blood.'

As Morson spoke, it began to snow. Lucy pictured Arthur and his shining knights swinging their swords to the bitter end as blinding snow swirled around them while their enemies closed in for the kill. The flakes were an astonishing white against the deep red of the sky.

'Beautiful,' Morson commented. 'No one could ever accuse Satan of not having an aesthetic sense. He's the greatest artist of all, don't you think? No one knows how to manipulate beauty like Satan. His understanding of humanity is peerless. All our weaknesses are laid bare for him. He knows every button to press. That's why he has so much power over us.'

Lucy suddenly understood with whom she was dealing. People who spoke of Satan in that way could only be one thing. 'You're Gnostics, aren't you?'

Morson smiled. 'You are too, Lucy. You just don't realise it yet.'

'I don't believe in any of these things. I mean, everyone else says Lucifer and Satan are the same person but, for you Gnostics, Lucifer is one of your most revered figures while Satan is your most hated enemy. Satan is Jehovah, the Creator, Allah, God, Yahweh, Rex Mundi, the Demiurge or whatever else it is you call him.'

Morson snorted. 'How could Lucifer be Satan? Lucifer is the Angel of Light, standing on the right hand of the True God. Satan is the monster who tried to usurp the True God. He was expelled from heaven and, in revenge, he created this world of matter – hell itself. It says in the Bible that it took six days to create hell, and on the seventh day Satan rested, satisfied with the abomination he'd constructed. How could any person worship that beast? How could they possibly confuse him with Lucifer? Human history is full of perversity, but that comparison is the most obscene of them all.'

'Are you going to kill me? This whole thing is building up to some form of sacrifice, isn't it? Am I the lamb being led to the slaughter?'

'You keep mistaking us for our enemies, Lucy. Sacrifice, animal or human, is repellent to us, but not to Satan, or Jehovah as you choose to call him. He always preferred blood and horror. All of us have memorised the tale of Cain and Abel so that we never forget, even for a moment, Jehovah's sickening savagery.'

Morson stared up at the falling snow and recited a passage from the Bible: *And Abel was a shepherd, and Cain a husbandman. And it came to pass after many days, that Cain offered, of the fruits of the earth, gifts to the Lord. Abel also offered of the firstlings of his flock, and of their fat: and the Lord had respect to Abel, and to his offerings. But to Cain and his offerings he had no respect: and Cain was exceedingly angry, and his countenance fell.*

'Don't you understand?' Morson said. 'Cain was a vegetarian who offered the Creator fruit and vegetables that he'd grown by his own ingenuity and toil. But the Creator detested such things. He wanted the sacrificial blood and gore that Abel offered. Right there, in that fatal preference, even the blindest person ought to be able to see the truth. Cain is gentle, a farmer, his thoughts turned towards the True God. Abel is a bloodthirsty savage, a killer hunter, who feasts on flesh and revels in slaughter. Who can doubt that the God Abel worshipped was Satan?'

'But Cain killed Abel.'

'It was self-defence. When Abel saw how contemptuous Jehovah was of Cain, he took that as a sign that an even better sacrifice to Jehovah was Cain himself. He stalked Cain as if he were the prey he hunted every day, and attacked him in a small glade. Cain managed to overpower him and use Abel's weapon against him. No murder was done. The only person with murder in mind was Abel, Jehovah's beloved.'

Lucy was unsure how to respond. The story had a chilling logic. She'd always found the tale of Cain and Abel problematic. Why would God despise the fruits of the earth? Why would he prefer animal sacrifice? It was stated as a simple fact, one not apparently in need of any explanation. Yet wasn't it vile that God wanted things killed rather than grown to honour him? In the name of God, hundreds of millions of people had been put to the sword over the centuries. Didn't God's glorification of Abel and contempt for Cain show that's exactly what he desired? An arrogant, violent, blood-soaked, angry and vengeful God? That sounded like a perfectly good description of Satan.

When Muslim hijackers slaughtered thousands of Americans in the cruellest and sickest way, was it an act done in the name of a god of love and compassion? Or was the 'Allah' of those hijackers a creature that feasted on human sacrifice, that bathed in blood and gloried in the multiplication of pain and misery? Not Allah – *Satan*.

The Inquisition, the endless pogroms against Jews, the Crusades, the massacres perpetrated by Muslims and Hindus in India, the Beslan Massacre, the Moscow Theatre siege, crucifixions, martyrdoms, beheadings, the burning of witches, the extermination of heretics, the endless litany of death, the sanctification of slaughter…all done in the name of God, or of Satan?

'You have no idea how special you are, do you?' Morson said. 'You're the last person in the world we'd ever harm. All of us have sworn to protect you. We'd die for you.'

Snowflakes fluttered around Lucy. 'Stop saying that. It sounds crazy. You've kidnapped me, that's the truth of it.'

'Lucy, it doesn't matter that you don't recognise how extraordinary you are. In fact, I'm glad you don't. Imagine how insufferable you would be if you thought you were a Messiah. I assure you, the very last thing the world needs is a second Jesus Christ.'

'Tell me what you want with me.'

'All in good time, Lucy. You feel we kidnapped you. By the time this business ends, you'll understand that you're our guiding light. You don't yet see the clear path, but you will, and then you'll know that we've merely taken you into our custody for your own protection. There are those out there who wish you only harm. They'll kill you without hesitation if they get the chance. Those soldiers you were with before, they wanted to kill you. After a little persuasion, your precious Cardinal Sinclair told us that they were Swiss Guards and they had orders to eliminate you. Hardly your benefactors. We're your family now, Lucy. You're one of us. You always have been.'

'Stop talking in riddles.'

'It would be wrong to burden you with knowledge of what's in store for you but, when the time comes, I have no doubt you'll know exactly what you must do. The future of humanity lies in your hands.'

Lucy twisted away from him, breathing in hard. A thin layer of snow now covered the plateau, but everything was tinged red, as though the world were being viewed through some bloody prism. Even her white winter uniform looked as though a fine film of blood was sprayed-painted over it.

'Have you never thought about your name, Lucy? Names are of crucial importance. Take mine – Samuel Morson. Of course, Samuel could scarcely be my real name. What would a Gnostic be doing with a popular Hebrew name? But we played the game, trying not to draw too much attention to ourselves. My Gnostic name is actually Sammael – one of the names for the Angel of Death. As for Morson, that means *son of Mors*. Mors was the Roman god of death.'

Lucy gazed at Morson's face, a tough soldier's face. He must have seen a lot of action, witnessed death at close quarters too often. He had those eyes that seemed to stare permanently into the far distance.

'Your name has a lot of death in it, doesn't it?' she said. 'Hardly what one would expect from a follower of Cain given what you were just saying.'

'The *death* in my name refers to an altogether different type of death: a glorious, desirable death, one that will set free the whole human race.'

'I don't understand.'

Morson smirked. 'What's your opinion of Yehoshua ben Yosef?'

'Who?'

'Isn't it odd how so few people know the name of the god they supposedly worship? Yehoshua ben Yosef is Jesus Christ's real name. *Jesus* is simply the Greco-Roman version of the Hebrew name Joshua. Joshua is itself an anglicised version of Yehoshua, and means *Yahweh is Salvation* – no name could be more repellent to a Gnostic than that one. As for *ben Yosef*, that means son of Yosef – Joseph. So, Jesus Christ is plain old *Joshua son of Joseph*. Josh to his friends. Or maybe Yehosh.' He grinned and traced a smile in the snow with his boot.

'How long do you think Christianity would survive if every Christian were forced to call Jesus by his real name? How many Christians would kneel to Yehoshua ben Yosef? Within hours, Christianity would crumble. Only by giving a Jew a Greco-Roman name was it possible for Gentiles to worship a Jew. A whole religion founded on a fake name. It's almost funny, don't you think?'

Lucy thought of all her hours in church, saying prayers, going to confession, seeking absolution. All in the name of Yehoshua ben Yosef? Morson was right. It sounded strange, wrong. Did it mean she was anti-Semitic? Maybe, deep down, no matter how much the thought appalled her, that's exactly what she was. And when she was shocked or upset, she often said *Jesus*. It wouldn't work if she had to say *Yehoshua*.

'Take Christianity itself,' Morson went on, 'now there's another strange word. *Christ* comes from the Latin *Christus*. That derives from the Greek *Kristos*, meaning anointed one. And that's the Greek translation of the Hebrew *mashiah*. From mashiah we get Messiah. So, Christianity is the religion of the worshippers of the Anointed One, the followers of the Messiah. But Joshua Christ or Yehoshua Mashiah doesn't have the right ring, does it? They just don't cut it. No one would want to be *that* type of Christian. Would they rather be Mashiasts instead? I don't think so. Maybe they'd prefer to worship a new Messiah – you, for example.'

Lucy stared at the red-tinted River Cam wending its way north. Maybe she should have laughed at Morson's suggestion, but she didn't. 'I don't have the right name either. There's nothing special about Lucy Galahan.'

'You really have no idea, do you?'

'I'm at the bottom of the food chain. No one tells me anything.'

'Lucy comes from *lux*, the Latin word for light.' Morson's eyes gleamed. 'It's no mistake you're called Lucy. Only the light can defeat the darkness.' He scrunched his foot in the snow. 'I love snow. It renews the world, temporarily wipes away the ugliness. The air is much fresher.'

'But snow turns to slush,' Lucy said. 'My name is just an accident. My father liked it, that's all.'

'There are no accidents. Has it never surprised you that your surname is so similar to the name of one of the successful seekers of the Grail?'

'Galahad?'

'He found the Holy Grail, and you will too.'

'I told you. It's pure coincidence about my name.'

'Is it? Your mother's name was Perivale, right? Perivale – a corruption of Perceval, another of the three knights who found the Grail.'

Lucy felt her face flushing. It had never even occurred to her before. Perivale and Galahan. How could those names be coincidental? There was only one other knight who found the Grail – Bors, the most ordinary of the three knights. Maybe Morson was right. Maybe her destiny was to be some sort of female Bors. An ordinary woman fated to find the Grail, bearing the names of the two most famous of the Grail finders – Galahad and Perceval.

'How do you know so much about me?' she asked.

'Nothing about your life is accidental. It's no accident who your parents were, what their names were. We've tracked your life from the very moment you were born. Everything you've ever done is known to us.'

Lucy's head throbbed. Her life, she felt, was being stolen from her. Others knew more about her than she did. If these people were watching her all the time, why weren't they watching when her father jumped off a cliff? Why didn't they help? Why didn't they stop it? Why didn't they spot her mum's cancer? Big deal if they watched. They certainly didn't help.

'Only one name is as special as yours, Lucy. My former captain's name is *Lucius*, the male equivalent of Lucy.'

Lucy began to shiver. She had an intuition. They were going to pair her with this Lucius, weren't they? A marriage? In this chapel? The unholiest alliance of all.

46

Vernon stood on the foredeck and gazed out to sea. Kruger had told him to go and get some air, to try to clear his head. The ship was some sort of pleasure cruiser painted battleship grey. Kruger jokingly referred to it as the 'Vatican's Navy.'

A fog was descending over the Bristol Channel and it was almost impossible to see anything. The ship had been forced to slow right down. Kruger's men were all asleep in one of the lounges where tourists must once have laughed and chatted as they headed towards some scenic attraction.

'March to the sound of the guns,' was the advice of an old military maxim. Here, they were doing the opposite, heading away from Lucy. Vernon thought it was ridiculous. He put his hand in his pocket, took out his mobile phone and stared at the screen. *No Signal*. The whole network was probably down. By now, the country's infrastructure must be falling apart. Fuel running out, motorways blocked by abandoned cars, trains at a standstill. All the old certainties, all the conveniences of civilisation, everything that had been taken for granted for so long, all finished.

'We have a satellite phone,' a voice said.

Vernon spun round and found Kruger behind him, looking pale and exhausted. This dim light made everything seem worn out. A fading world. Everything sliding, bit-by-bit, into oblivion.

'I spoke to the Vatican a few minutes ago,' Kruger said. 'The Conclave is deadlocked. There's no sign of a new Pope. How we need one in this hour. It's almost midnight for humanity.' He put his hand on his forehead. 'The things that are happening out there...too much to bear.'

'What do you mean?'

'All of the volcanoes around Indonesia, the so-called Ring of Fire, have erupted. The eruption clouds are glowing white-hot and have merged into one huge, fiery ash formation, thousands of square miles in size. No one underneath it could possibly have survived. Relief agencies can't go near.' He bowed his head. 'Those poor people.'

It was obvious from Kruger's expression that there was more to come.

'America hasn't been spared this time,' he said. 'What they feared most has happened. Twelve category-5 hurricanes came together to form a superhurricane, more powerful than anything seen before on earth. It blasted through the southern states of the USA, and the whole of Central America. Everything in its path was obliterated. They're talking about tens of millions of dead. In the Canary Islands, after a volcanic eruption on the island of La Palma, a chunk of land slid into the sea, triggering a mega-tsunami. It generated a wall of water over one hundred and sixty feet high that crossed the Atlantic, devastating the Caribbean and most of the southeastern seaboard of America. All across the world there's famine, drought, and pestilence. It's as if the Riders of the Apocalypse have come in person.'

Vernon didn't know what to say. Words had become absurd.

'I'll show you to the satellite phone,' Kruger said wearily, and led him to the ship's bridge, where there was a special booth for the satellite phone and an accompanying satellite dish. Kruger turned and walked away, his shoulders sagging.

Vernon felt sick. This was already way past critical. No matter what happened now, the world would never be the same. Given the severity of the natural catastrophes, hundreds of millions were probably dead. Maybe billions by now. Anyone in far-flung locations who managed to survive wouldn't be receiving any help. In days, they'd be dead too. A long, lingering death. No wonder the sky was blood red. It was reflecting the scale of human agony.

He punched in the number for Commander Harrington, but wasn't confident of getting a line. The fog was as dense as he'd ever encountered, and the atmospheric conditions had been poor for days in any case. He was amazed when he got straight through on a clearish line. Harrington sounded tired, not with it.

Vernon spent the first few minutes explaining the status of the mission, the loss of the helicopter and the fact that Lucy was now in the hands of the Delta Force deserters. Harrington didn't seem to take much of it in. His tone suggested he thought the whole thing was a waste of time.

'Things are bad here,' Harrington said. 'We've had no fuel deliveries. No oil tankers have reached the UK. The gas pipes from the continent have been cut off. We're rapidly using up the country's emergency reserves. In two days, we won't be able to supply any electricity and gas to domestic households. We're expecting chaos.' There was so much weariness in his voice. 'Shit's happening all over the planet. Everywhere is affected. The estimate of the number of dead keeps rising. Scientists still can't agree on any course of action. The world is desperate now. No matter what, the DG wants you to keep going.'

Vernon rubbed his head. *Clutching at straws* came to mind. There was no doubt incredibly weird things were happening on this mission, but could they really be linked to the devastation happening across the globe? Kruger claimed Lucifer was walking the earth. In medieval times, no one would have required any further explanation. Now, in the age of science, it was too hard to credit. No matter the evidence of his own eyes, Vernon's mind wouldn't accept it.

'I have some information about the case,' Harrington said. 'I don't know how much use it will be to you, but you might as well have everything we've got.'

Vernon was astonished by what Harrington said next. 'Let me be clear about this, commander,' he responded. 'All these Delta Force guys are test-tube babies? Why the hell should that be?'

This revelation freaked him out. It suggested something cold and clinical, almost inhuman. As if this whole Delta Force thing was planned by mad scientists long ago.

'I've been told that test-tube techniques make it easy to select the sex of a baby,' Harrington said. 'I guess that explains how their parents made sure they didn't have any female offspring.'

'But why did the wives cooperate? Why didn't they want to have girls?'

'We can't second guess people like these.'

Harrington passed on fresh discoveries the DIA had made about the members of Section 5. Apparently, every one of them became immensely rich. The assumption was that they'd managed to help themselves to a share of the Nazis' looted treasure. Several of them became powerful industrialists, with a particular interest in mining operations. One of their operations was at

Oak Island, Nova Scotia. They also had mining interests near Rosslyn Chapel in Scotland, and Tara in Ireland, but their main interest was in the vicinity of Glastonbury. In each case, they had a licence for exploring for precious metals, particularly gold. Many of the world's finest goldsmiths were on their books, but not one of these goldsmiths was willing to tell the DIA what they'd been working on. 'Artworks of a religious nature for rich clients,' was all they were prepared to say.

'While we were clearing up the mess in the archive section,' Harrington went on, 'we discovered additional notes from the interrogation in 1945 of SS-Sturmbannführer Friedrich Veldt, the author of *The Cainite Destiny*. A lot more happened at his interrogation than was written up for the official report. Veldt was apparently upbeat until he was told of Himmler's suicide. He demanded to know what Himmler's last words were. He was told that Himmler made crazy comments in broken English. "*All fakes*," Himmler said. "*The real ones are lost forever. It's finished.*"'

'What were fake? Vernon asked.

'No one knows. But Veldt's mood apparently changed immediately. He became extremely depressed. After asking for a glass of water, he made an enquiry about a fellow SS-Sturmbannführer called Hans Lehman. When he was told that Lehman was dead, Veldt had some sort of fit. He made a comment about being the last of the priesthood. If he died, the *Secret Doctrine* would be lost forever.

'We discovered he didn't kill himself. In fact, he was desperate to live. Two Jewish officers forced a cyanide capsule into his mouth and murdered him. Everyone had seen the horrific film footage from Dachau and Belsen concentration camps, so no one condemned the Jewish officers. The whole thing was hushed up and made to look like suicide.

'The DIA discovered another thing. The man Veldt asked about – SS-Sturmbannführer Lehman – was one of the Nazi officials in charge of the looted treasures in Nuremberg. He wasn't dead at all. It turned out he was the person interrogated most frequently by the men of Section 5. In fact, they spent nearly all of their time with him. He died ten years ago, in Britain. And, listen to this – just before his death, he was in charge of converting a convent into an asylum: *Our Lady of Perpetual Succour* in Glastonbury.'

47

Back inside the chapel, Lucy struggled with a bad headache. She didn't want to ask for aspirin, to show weakness in front of Morson. Why all this waiting around? Sometimes she thought she was in a dark room, waiting for a photograph to develop – the photograph of her whole life.

Where was the captain, this Lucius, Morson had mentioned? It might have been a common name in Roman times, but she'd never come across a Lucius in her life. Was he the one they were waiting for?

Colonel Gresnick was nowhere to be seen. As for Cardinal Sinclair, he hadn't spoken for hours. He just sat there, resolutely staring at the altar, as if he expected it to open and God's host of angels to emerge to rescue him.

Morson tapped Lucy on the shoulder then led her to a small side room. Colonel Gresnick was sitting in a plastic chair in the corner. On one wall was a large framed oil painting of Longinus piercing the side of Jesus with the Spear of Destiny.

'So, Lucy, I don't believe you've been properly introduced to Colonel Gresnick,' Morson said. 'He works for the Defence Intelligence Agency in the United States. He came over here to liaise with your former boyfriend in MI5. They wanted to know why we deserted from Delta Force. Above all, they wanted to know why we were so interested in you and the Holy Grail. But you know the answers, Lucy, don't you?'

'I think you're collecting all four Grail Hallows,' Lucy said. 'I think you plan to use them in a special ceremony.'

Morson smiled. 'Who knows? – maybe you're bang on the button.' He turned to Gresnick. 'I thought the colonel here might be interested in our little chat. You never know, maybe he'll share some of his knowledge with us. From what I can gather, Mr Gresnick has been studying my organisation for quite some time.'

'What organisation is that?' Lucy asked, but she didn't get an answer.

'Well, we have a lot of time to kill until nightfall,' Morson said. 'That's when the action begins.' He gazed at the painting of Longinus. 'I'd like to tell you a story while we're waiting.' After finding plastic seats for Lucy and himself, he cracked his knuckles before beginning.

'There's a special mountain in the northern foothills of the Pyrenees in the Languedoc region of France,' he said. 'It's almost four thousand feet high and commands spectacular views. Last year, I climbed up to the fortress on the summit. The mountain is called Montségur, meaning 'Mount Safe', but in the spring of 1243, it was anything but safe. It was the site of the last stand of the Cathars against the Catholic Crusaders. Ten thousand soldiers besieged the stronghold, but although there were only a few hundred defenders, the siege went on for ten months thanks to the terrain being so intractable. It was impossible for the Crusaders to completely surround the mountain and cut off supplies to the Cathars. The Cathars had several expert mountaineers in their ranks who were able to come and go from the fortress, climbing down the sheer rock face on one side of the castle, easily evading the besiegers.

'Three peculiar incidents happened at the end of the siege. When the defenders finally realised their position was hopeless, they negotiated with the Crusaders and were offered abnormally good terms. All of the mercenaries hired by the Cathars were to be set free and the Cathars themselves would all be pardoned if they recanted their heresy. Any heretic who refused would suffer the normal penalty of being burned at the stake. The defenders asked for two weeks to consider the terms. It appeared they were trying to buy time to allow them to hold one last special ceremony inside Montségur, a ceremony that would take place the night before the official surrender. Some people have claimed the special date was the vernal equinox, 14 March 1244.

'There's no record of what happened that night, of what the ceremony entailed. What *is* known is that many of the mercenaries who would have been allowed to go free the following day instead converted to Catharism, knowing certain death awaited them.

'The following day, 15 March, over two hundred men and women who had refused to abandon their Cathar beliefs were led down the mountain to a stockade erected in a field. They were tied to stakes and burned to death en masse. That place is known to this day as "The Field of the Cremated."

'But the incident that lies at the heart of the mystery of the Cathars concerns what four members of the garrison did immediately after the end of their sacred ceremony. The four were the Cathars' most expert climbers. They had a very special job to do, one that has ensured that the Cathars have been veiled in mystery ever since.

'The Cathars supposedly had a great treasure that they wished to prevent falling into the hands of the Crusaders at all costs. The treasure, whatever it was, was somehow essential for the vernal equinox ceremony and had to be kept inside the fortress until that date, despite the risk that it might fall into enemy hands. With the ceremony over, the elite Cathar mountaineers were able to take the treasure away hours before the official surrender. The Crusaders found no trace of the treasure, and none of the garrison divulged a word about it despite being tortured.

'To this day, there are all sorts of bizarre suggestions about what the mysterious treasure was. Some claim it was a miraculous elixir that extended life and had special healing properties, a bit like the Philosopher's Stone, except this was literal rather than metaphorical. But, as a Gnostic sect, the Cathars hated the material world, so they would scarcely be looking for something that prolonged their stay in this hell. By the same token, they wouldn't wish to be cured of any life-threatening illness. Their ambition was to achieve Gnosis and die as soon as possible so they could go straight to paradise. That's why so many of them went willingly to the stake, even though they might easily have lived.

'Others claimed that the Cathars had the skeleton of Jesus Christ in their possession, thus proving that he didn't die on the cross and was never resurrected. Allegedly, the Catholic Church was so afraid of this secret being revealed that they went to all the trouble of wiping out the Cathars. This version of events is preposterous on every level. How could anyone in those days hope to prove that a skeleton belonged to Jesus? More to the point, it was one of the central beliefs of the Cathars that Jesus Christ didn't have a physical body, so how could they have his skeleton? You can see how easy it is for the Cathars to be misrepresented.

'Many people have said that the Cathar treasure was the Holy Grail itself, but why would anti-materialists place any value on a material object? It's ridiculous. Nor would their treasure consist of gold, precious stones, or any other type of material wealth.'

'So, do you know what the treasure was?' Gresnick asked.

'Of course I do.'

'What then?'

'On 30 April, you'll see for yourself.'

'What made the mercenaries convert to Catharism?' Lucy asked. 'I've heard that story before and it's always baffled me. I mean, by doing that they sentenced themselves to death.'

'Isn't it obvious? They were given incontestable proof of the truth of Catharism.'

'But only some converted,' Lucy objected. 'Others didn't. Why not?'

'Again, you'll have to wait for the answer but, I guarantee, you'll get it soon.'

'You seemed to imply there was some doubt about when the Cathars held their special ceremony,' Gresnick said.

'The vernal equinox wasn't the date of the Cathars' ceremony,' Morson said. 'The Catholic Church invented it because they hoped to wipe out all trace of the truth of the date most sacred to the Cathars.'

'What was the real date?'

'April 30.'

'The day Hitler committed suicide,' Gresnick said. 'The day of the supposed end of the world.'

Morson nodded. 'Why do you think Hitler made the defenders of Berlin fight so ferociously for so long against impossible odds? Just like the Cathars at Montségur, he was trying to buy time to allow a special ceremony to take place.'

'Why are you guys all white?' Gresnick asked. 'Is that one of the qualifications for taking part in this special ceremony you keep talking about? An Aryan Race thing?'

'Let's just say you'll never be one of us, colonel.'

'I'd never want to be.'

'Many have said that. Our own grandfathers said the same thing when the Nazis they were interrogating told them what I've just told you.'

'What changed their minds?'

'On 30 April 1945, the Nazis in Nuremberg were able to re-enact part of the ceremony performed by the Cathars.'

'So, you're saying your grandfathers had no Nazi sympathies before they questioned those officials?'

'They detested Nazism. That's why they were chosen. But when your enemy provides you with irrefutable proof of your error, what do you do? Keep pretending you're right when you know for certain you're not? Or do the unthinkable and join the enemy?'

'You're confirming the Nazis were modern-day Cathars?'

'The Nazis were Gnostics, and so were the Cathars. The roots of Nazism go as far back as you can imagine.'

'Back to Cain?'

Morson seemed startled for a moment, then he smiled. 'You've seen *The Cainite Destiny*, haven't you? But there's no way you could accurately interpret it. It defied everyone, even the great professor Reinhardt Weiss. He spent his life trying to understand it. He never did any serious academic work ever again as he ran down ever more bizarre speculations about the Nazis. But the truth is the most bizarre thing of all.'

'Professor Weiss was my grandfather,' Gresnick said.

Morson visibly blanched. 'So, you're Jewish as well as black?'

'I'm a Baptist, actually. My grandfather was Jewish, but he married a Gentile. As you know, Jewishness passes down the mother's line.'

'Nevertheless, you have Jewish blood. If I were you, I'd start saying Kaddish. That's what your sort calls the prayer for the dead, isn't it?'

'My sort? You're a real Nazi, aren't you?'

'You know nothing about the Nazis.'

'I know they were deranged, genocidal psychopaths.'

'They're so far beyond your comprehension, you could never begin to guess their true nature. Your grandfather had many theories, but they were all wrong. He had no evidence, and nor do you.'

'Are you afraid of the truth, sergeant? Afraid of what my family discovered?'

'I could never be afraid of you, Gresnick. Tell me what you think you know then I'll tell you how wrong you are.'

'Well, I know all about the occult roots of Nazism. The senior Nazis thought Cain was the father of the Aryan Race. Cain, they believed, was blue-eyed, blond, with pale skin, while his brother Abel was a classic Semite – brown-eyed, dark-haired with sallow skin.

'The Nazi leadership, for obvious reasons, didn't openly divulge that they were Gnostics. Only senior Nazis knew they had inherited the mantle of the Cathars and the Knights Templar. They hated the Jews because the Jews were the self-proclaimed Chosen People of Jehovah – Satan, as the Nazis saw him. After they dealt with the Jews, they would have turned their attention to the two other peoples of "the Book" – the Muslims and the Christians; Satan worshippers as far as the Nazis were concerned. They weren't fighting a political war; it was a Gnostic Holy War.

'Their ultimate mission was to assemble all of the Grail Hallows and the Ark of the Covenant because they believed that with these they could somehow correct the mistake made by their alleged ancestors – the people of Atlantis – when they accidentally destroyed their own island. That's why the Nazis carried out excavations at sites of religious significance all over the world and why they were always interested in rare religious artefacts.'

'What went wrong for the Nazis?' Lucy asked.

'My grandfather believed the Nazis failed because they were unable to identify the true Grail Hallows and the real Ark of the Covenant. Many high-quality fakes existed and it was impossible for the Nazis to verify which ones were genuine. Their plan depended on having the authentic objects. Only those possessed true occult power.'

'What were they planning to do with them?' Lucy asked.

'Morson has all the answers, don't you sergeant?'

Morson smirked. 'OK, colonel, you're on the right track. And within thirty-six hours, you'll know exactly what our plans are.'

'I also know who the Nazis believed Cain's real father was,' Gresnick said. His tone, Lucy thought, was deliberately provocative.

Morson's eyes flickered. 'And who might that be?'

Gresnick's reply couldn't have been more shocking.

'*Lucifer.*'

48

Vernon stood at the prow of the ship trying to see through the fog. Everything had become still, quiet. Only the engines made any sound. His whole life, he felt, was vanishing into a fog like this, one somehow originating from Lucy. From what Harrington said, it was as though her whole life was predetermined, even her breakdown. But that meant he was part of the script too: a puppet in the Lucy Show. Each string was being cut and he was just one snip away from falling down and never getting up again.

Nothing that happened lately had truly sunk in. How could it? It was as though the world, reality itself, were turning inside out. The reflections were stepping out of the mirrors.

It was over an hour before the fog lifted, revealing a world bathed in red, the water picking up the sky's colour. A new Red Sea. The light gave Vernon a headache. His eyes couldn't adjust to this new red world.

He assumed they were a long way up the Bristol Channel now, probably deep into the Severn Estuary. Kruger said they would be going past the Bristol Docks, up the River Avon and into the centre of Bristol. He wondered what they'd find upriver. A calm city? Bedlam? If Bristol were anything like London, it was probably a ghost town by now.

It disturbed him how rapidly London had changed from a thriving, world-famous city to a deserted shell. What happened to the famous spirit of the Blitz? People had got on with their lives back then. Nowadays they cowered in their semi-detached homes with their families, watching the TV and hoping for someone to come along and make everything better.

Kruger joined him as they navigated past the docks.

'Completely deserted,' Kruger said. 'It's creepy, don't you think?'

The red sky was almost scarlet now. Vernon had never seen anything so ominous. Did God weep tears of blood? Nature, God – how ever you wished to say it – was repulsed by humankind. Time to end it all?

'Are you ready to meet your maker?' Kruger asked, holding his hands in front of him as though praying. 'As a kid, when I heard people talking about Judgment Day, I always tried to picture what would happen. Did everyone get in line? Did we all hear each other's sins, hear judgment being pronounced and sentence passed? Did billions of people stand in a vast, milling crowd in front of God with a vast escalator to heaven on the right and a bottomless trapdoor to hell on the left?'

'Or maybe nothing happens,' Vernon said.

Kruger shook his head. 'Even now, you doubt. Can't you see what's happening? It's all around us. All the signs.'

Vernon stared down at the water and watched the ship cutting through the waves. Everyone has to take some role or other in life. It was his to be Doubting Thomas. Why not? Better than Judas. Better than the other Apostles. They were so anonymous, he'd forgotten most of their names. What puppet should you play in the puppet show at the end of the world? No strings attached.

Everything on the river was deathly silent. He closed his eyes and tried to think of a prayer, but he'd forgotten them all. Just a sentence here and a line there. Patchwork prayers, cobbled together. *Our Father which Art in Heaven The Lord is with thee. Lead us not into Temptation and Blessed is the fruit of thy womb Jesus.* Meaningless, random words. He couldn't remember if he'd ever understood what they meant. Did he ever believe? *Really* believe? He had little doubt the world was indeed ending, yet he still couldn't work out what to believe in. Which God was the True God? Did God even exist?

When he opened his eyes, he wanted to throw up. Hundreds of dead ducks, swans and geese were floating downriver towards them. Water rats nibbled at their half-chewed entrails and eyes. The corpses gave off a nauseating smell. The miasma of cadavers, the vapours of the dead. The air itself seemed to be rotting.

They passed a beautiful marina where many millionaires must have lived the high life not so long ago, but now all the windows of the luxury apartments were smashed, and it appeared everything had been looted. Luxury yachts, sunk, now lay like shipwrecks in the marina. Ghost ships. A ghost world. Only echoes of people remained. Where had they all gone? Vernon remembered hearing that at Hiroshima when the atomic bomb detonated, all that was left of one person was his shadow on a wall. Maybe that was the fate awaiting us all.

Without warning, thousands of crows erupted into the sky, their flapping wings generating a deafening whooshing noise. They had congregated on the roof of a nearby office block. Vernon involuntarily ducked. He hated crows. They circled above the ship for a few moments then flew off towards the centre of Bristol.

The ship passed under several bridges. There were no cars on the bridges, no signs of police or soldiers. No roadblocks. It seemed the army hadn't bothered establishing patrols here. In London, much of the city was cordoned off. Tanks crawled through the streets, together with long lines of military trucks and armoured personnel vehicles. Here, nothing. Maybe the military had stayed outside the city, deciding nothing could be salvaged. Just how bad were things in the country as a whole? The hysteria in London had been growing, becoming almost palpable. People were losing their reason as they began to realise this really might be the end.

How would it come? An enormous explosion? A blinding light? A tidal wave, perhaps? Maybe a superhurricane. Smoke and ash from earthquakes blotting out the sun? A sudden freeze? A nuclear winter? A fire might rage across the earth, boiling the seas. Anything was possible. A *Room 101* for every member of the human race.

Vernon glanced at Kruger, but he didn't return his gaze.

The crows Vernon had seen earlier were now lined up along the near riverbank. He couldn't help trembling. Were there birds like these all over the world? – the watchers at the end of the world, only their black eyes left to see. So much decay for them to feed on. The world was consuming itself, burning its own flesh with its volcanoes. Eruption columns stretching ten miles into the sky. Gas, ash and rock. Lightning cracking open the crimson sky. Magma flows. Superheated gases, pyroclastic flows. Boiling, bubbling seas. Molten lava. A world tearing itself apart as all of its fault lines opened at once. Hurricanes, cyclones, tornadoes – the planet cast to the winds. Tsunamis, maelstroms and monsoons. A drowned world.

All the portents that the world was ending were undeniably in place.

Vernon was startled by a burst of gunfire. An army speedboat raced downriver towards them. It sped past, swung round and started moving parallel to the ship. Kruger signalled to his men not to shoot.

'This is a restricted zone,' a voice said over a tannoy. 'We'll fire on you if you don't turn back immediately.'

Kruger handed Vernon a megaphone. 'Talk to them.'

'I'm James Vernon of MI5,' Vernon said, trying to sound as authoritative as he could. 'I'm on a special mission. These men are taking me to Bristol.'

'We have no information on that.'

'Check with Thames House. You can go straight to the DG. She personally authorised it.'

'Who's your direct superior?'

'Commander Charles Harrington.'

As the officer contacted MI5, Vernon stared at the four soldiers on the deck of the patrol boat, one of them behind a large machine gun. They were spaced out – drugged or drunk. It wouldn't be long, he thought, until they were trigger-happy. *Apocalypse Now* wannabes. A disaster waiting to happen.

'I can't get through to Thames House,' the officer said after a couple of minutes, 'but I'm going to trust you and let you go ahead. I have to warn you that central Bristol is extremely dangerous now. A curfew is in effect from 10 p.m. to 10 a.m. Most of the population have been evacuated to temporary camps outside the city. I don't know what you want in the city centre, but believe me, it's not there anymore. Everything has been looted.'

'I'll take my chances.' Vernon waved unenthusiastically as the patrol boat sped off. So, martial law had been declared after all. It had only been a matter of time.

The ship travelled onwards, the only visible craft on the river now.

On the right bank, dilapidated bonded warehouses loomed up: old and Gothic, with dark, almost black brickwork, and every window broken. They looked centuries old, probably from the time when Bristol was a flourishing port with an active slave trade. Dark, louring, full of relentless rows of small arched windows with bars over them, they resembled a Victorian prison or maybe a lunatic asylum. Another image sprang into Vernon's mind – the warehouses from that creepy old silent movie *Nosferatu*. He couldn't remember if that film was monochrome or sepia. The whole world seemed sepia now, and even the sepia was fading. Would all the colours of life eventually disappear and leave everything in black and white? Or a planet of nothing but grey. Was that the best way for the world to meet its end: colourless, bleached, nothing but white bones left in the sun?

Further on, an old cruise ship appeared, sunk in mud. Vernon remembered it well – a disco ship with a rotating dancefloor that once attracted thousands of young clubbers. Not anymore. The music was long since over.

The ship kept ploughing forward. By now, nearly all of Kruger's soldiers were on deck, staring at the ruins of the city. Multicoloured pigeon lofts on a hillside were on fire. Trapped pigeons made a pitiful screeching sound as they tried to escape their cages. Every now and again, one broke free, its wings burning. It rose a few feet before crashing back in a blazing death spin; a tiny ball of fire in the gloom.

Thousands of pages torn from hard-core porn magazines drifted past the ship. Many of them had washed up on mud banks, covered with green slime.

'A trip along one of the rivers of hell, huh?' Vernon muttered. 'Civilisation has broken down. Even if we survive this, how can it all be put back together again?'

'There are no good outcomes,' Kruger responded. 'Everything's going to change, one way or another.' He put his hand on Vernon's shoulder. 'Let's go ashore. See what the people are like.'

Vernon felt a tremor of apprehension. 'Is it worth the risk? I mean it's only the dregs of humanity out there now.'

'I want to know what this brave new world is like,' Kruger replied.

They stopped at a mooring point then six of them stepped onto a wooden pier and cautiously made their way to the quayside. The first building they came to was an old Victorian structure, painted in gloss white, called the *Dead House*.

'What a name,' Vernon muttered. He stopped to read a plaque on the door. It said the Dead House belonged to the river police and it was where bodies found in the Avon were laid, pending identification.

Kruger opened the door and stepped inside, swinging his pistol in an arc. He came out quickly, pale.

Vernon's curiosity got the better of him and he pushed open the door and went in. There was a dreadful smell. In the corner of the plain room, two corpses lay on tables. Rats were crawling over them, silently feasting on their faces. Vernon retreated fast, letting the door slam behind him.

While he tried to see where the others had gone, a man and a woman came scurrying towards him. They squealed, clutched each other then raced into a peculiar building, shaped like Noah's Ark.

A sign on the door said, 'Only the Elect 144,000 are to be saved. Their names are recorded in the Book of Salvation. Is yours one of them?'

All the religious nuts are out and about, Vernon thought, gazing at the odd building. He could picture all the millions of Christian fundamentalists in America standing on hilltops with arms outstretched, awaiting the Rapture – the magic moment when the chosen vanished from this earth as God raised them up to Paradise.

He pushed open the door. Scores of men and women were on their knees, mumbling and praying, some talking in tongues. Some exhorted God with their hands outstretched and their eyes glazed over.

For a moment, Vernon was nauseated. Who were these people praying to? Their delusions, their lack of intelligence, their deficient education?

None of the congregation looked up at Vernon. They were all too caught up in their religious ecstasies. Maybe that was the best way to face the end – out of your skull, overdosing on false beliefs, gorging on whatever comforting lies and emotional crutches you could find. Vernon preferred the hospice solution; the large injection of morphine. He'd never taken hard drugs in his life. There was something enticing about slipping away during your first major league drug trip.

Depressed, he wandered back out, soon finding himself in the square of a luxury estate called *Blue Anchor Court*. Just when he thought he'd lost the others, they strolled into the centre of the court, almost nonchalantly.

'Listen,' Kruger said, raising his hand to stop his soldiers. 'What's that?'

The sound was unmistakable – an ice cream van, playing *Three Blind Mice*. It was so discordant. Why would an ice-cream van be here in the middle of this ghost city?

'There can't be any vans here now,' Vernon said. 'The city has been shut down.'

They went looking for the van and found it parked a street away, outside a tower block. As soon as he saw it, Vernon knew something was wrong. No one was inside, and there were no customers. Just that tune playing. *Three Blind Mice*, over and over again. Vernon hated it. *Stop*. Just stop, for Christ's sake.

He went over to shut off the damned sound. Staring into the service hatch, he saw that all the ice cream in the trays had melted. A severed hand rested in a tray of melted vanilla, a grotesque raspberry ripple.

Kruger opened the front door and switched off the jingle. 'There's a body inside,' he said.

Vernon went round to look and instantly put his hand over his mouth. The ice-cream vendor had been hacked to pieces by machetes.

'Let's get out of here,' Kruger said.

At the corner of the street, they found an electronics shop. Plasma TVs were in the window display, lying amongst broken glass. Several of the TVs were missing, probably looted. The rest were sitting there in pristine condition.

'Look,' Kruger said, pointing at the tiny glowing red lights on the TVs' control panels. 'Their standby lights are on. There's still power.'

He went into the shop and, a moment later, all the TVs came on. Half of them showed BBC *News 24*, probably the only channel still broadcasting. On the others, there was nothing but static. Dead channels. Vernon stared at the bursts of meaningless noise. Was the whole world like that now? Blank transmissions. Dead air.

On the BBC screens, a stressed-out male anchorman gazed grimly at the camera.

'I can't hear anything,' Vernon shouted to Kruger.

A moment later, the sound came on, and the picture changed.

'Jesus,' Vernon gasped. A picture of Raphael's mural had appeared.

'Today, the Vatican revealed the existence of an unknown masterpiece by Raphael,' the anchorman said. He seemed incredulous as he read from his teleprompter. 'The mural is said to give the date of the possible end of the world. That date is 30/4/2012, under thirty-six hours from now. Vatican officials claimed that the mural identifies someone living today who can prevent the destruction of humanity. They have asked the whole world to pray for Lucy Galahan. Ms Galahan is reported to be a thirty-year-old English Catholic whose current whereabouts are unknown. The Vatican refused to comment on a claim that Ms Galahan is in fact a mental patient. A former lecturer at Oxford University, Galahan wrote a controversial analysis of the Holy Grail legends a couple of years ago in which she maintained that they concealed a heretical secret.'

A picture flashed onto every screen – the glamorous publicity photograph Lucy had used for the dust jacket of her book.

'The world's last hope?' a caption said under the picture.

49

'In a bombed-out library in Berlin in late 1945, my grandfather came across an ancient manuscript by a Gnostic sect known as the Ophites,' Gresnick said. 'They got their name from the Greek word *ophis* – serpent. They were snake handlers and practically worshipped snakes. The remarkable thing about them was that they had an entirely different take on the story of what happened in the Garden of Eden.'

Lucy thought some of the ideas she had put forward in her book were outlandish, but Gresnick was doing his best to prove they were distinctly sober.

'I have your attention, I see.' Gresnick stared hard at Morson. 'In this version of the story, a stranger arrived in Eden bearing an extraordinary birthmark – a double serpent on his forehead. Through time, the myth became confused and people came to believe that an actual serpent appeared in the Garden of Eden. The stranger spent all of his time with Eve, telling her amazing things. He said he had secret knowledge of the true nature of the universe. He called this special knowledge *Gnosis*, and the *Tree of Knowledge* was his symbolic way of representing Gnosticism. Good and evil, he said, were entirely different from what Adam and Eve were taught by Jehovah.

'So, the legend arose that Eve was tempted by a serpent to eat the forbidden fruit of the Tree of Knowledge of Good and Evil. In fact, what happened was that she was taught Gnosticism by the serpent stranger. There was no literal Tree of Knowledge in Eden, and no forbidden fruit. After all, why would Jehovah create a Tree, put it in the middle of the Garden of Eden and then stop Adam and Eve eating from it? That made no sense, even for Jehovah. If he had done that, he himself would have been guilty of tempting Adam and Eve. What *was* forbidden was any knowledge that challenged Jehovah. Gnosticism was *the* forbidden knowledge; forbidden because it was the very first heresy – Original Sin.

'Eve managed to persuade Adam to listen to the Gnostic ideas; hence the myth that Eve tempted Adam to join her in eating the forbidden apple. What she kept secret was that she was pregnant, and Adam wasn't the father. The first person born on the earth, according to the Old Testament, was Cain, the first true human being. His brother Abel soon followed, and this time Adam *was* the father.

'When they grew up, the difference in appearance between Cain and Abel was obvious. They fought over their parentage, and, on Cain's birthday, Abel tried to kill Cain – with an old spear he'd found.'

'I've heard enough,' Morson said. 'Go back into the other room.'

'No,' Lucy said, 'I want to hear this.' She was surprised when Morson shrugged and gestured to Gresnick to finish his story.

Gresnick allowed himself a smile.

'Cain wrestled the spear from Abel and slew him. He knew he could no longer live with Adam and Eve and fled eastwards. The Old Testament said he was banished to the Land of Nod, but there's no such place. *Nod* simply means wandering. In other words, he began a nomadic life. He eventually settled in Canaan, *Cain's Land*, the same territory Jehovah later promised to Cain's mortal enemies: the Jews, Jehovah's Chosen People.

'The Old Testament also says Cain was branded by God. That too was false. Cain, like his true father, had a double-serpent birthmark – the so-called Mark of Cain. For some reason, it only became distinct once a year: April 30, Cain's birthday, and, following Abel's death, the anniversary of the first killing in human history.'

'SS,' Lucy said.

'Pardon me?'

'Don't you see? If the Nazis are linked to Cain, that's why the SS adopted two sig runes for their insignia. The Ss represented the two serpents.'

'They also had the Death's Head symbol, just like the Knights Templar,' Gresnick said.

Lucy felt her brain sparking. It was all flooding back to her, all her old academic enthusiasm.

'And the swastika,' she said. 'That was an ancient Hindu symbol for reincarnation. The Gnostics called reincarnation metempsychosis – the transmigration of souls. Any soul, trapped in a human body, that failed to achieve Gnosis was condemned to be reincarnated in a new body, and live again in the material world. So, the Nazis chose the swastika to show their Gnostic allegiance and their belief in reincarnation as the penalty for remaining wedded to this world. The swastika is just two square Ss stuck together at right angles, another form of the Mark of Cain.'

Gresnick smiled. 'Cain and his people became famous for technological accomplishment, and they spread far and wide from Canaan, building great cities wherever they settled. Their most famous city was an architectural and engineering marvel, full of people from all over the world, speaking different languages – *Babel*.'

'And that became Babylon,' Lucy said. 'And centuries after Canaan fell to the Hebrews, becoming the land of Israel, the Babylonians invaded, sacked the Temple of Solomon in Jerusalem, and carried off all the treasures it contained, including, perhaps, the Ark of the Covenant.'

Gresnick nodded. 'Some Babylonians took to ships and went looking for new lands to settle in, and the rumour was that they took the Ark with them. They went to the far North, to a land that legend said lay beyond the north wind. It's called Hyperborea in Greek. The Latin name was Ultima Thule, or, usually, just Thule: the land at the end of the world.'

Lucy tried to gauge Morson's reaction, but his face was expressionless.

'The people of Thule made another great journey,' Gresnick continued, 'to the most famous island of all...*Atlantis*. According to legend, Atlantis was destroyed over two and a half thousand years ago on none other than April 30, following an apocalyptic religious ceremony. The rumour was that the Ark of the Covenant was the centrepiece of the ceremony.

'The few survivors then spoke of finding a new Atlantis, a lush land marked by a special star called *Merica*.'

Lucy almost clapped her hands. '*America!*'

'That's right. America wasn't named after Amerigo Vespucci. It got its name because the people who discovered it thought it was the mythical Gnostic land that lay under the shining star *Merica*.'

'So, who *did* discover America?'

'The Knights Templar, Lucy. The Templar Fleet that sailed off in 1307 to escape the Catholic Church's persecution had no choice but to find a new land, beyond the reach of the papacy. Once they discovered America, they kept it a closely guarded secret. They made sure no word got back to Europe, knowing that if anything leaked out, the Pope would send an armada against them to conquer them and seize their new country.

'It wasn't until the end of the fifteenth century that they changed their strategy. They had lost many men in wars against the Native Americans, and the knights were unhappy about having to take squaws as wives. Their settlements were failing. They needed an influx of Europeans to make America viable. The Templar they chose for their most vital mission was one of the most famous men in history – *Christopher Columbus*.

'Columbus knew exactly where the New World was for the simple reason that he already lived there. That's why no one is quite sure whether he was Italian, Spanish, Catalonian or Portuguese. In fact, he was *American*. Isn't it the ultimate irony? The so-called discoverer of the Americas was an American all along.

'When the ships *Santa Maria*, *Niña* and *Pinta* embarked from Spain in 1492, they changed their sails as soon as they were out of sight of the land, and raised new sails emblazoned with the red Cross pattée of the Knights Templar. A Scottish Templar called Sir John Drummond was the man who drew up the maps and charts they used on the voyage.

'The history of America is largely the history of persecuted religious minorities, and the very first were the Templars. America is the country of the Knights Templar – a Gnostic country, Freemasonic. It's the new Atlantis, the cherished home of the Illuminati, their bulwark against the power of the Vatican.'

Lucy had never heard anything like it. This was amazing.

At last Morson intervened. His comment startled Lucy.

'And it's where my colleagues and I come from.' He had the weirdest smile. 'If you look at the night sky, you'll see that *Merica* is shining more brightly than ever.'

50

The world's last hope. Vernon stared at the nearest plasma screen. It was impossible, but the words were right there, being broadcast to everyone who still had a working TV. Lucy truly was special. He assumed the Vatican had taken the decision to give publicity to her to offer some hope to the world...to let people know there was still a chance. Even so, he felt it was a desperate act.

The plasma screens showed a succession of pictures from across the globe. They focused on huge screens set up in St Peter's Square, Times Square, Trafalgar Square, Paris, Berlin, Vienna, Prague, Tokyo, Beijing, Moscow, Jerusalem, Cairo – everywhere on earth that could still broadcast pictures. In some of the places, huge crowds were thronging around the screens; in others there were only a handful of soldiers; in others no one at all. Every big screen displayed exactly the same image: *Lucy*.

A flustered young reporter appeared in the centre of St Peter's Square, as hundreds of thousands of Romans knelt to pray.

'I've never known anything like this,' the reporter said. 'I'm hearing that every TV set on earth is simultaneously broadcasting this unknown woman's picture. If the Vatican is correct, the lives of all of us lie in her hands. The great artist Raphael apparently knew this moment was coming five hundred years ago. I really don't know what to say. Can it be true? I'm sure there's not one of us who wouldn't give anything to believe that, against all the odds, someone might be able to save us. But a mental patient?'

Vernon and Kruger stared at each other.

'Why did the Vatican do it?' Vernon asked. 'It's mad to publicise this.'

'Everyone needs hope,' Kruger replied. 'Lucy is the *only* hope.' He turned round and called to his men.

As they walked back towards the ship, they found hordes of rats scurrying in and out of deserted houses. In a stairwell, an old-fashioned automaton in a harlequin costume was lying on its back, clashing cymbals together, its small legs futilely kicking into the air.

Vernon gazed at the crazy spectacle. The automaton's arms moved more and more slowly, its batteries running out. After a few seconds, it stopped completely, its cymbals failing to clash one last time. Was that what was happening to the world? Everything running down.

'Come on, let's get out of here,' Kruger said.

Back at the ship, they got underway as quickly as they could. In the distance, columns of dense black smoke rose into the sky – several districts of Bristol were in flames. Unless it rained, the city would burn to the ground.

They manoeuvred into the central harbour and docked. The water was choked with bloated corpses, many with stab wounds and gunshot injuries.

'Look at the bodies,' Kruger said. 'Their eyes have been removed.'

Vernon gazed down at the mass of dead flesh. 'They must have gone crazy,' he said.

They disembarked. In the dock was an impressive yacht, the sort a billionaire might buy. Painted glossy black, it had a towering golden cross on its prow. It was sitting at an awkward angle and Vernon realised it was holed beneath the waterline. If it were in deep water, it would have sunk.

'Shall we check it out?' he asked Kruger.

The sergeant nodded. He ordered his soldiers and the handful of SAS men to wait while he and Vernon went onboard.

As soon as Vernon stepped onto the ship, he had a bad feeling. The vessel had a ghostly quality, as if it were the sister ship of Dracula's ship that ran aground with a dead crew.

Pistols in hand, they went below. It looked like there had been a frantic firefight onboard. Several dead men in sailors' uniforms were lying around. They had no eyes. The word *Repent* was scrawled on one wall.

When they reached the flooded hold, Vernon and Kruger stopped. Hundreds of eyes were bobbing up and down in the water. On the far wall, written in what looked like blood, was a quote from the Bible: *If thine eye offends thee, pluck it out.*

'Madness,' Vernon mumbled. He retraced his steps as fast as he could, with Kruger close behind. The people had turned into savages, going on religious-inspired killing sprees. If Bristol had gone this way, what were things like in London?

Kruger hurried over to a fenced-off compound at the edge of the harbour. He took out a key and unlocked a padlock, then pushed open the gate. Inside was a large storage facility. The sergeant heaved open the door and Vernon followed him in.

'Help me with these.' Kruger stood beside black tarpaulin sheets covering several vehicles. They turned out to be olive-green United Nations military Humvees: the closest a car could get to a tank.

'Where did you get these?'

'Let's just say the Vatican was owed a few favours.'

Kruger ordered the wounded Swiss Guard to be placed in the lead Humvee, with the two injured SAS men. 'We'll drop these men off at an army base. They can get proper medical treatment.'

'Where are the rest of us going?' Vernon asked.

'That's up to you. Have you remembered where the battle of Camlann was fought?'

Vernon shook his head.

'In that case, we're going to Glastonbury.'

Vernon was furious with himself for forgetting. He stared at the ground and noticed a discarded wrapper from his favourite chocolate bar – *Cadbury Whole Nut*. He started laughing. 'It's OK,' he said. 'I know exactly where Lucy is.'

51

Sergeant Morson and Gresnick had left the room, leaving Lucy alone. She stared around the plain room, then at the painting of Longinus with his famous spear. Was it really possible that the spear contained the power people claimed for it? In the painting, it was just an ordinary Roman horseman's lance but, according to some people, it was a Hebrew spear, as old as the human race. How could a spear contain mystical power? One theory claimed that one of the nails used to hammer Jesus to the cross was embedded in it. Was that enough to turn it into a magic spear?

Morson came back in and drew up a chair next to Lucy.

'*We're* your friends, Lucy. That fool of a cardinal back there could never help you. As for Gresnick, he's a soldier. He knows his duty. Believe me, if he gets the chance, he'll kill you without hesitation.'

'*Everyone* says they're my friends. I think you all want to kill me.'

'We could never harm one of our own. Deep down, you know who you really are. I mean, below the surface.'

'What are you talking about?'

'You *see* things, don't you? Sometimes, you have strange feelings. Maybe, at times, you don't think you're here at all. Your sense of identity is weak: practically non-existent at times.'

Lucy squirmed. It was true. Sometimes she thought she was in the wrong skin. The world was out of kilter, or she was.

'Life nauseates you at times, doesn't it, Lucy? That's why you ended up in an asylum. You know this world is *wrong*.'

'I don't understand what you mean.'

'You understand all right. You just can't come to terms with it. For most of us, we never get into the situation where we start *remembering*. Only the most special amongst us can contact the past.'

'I'm not getting you.'

'We questioned the cardinal. We wanted to know exactly why he was so interested in you.'

'It was the mural.'

'That's right – *our* mural. Julius II was a Grand Master of the Illuminati.'

So, she was right. Lucy almost conjured a smile. 'What about the late Pope?'

'Julius IV was a fool: a good Catholic to the end. He refused to believe that any of his predecessors could be a heretic. He'd heard all the rumours regarding Julius II and decided the only way to scotch them was to give himself the same name.'

'And Raphael?'

'He was paid well to create the mural according to a very specific brief. He didn't suspect anything, although he couldn't understand why he was told to leave one panel blank.'

Lucy looked up. 'The panel that looks like...'

'Well, it obviously wasn't painted by Raphael.'

'Then who? I certainly didn't do it.'

'But you did, Lucy, you *did*.'

52

Lucy couldn't take it in. Morson was insistent that she had painted the final part of Raphael's mural and said he could prove it. He made her sit at a small table with a paper and pen.

'Have you ever heard of automatic writing?' he asked.

'Psychiatrists use it. It's a technique to release the contents of a person's unconscious mind.'

'*Exactly*, and that's what we're going to do now. I want you to close your eyes and concentrate on the mural. I want you to think of each panel in turn, starting from the top left and working your way round clockwise.'

'And then what?'

'For each panel, write down anything that comes into your head.'

'But it will be gibberish.'

'We'll soon see. Let's get started'

Lucy shut her eyes and thought of the mural. It was incredibly vivid, almost as if it were hardwired into her brain. A much crazier idea occurred to her: it was in her mind from the moment she was born. How was that possible?

Each of the panels was so clear it was almost alive. Words were swirling around each panel. Not sixteenth century Italian or Latin words. Not English or Spanish, but French: *old French*. She began moving her hand, scribbling. The words were pouring out of her at a tremendous speed – words she'd known all her life, yet that meant nothing to her.

In under a minute, she was finished. She slammed down the pen and opened her eyes. She had no idea what she'd written. In front of her was a neat list of comments in old French. When she handed Morson the paper, she expected him to be disappointed.

'That's not my handwriting,' she pointed out. 'And I don't know modern French let alone old French. I know I wrote it, but...I can't have.'

'Yet you did. Even though I was expecting it, I can scarcely believe it. It's word perfect.'

'Surely what I wrote is gibberish.'

'Lucy, didn't Sinclair tell you about the attempts of the papacy to understand Raphael's mural?'

'He said they consulted several people, including Nostradamus.'

Morson smiled. He reached into his breast pocket, and brought out two folded pieces of paper. Placing them on the table, he smoothed them out, then stepped back.

Lucy studied the first piece of paper. 'But this is what I wrote. I mean it's *identical.*'

'I've just given you the notes on Raphael's mural that Nostradamus presented to the Vatican. He was only seventeen at the time, but his unique talents were already apparent, bringing him to the attention of all the great courts of Europe. The other page is the translation we made into English.'

Incredulous, Lucy picked up the sheet and read the translated list:

1. The seed of destruction. Light from dark. The creeping evil. Grand illusion. The Satan particle.
2. Rebellion or revolution? Eternal war or assassination. Death the only escape. Only one.
3. They are liberated. They are enslaved. They have peace. They have war. Heaven and Hell.
4. Temptation. Resistance. The road to paradise. The hardest road of all. The sacred stone of heaven made. The tree has no bark, no branches, and no fruit. Look to the Stone of Destiny.
5. Son of freedom. Take possession of their most special weapon. The original. The progenitor of all weapons. Strike the first blow.
6. Knowledge redeems. Infamy's stain is the Redeemer's sacred mark. By this sign shall you know your friend from your enemy.
7. In all his glory. Name him and he must answer the summons. The immutable law. Deliverance is possible.
8. The wise man. The holy man. The fool. The snare. The killing house.
9. He who is greater comes after. The saviour. The prophet.
10. Betrayal. Assassination. The conspiracy.
11. The double death. The death of hope. The promise of deliverance.
12. Which the betrayed and which the betrayer? The silver calculation.
13. They killed God. They collected his blood. They showed the way.
14. The tomb. The descent into a deeper hell. The defeat of death. Life everlasting promised. The threat of return.

15. The mount of salvation. The mount of damnation. The treasure of heaven. The holy stone.
16. My face. The Redeemer's face. The face of Abaddon. A moment will decide all. In the blue. Decision Point. Salvation. Damnation. Choose. Destroyer or Messiah.
17. Arthur's conception. Only the chosen one can do what no other can. The suffering place. The death plunge. Death of one, or death of all.
18. Beware the carrion birds. Hope vanquished. Killed by lance or sword? Which lance? True or false? Mordred's bane.
19. Bring me his head on a plate. The wrath of God. The hard path to paradise. You must go under the earth to find the truth. Beneath the water that freezes.
20. Rebuilt. A second chance. Correct the eternal wrong. Your soul. The false chalice.
21. The Question. For eternity. Your soul.
22. In all guises. The message spreads. Choose.
23. The Cainite Destiny.
24. Look in the mirror. Salvation or Damnation. The Last Judgment.

****

At first, the cryptic comments were nonsensical to Lucy, almost random, but the more she looked at them, the more they made some sort of mad sense.

'You're beginning to believe now, aren't you?' Morson stood over her. 'I ought to tell you another thing. On 30 April 1520, a day after Raphael's funeral, it was Nostradamus who painted the final panel of the mural.'

53

Lucy stared at Morson, trying to absorb what he'd said. If he was right, there was only one conclusion.

'Reincarnation is a reality,' Morson said. 'We've all been reborn many times, and unless we achieve Gnosis, we'll keep on being reborn. Until 30 April, that is.'

'You can't seriously be suggesting I'm Nostradamus.'

'Is it really so difficult to accept?'

Difficult? – it was *impossible*. Lucy didn't know what to say. Morson started explaining it to her again, but his words washed over her.

'The reason you know what Nostradamus wrote is that they're your own words: those you wrote when you lived as Nostradamus. In your convent, you simply repainted the same picture you painted five hundred years earlier. The mental problems you've been having weren't caused by your parents' deaths. Perhaps those were the trigger, but the real cause was that your past life as Nostradamus was coming back to you, forcing its way into your consciousness. It would have seemed like voices in your head; another personality taking shape within you.'

'Reincarnation,' Lucy mumbled. 'There's no such thing.'

'No? Hundreds of millions of Hindus believe in it. The ancient Greeks did too. The Cathars believed in it. Every Gnostic sect did. It's the oldest rule of all – any soul that doesn't achieve Gnosis will come back, and keep coming back.

'What you have to understand, Lucy, is that we each have a soul-line as well as a bloodline. Our bloodline is the list of physical ancestors genetically related to us. The soul-line has nothing to do with genetics. Each time our body dies, our soul must find a new host. Most of us forget our previous soul incarnations, for the sake of our sanity. Only the highly sensitive, or those in deep trauma, gain access to their soul pasts. That's what's been happening to you for these last months. Nostradamus is the most powerful of your previous soul incarnations. All of his life experiences have been flooding into your subconscious, and finally your conscious mind. There was no multiple personality syndrome, no Dissociative Identity Disorder. All of your symptoms related to your soul's memories of its time as Nostradamus.'

'I can't accept that.'

'Many powerful people have had no problem with this. In fact, they rejoiced in it. General Patton was certain he was Hannibal in a past life. It provided an instant explanation for why he was such a brilliant general. Forget West Point, it was his soul-line that made Patton a military genius.

'Heinrich Himmler believed that in a past life he was Sejanus, the Emperor Tiberius's ruthless right-hand man; he was Tomas de Torquemada who drove the Jews from Spain; he was Sir Francis Walsingham, Elizabeth I's spymaster; he was Joseph Fouché, Napoleon's chief of police and founder of the modern police state. Always, he was the second-in-command to a powerful ruler. That's the role best suited to his soul-line.

'Adolf Hitler was Nebuchadnezzar, the Babylonian destroyer of Solomon's Temple in 586 BCE; he was Herod the Great who tried to kill Jesus as an infant; he was Titus, the general and future Roman Emperor who destroyed the Second Temple in 70 CE; he was the Emperor Hadrian who expelled the Jews from Judea in 135 CE; he was King Edward I who banished the Jews from England in 1290 CE. In all of his incarnations, he was obsessed with the destruction of Jews.'

'Why did Hitler hate them so much?'

'That's simple. He was the reincarnation of Cain.'

54

Lucy munched on some bread and cheese that Morson had given her. She was still in the small side-room, but now Sinclair and Gresnick had joined her. Morson supplied them with some slightly stale bread, a lump of Cheddar and a jug of water then locked them all in. Lucy did her best to concentrate on the food and block out everything Morson had told her about her past as Nostradamus.

Gresnick stood with his ear pressed to the door. 'Something's going on out there. The soldiers are moving around.'

'What do you think they're doing?' Sinclair asked.

It was the first time Lucy had heard the cardinal's voice for quite a while. She wondered if this was his ultimate nightmare; being surrounded by unashamed heretics who held his beliefs in contempt, and there was absolutely nothing he could do about it. Back in Rome, he was an immensely powerful man; here, *nothing*. They treated him like a buffoon, too feeble to pose any threat.

'It's dark outside now,' Lucy said. 'Didn't Morson say the action would begin at nightfall?'

'A ceremony of some kind?' Sinclair asked.

They began discussing the different information they had between them: Gresnick's knowledge of *The Cainite Destiny*, and the work of his grandfather and his parents, all the news he had gathered concerning the theft of holy relics and the natural disasters occurring worldwide.

As for Sinclair, he knew about Raphael's mural and the Vatican's take on recent events. Also, as the head of the latest guise of the Holy Inquisition, he was an expert in the heretical beliefs of the multitude of Gnostic sects that proliferated around the time of Jesus.

Lucy had her unique inside knowledge of Raphael's mural, plus the information Morson had given her, and all of the expertise from her time at Oxford. Not forgetting all the material in her controversial book.

Between them, they were convinced they had the keys to what was going on. They agreed to share as much as they knew that seemed relevant. Sinclair started the ball rolling with an introduction to the different Gnostic heresies.

There were at least eighty distinct sects, he said, each emphasising a slightly different aspect of Gnosticism. The Mandaeans glorified John the Baptist and reviled Jesus whom they claimed falsified John's message; Priscillians opposed marriage and procreation as things of the Devil; the Borborians, in the throes of sexual excess, ate faeces and drank menstrual blood; the Ophites revered the serpent in the Garden of Eden for providing humanity with the secret knowledge that Jehovah sought to suppress; the Sethians believed that Noah's Flood was Jehovah's attempt to destroy the descendants of Cain; the Cainites exalted Cain as the greatest resistance fighter against Jehovah's tyranny; the Valentinians believed that once a man achieved Gnosis, nothing he did from then on was sinful, resulting in licence to do anything; the Montanists were celibates who condemned marriage and childbirth; the Basilideans believed that Jehovah wickedly helped the Jews to subjugate other nations and thereby created the strife with which the world was now plagued; the Carpocratians believed that sin was the path to salvation. And so it went on; every conceivable attack on Jehovah and those who worshipped him.

'I think we can agree *The Cainite Destiny* and Raphael's mural are what we have to focus on,' Gresnick said. 'The answer lies there, I'm certain of it.'

'The Grail Hallows are the solution,' Lucy said. 'They feature in the mural, and they're also mentioned in *The Cainite Destiny*.'

'I agree,' Gresnick said. 'My grandfather was certain the Cathars and the Knights Templar once had all the Grail Hallows in their possession, but lost them during their persecution by the Catholic Church. The Freemasons searched for them, and latterly the Nazis took up the quest. My grandfather suspected that if the Grail Hallows were assembled in one place at one time, they would become a source of incredible power. The Nazis, he believed, wanted to use that power to destroy the earth.'

Sinclair nodded. 'All of the Gnostic sects agreed the material world was evil. Logically, the ultimate desire of Gnostics must be to end the world. If the Nazis were descended from the ancient Cainite sect then *The Cainite Destiny* makes perfect sense.'

'OK,' Gresnick said, 'the Nazis searched for the Grail Hallows. Either they didn't manage to collect all of them, or one or more of them were fake.'

Sinclair agreed. 'Practically every religious relic has been faked. The Middle Ages saw a lucrative trade in holy relics. Several chalices in Europe lay claim to being the Holy Grail. There are several possible Spears of Destiny.' He stared at the painting of Longinus. 'Fakes won't work,' he said, 'no matter how much you believe in them. You must have the real thing. I believe that Raphael's mural reveals where the genuine relics are hidden, but only one person can actually locate them.' He turned to Lucy.

Gresnick nodded. 'This is all about you, Lucy. That's why Morson said you were the most important person in the world. Without you, they'll never manage to collect the true Grail Hallows. And without them they're sunk.'

55

Sergeant Morson came into the room, carrying a Bible. A big, powerful man with cropped blond hair, he had a way of dominating any room he entered. Lucy felt that she physically shrank whenever he stood near her.

'Having a cosy chat?' He threw the Bible at Cardinal Sinclair. 'Does the truth sicken you? Is that why you cling to this book of lies?'

Sinclair glared back at him, but didn't say anything.

'A priest,' Morson said, 'is a person who, in the name of nothing but the truth, tells nothing but lies. The bigger the lie, the more ferociously it's proclaimed as the truth. Lies are bathed in incense and paraded around in front of the deluded masses as though they're the most unshakable cornerstones of reality, when in fact they can't even support themselves.'

'And you think Gnosticism is the answer?' Sinclair retaliated. 'A "religion" that claims the world is evil.'

'Your predecessors sat in the Tribunal of the Holy Inquisition to pronounce judgment on my predecessors. Why don't we take this chance to put the People of the Book on trial? Shall we examine the claims of the Jews, the Christians and the Muslims? What do you think, cardinal? Or do you feel comfortable only when you have torture chambers at your disposal?'

'Say whatever you like. It won't change a thing. Heretics have cried in the wilderness for millennia and their voices have always faded to nothing.'

'Their voices haven't gone, cardinal. Far from it. We have the Book of Moses in our possession. This reveals exactly what Jehovah said to Moses when the Hebrew prophet disappeared for forty days and nights on the summit of Mount Sinai. It's the most savage book you could ever imagine. Jehovah is revealed in his true colours: the Anti-God, God through a glass darkly. An inversion, a perversion, a black hole from which light, hope and truth can never emerge. A better name for the Book of Moses would be the Gospel According to Satan.'

'I don't believe you,' Gresnick said.

'Of course you don't. That's why you worship false gods.'

'You're taking everything out of context, twisting everything.'

'Am I? Beneath the Dome of the Rock on Temple Mount is a huge, rough-hewn lump of rock. This is what Temple Mount is all about, what makes it the most sacred site on earth. This rock is sacred to Jews, Muslims and Christians because they all believe this was the spot where Creation began. This rock was the first material object ever created in the universe, touched directly by the hand of God.

'And this is the same spot from where Mohammed allegedly ascended to heaven. But it's also where Abraham, the first Jew and the patriarch of all three religions, planned to sacrifice his son Isaac. Can you imagine any good god asking his chief prophet to sacrifice his own son? And can you imagine any sane prophet contemplating it? Only Satan would make such a request, and only a Satanic prophet would be prepared to carry it out. Of course, the apologists for this Satan say that he didn't intend that Isaac should actually be killed. So why even suggest it?

'Never forget, Jehovah preferred the animal sacrifice of Abel to Cain's vegetarian offering. From the start, he showed his bloody intent. First animal sacrifice, then human. Suicide hijackers screaming Allah Akhbar as they fly planes of ordinary people into skyscrapers – that's *Allah*'s will. Christian pilots dropping atomic bombs and destroying tens of thousands in the blink of an eye; wiping out women and children and calling it "collateral damage." That's *God*'s will. Jewish gunships blowing up a Palestinian family having a picnic on the beach, Jewish soldiers shooting children dead for throwing stones, driving excavators over human rights protestors – that's *Jehovah*'s will. This is no God, this is Satan: the god of evil, of human slaughter on an industrial scale. This is the mechanisation of massacre.

'And these people who worship Satan – the Jews, the Christians, the Muslims – have the nerve to talk of the need for tolerance and multi-culturism. How can these people dare to look each other in the eye? How can they bear to be the next-door-neighbour of someone they think is going to hell? Do they nod at each other in the morning and exchange hypocritical pleasantries? Can there be anything more stomach churning? Yet you disagree with me that Satan created these religions.

'At least Hinduism got it right about reincarnation. If we have an eternal soul, why would we be allowed only one chance to lead a good life? Why not two, ten, a thousand, as many as it takes? Why just a one-time opportunity, with hell waiting for you if you get it wrong?'

'And what about the Gnostics?' Cardinal Sinclair said. 'What good can come from claiming the world is evil? It's insanity.'

'Insanity? Well, we don't believe in sending anyone to hell. We think hell is already here. Our mission is to free everyone. We want to bring every lost soul back to the True God. The Jews, the Christians, the Muslims, the Hindus, the Buddhists, the atheists – everyone – we want to save them all, to restore every lost soul to paradise. Even all the people who have hated us, persecuted us, fought us, resisted us – even *they* will be saved. Even you, cardinal. You want to send me to hell and I want to deliver you to heaven; yet you claim your religion is superior to mine. The Muslims want to blow me up while I want to lead them to heaven. The Jews want to damn me forever because I tell them Jehovah is Satan, yet I want them to join me in paradise, to be bathed in the light of the one True God. Gnosticism is the only moral religion, the one true religion of love, peace and forgiveness.'

'What about the Holocaust?' Gresnick snapped. 'Doesn't that disprove everything you've said? That was the most horrific act in history and it was ordered by the Gnostic leaders of Nazism.'

For once, Morson looked embarrassed.

'I agree,' he said after a few moments. 'We'll always be ashamed of that. We abhor pointless violence, and the Holocaust had no point at all. There was a particular context for it is all I can say. It's not an excuse, but it explains why it happened.

'After Hitler conquered France, one of the first places SS soldiers went was the Gothic cathedral of Chartres, where they began digging in the crypt, looking for the Ark of the Covenant. Chartres was long suspected of being the home of the Ark for a very simple reason. In the north porch of the cathedral are sculptures depicting the Ark of the Covenant, and on a pillar is a Latin inscription saying *Hic Amicitur Archa Cederis*, meaning *Here is hidden the Ark of the Covenant*. The SS found something buried below the crypt and had no doubt it was the missing Ark.

'Hitler was elated. Then more incredible news reached him. He always believed that two of the Grail Hallows – the dish and the Holy Grail itself – were hidden in England and that he'd have to conquer England before he could claim them. But SS digging operations in the Languedoc discovered a chalice and dish near the village of Rennes-le-Château, and they seemed authentic. Hitler was astonished. This meant, he thought, that he had all four Grail Hallows – the chalice, the dish, the Spear of Destiny from the Hofburg Palace in Vienna, and a matching sword from the same place: the so-called Sword of St Maurice – and he also had what he thought was the authentic Ark of the Covenant. In other words, he had everything he needed for the most sacred ceremony of all.'

'Which is?' Gresnick said.

'You'll find out when April 30 dawns.'

'So, what happened with Hitler and his ceremony?' Lucy asked.

'On 30 April 1941, perhaps the high watermark of Nazism, Hitler and twelve senior members of the SS went to Montségur. French peasants reported that hundreds of German aircraft flew over the fortress in strange formations. One of the formations was a swastika, and another the Cross pattée. Of all the men who attended the ceremony, only one was still alive by the end of 1945: SS-Sturmbannführer Hans Lehman. We'll be performing the same ceremony within thirty-six hours...with a few new elements added.

'All I can say is that Hitler's ceremony failed and he was devastated. Some say his mind cracked and he was never the same man again. He blamed his failure on Jewish machinations and, that very day, he formulated his plan for the Final Solution. It was the act of a desperate man, his judgment damaged beyond repair. In June 1941, he launched the invasion of the Soviet Union, the home of what he regarded as Jewish Bolshevism, and the Nazis' long march to defeat began.

'I don't intend to defend Hitler's actions. After 30 April 1941, he was deranged as far as I'm concerned. Lehman believed so too. But our crimes of the past are behind us. On 30 April 2012, there will be no mistakes. The age of the Demiurge's false religions, his *reign of terror*, is almost over.'

'The Catholic Church has seen thousands like you in the past,' Sinclair said, standing up. 'We'll endure long after you've vanished.'

'Really? Let me tell you what the collective message of the people of the Book is: hatred, slaughter, division and death. That's what the children of Abraham believe in. Their two central propositions are: *if you don't agree with us, we'll kill you*, and, *if you don't agree with us, you're going to hell*. And yet they call themselves good, decent people.

'The irony is that the question of hell is already settled. According to the Christians, every dead Jew is in hell. All those Holocaust victims – straight to hell. The same is true of Islam. Islam's great Prophet is in hell. Not as speculation, as fact. Even as we speak, all those Muslims who say *Peace be upon him*, are referring to a person currently in hell, suffering all its torments. If Mohammed *isn't* in hell at this very moment then all the Christians are wrong and hell is full of popes and saints. Don't you think that's amazing? The game is long over, but no one knows the score even though their eternal souls depend on it. In this game of life, with heaven as the reward for winning and hell the punishment for losing, the right way to play the game is already known in every detail, yet the creator of the game refuses to reveal the results of the billions of games that have already finished. Only when our lives are over and it's too late for us to change our game plan, do we learn the scores.

'If Mohammed is even now in hell, why doesn't God let the Muslims know so that they can change their wicked ways? If the popes and saints are in hell, why doesn't Allah put the Christians out of their misery? If heaven is full of Jews, why doesn't Jehovah tell the Christians and Muslims that they've got it fatally wrong? No game could be more deadly than this one. What sort of sick mind devises such a thing? Only a *Satanic* mind.

'Which sane person could deny that Judaism, Christianity and Islam are the work of Satan? They float on a sea of blood, of crosses of the dead stretching in every direction. There's no love, just hate; no peace, just war; no compassion, just limitless cruelty. Humanity's greatest benefactor would be the person who put an end forever to these mad Devil-inspired religions.'

'And you think she's sitting over there?' Gresnick said slowly.

Morson nodded. 'In a few hours, Lucy will deliver us from hell.'

56

The door was unbolted and swung open slowly. Footsteps receded. What was going on? Morson had left them an hour earlier. None of them liked to admit it, but his outburst had unsettled them. Sinclair declared that heretics often sounded persuasive on first hearing, but some reflection soon revealed how absurd their arguments were. It didn't sound as if he believed it himself.

Gresnick got to his feet and crept to the door. 'There's no one here. They've all gone.'

Amazed, Lucy and Sinclair joined him at the doorway. The chapel was deserted.

Lucy hurried to the front entrance. When she threw open the door, she involuntarily stepped back. A black carriage with four jet-black, blinkered horses stood on the driveway – a *hearse*. Two men in black top hats and frock coats sat in the seats at the front.

The hearse had glass windows. Lucy, peering inside, was confronted by a black coffin, covered with wreaths of black flowers.

Other men in top hats and tails appeared from the sides of the chapel and marched in procession to the rear of the carriage. They drew out the coffin and hoisted it onto their shoulders.

Lucy thought the men were wearing white makeup. They looked ghostly, like creatures who'd stepped through a portal from another world. Many other men now appeared, all in the same strange garb, with the same chalk-white faces.

Gresnick and Sinclair were right behind Lucy now.

'What's happening?' Gresnick asked.

'Devilry,' Sinclair said, stepping out onto the snow. One of the mourners pointed a pistol at him and motioned at him to go back in. The man came over and handcuffed Sinclair and Gresnick.

Stillness settled. There were no sounds. The night had died somehow. There was something odd about the coffin. Lucy could tell it was connected to her in some way, but she didn't know how.

Eight men carried the coffin into the chapel, with the others following. The coffin-bearers marched up the central aisle and placed the coffin on a black catafalque. All of the men saluted. One of them, with white gloves, removed the coffin lid.

Lucy realised she was expected to go forward and look inside the coffin. Everyone cleared out of her way as she walked down the aisle. As she got closer to the coffin, her legs carried her increasingly slowly, as though she were wading through molasses. Yet there was nothing in the coffin that could possibly scare her. Her own ghosts were far away.

Reaching the foot of the coffin, she glimpsed a figure inside, covered by a white shroud, its face hidden by a white muslin veil.

'Who is it?' she whispered to the man with white gloves, but he didn't answer.

She edged along the side of the coffin, trying to see through the veil. Why had the soldiers gone to all this trouble? Was it one of their colleagues who'd been killed in the fighting at Tintagel? Yet she couldn't free herself of the feeling that it was designed for her benefit. But why? The last thing she wanted to do was look at a corpse.

She remembered the day when she and her father went to the funeral parlour to look at her mother lying in her coffin. She and her father held hands as they went inside, praying for the strength to get them through the ordeal. Her dad took one look at his wife's face then turned away, covering his face as he started to sob. She'd never seen him cry. He sat down on a seat and didn't look up again.

Lucy gazed down at her mother's face, and placed her fingers lightly on her mum's cheek. The skin was waxy and ice-cold. No longer human, the lifeblood long gone. The soul? That was the critical question, of course. If people didn't have souls then that was that. She would never see her mum's face again, except in photos. 'The enchantment of summer does not last long,' her mother wrote in her last diary entry. Those were the words Lucy put on her wreath of red roses. Leaning over, she kissed her on the lips and whispered, 'Goodbye, mum.'

When her father was lying in the same funeral parlour several months later, she refused to look. She couldn't go through it a second time. Looking at the dead makes death part of you too. Corpses are mirrors. They put intimations of your own death in your mind.

Sergeant Morson, dressed like all the others, came and stood beside Lucy.

'*Why?*' Lucy whispered.

'You need to know who you are, Lucy. I want you to see that you're one of us, that you've *always* been one of us. Remove the veil and see for yourself.' He took a step back.

As Lucy's hand hovered over the man's face, she was certain she shouldn't look. It simply wasn't right. She was in the same position as the tourist who found her dead father in the sea at Tintagel. But her hand stretched down into the coffin, and her fingers touched the soft muslin veil. She stared hard, trying to see through the material to the face beneath. A man, she decided. Not young, so not one of the soldiers. What on earth did Morson expect from her?

Slowly, she drew back the veil. Her eyes grew ever wider as more and more of the face was revealed. Before she'd gone halfway, she stopped dead, her hands dropping to her side as though she'd been electrocuted.

Oh, Jesus Christ, this can't be.

She held her hand over her mouth, trying not to vomit. She couldn't breathe. All of her limbs were going numb. Staggering over to the pews, she managed to flop into a seat before her legs buckled beneath her. She wanted to scream, but her mouth just hung open.

Sick.

These people were monsters.

57

The convoy of Humvees didn't reach Cadbury Castle until nightfall. The vehicles drove over snow-covered fields to get as close to the hill as possible, the noise of their engines drowned by the high wind.

The Battle of Camlann, Vernon now remembered all too clearly, allegedly took place on the grassy fields between the great mound of Cadbury Castle and the banks of the River Cam, the fields churning into a muddy quagmire as first snow and then rain lashed down on the battlefield that day. Lucy, when she brought him here three years ago, tried to conjure the scene for him. King Arthur was inside Camelot with his small army. Crossing the river was Arthur's nephew Mordred with his much larger army of rebels. Logically, Arthur should have remained inside the fortress and tried to resist Mordred's siege. Instead, he and his few remaining loyal knights rode out in their finest, most glittering armour. The last charge of chivalry.

Vernon stepped out of the Humvee, his boots crunching into the thick snow. In London, snow rarely fell and didn't lie long. Here, the snow was several inches deep. In the headlights of the Humvee, he gazed at it as it glinted and sparkled like a crystal field, but Kruger quickly ordered all lights to be extinguished.

All around Vernon, the other soldiers fanned out, including the handful of remaining SAS men. There was no smalltalk, just professionals doing their job.

'Can you feel it?' Kruger whispered. 'There's something out there.'

Vernon nodded. He'd felt it long ago.

'Look up there.' Kruger pointed at the northern sky.

Vernon squinted upwards and spotted a small, intense bright light, like a star.

'The sign of Satan.' Kruger made the sign of the cross. 'He's *here*. You know it, don't you? This is his mockery of the Star of Bethlehem.'

Sherlock Holmes got it wrong, Vernon thought. Not even the impossible can ever be ruled out. He was certain Lucifer was really out there. There was no point in denying it, no reason to struggle with the impossibility of it. It couldn't be true, yet it was. 'What are we going to do?' he asked. He remembered what Kruger had said earlier about the possibility of killing Lucifer. Silver bullets just didn't cut it. Crucifixes, Holy Water, garlic – all useless. They certainly didn't have the Ark of the Covenant at their disposal.

'We have to take any chance we get to rescue Lucy,' Kruger said.

'But how do we fight the supernatural? We don't have the right weapons.'

'We have our faith. Now, let's get going.' Kruger led the way up the steep slope to the plateau of Cadbury Castle.

It was a difficult climb. The soldiers kept slipping as they made their way up the snowbound hill, through the frozen trees shedding tinkling ice crystals. A blood-red moon hung above the mound, casting the same sickly red light as the daytime sun.

After clearing the trees, they reached the lip of the mound. In the far corner of the plateau, lights were visible.

Kruger raised his night-vision binoculars to take a closer look. 'It's a Templar church,' he said. 'There's a hearse outside.'

'A hearse? You don't think...'

'Trust me, Lucy's not dead.'

Vernon felt the chill seeping through his uniform and into his bones. Would this nightmare ever be over? He was exhausted, physically, mentally, every which way. Yet, somehow, he knew his true trials hadn't even begun.

'There are no sentries outside,' Kruger said. 'We'll surround the church. They won't be expecting us in this snowstorm. It's perfect cover. The falling snow will cover our tracks. We'll go straight across the field and then surround the chapel. If there's a back entrance, we'll split in two and storm the front and back doors simultaneously. Otherwise, we go through the front. We use flash and stun grenades to disorientate them. We'll have maximum surprise.'

All of the troops nodded.

It sounded so good in theory, Vernon thought. Yet *that* creature was out there. How could they beat the Prince of Darkness?

58

Lucy held her head in her hands. 'No,' she mumbled, 'it's not real.'

Morson sat down beside her and clasped her hand.

'I buried him,' Lucy said. 'That can't be him.'

'You buried a box of rocks, Lucy. We took your father's body and embalmed it. It was our right.'

'What do you mean?' The words came out of Lucy's mouth so quietly she wasn't certain Morson heard them. Her fingers groped for her locket, the one she found back at Merlin's Cave. Now it hung from her neck, her most precious object. She raised it up and kissed it.

'Let me see that.' Morson gestured at her to hand it over.

'I'll never let it go.'

'That's not yours. You took it from your father, didn't you?'

Lucy clasped it to her chest.

'We all have one of those,' Morson said. 'It has the letters *DA* engraved on the outside.'

Lucy was startled. She'd always been curious about those two letters. Her dad said they stood for Latin words that were particularly dear to him, but he never revealed what they were.

'Deus Absconditus,' Morson said. 'It's Latin for *Hidden God*.'

'The Gnostic god?'

'The True God, the *only* God,' Morson said. 'Hidden from all those in thrall to the Creator of this hellish world.' He pointed at the locket. 'Flip it open.'

'I found it near where he drowned. It has my picture inside.'

'Under your picture, you'll find one of our most sacred symbols – the Death's Head.'

Lucy did what Morson suggested, but she was just going through the motions. She already knew he was right. Slipping out the small photo, she gazed at the intricately etched Death's Head underneath.

'I told you, Lucy – you've always been one of us. Your father was our Grand Master, our High Priest, the man with the most illustrious bloodline in the world. He could trace his lineage all the way back to the beginning...to our earthly lord and master.'

'You're saying my father was a direct descendant of Cain?'

'That's why you're the Chosen One, Lucy.'

'But why did he kill himself? Why did he leave me? He never told me anything about this. Not a word. I can't believe you took his body.'

'He wasn't in his right mind at the end, Lucy. When he went to Tintagel, he was trying to locate the Sword of Destiny – the one you found. He wanted to give it to you, to explain things, but he couldn't discover any trace of it.'

'You're saying he didn't kill himself at Tintagel? He slipped, or something?'

Morson shook his head. 'No, he definitely took his own life. He had to. After all, he'd committed a terrible crime.'

'What?'

'A crime against Gnosticism, against the beliefs he'd held all his life: the crime of *love*. He loved his wife and, above all, he loved you.'

Lucy shook her head. 'How can you say that love's a crime?'

'Love was Satan's deadliest gift to mankind. When Pandora opened her box, the first and greatest evil to fly out was love.'

'I don't understand.'

'Love is the glue that keeps souls attached to this world, stuck in this hell. It mires us in misery. Love glitters and seduces. No one would endure one moment of this hell if they felt nothing but the pain. It's the love that allows people to bear it. Love traps us, keeps us in the snares of the material world, this false world of the false god. Yet you, better than anyone, know that the underside of love is pain, the worst pain of all.'

Lucy looked away. Morson, in his mad way, was right. Love is poison. A beautiful poison, but poison all the same. The first taste might be paradise, but what followed was hell.

'What are you going to do with the body?'

'Our tradition is to give our Grand Master a Viking funeral.'

Lucy had no objections. When the funeral director asked her all those months ago how she wished to bury her dad, she almost chose the cremation option. As a Roman scholar, he would have approved of leaving this world in the same way as Julius Caesar, on a funeral pyre.

'A ring,' she said. 'My father always wore a ring. Have you got it?'

'The ring was passed on to your father's successor as Grand Master. I've spoken to him on the phone, but I've never met him. His identity is a closely guarded secret.'

A scuffling sound behind them made Lucy twist round. Colonel Gresnick was standing in the centre of the aisle. His handcuffs were gone, and he was holding a pistol. Lucy gasped. The pistol was pointed straight at her head.

'Get over here,' he barked.

Lucy glanced at Morson. His face was curiously blank.

'Don't look at him,' Gresnick shouted. 'He can't help you. Just do as I say and step over here.'

Lucy got to her feet. She'd started to like Gresnick. They had so much in common, so many reasons to be on the same side. Now, she realised, she didn't know him at all. He was going to shoot her, wasn't he? Morson was right all along – only he and his men were interested in protecting her. Her heart pounded as she made her way towards the colonel.

'I'm leaving here with Lucy,' Gresnick yelled, 'so I want all of you to back off.'

'You're not going anywhere.' Morson stood up. He and his men drew their pistols.

Gresnick grabbed Lucy, twisted her round, with his arm round her neck, and prodded the barrel of his pistol against her temple. 'I swear, I'll shoot her.'

All of the soldiers raised their pistols and pointed them at Gresnick.

'Don't make me do it,' Gresnick said. 'You know I won't hesitate.'

'I'll count to three,' Morson said. 'If you don't hand over Lucy, we'll shoot you. One…Two…'

Gresnick dropped his pistol and released his hold on Lucy. She darted back to Morson's side.

'I don't understand,' Gresnick said. 'You were willing to let me shoot Lucy. Your whole plan depends on her.'

Morson smirked. 'No wonder the DIA are so unsuccessful. Intelligence is useless if it's detached from psychology.'

'What?'

'You had a pistol, colonel, and you had Lucy. If you had intended to kill her, you would have done it instantly. You value your own life too much, or perhaps you value Lucy's as much as we do.'

Gresnick stared at the ground.

'Put the colonel and the cardinal in one of the middle pews,' Morson ordered. 'This time, use ankle restraints as well as handcuffs. I don't want…'

He stopped, and all of his men spun round.

Machine-gun fire had erupted outside.

59

Vernon sheltered behind the small stone wall he'd found during the mayhem. His heart was thudding so much, he thought he'd pass out.

Jesus Christ, what had happened? It was as if those things were waiting, as though they knew all along.

They had been advancing over the plateau towards the chapel. Snow was falling. The night was strangely beautiful. Vernon always found snow magical. It transformed old, tired sights. It was like a wonderful rejuvenating powder being sprinkled over the earth.

Then the snow-covered field simply rose up. Vernon gasped as thousands of ravens shook off the snow they'd lain beneath. As the birds flew upwards in a huge, flapping mass, the snow fell from their wings like white rain. It was terrifying and stunning at the same time. The ice the ravens had dislodged tinkled like weird musical chimes as it fell back to the earth. As the ravens accelerated upwards, they merged with a storm. The wind whipped across the plateau, full of snow and ice, stinging Vernon's eyes so much he couldn't see properly. All of his colleagues seemed to be swallowed up by the night. He was alone, lost.

Every raven cawed, creating a hideous cacophony as they wheeled and fluttered in the night sky. Then they started to swoop down like Stuka dive-bombers, with the same terrifying screech.

Vernon heard the staccato of machinegun fire. He threw himself onto the snow, and reached for the Uzi machine pistol Kruger gave him earlier. Through the snow flurry, he saw vague shapes moving around. An SAS trooper sprinted past him, spraying bullets into the air as a seething cloud of ravens attacked him. Scores of ravens fell out of the sky, their blood splattering onto the snow, but soldiers were letting out horrific screams too. No one could survive these aerial attacks. There were just too many ravens.

That was when Vernon crawled away to a wall beneath the cover of some trees. He sat there, breathing hard, his back pressed against the wall. The ravens were protecting the chapel, he realised. God Almighty, it was as if they had human intelligence, or something was controlling them.

Through the blizzard, an immense dark shape appeared. At first, it was high above the ravens, but it soon came swooping down, passing in front of the bloodshot moon. For a moment, the moon flickered, as if its light were being sucked in by a black hole. The shape seemed to have huge beating wings, distorting the air, generating overwhelming blasts of wind turbulence.

'Christ save us,' a soldier shouted.

Vernon recognised Kruger's voice and tried to see where he was.

The dark shape swept low over the field, beating its wings.

Vernon could see a little more clearly now. Most of the soldiers had thrown themselves onto the snow and were firing upwards from their prone positions. Kruger tossed a grenade into the sky, straight at the shape. There was a pause, almost silence, and then an explosion.

The clatter of machine-gun fire began again, yet it sounded desperate.

Kruger came running out of the chaos and threw himself towards the wall where Vernon was hiding. 'It's slaughtering us,' he screamed. 'We have to get out of here.'

'We can't leave,' Vernon blurted. 'Lucy's still in the chapel.'

'I should have killed her when I had the chance.'

'*What?*'

'Open your eyes, you fool. Lucy Galahan is the child of the Devil. If we let her live, the whole world will perish.'

Vernon pushed him away and ran out from behind the shelter of the wall. Immediately, the vast, dark shape appeared above him. He tried to scream, but the noise stuck in his throat. The creature was beating its wings, closer and closer to Vernon. He held his hands to his ears, trying to shut out the deafening sound.

'God help me,' he screamed…but everything was going black.

60

Lucy was astonished by how unfazed Sergeant Morson was by the gunfire. 'No one's going to harm you, Lucy.' He strode towards the door where his men were busy changing back into their camouflage uniforms. 'I want a patrol ready in five,' he barked. 'Reconnaissance only.'

'Shouldn't we be on full alert, sir?' one of the men asked, just as the shooting outside ended. Then the only sound was the ravens' high-pitched cawing.

'Trust me, it's just corpses out there now.'

As Lucy watched a handful of soldiers troop outside, she was certain it was Kruger and his Swiss Guards who had tried to assault the chapel. Coming to kill her, or rescue her? Everything was so confusing. Did it make sense to talk of good people and bad? Morson, Kruger, Sinclair and Gresnick all had their own agendas. Her father was mixed up in it too. She never expected that.

It was appalling to think of the Swiss Guards lying frozen out there in the snow, being mutilated by the ravens. To die so far from home. Maybe one or two escaped. She hoped Kruger was still alive. It was too cruel for both brothers to be dead. Someone would have to inform their mother. It would break her heart. Her two strong, proud sons throwing their lives away. In pursuit of what?

She sat in her usual position in the front pew, and found herself studying the elegant stained glass windows. It took her a moment to notice something odd: in the pane showing the Crucifixion, every figure other than Jesus was smiling. His death was a cause of celebration, it seemed. No wonder no priest came here.

After quarter of an hour, the front door flew open and the patrol returned carrying an injured man. They laid him on one of the pews at the back and Lucy went forward to see if she could help.

'Oh, my God – *James.*' She reached out, trembling, towards him. Unconscious, not dead. He'd survived the helicopter crash, and now this.

'That man takes a lot of killing,' Morson muttered.

Lucy glanced back at Gresnick. He had twisted round and was gazing at James. Was it true what he said, that James had planned to kill her? Apart from her parents, she'd never trusted anyone as much as she did James.

'Let me look after him,' she pleaded.

Morson frowned. 'Like father, like daughter. For all our sakes, I ought to kill him right now.'

'Please, don't harm him.'

Morson stared at the altar. 'I'll decide about him later. Right now, Lucy, it's *time*. One of the Grail Hallows is in this chapel. *Find it for us.*'

61

Everyone stopped to stare at her. Sinclair and Gresnick glowered. Lucy didn't want to leave James, but she knew she mustn't antagonise Morson. Slowly, she forced herself to walk round the chapel, staring one by one at the Stations of the Cross. Yehoshua ben Yosef she mouthed to herself. Just as Morson said, it didn't seem right. Names were so important. Did they define your fate? *Lucy Galahan.* Was she standing here in this chapel simply because she had that name? If she were Jenny Brown, would she be at home with her husband and children, praying for the Prime Minister to save the country?

She turned away from the stained glass windows and walked along each pew, trying to sense something, but nothing came to her. Why should she be helping Morson anyway? When he told her that her father was their leader, she automatically felt it right to help him and his men. Yet she still had no idea of what their ultimate plan was. They would collect the Grail Hallows and conduct some ceremony, but then what? Was Gresnick correct that maybe the Grail Hallows were a super-weapon?

Morson was a man with no love in his eyes, just like Kruger. Was it right to ally yourself with people incapable of love? She agreed with him that love could be the worst thing of all – she'd thought it often enough – but a world without love; was that a place where humans could live? Wouldn't it be the worst hell of all?

She glanced at James lying stretched out on the back pew. One soldier was administering smelling salts to him. He wasn't badly injured, it seemed.

It broke her heart when she'd had to end their relationship, but she didn't have any choice. Love paralysed her. She couldn't think or relax knowing it was sure to end. Being neurotic about a love affair ending is, she realised, the same as ending it.

Much as she wanted to care for James, she also felt uncomfortable being near him. It was hard to believe that she had her former lover behind her and her dead father in front. Love and death. They were inextricably linked.

She went down the right-hand aisle, and round the back of the altar, approaching it from the opposite direction from where her father's coffin lay. It unnerved her to have to look at that black box. Earlier, she'd insisted on having the lid put back on.

When she stopped in front of the altar, her fingers tingled. All along, she'd known that if there was any object hidden in the chapel, the altar was the key. It was the chapel's only original feature.

Reaching under the altar, she let her hands roam across the cold marble. Near the edge of the altar, a burning sensation spread through her fingers, the same feeling she got when she touched the sword in Merlin's Cave.

She retreated a few steps and bowed her head, almost ashamed of what she was doing. 'It's inside the altar,' she said quietly. 'In a hollow compartment.'

Morson signalled to one of his men, and the soldier returned seconds later with a sledgehammer. He went over to the place indicated by Lucy and began smashing the altar apart. Soon, he'd cracked it open, revealing the hollow section Lucy had predicted. He quickly hammered away the surrounding marble then seized the lance hidden inside.

Lucy was expecting Morson to be overjoyed. Instead, his face had turned pale. The soldier handed him the spear and stepped away.

'Isn't that what you wanted?' Lucy asked, puzzled by Morson's reaction.

'I was dreading this moment because I don't understand what it means.'

'I don't follow.'

'The one thing we were always certain about was that we already had the real Spear of Destiny in our possession. Hitler himself held it in his hands in the Hofburg Palace in Vienna in 1938. There was no doubt it was the right one. It glowed in his hands, exactly as legend said it would. At the end of the war, General Patton arranged for it to be sent to America while a fake was returned to the Hofburg.'

'General Patton was one of *you*?'

'Have you ever heard of Section 5?' Morson asked.

Lucy nodded. Gresnick had been keen to emphasise the significance of Section 5 in their earlier conversation. She'd found it incredibly intriguing.

'Patton became a believer when Section 5 had a chance to speak to him and present him with the facts,' Morson said. 'Everything they said made perfect sense to him. It was all in accord with his existing beliefs about being a reincarnation of Hannibal and so on.'

'But Hitler's spear must have been a fake too,' Lucy said. 'This is the real one. I'm sure.'

'I can't believe that. What I know, though, was that there were always two spears claiming to be the authentic one used by Longinus. We have the spear that was once part of the Imperial Regalia of the Holy Roman Empire. As for the other, perhaps this is it.'

'You mean the Spear of Antioch, don't you?' Lucy was familiar with the story of the rival spear. During the First Crusade, the city of Antioch was under siege by a large Muslim army and likely to fall at any time. A Christian monk claimed he'd received a vision from St Andrew saying that the Holy Lance was buried in St Peter's Cathedral in Antioch. A lance was duly found and the next day the Christian army marched out with the lance held aloft in front of them and won a famous victory.

Morson nodded. 'Even at the time, many people were convinced the Antioch Spear wasn't genuine. We never took it seriously, yet you're the Chosen One and you've found this spear for us. For all I know, this is indeed the Spear of Antioch, brought back to England from the Crusades and eventually hidden here.'

'There are only four Grail Hallows,' Lucy stated. 'All of them unique and distinct objects. There can't be two spears.'

'Fakes have always been our main problem,' Morson said wearily. 'Fake Grails, fake spears, fake swords, fake dishes. We're not the only ones plagued by fakes. Look at the Catholic Church. Fake pieces of the true cross, fake bones of the saints. The Turin Shroud – a fake. It actually shows the body of Jacques de Molay, the last Grand Master of the Knights Templar. Because de Molay rejected Jesus, the Inquisition subjected him to a mock crucifixion and a fake burial in a shroud. After, he was burned at the stake on a small island in the River Seine in the centre of Paris. So, the Turin Shroud was bogus like everything else. Fake miracles. Fake visions. Fake cures. But you can never underestimate the power of false beliefs, can you? Many more people have died for the sake of fantasies than for the truth. For us, only the truth suffices. We must have the authentic Grail Hallows.'

'I don't understand something,' Lucy said. 'If you thought General Patton took the genuine Spear of Destiny to America and gave a fake back to the Austrians, why did you raid the Hofburg Palace? Colonel Gresnick told me you raided seven different locations. If you're using me to find the Grail Hallows, why did you carry out those raids?'

'We had nothing to do with them,' Morson replied.

62

Lucy was astonished. Gresnick had made a huge play of those raids. Now, it appeared, they were a spectacular red herring. How was that possible? Didn't Gresnick say the evidence showed that only a Special Forces team could have carried out the raids?

'We were furious when we found out about those incidents,' Morson said. 'It drew attention to something we wanted kept quiet.'

'So, who was responsible?'

'I have no idea.'

Lucy was baffled. 'That spear you're holding is genuine,' she said again. 'I swear it.'

'That's what worries me. What better way to destroy us than to send us a false Messiah?'

Lucy was startled. How could Morson think she was a fake when she'd never once claimed to be anything special?

'We've become trapped by the past,' Morson said. 'At all times, we were trying to find ever more secure ways of protecting our secrets, better ways of confusing our enemies, misleading them as to our true intent. But, over time, we lost many of our records. On several occasions, the most important members of our brotherhood were killed before they could pass on their secrets. Now it's practically impossible to be sure of the truth.

'There was only one place that told the unadulterated truth: the history of Gnosticism going right back to the Garden of Eden and up to the siege of Montségur. It was the Cathar Bible, one of the two great treasures smuggled out of Montségur before it fell to the Catholic Crusaders. The treasures were buried in separate locations. The Bible was concealed in a cave somewhere in the Sabarthès Mountains. Crusaders captured the knight who hid it before he could reveal the location to other Cathars. He was taken in front of the Inquisition and tortured, but didn't give anything anyway. They burned him at the stake.'

'So, it was lost forever?'

'As it turns out, no. It turned up two centuries ago in Carcassonne. It's now in the Rare Book Library of Yale University.'

'In that case, what's the problem?'

'It's been dubbed the most mysterious manuscript in the world. In fact it's become a sort of Holy Grail itself. Codebreakers and cryptographers all over the world revere this book above all others. They have no idea it belonged to the Cathars. They call it the *Voynich* manuscript in honour of the man who brought it to public attention. Experts say there's nothing like it. It's written in an unknown script and contains numerous inexplicable illustrations. No one has come anywhere near deciphering it.'

'So, how do you know it's the Cathars' Bible?'

'We have other Cathar documents. They're written in the same script and they contain similar illustrations. The trouble is, only the elite brotherhood who led the Cathars knew the language, and they were all killed, most of them at Montségur.

'The Knights Templar took over where the Cathars left off. They created a new brotherhood and were able to put together much of what was lost, but not everything. The simple fact is that there are holes in our knowledge. We try to fill in the gaps as best as we can, but it's never easy. The Templars themselves were largely wiped out, and again vital pieces of the jigsaw were lost. That, ultimately, was why Hitler failed. He acted on false information. He used fake Grail Hallows. But he didn't doubt the authenticity of the Spear of Destiny for a second.'

'What makes you think you can do any better than Hitler?'

'Because a member of our organisation rediscovered one of our most valuable treasures – Raphael's mural. The mural was Julius II's attempt to preserve our beliefs, but it vanished from our awareness for centuries because it was so inaccessible. Of course, the mural led us to you.'

'But you said I might be deceiving you, that I was a false Messiah.' Something else occurred to Lucy. If everything Morson said about reincarnation was true, a mechanism might exist to rediscover lost history. If you could tune into the memories of your previous souls, the past would open like a book. Maybe the knowledge of the Cathar Bible wasn't gone forever. Maybe someone with the right soul-line could retrieve it.

Perhaps some souls had a vastly superior ability to remember their previous existences. Maybe they were so attuned to their soul-lines, so capable of gaining knowledge and insight from them, that they might seem to possess magic powers. Was it possible that someone like Nostradamus didn't so much see the future as predict how souls were likely to behave in the future? If a soul, such as that of the Emperor Titus, had a lethal hatred of Jews, wouldn't it be logical to predict that the same soul, in the future, would persecute Jews with the same passion, but with greater resources at its disposal? That, then, would be a prediction of the rise of Hitler and the creation of death camps...but it wouldn't be a question of seeing the future so much as projecting the past into the future.

'There's no going back now,' Morson said. 'Besides, you've already brought us the Sword of Destiny.'

'It's just a sword,' Lucy objected. 'You don't know if it's special or not.'

'But I do. Most people, if they were faking the Sword of Destiny, would have tried to use some medieval sword supposedly linked to King Arthur. They wouldn't realise that the Sword of Destiny had no connection with Arthur. It was the sword used to behead John the Baptist. It's an ancient sword from the time of the Roman occupation of Judea – exactly what you brought us. I have no doubt it's authentic.'

'Which sword did Hitler think belonged to the Grail Hallows?'

'I think I mentioned it before: the Sword of St. Maurice. It was kept amongst the Imperial Regalia of the Holy Roman Empire, as a partner to the Spear of Destiny, itself sometimes called the Spear of St. Maurice. Maurice, or Mauritius to give him his Roman name, was the commander of the Theban Legion. He and his men were Christians. In 285 CE, the Emperor Diocletian, who despised Christianity, ordered the legion to be decimated unless they abandoned their beliefs. Maurice refused to carry out the order and so did his men. The entire legion was then executed. The Church made Maurice a saint for his supreme sacrifice.

'Maurice was said to have possessed the Spear of Destiny when he led the Theban Legion, so the theory arose that his sword might also be sacred. As an ancient Roman sword, it looked similar to the one you found. That, of course, is the problem. It's so difficult to separate the genuine ones from look-alikes and fakes. The Spear of St Maurice was genuine, the Sword of St Maurice just an ordinary soldier's sword.'

Lucy was amazed by how complicated all of this was. Was there any realistic chance of bringing together the true Grail Hallows? It appeared impossible. Maybe that was no bad thing, but her intellectual curiosity was growing. What would happen if the genuine Hallows were actually assembled? Would it be a supreme moment of destiny? She almost hoped it would happen.

But everything connected with the Grail Hallows was coded. In fact, it was probably the most elaborate code ever created by humanity. It had to be since the Gnostics' enemies were so ruthless. The Cathars and the Templars were practically exterminated by the Catholic Church. Tens of thousands died. For secrets to survive the Inquisition, they had to be so good that those who kept them would scarcely know what they were concealing. The safest secret was the one no one knew was a secret. The Grail stories had reached that status.

Every part of the tale had pitfalls. Many people thought that the sword that King Arthur pulled from the stone to prove his legitimacy was Excalibur. In fact, the sword in the stone and Excalibur were two entirely different things. The Lady of the Lake gave Excalibur to Arthur. The sword in the stone conferred legitimacy, Excalibur mystical power. The sword in the stone reflected a real, physical sword while Excalibur was a symbolic, spiritual sword. Almost everything in the Grail Romances was conducted at both the literal and symbolic level.

The Lady of the Lake was the symbolic representation of Sophia, the Gnostic personification of wisdom. The Lake was the pool of mystical knowledge – Gnosis. Excalibur represented the sword of Gnostic truth that cut through the lies of the other religions and led the deserving to Gnosis. If you died before you attained Gnosis, you had to return the sword. That was why Arthur's last act was to ask Sir Bedivere to throw Excalibur back into the lake. He had failed to achieve Gnosis because of his obsession with Guinevere, and his personal failure.

Most would miss the story's underlying meaning. They would take the Grail legend at face value as a romantic story, and nothing else. But even when you thought you'd grasped what was really going on, you'd usually discover there was a deeper layer still. It was the ultimate Russian Doll. Was there anyone alive who knew the identity of the final doll in the collection?

Lucy stared at Morson. She'd missed something, hadn't she?

'You said two treasures were removed from Montségur. You only mentioned the Cathar Bible. What was the other?'

Morson swept his hand over his short hair. 'The brotherhood found it at the end of the nineteenth century in the French village of Rennes-le-Château. It's in a safe place now.'

'What is it?'

'Something so wondrous it's beyond human imagining.' His face became hard. 'And it will prove once and for all whether you are a false Messiah.'

63

Lucy had been given a mat to lie on. She was exhausted but couldn't sleep. Every time she closed her eyes, they opened again moments later. Her gaze kept drifting towards the lantern Morson had placed on the half-demolished altar, now the only light in the chapel. He'd ordered everyone to get a few hours sleep before they set off at dawn for their next destination. He'd given no indication of where that might be.

Lucy watched the light reflecting from the lid of her father's coffin. She couldn't decide if she was appalled or comforted knowing her dad's body was so near. As for James, she was just as undecided about his proximity. Part of her felt elated, while another part was freaked out. Raking over her old feelings was the last thing she wanted to do. She wouldn't know what to say to him. The words would dry in her mouth as she tried to communicate how much she still cared for him, while she struggled to avoid being sucked back into the horrors of love.

How could anyone sleep well in times like these? How many hours of life were left? She kept wondering about the second of the Cathars' treasures. What could it be? Some said it was the Holy Grail itself, but the Cathars hated all material objects. A Bible was OK as the first treasure because it had nonmaterial value. Could the second be another source of knowledge? An earth-shattering secret, perhaps? Morson said it was something that could prove whether or not she was a false Messiah. How could she be false when she never claimed to be the Messiah in the first place? Morson had clearly meant it as a threat. What did he intend to do if she failed his test?

****

A soldier was looking down at Lucy, his hand pressed over her mouth to stop her screaming. He didn't say anything, just gestured towards one of the small side rooms. She realised she must have drifted off to sleep. Now, instantly, she was fully alert.

In the dim light, she could see Gresnick, Sinclair and James standing in the doorway. The other soldiers were asleep. What was going on?

She tiptoed to the other room. The soldier who'd woken her followed, carefully closing the door behind him.

'I'm the only guard on watch,' he whispered. 'Punch me as hard as you can,' he said to Gresnick, 'then tie me up. I've opened the side door. You can slip out that way. You'll probably have half an hour before they discover you've gone. Take my flashlight.'

Without hesitating, Gresnick stepped forward and slugged the soldier in the jaw. The soldier slumped to the ground. Gresnick quickly tied him up. 'Let's get out of here.'

They sneaked out of the side door and emerged into the freezing night. Snow still covered the ground. Lucy felt ill. Something was out there, the same presence she'd sensed at Tintagel. She was certain it was something not of this world, and the thought terrified her. She tried to block out all awareness of the thing.

The hearse was still there, the horses tethered to a fence and shivering in the cold.

'Get into the back.' Gresnick gestured towards the hearse with his flashlight. 'I can drive one of these things.'

Cardinal Sinclair climbed on top while Gresnick untied the horses, stroking them to keep them quiet.

Awkwardly, Lucy climbed into the back with James. It was spooky to be in the same place where her father's coffin once rested. It was even spookier to be with James. She had no idea what to say to him, and he was just as hesitant. He struggled even to look at her. It amazed her that he was in a fit enough state to be here. Last time she saw him, in the helicopter wreckage at Tintagel, she was convinced he was dying.

The carriage moved off, the sound muffled by the snow. It was so dark it was virtually impossible to see ahead. One tiny bright light stood out in the northern sky. Lucy shuddered. Was that Morson's *Merica*?

James lay with his back to her, breathing heavily. She wondered if she should reach out to him, maybe put her hand on his shoulder. What would it be like to touch him again? But she couldn't, not after the way she'd treated him. Should she apologise? Tell him it was all a mistake? She had no idea what to do and turned away.

The carriage shook from side to side as they found a rough path through the woods and down Cadbury Castle's steep slope.

She wanted to know who had helped them escape. Some sort of double agent? It must have been the same person who released Gresnick from his handcuffs earlier that night. Maybe the soldier had doubts about Morson's plans. Another thought occurred to her. Maybe it wasn't such a good thing to have escaped. Morson's religious opinions were vile, but also hard to disagree with. It was so difficult to know what to think. Good and evil were merging.

'That soldier back there,' Gresnick said eventually. 'He worked for the DIA a couple of years back. He said he recognised me. He couldn't go along with the others any longer. He said they were going "too far, *crazy too far*." He recently met a girl back home. It changed his outlook on things.'

Lucy frowned. It was all so grimly predictable. *Love*, the axis around which everything revolved. She didn't think the soldier had much of a future. Morson was sure to uncover him.

She wondered where they were going. To the nearest army base, the nearest town? Glastonbury wasn't too far. Maybe she'd end up back at her convent. Wherever they were going, it would be difficult getting there. There was no roadside lighting and the snow was swirling in the wind.

After a few minutes, the carriage stopped. Gresnick pointed his torch at a signpost at a roundabout.

'We can go to either Glastonbury or Cheddar,' he yelled. 'Which way, Lucy?'

For a second, she was speechless. Why was Gresnick asking her? Not so long ago, he'd pointed a pistol at her head. 'Are you sure you want me to decide?'

'This is all about you, Lucy. I trust you to do the right thing.'

Do the right thing? Lucy had no idea what that was. She was operating on pure instinct now. To go back to Glastonbury was to go back to her cell, to close the door and wait for the end. There was a time in the last twenty-four hours when that would have been her preferred choice. Now, she wanted something else. *Closure* – of who she was, of Raphael's mural, of whatever role Morson claimed was hers.

'Cheddar,' she said. 'There's a famous Gorge there that I visited it as a kid.' She stared at the bright star in the sky. 'And it contains a cave called King Solomon's Temple.'

64

They had been on the move for over an hour. There were no signs of pursuit. Lucy had expected to see flares exploding in the sky and hear the sound of Morson's trucks, but there was nothing. The snow hadn't let up. That meant it would be impossible to follow their tracks. She wondered if Morson would know to go to Cheddar Gorge, or if he had been expecting her to choose Glastonbury as the next logical move.

They were making slow progress in the dark and heavy snow. Luckily, Gresnick had managed to light a couple of lamps on the side of the hearse, so they had just enough light to see the way ahead, but the main road had vanished beneath the snow. Gresnick couldn't be sure he was heading the right way.

Lucy reckoned they had put about four or five miles between them and the chapel; enough to make it unlikely Morson would find them, at least until morning. This part of the country mostly consisted of fields and woods, so she wasn't surprised when they began to make their way through the edge of a forest.

She sat up, hunched like a ball, clasping her knees and staring ahead. All the time, she was aware of James. He was lying on his side, asleep. She wasn't relishing the moment when they'd have to talk. With all their history, every word would be loaded with unspoken meanings. It was so long since she last deciphered language like that, words that were all subtext and practically meaningless on the surface.

As the carriage made its way through the trees, the road grew narrower. They had probably strayed off the main road and onto a country track. Maybe they were going in the wrong direction. How could they tell? They might need to stop and wait until morning to find their bearings.

As they moved deeper into the forest, Lucy huddled up even more. She was certain they were being watched from the trees. Strange sounds broke out all around. She imagined the floor of the forest had come to life, and millions of insects were crawling towards them.

The trail disappeared and a dense screen of trees blocked their way. The carriage stopped.

'We can't go any further tonight,' Gresnick said.

'We'll freeze,' Cardinal Sinclair objected. 'We need to light a fire, get some proper shelter.'

Gresnick nodded. 'I'll go on a reccy, see if I can find a better spot.'

Lucy got out of the back of the carriage and stood shivering in the dark. The trees swayed in the wind. Their branches kept making odd, creaking noises. She'd never been anywhere quite so creepy.

Sinclair came over, rubbing his hands together. 'Hungry? I found a packed-lunch stuffed under the driver's seat: a couple of sandwiches, some chocolate bars, a couple of bags of peanuts and a carton of orange.'

'Not right now,' Lucy said.

'How are you bearing up? You've been off your medication for a while. Are you feeling a bit strange?'

'I'm OK.'

'What about James?'

'He's asleep.'

'We'll let him rest.'

'Cardinal, I never got the chance to thank you properly for what you did for me back at Tintagel. You saved my life.'

'It was for all our sakes, Lucy. There's only one thing Morson and I agree on: you are destiny's child.'

Lucy couldn't help smiling. As a teenager, she used to listen to a girl-band with that name. She and her friends learned all their dance moves, using them to terrorise the boys at school discos.

'What do you think will happen next?' she asked.

'We're all in God's hands now.'

'Do you believe God would destroy the world to stop Morson doing whatever it is he's planning?'

'God once drowned the world, Lucy. Only Noah and his Ark were saved. Why should he let anyone survive this time? If he does spare us, it will be thanks to you.'

'But I have no idea what I'm expected to do.'

'Just be yourself. That's all anyone can ask of you.'

Gresnick came back out of the woods, his torchbeam piercing the dark. 'I've found somewhere. It looks like a ruined abbey. There's a room with a fireplace. We can stay there for the rest of the night and set out at dawn.'

They found a sheltered spot where they tied up the horses.

'Come on, Mr Vernon,' Gresnick said, waking James, 'we have to move.'

Lucy watched as James stiffly emerged from the back of the carriage, a dazed look on his face. He briefly glanced at her then turned away again.

After tethering the horses, Gresnick led the way through the trees, his boots sinking into the flaky snow.

'God have mercy on us.' Sinclair stopped abruptly.

'What is it?' Gresnick spun round. 'Did you see something?'

'There are wolves in the woods. They're everywhere, staring at us. They have bright yellow eyes.'

They all halted. Lucy peered into the darkness. Sinclair was right. There were yellow eyes all around them. But this was insane: England didn't have any wolves. They were hunted to extinction long ago.

'Why are they so quiet?' Gresnick whispered. 'They're not moving a muscle.'

Sinclair fidgeted with the crucifix round his neck. 'It's as if they're waiting for someone – *something* – to give them orders.'

'Let's get moving,' Gresnick said.

The ruined abbey was just a few metres further on, in a clearing near a stream. The light from Gresnick's torch reflected in the dark water. Drops of snow peppered the surface, melting into it. It made Lucy think of white confetti showering down on newly laid tarmac.

A graveyard full of snow-covered headstones stood in front of the abbey. They had to walk through it to get to the entrance of the room Gresnick had mentioned. Made of sandstone, with a hole in one corner of the ceiling, the room had a large fireplace with blocks of old chopped wood stacked in front of it. A rear door led to other rooms of the abbey. Gresnick checked them out with his torch.

'They're safe,' he said. 'They're all like this one: holes in the ceiling and a few gaps in the walls, but there's no way wolves can get in. There's even a toilet – well, a room with a hole in the ground.'

'We need to barricade ourselves in,' Sinclair said. 'Then we can light the fire and settle down for the night.'

Gresnick and James found some boxes and wedged them in the doorway. Lucy took the chance to visit the toilet. It was as grim as Gresnick had hinted.

Gresnick used a lighter to ignite the firewood. It didn't take long to get a good fire burning. The crackling wood mesmerised Lucy. She stood near it, holding out her hands towards the flames. It seemed miraculous to have found this place in the woods, a sanctuary from all the madness.

'Have you heard of the story about Kafka and his friend Max Brod?' she asked Gresnick. 'They were discussing hope, or, rather, Kafka's lack of it.'

'No, what did they say?'

'I think about it a lot. Brod wondered if there was any room for hope in Kafka's bleak world. Kafka replied, "*Oh, plenty of hope, an infinite amount of hope – **but not for us**.*" I can't get those words out of my mind.'

Gresnick nodded. 'I can see why.' He brought his head down towards hers. 'What about you – do you think there's hope?' Leaning into her, he gently put his hands on her upper arms and held her for a moment.

She looked at him and didn't know how to respond. Again, she was aware of how attractive she found him, and how *wrong* it was. She wanted him to put his arms right round her and hug her, to protect her. A shudder ran through her. How could she be so disloyal to James? 'I'm tired,' she said, stepping away.

Gresnick reached out and gripped her arm. 'Wait, there's something I have to tell you.'

Lucy looked at him. 'What?'

'I lied to you,' he said. 'James never said anything about killing you. I...I don't know why I said it.' He stared at the ground. 'I'm ashamed of myself.'

Lucy was appalled. 'How could you do something like that?'

Gresnick shuffled uneasily. 'When I met you, I didn't expect to...' He couldn't look Lucy in the eye. After an awkward pause, he said, 'I guess I was jealous of James.'

'I can't listen to this.' Lucy freed herself from Gresnick's grip then quickly lay down in front of the fire.

Struggling to get comfortable on the hard stone floor, she kept turning over. Her mind was flooding with alternate images of Gresnick and James. She was so confused. Part of her wasn't nearly as disgusted by Gresnick's revelation as ought to have been the case. He wanted to say that he was attracted to her, didn't he? She didn't dislike the idea.

She had only just managed to keep her eyes closed for a few seconds when the noise began: the baying of the wolves, a primal sound, as though the earth was travelling back in time. Their howling was so loud she thought it would carry for miles. She prayed Morson and his men wouldn't hear.

James got to his feet. 'Someone will need to stand guard. We have to make sure those wolves don't come any closer. I'll take the first watch.'

'Are you sure?' Gresnick asked.

'Yes.' James glanced at Lucy. 'Besides, I need to clear my head.'

65

James took Gresnick's torch and stepped into the next room. His worst fears were coming true. Lucy was *far* too friendly with Gresnick – he had no doubt he'd seen an unmistakable look of lust, even love, on Lucy's face when she'd let Gresnick put his hands on her a few moments earlier – and there was no ambiguity at all about the way Gresnick gazed at her.

Aggressively, he swept his torch round the ruins of the abbey. Ruined love. In the end, it all crumbles. Instead of joy at seeing Lucy again, he was experiencing something else, new and utterly unexpected. *Hatred.* Hatred because she rejected him, because she had such a hold over him, because she was so perfect. Above all, he hated her for being capable of feeling love for others. Was she already falling for Gresnick with his Hollywood good looks and his knowledge of the same obscure subjects that she enjoyed? In many ways they were a perfect match, and that was…unacceptable.

He pointed his torchbeam at the corner of the room. A rat stared back at him. He picked up a stone and threw it towards the vermin, making it scurry away. The stone hit something metallic and he went over to see what it was. He picked up a penknife, in good condition. He opened the blade and touched it. For a second, he stroked it, then abruptly jabbed it into his palm. Blood appeared. *Christ, what am I doing?* He wondered if something had happened to his brain in the helicopter crash, some subtle injury that was causing his behaviour to change. He sensed a rage within himself that he'd never experienced before. It frightened him.

It was so cold here, away from the fire. Shards of ice were growing inside him, jagging into his heart. Why was it that we loved only the ones who got away? They had a magical lustre that time couldn't diminish, unlike those who stayed with us too long and grew stale. Their skin that once seemed so golden and untarnishable all too quickly corroded – second-hand goods with no trade-in value. What price wouldn't we pay to bring back those who left us before we noticed the first specks of rust?

Lucy was more beautiful than ever, even in her white army fatigues. In the chapel back at Cadbury, she'd looked so different from everyone else. They all had camouflage uniforms, while she looked ghostly – or maybe saintly was the right word: pure and virginal amongst the hardened warriors. He'd sensed how uncomfortable she felt with him in the back of the carriage.

She didn't say so much as a word to him – and if he was being honest, he couldn't speak to her either – so he pretended to sleep. Every second pressed down on him like stone slabs on his chest.

It didn't take long, in this Gothic abbey, for the words of Keats' gothic poem that so haunted him as a schoolboy to come back to him. *La Belle Dame Sans Merci* – the beautiful woman without mercy – the perfect description of Lucy.

O what can ail thee, knight-at-arms,
Alone and palely loitering?
The sedge has withered from the lake,
And no birds sing.

O what can ail thee, knight-at-arms,
So haggard and so woe-begone?

It could so easily be about himself. No one ever mentioned the many knights who searched for the Holy Grail but got nowhere. He was one of *them*, the ones who never made it; those who were killed, lost, driven mad: the losers and failures no one spoke about, whose names no one remembered. Lucy was his Grail and she was further from him now than ever. It was impossible to believe there was once a time when he held her in his arms, made love to her, spent as much time as he wanted with her. The past was a mirage. He wished he could set fire to his memories.

He wandered over to the far wall, and looked out of a space where there must once have been a stained glass window. No sign of the wolves. If they were still out there, they weren't making any sounds. There was no noise at other than the faint crackling of the wood in the fireplace in the other room.

He repeated a line from Keats' poem, the one he found most poignant: *And no birds sing.* It was so long since he last heard birdsong. There was nothing he wouldn't give to hear just a few seconds of a bird chirping: a sign that life was normal, that the nightmare might end.

What happened to Kruger? All those men dead back there, killed by Lucifer. It seemed absurd to acknowledge that Beelzebub was actually alive and on earth. Was the creature in the woods now? Lord of the wolves, master of dark places. Was it possible to defeat him? Maybe only an angel like Lucy could manage it.

Sweeping the torch around him once more, he imagined that the shadows were plotting against him, that he had to kill them by stabbing his torchlight into them. There were so many weird shapes. This abbey was like one of those creepy ruins that vampires liked to colonize. It was easy to imagine their coffins in the crypt.

In its time, the abbey must have been a spectacular sight, a beautiful stone edifice next to a babbling brook in the middle of a forest. You couldn't get anywhere more picturesque. The monks who lived here must have found it an inspiring place. They could commune with nature, have as much isolation as they desired. Yet even this idyll crumbled, its walls collapsing, leaving a shell with only a couple of intact rooms.

He crept back towards the other room, noticing the dancing shadows cast by the fire, like the restlessness in his own heart. Would he ever manage to speak to Lucy properly? Or was she too preoccupied with Gresnick now? It seemed incredible that she was so friendly towards a man who'd made it clear he would kill her. Should he tell her that Gresnick promised to shoot her if it came to it? Gresnick was cold-blooded. How could Lucy be falling for his act? That ridiculously perfect smile of his. He was so *fake*.

Peering through a red pane of glass in a broken window, James saw something that made him think an ice-cold hand had gripped his heart.

Lucy was lying on her back next to the fire. Gresnick was leaning over her, his hand softly stroking her arm. The angle wasn't quite good enough for him to see clearly, but he could swear Gresnick was kissing her. The American's hand wasn't being pushed away by Lucy. There was no denying the physical intimacy between the two.

How could Lucy betray him like this? All those years of torturing himself, for what? OK, he was married, but only because Lucy rejected him. She was the woman he wanted to spend his life with. That had never changed, *not once*. Women can't love in the same way as men. They lack that blazing quality, the fire in the soul. Their aim is to humiliate men, to neuter them like dogs.

Now he understood why the grandparents and parents of the Delta Force deserters had opted for male-only offspring. Who could possibly place any trust in females? It was a contradiction in terms. Fickle, protean, they'd slip through any net you used to catch them. They themselves had no idea of what they were, and nor did they care. And the whole thing about test tube babies was clear too. Most Gnostics detested sex, seeing it as the worst instrument of Satan, the mechanism by which new souls were delivered into this hell. So, the test tube technique saved them from having to perform the act they most reviled.

James turned away, wanting to vomit. Had Lucy returned Gresnick's kiss? She loved the American, didn't he? He couldn't let this abomination of love flourish. He had to stop it. A shudder passed through him when he realised there was nothing he wouldn't do to thwart Gresnick. *To stop Lucy loving someone else.* Only then might the birds sing again.

66

When Lucy awoke, it took her a few moments to remember where she was. The fire was still burning and Gresnick and Sinclair were stretched out in front of it, asleep. The world's new style of dawn was throwing its customary red light into the room. Lucy didn't think she'd ever get used to it.

She felt a prickling on the back of her neck, and twisted round to see if something was behind her. For a moment, she thought she glimpsed a figure staring at her through a smashed pane of glass.

'*James?*'

There was no answer. She got up and went into the next room. Patches of red light fell onto the floor through the holes in the roof. A door was open in the corner. James was standing there with his back to her.

She felt uneasy. Should she go back and wake the others? She still couldn't think of anything to say to James. No words seemed to have the right shape. They lacked the meanings she wanted to convey. She had an urge to hug him yet, at the same time, the thought of being in physical contact with him made her squirm. She had buried her love for him as deeply as she could, yet it was always there, always asking why she'd turned her back on it. The reason was obvious enough. Love was a form of death. In the end, love died or the loved one died, so why put yourself through it? Despite herself, she found herself heading towards the doorway. She stopped just behind James. He didn't turn round.

'There's something beautiful about this light,' James said after a moment, then stepped into the small, overgrown garden at the side of the abbey. Lucy followed, her breath condensing in the cold air. The grass and the flowers were covered with snow. An old fountain, miraculously in full working order, sent a plume of water into the air, the water-drops gleaming with the red tinge of the sun. James wandered round to the far side. Lucy stayed where she was. She still loved him, but her heart felt as frozen as this garden. The things she wanted to say were locked inside, clinging to what little warmth remained.

'The soldier who freed us last night – you won't believe what he told me,' James said. 'He was a born traitor, he said. He told me that in previous lives he was Brutus, Benedict Arnold, even Judas himself. He couldn't control himself. Every group must have a traitor. He was a marionette, destined to betray his companions. How could anyone believe such a thing about themselves? None of us is fated to do anything. You know that, don't you, Lucy?'

Lucy didn't answer. Gresnick's version of what the soldier said was much more plausible. Why should the soldier tell a different story to James? Then again, why not? If he were the reincarnation of Judas, he could have any number of duplicitous tales to tell. Anyway, according to Morson, she was even more of a puppet than that soldier.

'What happened to Sergeant Kruger?' she asked.

'He was still alive when I left him. For your sake, I hope he's dead.'

'Why are you saying a terrible thing like that?'

'Because he swore to kill you. If he's alive, he'll track you down.'

Lucy turned away and trudged into the heart of the garden, stopping in front of a thorny bush. A single, absurd, red rose was poking through the thin covering of snow. Crouching down to smell it, she let the scent overwhelm her. She held one of the petals between her fingers. The feel of it, the texture, was exquisite. For a second, she could forget.

At the rear of the garden was the small graveyard they'd chanced upon the previous night. There was something about graveyards that made them so much more poignant when they lay beneath snow. Everything was starker, more in keeping with death. As Lucy walked between the headstones of the monks who once lived and worked here, she thought of her father. Had Morson gone ahead with his plan and burned the body on an open-air pyre on top of Cadbury Castle? It would have been a spectacular sight. The best way to commemorate her father.

Returning to the fountain, she put her hand in the water then instantly snatched it back. She gazed down and felt sick – the water was full of dead goldfish floating on the surface.

'It doesn't make sense, does it?' James said. He was directly opposite her, his body hidden behind the ornamental marble angel that formed the centrepiece of the fountain. 'I mean, it's freezing, but the water in the fountain hasn't iced over. How is this fountain working at all? I bet it hasn't functioned for centuries.'

'Dead fish,' Lucy mumbled, pointing.

'Everything dies.' James's voice sounded so strained.

Lucy deliberately kept her head behind the angel.

'I thought maybe you'd met someone else,' James said.

'What?'

'When you said you didn't want to see me anymore in your letter.'

Lucy bowed her head.

'But there was no one else, was there?'

Lucy remembered one of her conversations with Gresnick. He said he'd seen a DIA intelligence report on her, covering everything that had happened to her in the last year. James must have seen it too. A thin file. She'd done nothing except have a breakdown.

'How about you?' she asked. 'Is there anyone special?' She wasn't certain what she wanted the answer to be. An emphatic yes and, simultaneously, an equally emphatic no. Then she could remain frozen. For the last six months, she'd lived in a glass world where nothing ever changed. It comforted her. Nothing ever got worse; the most frightening nightmares were kept at bay.

There was a long pause. Too long? Long enough?

'No one special.'

****

James wanted to vomit into the fountain. Lucy had reduced him to a liar, made him deny his wife and his beautiful baby. Somehow, he was inside Keats' poem, living it, breathing it. He remembered one line in particular: *Full beautiful, a faery's child.* Was that Lucy? And, of course, the line that haunted him most: *And no birds sing.* Lucy was the one who stopped them singing.

Despite it all, he couldn't find it in himself to stop loving her. He remembered what one of his friends once said to him after he'd been moaning too much on a boozy night out: 'The only haunted house you'll ever enter, James, is your own past. All the ghosts are personal, and no one is ever leaving.'

Everything was on hold until he dealt with Lucy, one way or another. His own life had become estranged from him. He felt as though he were receiving news from a land far away, about someone he didn't recognise. Nothing was scarier than the fact that the person who was your best friend, your soul mate, could become unrecognisable to you in the blink of an eye. With a few words, they could kill your happiness.

The ancient Greeks said you shouldn't eat your own heart. He never understood what it meant, not until Lucy left him: if you bottle everything up, if you don't confide in someone, you'll end up consuming yourself.

'I haven't seen any sign of the wolves,' he said. 'We ought to get going again.' He pointed up at the sky. 'You see that bright light up there? I first saw it last night.'

Lucy nodded. 'I did too. It made me think of the Star of Bethlehem. Maybe someone special has been born somewhere in England.'

James peered hard. 'I swear it's getting bigger.'

67

Half an hour later, they were on the road again. All the wolves had gone, just as James had said. Lucy was worried the creatures might have attacked the horses during the night, but the horses were exactly where they left them, cold but otherwise fine. She and Sinclair climbed into the back of the carriage while James sat up front with Gresnick. It was a relief to be separated from James. The atmosphere between them was like a Chinese water torture, each drip inflicting agony. She longed to go back in time to when she could hold his hand without giving it a second thought, when they sat for hours without saying a word and didn't feel a trace of self-consciousness.

They found a route through the forest and soon reached a sign for Cheddar Gorge, saying it was fifteen miles away. As Gresnick drove the horses forward, Lucy stared back at the forest. In the pale red light of morning, with snow covering the treetops and the ruined abbey peeping out, it was utterly magical.

None of them spoke as the carriage plodded forward. Hours passed as they made slow progress towards their destination. They found an old barn with bales of hay and were able to feed the horses and get them in out of the cold for a while. There was running water, and they all had a drink. After a fifteen-minute break, they set out again.

Lucy kept expecting to hear the engines of Morson's trucks, but the sound never came. The occasional snorting of the horses and their heavy breathing were the only sounds that broke the silence. Further on, Gresnick said he saw a flash of light, as though the sun had glinted off a mirror, or the lens of something...binoculars perhaps.

'Morson?' Sinclair asked. 'He must have spotted us.'

'I don't know,' Gresnick said. 'Maybe it was nothing.'

Lucy felt uneasy. For a while, she'd had the sense they were being followed. Not by Morson and not by anything supernatural. She didn't say anything, but she feared it was Kruger's brother.

By mid-afternoon, an uncanny landscape had materialised in front of them. To the left was a desert of black sand, snowless and stark. Ahead were mountainous slopes covered with pebbles and huge boulders, the crests snow-capped. To the right, an impenetrable forest of black trees, snow-laden on one side, without a trace of snow on the other. Why was snow lying in some places but not others? Lucy didn't realise England contained terrain like this. But the hills were familiar enough – the Mendips, through which Cheddar Gorge gouged its path.

The carriage stopped in a designated picnic area for tourists. They all got out to stretch their legs and the men went for a toilet break. Lucy, dehydrated and hungry, didn't feel any need. She stood and gazed at the bleak terrain.

When the men had returned, they debated what to do next. It appeared that a landslide had cut off the main route through the Mendips. James went over to an information point that provided a large map of the local area. He confirmed that the main road shown on the map was exactly where the landslide had occurred. They would have to find another route.

'There's a track over the hills,' James said. 'It will take us straight to Cheddar Gorge.'

Lucy gazed at the hills in front of them. They didn't look inviting.

'Isn't there another road?' Gresnick asked. 'A long way round?'

'There are two other possible roads. One's about a mile away and the other's a further ten miles.'

'We can rule out the ten-mile trip,' Gresnick said. 'The other sounds perfect.'

'What if there's been a landslide there too?' James objected. 'Maybe going by foot is the best bet now. According to this map, we're only a couple of miles from the heart of the Gorge.'

'I'm not going hill-walking,' Sinclair said. 'Let's try the other road.'

James shook his head. 'What makes you think that road will be in any better condition than the one in front of us?'

Their bickering voices gave Lucy a headache. She turned away and went over to one of the picnic tables. Flopping onto a wooden bench, she sighed then looked back at James. When they went out together they never argued.

The others eventually came over to join her.

'We've agreed to meet back here in an hour,' James said. 'I'm going up the hilltrack to see if there's a clear route. The others are taking the carriage to check out the next road.' He held out his hand. 'You can come with me if you like, Lucy.'

She saw how eager he was for her to say yes. It was such a simple word to say, yet often the hardest. 'I'm tired,' she said weakly. 'I think I'll have to take the carriage.' Seeing how crushed James looked, she bowed her head and stared at the top of the picnic table as though it were the most interesting object in the world.

'*Christ!*' Gresnick yelled.

Lucy looked up. Far to the north, the brilliant light they'd seen before was vastly bigger, practically a second sun.

'That's heading straight for us,' Sinclair bellowed.

The light in the sky had transformed itself into a huge fireball travelling obliquely at incredible speed through the atmosphere, leaving a blazing trail in its wake. There was no question it was on a collision course for the earth.

Without warning, a light brightened the horizon and the air warped into a vast shimmering heat-haze. For an instant, it was as though the sky were splitting apart. Seconds later came a thunderous roar accompanied by a stinging, raging wind, so forceful it knocked them over. Gravel-sized stones showered down everywhere.

When the worst was over, they all slowly got back to their feet. A vast column of smoke was visible in the distance. There was no trace of the fireball any longer.

'My God, what happened?' Sinclair's voice was quivering.

'I think that was an asteroid,' James said. 'I remember reading about this type of thing. An asteroid exploded in mid-air over Siberia a century ago. Witnesses said there was a blinding light followed by a deafening thunder. They were knocked off their feet by the wind. Afterwards, it was estimated that trees were flattened over an area of eight hundred square miles. If it had happened over a major city, it would have been like a thousand atomic bombs going off.'

They all looked at each other. Birmingham and its satellite towns, with a population of several million, weren't so far away.

'Let's get moving,' Gresnick said. 'I don't think we have much time left.'

68

Lucy squeezed onto the same seat as Cardinal Sinclair as they set out again. She twisted round to glance at James as he marched up the hill. He looked so forlorn.

'That spear you found back there at Cadbury,' Sinclair said. 'We need to understand what significance it has. Why was Hitler so interested in the Spear of Destiny? How does the spear he took from Vienna relate to your spear?'

'My grandfather was obsessed with Wagner's opera *Parsifal*,' Gresnick interrupted. 'The Spear of Destiny plays a central role. My grandfather thought it proved Wagner was a Grand Master of a Gnostic cult.'

'My father used to love listening to Wagner too,' Lucy said.

'Wagner was never to my taste.' Cardinal Sinclair grimaced. 'I presume *Parsifal* is about Percival, the knight who found the Holy Grail. Where does the Spear of Destiny fit in?'

The horses had practically stopped and Gresnick had to urge them on with a riding crop. 'Wagner's opera is based on Wolfram von Eschenbach's book *Parzival*,' he said when they were going at a reasonable pace again. 'It's set in medieval Europe. A mountain castle called Monsalvat overlooks a forest and a beautiful lake in inaccessible terrain. Monsalvat is the Grail Castle, almost certainly modelled on the Cathars' stronghold at Montségur. The Grail King is called Amfortas and he's served by the Grail Knights; men who have vowed to protect the Grail with their lives.

'Their great enemy is Klingsor, a black magician of the highest degree who once tried to join the Grail Knights but was rejected because of his uncontrollable sexual lust. Insanely, Klingsor castrates himself to try to cure his condition, but the Knights still refuse to allow him to join their Order. So, Klingsor becomes their sworn enemy, pledging to do everything to destroy them.

'The Grail Knights guard the Grail Hallows, including the Spear of Destiny, but Klingsor manages to steal the Spear and later uses it to wound Amfortas in the genitals. It's a spiritual as well as physical wound that never heals no matter how many medicines are applied to it.

'From his dark castle, Klingsor, with the power of the Spear flowing through him, dominates all the lands around. Meanwhile, Amfortas lies in agony in the Grail Castle, tormented by his incurable wound, powerless to resist Klingsor and praying for the return of the lost Spear.

'A prophecy says that an innocent fool will find the Spear and cure Amfortas. Parsifal chances upon the Grail Castle and is allowed to witness the Grail Keeper's most sacred ceremony. In the great hall of the Grail Castle, Amfortas and the Grail Knights prepare to commemorate the Last

Supper, with Parsifal looking on. When Amfortas tries to remove the veil that covers the Holy Grail, the pain of his wound grows worse than ever.

'When the chalice is uncovered, it glows. Parsifal watches the strange ceremony, but takes no part and doesn't ask Amfortas any questions about his wound. Parsifal is then ordered to leave the castle and told never to return.

'Klingsor, aware of the prophecy regarding the innocent knight, guesses Parsifal is the knight in question and lures him to his wondrous castle. In the castle's magic garden, enchanting flower-maidens beg to make love to Parsifal but he turns them all down. Klingsor then uses a beautiful sorceress to try to seduce Parsifal. The sorceress is Kundry, a Jewish witch who was present at Jesus' crucifixion and who mocked him as he hung on the cross. Cursed to live forever because of her crime, she's despicable and tragic. It was she who, with promises of perverted sex, entrapped Amfortas, which led to the Grail King's wounding by Klingsor.

'When Kundry kisses Parsifal, the young knight recoils, but, at the same time, he's overcome by profound insights. He understands why Amfortas was tempted, and he feels the Grail King's longing and suffering. The world, he realises, is an unending circle of pain and despair. Only through compassion and renunciation of the pleasures of the flesh can the circle be broken. He's full of regret for the lack of pity he showed at the ceremony in the Grail Castle. Why was he so insensitive towards the Grail King? Now he knows what he must do to help Amfortas.

'Klingsor, thwarted, flies into an uncontrollable fury, and hurls the Spear of Destiny at Parsifal, but it miraculously stops in mid-air. Parsifal reaches up and grasps it. As soon as he does so, Klingsor's castle of enchantments disappears.

'For years, Parsifal struggles in vain to find the Grail Castle once more. It seems to have vanished from the real world. After many trials, he's allowed a second chance to enter the sacred castle. The castle is full of gloom, the Knights sunk in despair because they've been deprived for years of the spiritual sustenance provided by the presence of the Spear. As Parsifal brings the Spear close to Amfortas, the tip begins to bleed and he touches the King's wound with it. Instantly, the King's wound vanishes.'

'What did your grandfather think the hidden meaning was?' Sinclair asked.

'Parsifal is regarded as a symbol of Christianity, and Klingsor of paganism,' Gresnick said, 'and the story is about how the purity and compassion of Christianity triumph over the primitive passions of paganism.

'But a Nazi called Hermann Rauschning claimed that Hitler interpreted *Parsifal* very differently. Rauschning said he found the notes Hitler scribbled on his programme when he first saw *Parsifal*. Hitler, according to Rauschning, believed it was a story about the purity of blood – *racial hygiene*. Amfortas's incurable sickness was caused by his perverted sex with a Jewess. His blood had mixed with hers and was now eternally tainted. The Grail Knights' sacred task was to protect the purity of Aryan blood. Untainted blood was the secret of life – the real Holy Grail. Impure blood, racial mixing, on the other hand, was a catastrophe, leading to bestial breeds driven by primal, degenerate instincts.

'Klingsor's enchanted castle was the world of temptation where pure Aryan blood was in danger of being contaminated by non-Aryans. Parsifal was the great hero because his blood was never corrupted. He was able to resist Klingsor's blandishments and Kundry's offers of wild sex. The recovery of the Spear was the restoration of Aryan purity. Amfortas had sinned by having sexual intercourse with a Jewess. His genitals were the source of his downfall. When the holy Spear was used to touch his genitals, his blood was miraculously re-purified and he was cured. The Grail Castle was the perfect Aryan world. Klingsor's realm threatened that purity, and it was the task of all good Aryans to take the role of the Grail Knights and resist the corruption of their Aryan blood.'

'But you don't accept either interpretation, do you?' Sinclair said.

Gresnick smiled and shook his head. 'My grandfather believed Wagner was a senior figure in a German secret society known as the Order of the New Templars. Strongly Gnostic, the Order of the New Templars believed that the Grail Knights were the Knights Templar themselves. Amfortas symbolised Gnosticism, while Klingsor was Christianity. The Grail Castle was the True God's pure world of light while the Castle of Wonders was the material world of the Demiurge. Amfortas's incurable wound was the loss of so many souls from heaven to the evil world of matter. He could only be cured by the return of all souls to heaven. The lesson of Parsifal is that only an innocent fool can achieve that, using the Spear of Destiny. The Spear is the key, not the Grail. And...a final point...it's necessary that blood be shed.'

'You think I'm the innocent fool, don't you?' Lucy found it hard to look Gresnick in the eye.

'A nice, sensitive Catholic girl seized from an asylum? I'm afraid you fit the bill perfectly.'

'And you think I'll shed blood, that I'll kill someone with the Spear?'

'Yes.'

'But Parsifal didn't kill anyone.'

'Let's hope this turns out the same way, but I doubt it.'

Gresnick turned to Sinclair. 'What if Hitler somehow got it wrong, and the Vienna Spear is a fake?'

'Well, if that's the case then thanks to Lucy's efforts back at Cadbury, they now have the genuine Holy Lance of Longinus.'

Gresnick scratched his head. 'We're missing something, aren't we? All along we've been concentrating on the Grail Hallows and practically ignoring something else of equal if not greater power.'

'The Ark of the Covenant,' Lucy said. 'But didn't you say it was blown up in front of the White House?'

'I don't think that was the real Ark. No one who believed in its power would blow it up, and no one who didn't believe in its power would go to all the trouble of stealing it. And if everything that people say about it is true, I doubt it could be destroyed anyway. Besides, didn't you get the impression that Morson knows exactly where it is?'

Sinclair nodded. 'Nevertheless, I don't understand where it fits in. The Grail Hallows are all associated with Christianity, but the Ark is purely Jewish. It's never been mentioned in the same breath as the Hallows.'

'You're right.' Gresnick said. 'The Ark disappeared from Jewish history long before Jesus' time. He never set eyes on it.'

'What's your take on the Ark?' Lucy asked Sinclair. 'Do you think it's just a glorified treasure chest?'

'In the Bible, the Ark is a gold casket that contains not only the Ten Commandments but also the very secrets of Creation. It holds the answers to all of our questions about where humanity came from and where we're going. It's also literally God's throne on earth. Some people go further and say the Ark is the portable house of God: he actually lives inside it. Moses, they point out, would address the Ark directly and say things like, "Rise up, Lord, and let thine enemies be scattered and let them that hate thee run for their lives before thee." In a sense, the Ark *is* God. That's practically how the Jews regarded it. That's why they were so obsessed with it, and why it haunts them to this day. They've never recovered from its loss.'

'Hold on,' Gresnick said. 'Are you saying that to find the Ark is to find God?'

'According to the Jews, yes.'

Gresnick rubbed his head again. 'The Ark and the Spear of Destiny are both said to possess massive, unimaginable power, the power of God himself. Is that what this is really all about? The Gnostics are going to do something with the Spear and the Ark to unleash the power of Creation.'

'It looks that way, doesn't it?' Sinclair said. 'Maybe these Gnostics are planning something so sacrilegious it will bring the final wrath of God down on us.'

'What kind of sacrilege?' Lucy asked.

'That's what we need to work out. But don't kid yourself, Lucy. Morson is determined to make you part of it. You must prevent it. If you fail, the world will end in a matter of hours.'

69

James trudged up a stony path. He couldn't believe Lucy had refused to come with him. Was she deliberately torturing him? Always, he was supportive, understanding, loving, and all he got in return was to be treated like this. When he reached the summit, he turned and looked back. A frozen landscape stretched before him. It looked like the land of the dead. He could imagine millions of male ghosts as wretched as he was wandering through this snowlocked land, their hands trembling with misery, playthings of faerychildren like Lucy. All of them had the same story to tell, the tale Keats told so chillingly:

> *I saw pale kings and princes too,*
> *Pale warriors, death-pale were they all;*
> *They cried – 'La Belle Dame sans Merci*
> *Thee hath in thrall!'*
>
> *I saw their starved lips in the gloam,*
> *With horrid warning gaped wide,*
> *And I awoke and found me here,*
> *On the cold hill's side.*
>
> *And this is why I sojourn here*
> *Alone and palely loitering,*
> *Though the sedge is withered from the lake,*
> *And no birds sing.*

That was exactly where he was – on the cold hill side, with no birds singing: *Lucy's world*. An impossible word entered his head and for a second it took his breath away with just how absurd, how shocking, it was; a word he couldn't possibly associate with Lucy. Yet the word refused to go away, and he realised something inside him had changed in the most disturbing way. A switch had been flicked, an irrevocable switch. The word was so bold in his mind it might as well be written in the sky for everyone to see.

Evil.

Kruger was right – Lucy was the Chosen One of Lucifer. One of the ancient signs was a blazing, destructive light in the sky, just as they'd seen less than an hour ago.

With his mind harbouring ever-darker thoughts, he resumed his walk and found a small rope bridge crossing a chasm, with a river far below. Next to the bridge was one of those old telescopes he used to find at the seaside as a kid, where he could put in a coin and look at passing ships for a minute or two before a shutter came down and everything turned black.

On a summer's day, the view from here was sure to be spectacular. For a second, he longed to be a kid again, blissfully unaware of creatures like Lucy. He squinted through the eyepiece and was astonished to find that it was working perfectly. Someone must have jammed the mechanism.

He swung the telescope in the direction taken by Lucy and the others. It didn't take him long to locate their carriage. As he gazed at the terrain just ahead of them, his mouth fell open.

Jesus Christ, he thought, what the hell is *that*?

70

'Look how spooked they are.' Gresnick fought to control the horses as they struggled to turn away.

'What *are* those things?' Sinclair couldn't hide his alarm.

They were confronted by a vast field full of strange upright pointed structures that resembled flower buds or seed pods. Each was bright green and taller than a basketball player. It was like a scene from *Invasion of the Body Snatchers*.

'I saw one of those at Kew Gardens a couple of years ago,' Lucy said. 'They come from the rainforests of Sumatra.'

'So what the hell are they doing in England?' Gresnick was still struggling to pacify the horses.

'I can't remember their proper name,' Lucy said, 'but their nickname is *corpse flowers*. When they bloom, they make an appalling stink like the odour of rotting flesh. It can take these things up to six years to flower, and then they keep their bloom for only a couple of days. That's why people are so fascinated by them. Nearly every Botanic Garden in the world has one.'

'Look, all the snow is melting round the flowers,' Gresnick said. 'How did it get so hot all of a sudden?'

Lucy was trying to remember all the things she'd learned about these bizarre flowers. They could metabolise sugars to accelerate vaporisation and help spread their stench faster. The amount of energy they generated allowed them to produce a temperature several degrees above air temperature.

The horses didn't want to go anywhere near the flowers. They were snorting frantically, shying away, trying to go back the way they'd come.

'Something's near,' Lucy said. 'I've felt this before. *Something terrible*.'

'I feel it too.' Sinclair gripped the crucifix hanging round his neck.

Lucy expected to see the darkness of the past and future, darkness itself, rising up from behind the flowers.

As they watched, the structures began to open. They were like weird, organic chimneys belching out hot, putrid stenches into the air, vapours that would attract carrion insects. In seconds, the soil around the flowers came to life. The fetid odour had brought every insect from miles around.

'*Listen*,' Gresnick yelled.

There was an extraordinary buzzing sound, as if the air had an electric current flowing through it. The sky darkened as a cloud of flies appeared over the flowers. The whole area now smelled of putrefying flesh. Hundreds of thousands of flies, millions maybe, were heading from all directions towards the flowers – huge, rancid beacons of hell.

The odour was unbelievably foul now, as if the air were turning to poison. Lucy held her hand over her mouth and nose. The horses reared up.

'Jump off,' Gresnick shouted. 'I can't hold them any longer.'

Lucy and Sinclair both leapt off. Gresnick had to throw himself to safety as the horses stampeded away.

'Shit!' the colonel grunted. 'I think we've lost them for good.'

While he and Sinclair stared at the disappearing carriage, Lucy walked forward towards the nearest corpse flower. Black beetles were swarming over her feet, but she scarcely noticed. She gazed, transfixed, at the amazing structure with its velvety maroon interior. Reaching out, she touched the fleshy yellow upright stem. Without warning, it collapsed, as though its immense weight was suddenly too much for it. All across the field, other corpse flowers did the same, withering and dying.

Gresnick came over and put his hand round Lucy's arm. 'Come away from here. This place is dangerous.'

As he spoke, Lucy heard a scuttling sound. Tens of thousands of cockroaches emerged from the collapsed insides of the corpse flowers and swarmed towards her. Black rain lashed down, probably an after-effect of the asteroid explosion.

'*Run!*' Sinclair bellowed.

They sprinted away from the seething mass of insects and didn't stop until they'd put hundreds of metres between themselves and the corpse flowers.

Sinclair was exhausted. He vomited into a snowdrift at the side of the road. Lucy bent over too, gripping her knees.

Gresnick hauled her upright. 'Are you OK?'

She nodded. The stench of the corpse flowers clung to every part of her.

'Don't go off like that ever again.' Gresnick wrapped her in his arms. 'You're the most precious thing in the world.'

Lucy pressed herself against him and kissed him.

71

James turned away from the telescope, shaking. *No doubt now.* Lucy was mocking his love for her. She'd cast a new spell; found a fresh victim. He recalled a Biblical injunction: '*Thou shalt not suffer a witch to live.*'

His mind worked fast. The others would have to use this path to get to Cheddar Gorge. He would go down shortly to meet them then bring them back up here.

Staring at the rope bridge, he knew what he had to do. Clutching the penknife he found at the abbey, he walked towards the bridge. He carefully frayed the undersides of the main supporting ropes, trying to judge how to ensure it would collapse when someone got halfway across. He would send Lucy across the bridge first. And that would be the end of it.

A hard frost had descended as the sun started to go down. Everything was slippery. It would be dark by the time they were ready to cross so no one would notice the damage to the ropes. He stared at the narrow, winding river far below. Lucy would topple down there, the child of the Devil falling into the abyss. It was the right – the *Biblical* – ending. And then the birds would sing again.

****

It was a pitch-black night and the temperature was falling rapidly.

'A rope bridge? You didn't say anything about that when you told us about this track.' Gresnick stared incredulously at the flimsy structure, as he swung his torch from one end to the other. 'It doesn't look safe.'

'We don't have a choice,' James said. 'This is the only way to the Gorge. It's a tourist trail, so it should be OK.'

'It's either this or trekking for miles to find a ford or a proper bridge over the river,' Sinclair said.

'We don't have time.' Lucy had lost patience with all of this talking. She stared down into the chasm. The rushing water made a rumbling sound that echoed off the steep cliffs. The thought of crossing over that narrow bridge terrified her.

The full moon, garishly red, threw a queer light over the water. A line of beautiful white swans appeared, making their way upriver. Even in the red-tinted moonlight, they seemed brilliantly white, like creatures from another reality. They were so serene, oblivious to the chaos of the world. Even the river became calmer.

'Let's cross,' Lucy said.

'You go first,' James said.

'No, I'll check it out.' Gresnick glanced at James. 'You don't look so good, Vernon. Are you sick?'

'I'm fine.' But James's hands were trembling uncontrollably.

We don't want to take any chances,' Gresnick said, 'so no more than one on the bridge at a time, right?' He carefully made his way across the five-metres-long rope bridge.

Lucy prayed nothing would go wrong. James was as intent on the bridge as she was. She gazed at him and wondered how on earth she could possibly have kissed Gresnick. What was *wrong* with her? She was so confused. Should she confess? But James would hate her. She wanted to cross hand in hand with him. In the time when they went out together, she loved the way he never refused her hand when she wanted to hold his. So few men realised how much women appreciated it.

'Christ, that didn't feel safe.' Gresnick stood on the other side, looking back anxiously. 'You next, Vernon.'

'*No*, Lucy next. We need to get her over to the other side.'

Lucy shrugged. 'OK.' Gingerly she stepped onto the bridge and edged her way along, gazing straight ahead, gripping on tightly to the support ropes. *Don't look down.* The bridge started to sway beneath her feet.

'God, it's giving way,' Sinclair yelled.

'Your hand, quick!' Gresnick desperately stretched out towards Lucy.

She tried to grab his hand, but as she was reaching out, one side of the bridge collapsed completely.

Screaming, she thought she was toppling into empty space. It took her a moment to realise she was dangling, not falling: Gresnick had caught her.

'Hang on, Lucy. I can haul you up.'

She closed her eyes and began praying. *Out of the depths.*

When her eyes opened again, she was lying on her back, with Gresnick crouching over her. 'Are you all right?'

She feebly waved her hand in the air then rolled onto her stomach. She gazed across the chasm where James was staring at her, his face sheet-white.

'In God's name, are you OK?' Sinclair asked.

'I'm all right.' Lucy's voice hardly rose above a whisper.

'I knew it was mad to use this bridge.' Gresnick glared at James. Pointing his torch at the frayed ropes, he squinted hard.

'What is it?' Sinclair asked.

'I think those ropes have been tampered with.' Gresnick looked straight at James. 'You *bastard*.'

'Don't be ridiculous,' Sinclair said. 'James was next to cross.'

'But he held back, didn't he? He knew exactly how dangerous it was.'

'Lucy, you can't possibly believe I'd ever harm you.' James turned to Sinclair. 'It's an old bridge…it….' He sounded frantic.

Lucy wondered why Gresnick would make such an appalling accusation. James was obviously telling the truth. 'It was an accident,' she said.

Gresnick turned his back.

'What are we going to do now?' Sinclair asked.

'We'll find another way.' James looked at Lucy. 'We'll meet you at the top of Jacob's Ladder. Do you remember?'

'I remember.'

'Jacob's what?' Gresnick snarled.

'It's a long flight of steps leading down into the gorge,' Lucy explained. 'James and I went there a few years ago.'

'Just keep following the trail,' James said. 'It's not far. There's another bridge a mile down the track on this side. We'll meet you as soon as we can.'

****

'That was a close call back there.' Sinclair and James were scrambling over patches of black ice, making the rough track even more treacherous.

James nodded. He was trying to appear calm, but inside he was a wreck. When Lucy hung over the ravine for those couple of seconds, he was simultaneously willing her to fall and praying she wouldn't.

When he caught her gazing at him afterwards, with shock in her eyes, he felt stomach-churning guilt, yet it infuriated him that Gresnick was playing the hero. The American had declared his willingness to be Lucy's assassin. Now, it seemed, he was not only willing to do anything to save her life, he wanted to take her as a lover. The *Lucy Effect* – everyone succumbed to her in the end. The Devil's daughter.

'Strange, the bridge collapsing like that,' Sinclair remarked.

James was glad it was too dark for the cardinal to see him clearly. His eyes would betray him, he was sure. Sinclair was the Vatican Enforcer, the head of the organisation once called the Inquisition. He was certain to see his sins, lit up in neon. That was the purpose of the Inquisition, after all. To force your secrets out of you, one by one. Nothing concealed, the truth dragged out, ready or not. He had to change the subject, get the cardinal to think about something else.

'Cardinal, I've heard people claiming that the Knights Templar discovered something in Jerusalem – incontrovertible proof that Jesus was married to Mary Magdalene and had a child – and that they used this evidence to blackmail the Catholic Church and extort money to guarantee their silence.'

Sinclair laughed. 'It's amazing what credence is given to the most crackpot of theories.'

'What's the truth?'

'The truth is much stranger than any fiction, and nothing is odder than the story of how the Knights Templar were formed. In 1118, Hugh de Payens and eight other French noblemen turned up in Jerusalem. King Baldwin I greeted them warmly and, amazingly, allowed them to set up their HQ in a prime location on Temple Mount. For nine years, the knights didn't recruit a single person to fight the Muslims. In fact, they never left their HQ. There's practically no evidence of what they actually *did* do during those years. Everything was shrouded in secrecy, but it seems they spent the whole time digging in the foundations of Solomon's Temple that lay directly beneath their HQ. There had always been rumours that Solomon built secret passages, in which he hid his great treasure.

'It was clear that these knights were more interested in archaeology and treasure hunting than in protecting any pilgrims. What were they digging for, that's the question. Something that they knew was buried in Solomon's secret passages? The Ark of the Covenant, perhaps? Remember that the sole purpose of the Temple was to house the Ark. The Ark vanished from history over two and a half thousand years ago, and no firm trace of it has ever been discovered, though rumours abound.'

'What did they find?' James asked. 'I mean, the Templars were famous for their wealth. Did they find Solomon's treasure?'

Again, Sinclair laughed. 'The wealth of the Templars is no mystery. Every recruit had to donate all of his possessions to the Order, and many of these recruits were very rich. Noblemen from all across Europe made vast donations of money, goods and land. Don't forget, the Templars were the celebrities of Christendom – the poster boys to use the modern jargon – famed for never retreating and always fighting to the last man. They attracted all the patrons, all the sponsors, all the money. In addition, they were international financiers, inventors of the modern banking system.

'Far from threatening to expose shocking revelations about Jesus to the Pope and having their silence bought in return, the Templars didn't breathe a single word of what they discovered in Jerusalem. They acknowledged that they had looked for the Ark, but maintained they didn't find a thing.

'They were lying, of course, as the Inquisition eventually discovered. They confessed that what they'd actually been searching for was a set of ancient Gnostic parchments. These promoted the Johannite heresy that John the Baptist and not Jesus was the true Messiah. It transpired that the original nine Templars were all related to Cathar families and it seems they were sent on a mission by Cathars to retrieve lost documents that shed light on various Cathar mysteries.'

'You're saying they made no attempt to blackmail the Pope?'

'Of course not. The idea that they found proof of Jesus' alleged marriage to Mary Magdalene is laughable. What would constitute proof? A dusty document? The Vatican is full of dusty manuscripts seized from heretics propounding every weird and wonderful heresy conceivable. A painting of Jesus kissing Mary? Anyone can paint. Bones? So what? The world is full of them. Nothing could possibly prove that Jesus was married. Even if it were written in capital letters in bold red ink in a document called *The Gospel of Jesus*, it still wouldn't be credible. Heretics have always faked evidence to spread their lies.

'If nine knights arrived in front of the Pope to claim Jesus was a married man with a child, they wouldn't have left the Vatican laden with treasure to buy their silence...they wouldn't have left the Vatican at all. They would have gone straight to the stake.

'Besides, if they had anything remotely like proof of these crazy claims, don't you think they would have made them public as soon as the Vatican ordered their arrest? At that point, there would have been no possible reason to hold back. Yet not a shred of evidence appeared, demonstrating conclusively that they didn't have any in the first place.

'No, the Templars' game was to pretend to be the most faithful and loyal Catholics of all, while secretly spreading their vile heresy. Far from claiming that Jesus was married, they would have been the first to denounce such an idea, thus seemingly proving how orthodox they were. But the Catholic Church is always vigilant, and we eventually penetrated their secret world and exposed their heretical beliefs, practically indistinguishable from those of the Cathars.'

'But didn't I read somewhere that the Church actually absolved the Templars of heresy?' James asked.

Sinclair smiled sardonically. 'The Church was infested with friends and allies of the Templars. Their corruption was everywhere, even in the highest echelons of the Vatican. But the Pope saw through the pro-Templar propaganda and overturned that false verdict and rightly condemned them.'

James felt an uncomfortable affinity with the Templars. He knew exactly what it was like to lead a double life. When you conceal secrets, they start to burn through your soul. Sooner or later, they would melt all the way through and out into the open where the whole world would see them.

72

Lucy, straining to see in the dark, gazed down the hillside. Her parents brought her here to Cheddar Gorge when she was ten years old and her dad said he'd buy her ice cream if she could get to the top of Jacob's Ladder in under fifteen minutes. Although she slipped a couple of times, she made it in fewer than twelve and got a delicious Knickerbocker Glory as her reward.

She always thought racing up the 274 narrow steps of Jacob's Ladder was a big achievement: it was a feat certainly beyond her now. Even going down the steps looked strenuous.

Up here, on a clear day, tourists got a fantastic view of the Mendip Hills and the 300-acre Nature Reserve on the clifftops. The view was even better from the wooden lookout tower. On a summer's day, you could glimpse the peregrine falcons that nested in the high cliffs. She wondered if any were still here, or if they'd fled like the people.

It was also possible to see Glastonbury Tor in the far distance. In a strange way, her life had always revolved around Glastonbury. Her mum was always keen to tell her about Glastonbury's great myths and legends. To a child, they seemed wondrous. It was then that she developed her lifelong interest in esoterica.

On the summer's day when the family came here, they sat on the grass and had a picnic from a hamper. Lucy's mum told her the tale of the original Jacob's Ladder. Jacob, the patriarch whose twelve sons became the founders of the twelve tribes of Israel, was camping outdoors as he made a long journey. He rested his head on a stone and tried to get some sleep. He had a dream in which he saw a ladder extending from earth to heaven, with angels ascending and descending.

Lucy had longed to see those angels. As for Jacob, she disliked him when she discovered he bought the birthright of his brother Esau for 'a mess of pottage.' To her child's mind, she thought it strange that messy porridge featured in the Bible. Besides, it seemed nasty to steal your brother's birthright. Even worse, he impersonated his brother to get the necessary blessing of his blind father. It was the act of a sneak who'd do anything to achieve his goals: a cheat, a liar, a man without a shred of morality. The very name Jacob meant *deceiver*.

'The Gnostics hated Jacob,' Gresnick commented.

Lucy gazed at him for a moment. They'd hardly spoken since the incident on the bridge. She couldn't believe how vile he was for accusing James. Now, she was glad to return to some sort of normal conversation.

'I didn't know that.' But it was no surprise. She wasn't a fan of Jacob either.

'Israel was named after Jacob.'

'What do you mean?'

'Don't you remember the Bible story about Jacob and the angel?'

'Of course. Jacob wrestled with the angel all night long. Neither could gain any advantage.'

'That's right, but what happened next?'

Lucy shrugged.

'For fighting so well, the angel gave Jacob the name *Israel*, which means *One who struggles with God*. Ironic, huh? I mean, how can the Israelites, the Chosen People, be the ones who struggle with God?

'Gnostics reached what to them was an obvious conclusion. The Israelites are the Chosen People of the False God and it's the True God with whom they're struggling. The very name of their nation proclaims the truth.'

'How did the Gnostics interpret the story of Jacob's ladder?'

'They thought the descending angels were souls being lured to the earth by Satan. The ascending angels, on the other hand, were the souls who'd achieved Gnosis and could at last return to heaven.

'According to Jacob, he had his famous dream at a place called Bethel. The stone he rested his head on was known as the Bethel Stone. Legend says that the Bethel Stone eventually found its way to Ireland and then to Scotland, where it became known as the Stone of Destiny. The kings of the Scots were crowned on this sacred stone. The English king Edward I seized it during a war with the Scots and took it to Westminster Abbey, where it was then used in the coronation ceremony of English monarchs. But Scots believed that Edward was given a fake and the real stone never left Scottish soil. A prophecy said that if the true Stone of Destiny should ever leave Scotland, the world would end.'

'It's bizarre to hear Ireland and Scotland being mentioned in all of this.'

'Not really. For one thing, the Scoti, the people who gave their name to Scotland, were actually an Irish tribe. Apparently, it was common for ancient

Egyptians and Israelites who found themselves in trouble in their countries to flee to Ireland. It was a welcoming country, far from the reach of their enemies. And from Ireland it's only a short way to Scotland.

'The Scoti were supposedly named after a pharaoh's daughter called Scota, who left Egypt at the time of the Jewish Exodus.'

'Where did you hear this story?'

'It's in an ancient manuscript called the *Scotichronicon*. I've heard that the reason so little is known about Jesus between his teenage years and the ministry of the last three years was that he wasn't in the Holy Land at all. He was somewhere in the British Isles – Glastonbury perhaps, or Tara in Ireland. In Dunvegan Bay, off the Isle of Skye in Scotland, there's a small island called Eilean Isa, meaning *Island of Jesus*, where Jesus was said to have stayed for a while. The Outer Hebrides in Scotland have many local traditions claiming that Jesus, his mother and uncle, all spent time there.

'It doesn't end there. My grandfather found Gnostic documents claiming that many of the survivors of Atlantis made their way to Scotland, and that Scotland became the Ground Zero of Gnosticism, the epicentre from which Gnostic beliefs radiated across the world.'

Lucy smiled. The Scots she'd met in her life didn't strike her as the great, lost race of Atlantis. They seemed rather too keen on the *water of life*.

'You have a lovely smile,' Gresnick said.

'What?'

'You have no idea of how beautiful you are, do you?'

Lucy felt blood rushing to her face. 'Don't say that to me.'

'Why not? It's true. I can't help it.'

'But...*James*.'

'Come off it. James is a married man with a child.'

'James is *married*?'

73

'There they are.' Gresnick pointed his torch at Sinclair and James as they came trudging along the track towards the lookout tower.

'Give me the torch.' Lucy snatched it from Gresnick, and led the way down the steep steps of Jacob's Ladder. *Married*! She kept saying the word, until she barely recognised it any longer. In all the time she was with James, he never once lied to her. How could a man deny his own wife and child? But there was another emotion – jealousy. She ought to have been James' wife. Only now did she realise how lonely she was. In her stupidity, she'd driven away the only person who still meant anything to her.

As for Gresnick, what did he think he was playing at, saying those things? How could he think she had any strong feelings for him? She liked him and thought he was handsome, but that was as far as it went. It would take her the rest of her life to get over James.

'It's six p.m.,' Gresnick said. 'You know what that means.'

Six hours, Lucy thought, before 30 April 2012 – the most fateful day in human history. Could all the mistakes of a lifetime be repaired in six hours? Were people all over the world praying, screwing, screaming? Did it matter? She thought weeping was the right response. Six billion sets of tears on the last midnight of humanity.

No one spoke as they reached the bottom of the steps and set foot in Cheddar's great gorge. They made their way along the base of the limestone cliffs towards the entrance to the main cave that nature had painstakingly carved from the rock.

There were no lights, apart from Lucy's torchbeam. The world was lowering the final curtain and turning off the stage lights. There would be nothing left but void. Did anyone have the right answers to what life was all about? The Catholics, the Jews, the Muslims, the Buddhists, the Hindus? The Gnostics? Or any of the rest of the ranting voices proclaiming the absolute truth without a shred of evidence. At midnight, someone would be proved right, or maybe no one would. In a way, she thought that was the just outcome. Humanity wrong to the bitter end, still lying to itself as it exited the stage it had disgraced for so long. No curtain call required.

The Cheddar Gorge ticket office was abandoned, every door left open. Cheap souvenirs – guidebooks, crystals, precious stones, beads, miniature models of the Gorge – were scattered everywhere.

Lucy searched for a control panel and flicked a switch. Lights came on.

'Good, the generator still works,' Gresnick said, taking his torch back from Lucy.

They made their way to the entrance of the cave and prepared to go inside.

'Is this wise?' Sinclair asked. 'We could get trapped in there. If the entrance gets blocked, there's no escape route.'

'The third of the Grail Hallows is inside,' Lucy said. 'I'm going in.'

Sinclair put his hand on her shoulder. 'But we don't have the other Hallows. What's the point in continuing with this?'

'I have to do it.'

The opening in front of Lucy looked like a gaping hole in the earth – a hellmouth – but she strode forward, the others scurrying after her.

When she found herself in the dreary, grey entrance chamber, she remembered how disappointed she was as a child to see nothing but ordinary cave walls. *You'll see stalactites and stalagmites*, her parents had promised her. She'd seen those mysterious things in books and she was expecting to be instantly greeted by a host of wonders. Luckily, they were just round the corner.

She felt as though she were walking over her own footsteps of twenty years earlier, her present self haunting her former self, or the other way around. It always spooked her to retrace the steps of her past, ghosts colliding in the dark.

They went past a railed-off pit where a 9000-year-old skeleton was found in 1903, belonging to a man who'd been ritually sacrificed and buried. A fissure going deep into the ground was filled with dark water. As a kid, Lucy was convinced a monster hid in that water. It seemed more likely than ever.

On the right was a cluster of musical stalactites called *Ring o' Bells* that made chiming sounds if you struck them with a rod. They enchanted Lucy on her last visit, but now she barely glanced at them.

She led the group up a flight of steps then through a narrow tunnel. As they reached the end, a white stalagmite cascade known as the Frozen Waterfall confronted them. From there they emerged into a chamber called St Paul's because it reminded the man who discovered it of St Paul's Cathedral in London. Breathtaking when Lucy first saw it, it was no less impressive second time around.

Iridescent stalagmites, glinting in the artificial light, covered one wall. Then came a feature called Aladdin's Cave, like something from a fairyland, with its stalactites enchantingly reflected in an artificial pool. It was the sort of pretty grotto that, as a child, Lucy wanted to take back to her house so that she could crawl into it every night and soak up its magic.

She twisted round and saw that the men were all gazing, awestruck, at the spectacles within the chamber. But she got no sense that the third of the Grail Hallows – the enigmatic dish – was nearby.

The dish had an uncertain status. For a few experts, the gold, jewel-encrusted dish on which John the Baptist's was paraded in front of Herod was the true Holy Grail. Chrétien de Troyes, the first man to mention the grail, described it unambiguously as being held by a beautiful young woman using both of her hands. *Graal*, the precise word de Troyes used, was an old French word for dish. How could a dish be confused with a chalice?

'It's in the next chamber,' Lucy announced, her words echoing as though she'd thrown her voice from somewhere else. 'The chamber is called King Solomon's Temple. I think that's the right place to find a sacred object.'

She led the group along a short passageway and into the chamber. They went past another fabulous stalagmite cascade, and encountered three more striking formations known as A Pillar of the Temple, The Archangel's Wing and The Organ Pipes.

They came across a second frozen waterfall, much bigger than the previous one, this one known as Niagara Falls. Nearby was a feature called the Frozen River. Lucy stopped. Her fingers tingled, just as they did at Tintagel and Cadbury.

She remembered Nostradamus's cryptic words about this panel of Raphael's mural: *Bring me his head on a plate. The wrath of God. The hard path to paradise. You must go under the earth to find the truth. Beneath the water that freezes.*

Those final words: *Beneath the water that freezes.*

No mystery now. She stepped past a guardrail and clambered up onto the Frozen River, standing several feet above ground level. It was incredibly slippery and she was glad her army boots gave her a good grip.

'Be careful,' Sinclair said.

For a moment, the sound of the cardinal's voice startled Lucy. Why was he the one to speak, and not James or Gresnick?

She made her way along the strange white, solid river, holding her arms in front of her in case she had to grab hold of something to stop herself falling. Everything was covered with a thin film of water, sparkling under the electric lights. When she reached a miniature waterfall at the rear of the river, she stopped. Her whole body was electrified. She imagined that if the lights were turned off, she'd shine like a spectre. Was that what she'd become? – an unearthly presence, an anti-person. She haunted people, made them miserable.

Crouching down, she put her hand in a space behind the frozen waterfall. Her fingers stretched out, groping, and soon she touched cold metal. Instantly, a carousel of images spun in her mind. So much pain. *Blood*. A great arc of red. Pain. Darkness. *Death*. Calling to her through time.

She pulled out a spectacular, glinting gold dish, studded with rubies and emeralds: a platter fit to serve a king. John the Baptist's severed head, she didn't doubt, once rested on this, his hair matted with sweat and blood, his eyes still open, crusted with his last tears. It was presented to Herodias, Herod's wife, as the most perverse of gifts, following Salome's deadliest of dances.

Lucy sensed the dish's other use, something dark and strange. It was from this same dish that Jesus served bread to his disciples at the Last Supper. Why *that* dish? How did Jesus get hold of it in the first place? Joseph of Arimathea bought it from Herod, didn't he? The whole thing was a conspiracy against John the Baptist by Jesus and his followers. That was certainly what the Johannites believed. The dish, they considered, was the proof: a mockery of John's death, a sign of the conspirators' triumph. But it didn't save Jesus in the end. The Johannites struck back and avenged their leader.

Lucy found Sinclair standing behind her.

'Does it speak to you?' he asked.

'What?'

'The past reaches out to you, doesn't it? History whispers to you. You're so privileged.'

There was something odd about Sinclair's tone. Also, the way his eyes gleamed as he gazed at the dish...

'I'll take that off your hands, if you wish.' Sinclair gestured towards the dish.

Lucy shook her head. 'No, I'll hang onto it.'

She and Sinclair retraced their steps and joined the others. James and Gresnick were standing exactly where she'd left them, their expressions oddly vacant.

'What now?' Gresnick asked.

Lucy didn't know what to say. There was only one Grail Hallow left – the Holy Grail itself. Or, rather, the object Robert de Boron claimed was the Grail. Lucy had no idea where to find it. Raphael's panel showed a castle on a wooded mountain overlooking a lake. There was no such place near here.

'Well, first, let's get out of here,' Sinclair said.

Lucy gazed at James. There was such a pained expression in his eyes.

'What do you think, James?'

'This is your show.'

My show? That was the last thing this was. She was the puppet, unable to see the strings.

She headed for the path back to the entrance. They entered a large passageway, with boulders stacked on one side. She remembered from her childhood that this chamber contained a strange cave shaped like a black cat. She found it frightening back then. It had lost none of its creepy aura.

Walking fast, she led the group down a long flight of steps that broke out into a much larger passage, not far from where they'd come in.

'Stop!' Gresnick hissed.

Lucy looked quizzically at him. He put his finger over his mouth. She concentrated hard, trying to understand what had made him so agitated. Then she heard it: an engine ticking over.

'Morson's found us,' Gresnick said.

74

All the lights went out. Lucy shook her head, dismayed. Was it meant to end this way?

'What are they doing?' Sinclair whispered as Gresnick switched on his torch. There were no sounds of footsteps, no signs of pursuit. 'Are they just going to wait out there?'

'There's another way out,' Lucy said. 'There are lower levels to these chambers. They haven't been opened to the public because they regularly flood, but they exit further up the Gorge. They might be passable.'

'We don't have a choice,' Gresnick said. 'Let's get moving.'

Lucy took Gresnick's torch and swept it around the passageway. A *Do Not Enter* sign behind a roped-off area showed the entrance to the lower levels.

'We're not cave explorers,' James said. 'We might get trapped.'

'It's either this or Morson,' Sinclair said. 'I'm willing to take my chances.'

'We're wasting time.' Lucy marched off, pushing the security rope to one side.

Ducking under several low archways, she entered an enormous cave. As she made her way further in, she heard queer, scuffling sounds and bizarre echoes. She swept her torch round but it showed nothing other than damp cave walls. Green slime dribbled down in a few places.

Taking a few more paces, she found her steps becoming increasingly laboured. The cave floor was covered with some sort of glue.

'What is *this*?' Gresnick complained.

'It's shit,' James said. 'There's a bat colony here.'

Lucy pointed her torch at the cave roof, then nearly dropped it. A mass of bats was hanging there, twitching.

'Jesus Christ, they're everywhere,' Gresnick gasped. 'There must be thousands of them.'

Lucy stood there, transfixed. She pictured them swooping down all at once, a dense choking cloud heading straight for her. They were probably vampire bats. They'd suck every drop of blood out of her.

'We have to keep going,' Sinclair said. 'They're not doing anything. Our luck might hold.'

Lucy wasn't sure she could take another step. She switched off the torch for fear of attracting the bats. Darkness enveloped her. All she could think of was the bats, the terrifying sound they'd make if they attacked. Just a question of time. She was aware of something else – a feeling of unutterable dread. It was there at Tintagel, there at Cadbury, and now it had arrived here. Something malignant was following her – darkness, darkness itself.

'Can't you feel it?' she asked.

'Move,' Gresnick barked.

'I feel it,' James said. 'It's found us.'

'What are you talking about?' Gresnick snarled.

'There's no time.'

Lucy managed to struggle forward, but now she heard new sounds – writhing, scurrying, as though the walls and ground were coming to life.

Panicking, she switched on her torch again. Hundreds of thousands, millions maybe, of spiders, beetles, centipedes, ants and small black snakes were carpeting the cave floor, swarming all around her feet.

Unable to control herself, she vomited over the creatures nearest her feet. She felt as though her insides were dissolving.

Gresnick gripped her arm and dragged her away. They moved as fast as they could, under another low arch and into a fresh cave. Then they halted. The new cave was glowing yellowy green: the ground, the walls, the roof, everything.

'Fireflies,' James said. 'Adults and larvae.'

Firefly larvae, Lucy knew, were called glow-worms. In ancient China, they used to collect the glow-worms and fireflies and put them in transparent containers to make primitive lanterns. She'd always wanted to see them. Not anymore. They were terrifying, like the tiny lights of hell.

'Luciferin,' James said.

'What?'

'It's a light-emitting chemical. That's how these things glow.'

Luciferin – Lucifer's light. The luminescence of hell. That's what this was. That's why the sea at Tintagel glowed, and why this cave was glowing. Every dark creature glowed when their master was near.

Fear flooded every cell in Lucy's body. The cave's yellow-green luminescence was slowly changing to aquamarine, and she knew it wouldn't be long until it was pure blue: somehow, the world was conspiring to become her worst nightmare. Her forehead was saturated with sweat. She had a fever coming on, with hot and cold shivers running up and down her body.

'We're lost, aren't we?' Gresnick said.

Lucy shook her head. 'I promise you, there's a way out. I remember now what the tour guide told us when I came here as a kid. He said there was a passageway behind one of the waterfalls. It was where the men who found the caves first broke in.'

'So, we go back?'

She nodded, embarrassed by her mistake.

'There are pools of pitch in here,' James said. 'Can't you smell it?'

'So what?'

'If there's a spark, the whole place goes up.'

'Come on, let's get out,' Gresnick shouted.

Before they could move, the cave erupted.

'God preserve us,' Sinclair yelled.

All of the fireflies had become airborne. They were joined by an overwhelming, buzzing, seething mass of wasps, bees and hornets. Then the bats joined in from the adjacent cave, filling the entire chamber with their flapping wings and high-pitched squeaks. On the ground, all the insects had reappeared, and there were rats too, thousands of them.

Lucy screamed and pressed her hands against her ears to shut out the din. The gates of hell were wide open and hell's creatures were swirling and scampering around her like a whirlwind, but nothing touched her, not a thing.

As her torch futilely picked out individual creatures from the surging mass, she noticed that the front of her uniform, round her groin, was red.

Jesus, God. Bleeding? Her period? But it wasn't the right time of the month. It felt as though her insides were gushing out, her body attempting to invert itself. She sank to her knees, trying to scream, but unable to find any sound. Maimed. Cut. She thought of the Fisher King, incurably wounded, speared in the genitals by a black magician. The whole lower half of her uniform was red now. The blood was spreading everywhere. She patted herself in horror and then her hands became bloodstained too.

Is this how it ends? Surrounded by her worst fears, every nightmare come true.

Bats were swooping around Lucy's head, rats crawling over boots. All the safety barriers in her mind were collapsing. There was nothing left except the blue that always haunted her. The last circle of hell – the purest blue.

Flames leapt up. The creatures started to screech hysterically.

Was this how she'd die? Trapped in a vision of the inferno. Apocalypse now. Just as Raphael's mural predicted.

Amidst the bedlam – the chaos of wings, fangs, eyes, screaming, a maelstrom of movement, a glowing, fluttering whirlpool trying to suck her in, a seething pit of life and death – she heard one strong, determined voice: Gresnick's.

I've set the pitch on fire. We have to leave right now, Lucy...Jesus, you're wounded.

Wounded? Lucy shook her head. Physical explanations. Straight lines. Cause and effect. Things that made sense. But now, down here in the shadows, logic had lost its power. Only unreason existed here.

She felt pressure against her arms, oddly reassuring. She was being gripped, propped up – Gresnick on one side, James on the other. Her two knights. They would get her to safety somehow, she was certain. The smoke and the flames would kill every other creature in the caves.

They managed to retrace their steps. Lucy's head kept lolling back, and every few seconds she let out a whimpering moan. Had she been stabbed in the stomach? She panicked when she realised she'd lost the dish, but then she saw it in Sinclair's hands. He must have grabbed it from her in the confusion.

In minutes, they were back at the Frozen Waterfall.

Lucy's lungs were choked with smoke, stopping her from speaking. She pointed frantically at a small gap in the solid rock. Gresnick went in first.

'There's a narrow passageway. I can see an old door. I think Lucy's right – we might be able to get out.' The door was controlled by a rusting wheel mechanism. Gresnick gripped it with both hands and managed to turn it. 'It's moving,' he said. 'We're going to make it.'

Lucy felt an odd exhilaration, as if she were in control of her fate for the first time since leaving the convent. Still here. Still fighting. She took the dish back from Sinclair.

They all squeezed through the doorway and emerged into the outside world. A main road was in front of them and sheer cliffs behind. Before they had a chance to get their heads straight, they heard an explosion. The sky turned bright pink.

'Flare,' Gresnick said.

From left and right, shapes appeared – soldiers, pointing their assault rifles. Morson was in the centre of the group, with a pistol. 'Give me the dish.' He beckoned at Lucy with his free hand.

She didn't move.

'Have you had an accident?' he asked. He marched up and took the dish from her. 'Well, your journey's almost done. In a few hours, it will all be over. Now we're taking you to one of our most special places: Carbonek.'

'What's there?' Gresnick asked.

'The Holy Grail,' Lucy said.

75

Morson kept checking his watch. He had made Lucy sit upfront with him in the driver's cabin, vowing not to let her out of his sight again. He said they were going to a private estate set in a valley close to Glastonbury.

Lucy didn't take her eyes off the road. More snow was falling. The world was trying to hide its blemishes, she thought. There was a constant pressure in her abdomen, as though her guts wanted to dribble out. She didn't dare look down for fear of seeing how much blood was staining the lower half of her uniform. Looking in the rear-view mirror, she caught a glimpse of herself. Some creature stared back, like a murderer, her face smeared with blood, hair filthy and straggling, eyes sunken.

Best to close her eyes, to try to avoid seeing what lay ahead. Images flooded her mind. She was in a forest where every tree was made of mirrors, and the grass made from filaments of mirror.

Running through the mirrored woods in her bloodstained uniform, Lucy knew she was being pursued by something. Time? Love? Hate? Her face was reflected back from mirrored leaves dropping from the trees as a wind blew through mirror world. Everywhere, she was confronted by her reflection, fluttering to the earth. A million mirrored butterflies with her image trapped in their wings.

She tried to run faster, away from her life. Instead, she saw her past flashing up on the mirror trees, her personal history transformed into reflections hanging from branches, shaking in the wind.

Got to outpace the reflections, to escape from the forest. But when she emerged from the trees, she ran onto a mirrored lake. She stood in the centre of the gleaming surface. Her life in a mirror. A reversed life. And then it cracked. She toppled in, taking a cascade of mirrored shards with her.

Her eyes flashed open.

The two military trucks had stopped in the outer courtyard of a stone castle on the crest of a steep valley. *Carbonek.* It was one of the names given to the Grail Castle of legend.

'Get out,' Morson ordered.

Lucy clambered out, feeling dizzy. When she looked up at the sky, she was amazed by the spectacle. Thousands of shooting stars of every colour were showering down across southwest England. Her legs wobbled beneath her as she took a few steps across the snow-covered cobblestones.

'This is a recreation of Montségur at the time it fell to the Catholic Crusaders,' Morson said.

Lucy had never known of the existence of this place, even though it was so close to Glastonbury. It ought to be a famous landmark, yet she hadn't come across a single reference to it. It meant the owners controlled all the land around here, all the roads; that they could stop newspapers and TV channels reporting on it. These must be people of immense wealth and power. The puppetmasters standing in the shadows.

She twisted round, looking for James. He was with Sinclair, his head bowed.

Soon it would be 30 April, sixty-seven years to the day since Adolf Hitler shot himself in his bunker. People thought he chose that day to kill himself because the Soviets were within a few hundred yards of his bunker and might make a final breakthrough at any moment. Now, Lucy knew, April 30 was the Gnostics' most special day, the day when they believed the rule of Jehovah, the Demiurge, would end once and for all. Hitler had thought that day would come during his own lifetime, that he would instigate the final act. Instead, he ended his own world on April 30. Was the outcome Hitler craved about to come true now? It was still impossible to imagine that the heartbeat of the world was hours from being quenched.

'Everyone inside,' Morson barked.

Lucy joined the others as they trooped through the castle's portcullis and into a second courtyard, this time within the castle walls. At the rear was a tall, rectangular keep, lit by blue floodlights. A ghost castle.

In the centre of the inner courtyard was a black wooden tower with many ledges, each packed with ravens. Lucy shivered as she stared at the black birds. Every one of them watched her, tracking her as she moved.

Morson heaved open an iron door and motioned with his pistol for everyone to go inside the keep. They entered an entrance area, covered with familiar banners: the Square and Compasses of the Freemasons, the Rising Sun of the Gnostics, the Soul Bird of the Alchemists, the black over white flag of the Templars, the Cross pattée of the Templars, the Templars' Skull and Crossbones, the Cathars' blue swastika on a white background, the Nazi swastika and the lightning flash runes of the SS. Finally, the largest banner of all – two matching serpents – the Mark of Cain.

Lucy found it grotesque. It was so hard to accept that all of these groups were just different aspects of a single ancient religion whose sole aim was to destroy Jehovah's world. No one had ever guessed at such a link, but it all stacked up. All of these groups featured in well-known conspiracy theories.

Perhaps the truth was that there was only ever one conspiracy, stretching through history from the dawn of humanity.

Morson opened a second door at the far end of the entrance room and led them into a grand hall with a large fireplace, crackling with blazing wood.

A round table took pride of place in the middle of the hall, with a Nazi swastika painted in its centre. Lucy was appalled. That symbol had always nauseated her: the banner of the crematoria. Yet here it was, being paraded as some sort of knightly symbol, the emblem of King Arthur's valiant court. How could the chivalry of the shining Knights of the Round Table be linked to the horrors of Birkenau? It simply couldn't be true.

Morson's soldiers took up position all round the hall, leaving Lucy with Gresnick, James, Sinclair and Morson. One of the soldiers went towards a pair of black velvet curtains covering one of the walls. When he drew them back, Lucy gasped.

In front of her was a perfect reproduction of Raphael's mural. To the left of the mural was the bald-headed eagle that appeared on the front of the Great Seal of the United States of America and the back of the dollar. To the right were the pyramid and eye shown on the reverse of the Great Seal. Above the mural were the words of the official motto of America, *In God We Trust*, and beneath, *Novus Ordo Seclorum* – New Order of the Ages.

Sergeant Morson looked at Lucy. 'Now, do you understand?' he said. 'Everything that the world believes is separated is in fact connected. Who would have thought that a direct link existed between the Nazis and the founding fathers of the Unites States of America, that America is the Promised Land of Cain's descendants, that the American people are the new Templars, the new Cathars, the people in whom the power of Alchemy has reached its highest point. It's no accident that it fell to America's most elite soldiers – Delta Force – to bring this mission to its conclusion. The longest, most complex mission in history was always ours to finish.'

Out of the corner of her eye, Lucy noticed Cardinal Sinclair stepping forward. Morson spun round.

'Who told you to move, holy fool?'

For some reason, Sinclair seemed much more upright than before, taller. He held out his right hand, and the light glinted off a gold ring on his index finger.

Lucy's mouth fell open. *Her father's ring*.

Morson was transfixed. Like an automaton, he knelt down, bowing his head. He took Sinclair's outstretched hand and kissed the ring.

'I had no idea, *Grand Master*,' he said. Lucy gasped.

'Who else could it be?' Sinclair replied. 'What greater irony could there be than that the head of the Holy Inquisition was the arch heretic? – in the midst of the enemy's fortress, whispering into the ear of their leader. The last place anyone would look for the supreme heretic was at the top of the department charged with heresy hunting.'

'Of course. It seems so obvious now.'

'Now I'll summon the others.' Sinclair walked away and it was obvious this castle was somewhere he knew very well indeed. *It was his home.*

Lucy couldn't help herself and stepped forward to study the copy of Raphael's mural. Even now, it shook her to see her own painting lodged in there in one of the world's greatest works of art, created by her in a past life. If soul lines truly existed, it meant we were all inextricably tied to the past. The memories of our previous lives were buried inside us, part of our unconscious that bubbled to the surface every now and again, incomprehensible and terrifying. We were haunted by ourselves, by what we'd done in our past lives, by what others did to us. One life, *this* life, was problematic enough. To add hundreds of other lives was to multiply misery. It was a recipe for constructing hell inside our heads.

She gazed at each of the panels, following them round as they told their strange story, similar and yet dissimilar to the traditional Christian story of the world. Only the most brilliantly conceived depiction of heresy could be smuggled under the noses of the Vatican. It reminded her of the story of Hieronymus Bosch. Some said the Dutch painter was a high priest of heresy, yet the ultra-orthodox Spanish king Philip II loved his paintings. We see what we want to, don't we? Only those who know the code can read it.

Lucy heard an odd clanking sound and twisted round. Thirteen knights entered the hall wearing black mantles emblazoned with the scarlet Templar cross. Over each of their hearts was a silver skull and crossbones. The men had a terrifying aura, as though they'd brought the brutality of the medieval world with them. Even Morson looked uneasy. One of the knights carried a black box.

As Lucy retreated, the thirteen knights took up position in a straight line in front of Raphael's mural. The one in the centre took a step forward – Sinclair.

'We are the Invisible College,' he said, 'the governing body of the *Illuminati*. We are the Shining Ones, the Holy Light. In the past, a group known as the College controlled the Illuminati, but a shadow leadership was established to take over from the College if they should be killed or captured. In the 1930s, the College had become corrupted and consisted entirely of members of the Nazi Party. By the end of May 1945, all but one were dead, including the Grand Master Adolf Hitler who had perverted the true message of Gnosticism. The single survivor passed control to the Invisible College, all of whom were British. In fact, we're all Scottish now, bearing some of the most illustrious names in Scottish history: Bruce, Wallace, Douglas, Randolph, Keith, Moray, MacDonald, Fleming, Burns, Stewart, Maxwell, Hume and Sinclair.

'Many of those names were present at the Battle of Bannockburn, the greatest military victory in Scottish history. It was fought on one of the most special days of Gnosticism – 24 June, the feast day of John the Baptist. The

Scots won despite being massively outnumbered and up against thousands of English heavy cavalry, the medieval equivalent of tanks.

'It's fitting that Scots should be in control at the end. After all, a Scotsman discovered America. The outlawed Templar Fleet that sailed from France in 1307 was led by one of my ancestors, Admiral William Sinclair, the true discoverer of the Americas. A secret sailing route was established between the Americas and Scotland, controlled by my family. One of the main stopping points on the route was Nova Scotia – *New Scotland*. Another of my ancestors, Henry Sinclair, established a Templar base there.

'The Scots have always been at the centre of world events, and Scotland's own story reflects the Gnostic struggle. When the Scottish king Robert the Bruce was hiding in a cave from his enemies, he watched a spider struggling to spin its web and learned the Gnostic lesson of having to try, try and try again. The Gnostic mission was to deliver mankind from hell, to restore every lost soul to the embrace of the True God. America was Scotland's child, the superpower we created to help us fulfil our destiny. Fifty million Americans have Scottish blood in their veins. The Declaration of Independence is based on the Declaration of Arbroath, written in 1320 asserting the independence and freedom of the Scottish people and their right to make and unmake their rulers.'

He gave a signal and the knight holding the black box walked over to the round table, placed it on the edge of the table and opened it.

Lucy was revolted when the knight brought out a preserved head and laid it on top of crossed bones on a crimson velvet cushion.

'That's the *caput mortuum*,' Sinclair said, 'the dead head of the most mysterious man in history. Those are his thighbones. This is where the Skull and Crossbones originated.'

'*Whose* head?' Gresnick asked.

Sinclair smiled. 'Your grandfather's lifework was to understand *The Cainite Destiny*. He passed the task to his daughter and she to you. Well, here in Carbonek you'll find all the answers.

'Contrary to what Sergeant Morson believes, we've deciphered the Voynich manuscript. The man who looks after it in Yale University works for us. He made a breakthrough a few years ago, one he kept secret from the academic community. When he was on holiday in Carcassonne in France, an antiquarian book dealer offered him an original manuscript of Chrétien de Troyes' book *Conte del Graal*, the source of the first Grail story, together with a second unknown manuscript. The main manuscript was written in old French, the second in gibberish as far as the book dealer was concerned. What he didn't know was that it was exactly the same "gibberish" that appeared in the Voynich manuscript. Our inside man was certain the second manuscript was also the *Conte del Graal*, but written in the Cathars' secret language. By comparing the two manuscripts line by line, our inside man was able to finally decode the language of the Voynich manuscript and provide a full translation.'

Lucy gazed at Gresnick. Despite everything, his eyes were gleaming. He was hanging on Sinclair's words.

'The Voynich manuscript says that after the disaster at Atlantis, the religion of Cain was almost destroyed. All of the high priests died, and the religion was extinguished with the exception of a few fragmentary pages of the *Book of Cain*. A few survivors reached Scotland. From there, a few ventured back to the Middle East, in an attempt to rediscover their religion.

'The man to begin the task in earnest was John the Baptist. He used baptism to symbolise the process of embracing Gnosticism. To immerse yourself in water, he said, was to show your willingness to bathe in the sea of true knowledge. But John always maintained that a second, greater man was to follow him. He made his famous statement: *After me One is coming who is mightier than I, and I am not fit to stoop down and untie the thong of His sandals.*'

'That was about Jesus, wasn't it?' James said.

'Don't be absurd.' Sinclair's face instantly darkened. 'John the Baptist despised Jesus. He called him a liar, a deceiver, an occultist and sorcerer who led astray his followers. One of his most famous quotations about Jesus was: *He perverted the words of the light and changed them to darkness and converted those who were mine and perverted all the cults.* On another occasion, he said: *Do not believe him because he practises sorcery and treachery.*' Sinclair pointed at the preserved head. '*That's* who John thought the Messiah was.'

'It's Simon Magus, isn't it?' Gresnick said.

'Very good, colonel. Simon Magus is the most overlooked figure in history, the lost prince of humanity, a man so brilliant, so knowledgeable, so capable of extraordinary feats, that people thought he was a magician. The Simonians, the Gnostic sect that most revered him, said he was God come to earth, just as the Christians said about Jesus. Irenaeus, one of the early leaders of the Christian Church, branded Simon Magus "the father of all heretics." Eusebius in his *Ecclesiastical History* declared Simon the "first author of heresy." He was accused of being the founder of Gnosticism.

'Some experts think that the beliefs of the Cathars and the Knights Templar can be traced back to the Johannite Gnostic sect. In fact, the Johannites were only a minor influence. The Simonians and the Cainites were the true forbears. Both were inspired by Simon and were based on the lost religion of Atlantis, the religion Simon rebuilt.

'The Templars were said to worship a head called Baphomet. The head right in front of you is the very object. They didn't worship it because they would never have worshipped any material object, but they thought it brought them closer to the True God. If you apply the code-breaking Atbash Cipher to *Baphomet,* you get the ancient Greek word *Sophia* meaning *wisdom*. That's what Simon was – the Father of Wisdom, the man who recovered the lost knowledge of Atlantis, who restored Cain to his pre-eminent position amongst men.

'Simon was the reincarnation of Cain, just as Hitler was. Jesus Christ was the reincarnation of Abel, and so was Stalin. When Cain and Abel are reincarnated at the same time in history, the world is always plunged into terrible conflict.

'If things had turned out differently in the conflict between Simon and Jesus, Simonianism would now be the official religion of much of the world, and Christianity would be a forgotten cult. But Jesus, tragically, won.

'Many Simonians and Johannites pretended to become Christians but they were told: When Jesus oppresses you then say: *We belong to you. But do not confess him in your hearts or deny the voice of your Master, the high King of Light, for to the lying Messiah the hidden is not revealed.*'

'What happened to Simon Magus?' Gresnick asked.

'When John the Baptist was executed because of Jesus' conspiracy, Simon knew he would be the next target. He fled – to Scotland. Jesus then proclaimed himself the Messiah, sickeningly claiming to be the one prophesied by John the Baptist. Simon struck back, using two of his secret followers – Caiaphas, the High Priest of the Temple, and Pontius Pilate, the Roman Governor. Jesus was crucified on the mount of Golgotha, the place of the Skull, but his body vanished after his death. Either it was spirited away by his followers, or Jehovah the Demiurge caused it to vanish. Whatever the case, the story caught the world's imagination and the abomination of Christianity took root. Simon, who returned to Judea after Jesus' death, couldn't stop its rise and was eventually executed by Christian assassins, with the same sword that struck off the head of the Baptist. The severed head was displayed on the same platter that John's was once placed on. The head, the sword and the dish were preserved as holy relics, the only objects valued by Gnostics. The head is over there, and Lucy has found the sword and dish.'

'But that's not how Simon Magus died,' Gresnick said. 'He had a confrontation with Simon Peter in the Roman Forum in front of the Emperor Nero. Simon Magus levitated to demonstrate his magic powers, and Simon Peter prayed to God to cast him down. Simon Magus fell and died at the Emperor's feet.'

'That story was invented,' Sinclair said. 'It symbolised the struggle between Christianity and Gnosticism to become the official religion of the Roman Empire.'

'There's something I don't understand,' Lucy said. 'How did the sword and the dish end up in England?'

'Caiaphas hid them in the underground passages of the Temple. The nine original Knights Templar dug them up and eventually it was decided England was the safest place to store them. They were concealed in places connected with the Arthurian legends. Tintagel was where Arthur was supposedly conceived, and the main cave in Cheddar Gorge was supposedly where King Arthur and his ghost army lie sleeping, ready to ride out to establish a new Camelot.'

'But why did the Cathars and the Templars become so fascinated by the Arthurian romances?' Gresnick asked. 'Why did they start linking Biblical events with Celtic stories?'

'Some stories are archetypal. They have a pattern that repeats over and over again, across different times and cultures. The most archetypal story of all is the Quest for the Holy Grail. It maps almost exactly to what was going on in Judea in the first century CE.

'In Lucy's book, she identified Judas as Mordred, Jesus as Arthur, John the Baptist as Merlin, the twelve apostles as the Knights of the Round Table, full of good intentions but suffering from their human limitations. She wasn't sure about Guinevere. Mary Magdalene, she speculated.

'In fact, Jesus is Mordred and Simon Magus is Arthur. The Knights of the Round Table are Cain's original priesthood. Salome is the enchantress Morgana. Guinevere is Helena, Simon Magus's lover. Simon Peter, the future first pope is Lancelot. Once, he was Simon Magus' right-hand man before switching sides. He and Helena had an affair.

'Camelot is the heaven of the True God. The forces that threaten to destroy it are the temptations offered by Satan to lure souls away from the light. The Wasteland is the spiritual desolation of the material world. The catastrophic relationship between Lancelot and Guinevere shows how lust can destroy the perfect kingdom, how souls are lured to their doom by sex. Arthur broods over Guinevere's adultery and Camelot falls apart, paralysed by a spiritual malaise. Civil war breaks out, and the only thing that can restore Camelot is a worthy knight who can find the Holy Grail. The Grail Quest is the arduous search to restore lost purity, to return to the True God.

'We are both the Grail Castle and the holy Knights who protect it. Down the centuries, we've been forced to live in the shadows to hide from our enemies, so the Grail Castle has become a mystical, elusive place. It's an epic journey to reach the Grail Castle because, to do so, you have to achieve Gnosis. That's what Galahad, Perceval and Bors all achieved; that's why they were allowed to find the Holy Grail. Outside is the Wasteland, the hell ruled by Satan.'

Lucy was amazed as she listened to Sinclair. In her mind, she was correcting all the mistakes in her book. At the start of her book, she quoted Jung who was fascinated by the Grail all his life: *The stories of the Grail had been of the greatest importance to me ever since I read them, at the age of fifteen, for the first time. I had an inkling that a great secret lay hidden behind those stories.* Lucy believed she had discovered the secret. Now, she realised, she'd scarcely begun to understand what was going on.

'Was there a real King Arthur?' she asked.

'Arthur was a warrior chieftain in what is now Scotland and he fought Angles and Saxon invaders. He was victorious, and the North of Britain retained its Celtic identity. Arthur went far north to the Highlands and established Camelot. It was built on a small island at the confluence of three lochs, on the site where Eilean Donan castle now stands. The Isle of Avalon was the nearby Isle of Skye. The Battle of Camlann was fought at the Kyle of Lochalsh, the strip of mainland opposite Skye. Merlin was a Celtic Druid. The whole story was appropriated by the English and relocated to the southwest of England. The Welsh and the French also have versions.'

Sinclair gazed at his watch. 'There's not much time left. Now we must prove once and for all that we can trust you, Lucy.'

'What do you mean?'

'Do you know how many seats are placed at the Round Table?'

'Thirteen. Twelve knights and King Arthur.'

'Indeed. The Round Table is the counterpart of the table of the Last Supper; thirteen places – twelve apostles and Jesus. One of the apostles is a traitor – *Judas*. In the Gnostic version, Simon Magus replaces Jesus and Jesus replaces Judas. But a traitor's seat always remains.'

'The Siege Perilous,' Lucy said.

'That's right: the Siege Perilous, the perilous seat, the Judas Seat. When the Round Table met, one of the knights had to remain standing because only the purest of knights could sit in the Judas Seat. Only one knight fitted the bill – Galahad, the purest knight of all.' Sinclair pointed at his version of the Round Table. 'We have our Judas Seat too, or should I say *Jesus Seat*. All the chairs are black bar that one, which is red. Anyone with impure motives who sits in that seat will die. We don't know how it works, but it does. Any traitors, liars who haven't confessed their lies, those who play others false, will perish if they sit there. In Dante's *Inferno*, the lowest circles, those closest to Satan, are where traitors are consigned. In the final, deepest circle, the ninth circle, are Judas, Cassius and Brutus, the three greatest traitors of them all. Except Judas shouldn't be there at all. It ought to be Jesus.

'Now, we'll all take our turn in the seat, to prove that we are who we say we are, that our hearts are true.'

Sinclair sat down on the red chair without mishap, followed by each of his twelve companions. Morson took his turn, then each of his soldiers.

As Lucy watched, she wondered what would happen to the soldier who helped them escape from the chapel at Cadbury. She could see him near the back of the line. As he got closer, he looked increasingly like a trapped animal. At the last moment, he collapsed onto the floor, clutching his stomach.

'Behold the traitor,' Sinclair shouted. 'Force him into the seat.'

The man was grabbed by three soldiers and pushed into the seat. As soon as they let go, the seat collapsed beneath the man, a section of flooring opening up. A livid flame soared up through the gap in the floor. After the screaming stopped, a smell of burning flesh spread round the hall. The seat reappeared, in pristine condition.

'Now you,' Sinclair said to Lucy.

'I'm not doing it.'

'Above all, we must be sure of you. If you've always been pure of heart, nothing will harm you.'

Lucy didn't move. She didn't want to go anywhere near that seat.

Sinclair gave a signal to Morson. The sergeant pointed his pistol at Lucy.

'I told you we'd discover if you were a False Messiah. You know I won't hesitate to shoot if you don't prove yourself.'

'Sit down, Lucy,' Gresnick urged. 'You'll be fine.'

Fine? That seat was one step from an inferno. Lucy stared at Morson. His face was hard, his eyes unblinking. He looked exactly like Captain Kruger had at the convent. He would definitely pull the trigger.

She sat down. Nothing happened. *Nothing*. She got up and walked away.

'Thanks be to God,' Sinclair said then turned towards James. 'Now, what about the man who claims to love you. Are you pure of heart, Mr Vernon? Are you worthy of Lucy's love? Or are you a traitor?'

Lucy got the impression James was doing everything in his power not to look at her. He took a few steps towards the seat then halted.

'I can't do it.'

'I knew it,' Gresnick shouted. 'He sabotaged the rope bridge. He tried to murder you, Lucy.'

James stood there open-mouthed, unable to respond.

Lucy was sickened. Some things you'll stake your life on, like the unconditional love of your parents. They're the foundations of your life. Everything else may collapse around you, but not those. James had joined her parents as one of her foundations. Now, they had all collapsed.

'You disgust me,' Morson snapped at James, 'but you're not going to die just yet. We have other plans for you.'

'They ought to force you to sit, you bastard,' Gresnick snarled. He lunged towards James, but was dragged away.

'Enough,' Morson said. 'We've learned all we needed to know.'

'The True God has given us this gift for testing men's souls, and he has given us you, Lucy,' Sinclair said. 'You have found three of the Grail Hallows. Now you must find the last – the Holy Grail itself.'

76

Lucy tried not to look at what was in front of her. She gazed back up the valley, at Carbonek Castle on the crest, a red moon sitting above it. The valley, deep in snow, was illuminated by pale blue floodlights hidden within the woods that lined the valley.

Sinclair had brought her to an ornamental stone bridge built across a circular lake at the foot of the valley, but he hadn't allowed her to change out of her bloodstained uniform. He claimed that her soul, knowing how close it was to freedom, was detaching itself from its physical jail, causing her bodily functions to go haywire. She was unconvinced. She felt repulsive.

They were alone at the centre of the bridge while the others were gathered at either end. She prayed that the last of the Grail Hallows, the most famous of all, was concealed somewhere in the stonework of the bridge.

'Where do you want me to look?' Her voice was scarcely audible.

Sinclair stared at her. 'You know where, Lucy. In the blue, Lucy. *In the blue*.' He stabbed his finger at the lake.

'Before this bridge was built, one of my predecessors ordered his men to drain the lake and do a fingertip search. They inspected every inch to find the Holy Grail. They didn't manage it. Only *you* can do that. You're Galahad's successor. Do you know what symbol he wore on his white mantle?'

Lucy shook her head, her face burning with the night's coldness.

'He wore a red Cross pattée like the one on my mantle. Galahad was one of us – *a Templar*.'

'But you're wearing black.'

'We wear black because Cain's priesthood did; the same reason why Hitler's SS wore black. They, like us, displayed the Death's Head. Today, more than ever, that's our most sacred symbol.'

'Why?'

'Because this is the eve of the Apocalypse. In a few hours, the world will die.' He gave a signal and all around the circular lake, blue floodlights flickered on, bathing the lake in intense blue.

Lucy gazed at the lake, at the reflections in the surface of the water – her terrors taking shape: blue shadows and whispers, all her blue nightmares coming true.

'You've heard the legend that Joseph of Arimathea hid the Holy Grail in a well at the foot of Glastonbury Tor. It was no legend. The Knights Templar, at the end of the twelfth century, searched the well and found the Grail. They brought it here. The Holy Grail lies hidden at the bottom of this lake. You can find it for us, Lucy. Everything reaches its fruition in you. You're the first and last, the beginning and the end, the alpha and the omega.'

'Don't say that.'

'It's true.'

'How can it be true? I'm *terrified*. I can't go into that water.'

'This is the way it must be, Lucy. These are the most momentous hours in human history. Nothing great can be achieved without sacrifice. You must overcome the most difficult opponent of all – *yourself*.'

Lucy tried desperately to think of something to say. Anything to avoid the water...the *blue*. 'Colonel Gresnick told me religious sites were raided all over the world,' she said, 'places associated with the Grail Hallows and the Ark of the Covenant. He thought Morson was responsible but Morson denied any knowledge of it.'

Sinclair smiled. 'I ordered the raids.'

'*What?*'

'They were a calculated ruse. We already knew none of the sites contained anything we were looking for, but our enemies weren't aware of that. We wanted to sow confusion, to put religion at the forefront of people's minds as the cause of the worldwide disasters. A member of my Round Table was in charge of an elite Scottish commando unit supposedly on secret training exercises in the Arctic. They were the ones who performed the raids, not the Americans. Morson wasn't even aware of our existence until now. All he knew was that there were influential people in Britain who could assist him with his mission.'

'Why use Morson at all? You already had your own Special Forces unit.'

'It was Morson's captain we were interested in.'

'The captain? Why?'

'Because your task is impossible without him.'

'I don't understand.'

'You'll soon have all the answers, Lucy. Right now, you must fetch the Holy Grail.'

Lucy remembered that Morson said something about his captain having a significant name. *Lucius*, that was it, wasn't it? The counterpart of *Lucy*. But what was the captain's surname? Did Morson tell her? She couldn't recall. As she stared at the glowing water, she started to cry. 'I can't do this.'

'You'll do it for the sake of the oldest of sins – love. If you don't dive for the Holy Grail, we'll kill James Vernon.'

Morson was standing beside James, gripping his arm. In her mind, Lucy heard Gresnick's voice: '*Let him die. He tried to murder you. Don't help these people.*'

Sinclair nodded at Morson and the sergeant put his pistol to James' temple. James closed his eyes and braced himself.

Lucy turned away and watched the spotlights reflecting off the surface of the water. She'd never seen water so blue: the colour of suffering, the measure of pain. No matter what James did, she couldn't watch him die. It was unthinkable. 'Give me a blindfold,' she said.

'But you won't be able to see anything under the water.'

'I don't need to.'

Sinclair reached under his mantle and brought out a black cloth covered with a silver skull and crossbones. 'I was intending to wrap the Holy Grail in this.' He blindfolded Lucy then helped her onto the parapet of the bridge.

She stood for a moment, dangling in the breeze. The water, she knew, would be ice cold. She was in a heavy army uniform, and she couldn't see a thing. This would be the most difficult dive of her life. *God help me*, she mouthed before plunging into the water.

At first, she felt nothing but the numbing, overwhelming shock of freezing water. The lake was much deeper than she expected and her uniform dragged her down to the bed of the lake. As she touched bottom, something remarkable happened – she felt her old strength returning, the experience born of a thousand dives.

Twisting round, she pointed herself towards the surface. Even with her blindfold on, she could see a blue glow. She'd found herself in the interior of the colour blue, inside its core, absorbed by it. It was in her heart, her mind, every cell. Her *soul* colour. Her body started to shake. Waves of distorted sounds bombarded her. She realised they were human voices; just whispers at first but rapidly amplifying. Hundreds of them: men, women, children, even babies. They were talking to her, telling her things. Voices in her head. They were back, worse than they ever were in the convent. *Losing it*. Her recovery, her *cure*, was all an illusion.

She struggled for breath. Got to get back to the surface. *Air*. Kicking off from the bed, she pushed her way upwards through the water. She rose fast, the water seeming to part in front of her. Reaching the surface, she took in as deep a breath as she could manage, trying to release the burning sensations in her lungs.

'Anything?' Sinclair shouted.

She didn't answer; just tumbled and dived again. The voices were still bombarding her. She imagined hundreds of ghost swimmers, different shades of blue, all of them translucent, surrounding her. *Like angels*. At last, she understood. They were her soul-line, her past lives. All talking to her at once. All together. She was whole again, all her pasts reunited. Everything she was, had been, or ever could be. Linked through time and space. Connected for eternity. She cut through the water effortlessly, just as she did in the old days when her mum and dad were still alive.

Groping amongst the reeds on the bed of the lake, she imagined her father's hands guiding her. When she was a baby, he involved her in a strange ceremony. Surrounded by men in black robes with the skull and crossbones on their silver rings, he plunged her into a river. He spoke in a language she'd never heard before. Was it Aramaic? It was all for *this*, wasn't it? All along, it was her destiny. A water child, born to find the Holy Grail in the blue.

She visualised the Grail's location. Others had searched for it and found nothing. Why? Buried somehow, or concealed. In the sand and gravel beneath the reeds? Concentrate harder, she thought.

Her fingers touched a boulder amongst the reeds. Instantly, an image flashed into her mind. It had been deliberately hollowed out, hadn't it? The Grail was concealed inside that rock. Then the hole was sealed with gravel and the boulder placed in the centre of a reed bed.

Feeling around the boulder, she located the gravel in the seal and cleared away as much as she could. Reaching inside, she touched something regular, cold and metallic. A current surged through her, more powerful than anything she'd ever experienced, firing up every cell in her body.

The souls all around her, all her pasts, were visible. Even though she was blindfolded, she could see them clearly, as real as she was, smiling at her. And foremost amongst them was Nostradamus. The entire lake had lit up, every molecule of water glowing, a pool of eerie light. She pictured the glow extending to the bridge, the snow-covered valley, to the dark woods on either side, the castle on the crest. *Everywhere.*

She kicked up to the surface, clutching the Grail. As she clambered out of the lake, everyone rushed towards her.

'My God, she's got it,' Sinclair yelled.

She stood up and pulled off her blindfold. In her hand, she had a silver chalice, radiating light, making her skin translucent. She'd never seen anything so beautiful. Soon, all the others had joined Sinclair. They stared at her as she stood there at the edge of the lake in the snow, in the eerie glow of the Grail. They kept staring.

It was impossible, yet it was true: she was holding the Holy Grail.

77

'Give it to me.' Sinclair didn't take his eyes off the Grail for a moment. Lucy handed it over, oddly relieved. The world had desperately sought this object for centuries. Now she'd found it, and, because of that, the world might end. She didn't want anything to do with it.

Sinclair held it up and turned it round to gaze at it from every angle. 'Isn't it strange? So many people have searched for this, believed in it, worshipped it. All of our problems would be solved, they thought. Yet, this is a false grail, a deliberate deception, our greatest trick.'

'What do you mean?' Lucy was astonished.

Sinclair turned away and began leading everyone towards Carbonek.

Lucy hurried after him. 'But that *is* the Grail.'

Sinclair gave a wry smile. 'Since the time of the Cathars, Gnostics have believed that the way for people to escape the wheel of suffering is to solve the Grail mystery. For us, knowledge is everything. Faith and good works count for nothing. Life is an intellectual process. Salvation is for clever people, not for those who have nothing but blind faith to offer. Those who have achieved Gnosis know exactly what the Grail Question represents.'

'But the Grail Question is about showing compassion for those who suffer,' Lucy said. 'It's nothing more.'

'You're wrong. The Grail Question is the most profound question of all. It comes in two forms. The Grail Seeker is supposed to ask the wounded

Grail King, *What ails thee*? To a Christian, it sounds like an expression of simple compassion, just as you said, but to a Gnostic it means something very different. The Gnostic is asking if you are aware that something is fundamentally wrong with the world. What ails all of us is that we are jailed souls on a prison planet.

'The second form of the question, the main version, is the one Perceval failed to ask the Grail King after he was first shown the procession of the Grail Hallows: *Whom does the Grail serve*? To a Christian, the straightforward answer is that it serves the Grail King. For Gnostics it means *do you believe in the True God or Satan*? The Grail and the Spear are Christian symbols. The Sword and the Dish are Gnostic symbols relating to John the Baptist and Simon Magus. Christ, the son of the Creator, is the spawn of Satan, while John and Simon are servants of the True God.

'The procession of the Grail Hallows, in which the competing symbols are paraded side by side, signifies that you are being offered the choice between two radically different religions. At the end of the ceremony, you must make your choice. The answer you give to the Grail Question determines your fate. A Gnostic answers that the Grail and the Spear serve Satan while the Sword and the Dish serve the True God. If you don't give that answer, or if you fail to ask the question in the first place, you'll never again be admitted to the Grail Castle.'

Lucy absorbed Sinclair's words. It astounded her that one of the most sacred objects in the world could be so misunderstood. Far from being something you would want to find – the culmination of your spiritual journey through life – the Grail was something to be shunned. The real idea behind it when Chrétien de Troyes, Robert de Boron and Wolfram von Eschenbach first wrote about it all those centuries ago was that you should approach it with extreme caution, that it had a deceptive, seductive, ever-changing quality. Finally, the message was that you should avoid it at all costs.

Each writer deliberately called it a different thing – a dish, Christ's chalice or a stone from heaven – so that people would feel compelled to unlock its mystery, and, hopefully, eventually find their way to the Grail Castle, the world of Gnosticism, where they might at last discover the truth.

But the three Gnostic writers failed. In their attempts to conceal their true intentions from the prying eyes of the Inquisition, they added too many layers of code and symbolism. The mystery was made all but impenetrable. Even many Gnostics didn't understand it. It was a secret to which only the elite had the key, and even they came perilously close to losing it.

****

When they got back to Carbonek, Lucy was allowed to have a shower and change out of her filthy uniform and into a fresh one. Returning to the Great Hall, she discovered a ceremony in progress.

The preserved head and bones of Simon Magus had been placed on a gold table. Sinclair and his twelve knights were kneeling with their arms outstretched. Morson and his soldiers were at the back of the hall, while Gresnick and James stood as far apart as possible. James looked ill now, like a ghost.

'We acknowledge Baphomet, the Father of Wisdom,' Sinclair and his men chanted. 'He is our guiding light, our inspiration. He showed us the path to the truth, to the kingdom of the True God.'

They stood up and Lucy noticed that they had placed a large gold crucifix on the floor in front of Baphomet.

'We abuse this obscene cross,' the knights cried. 'We spit on it, trample on it, urinate over it, smear excrement over it. We renounce Jesus Christ, we denounce Jesus Christ. Jesus Christ is a false prophet, the arch traitor, the progeny of Satan, rightfully killed by Baphomet's loyal servant Longinus.'

On either side of Baphomet, set back by a few feet, were two more gold tables. On one lay a spear that Lucy hadn't seen before, together with the newly found Holy Grail; on the other were the sword and dish Lucy had retrieved from Tintagel and Cheddar.

'Now, it's time for the ceremony of the Grail Hallows,' Sinclair announced.

Two thrones, like those King Arthur himself might have sat on, were brought out and Lucy was commanded to sit on one. Sinclair took the other. The lights in the hall were turned down until the only illumination came from two candelabra, each containing about twenty candles.

The Grail Hallows were collected by four of Sinclair's knights who carried them in procession in a circle around the preserved head then around each throne. All four objects glowed in an unearthly aquamarine colour, as though they didn't properly belong to this world but some higher plane.

Lucy found it incredible that she was involved in this, a ceremony at least eight hundred years old, revealing the ancient beliefs of the Cathars and the Knights Templar. History had come to life.

The knight holding the spear stopped in front of Sinclair. All of a sudden there was palpable tension. What the hell was happening? The other three knights looked on.

'Do it,' Sinclair shouted and visibly braced himself.

The knight took a step forward and plunged the spear into Sinclair's inner thigh.

Oh, God. Lucy couldn't believe what she was seeing. Blood spurted out of Sinclair's leg. It looked as though one of his main arteries had been sliced open. The four knights ignored him, went back to the gold tables and laid down the Grail Hallows.

'Say the words,' Sinclair barked at Lucy.

She gazed at his blood dripping onto the floor and wanted to throw up. Why had he done it? He could die in minutes. Why was no one intervening?

She started to get to her feet, intending to go over to help him, but he angrily shook his head.

'Say it,' he repeated. 'For God's sake.'

'I don't know what you want me to say.'

'Of course you do.'

Lucy was horrified. Everyone was looking at her. Then she remembered their earlier conversation. He was prompting her to ask the Grail Question, wasn't he? 'What ails thee?' she asked hesitantly, the words echoing in the great hall.

'This false world, this *hell*, ails me,' Sinclair answered. 'This world was created by the Father of Lies, the Prince of Darkness.' He gritted his teeth. More and more blood streamed down his leg.

Two Grail questions, Sinclair said, didn't he? 'Whom does the Grail serve?' Lucy asked, and for a moment she could genuinely imagine herself as Perceval, the innocent fool.

'The false Grail serves Satan. The true Grail serves God.'

Lucy stood up. For some reason, she was certain there was a third question, one that had never been revealed because it was the key to this secret ceremony. 'Which is the true Grail?' she asked.

'*You* must choose.'

Lucy turned away from Sinclair and stared at the two gold tables. If she chose the spear and chalice, she'd be choosing Christianity over Gnosticism, and the opposite if she chose the dish and the sword.

But Gnosticism was all about hidden knowledge. Even in the most sacred ceremony, the truth would be concealed somehow. Something was missing. She was convinced of it. There had to be mystical, transcendent knowledge. Was it possible that the true Grail wasn't amongst these items? That would be the final irony – the Grail Hallows didn't contain the Grail at all. As soon as she thought of it, she knew she was right. That was the final secret. The Grail was an Otherworldly object. It lay *beyond*.

Walking slowly, aware of Sinclair's eyes desperately on her, she went over to the copy of Raphael's mural. She stared at it. The Grail was somewhere in this picture, the *true* Grail.

Placing her fingers against the lower panels of the painting, she let her fingers run over the separate panels. Just as she reached her own panel at the centre of the bottom row, she realised something wasn't right. There were fine cuts down the sides of the panel. As she pushed with her fingers, the panel gave way. A flap had been deliberately cut into it. Carefully, she raised the flap. Behind it was a small alcove, the size of a large brick, with a carved wooden box wedged into it. She opened the door of the box and peered inside. It contained a beautiful emerald globe, the size of a paperweight. Taking it, she turned to face the others.

'*This* is the Grail.' Now she understood exactly what was expected of her. She walked over to Sinclair and, without hesitating, pressed the emerald orb against his open wound.

Sinclair's thigh glowed. All of his veins and arteries were visible through his mantle and chainmail, glowing. She could practically see the blood vessels repairing themselves, sucking back the lost blood. In seconds, the fatal wound was healed.

Sinclair stood up, smiling. 'Only once before has the ceremony been successfully completed: by Galahad, and now by Lucy Galahan, the new Galahad.'

Lucy didn't know what to say. She was overwhelmed.

'The true Holy Grail never had anything to do with Christ,' Sinclair said. 'It was no chalice and it was never used at the Last Supper. It never collected any blood. We invented that story to fool the Christians. The rumours of the Cathars having the Grail at Montségur were true. They smuggled this out the night before the castle surrendered to the Crusaders. And now I'll call the Holy Grail by its true name – the *Lucifer Stone*.'

Lucy was astounded.

Sinclair said that this stone was unique because it was the only material object in existence that wasn't created by Satan. Instead, Lucifer, the True God's brightest angel, made it, its purpose to allow him to take human form in this material world. He threw it from the sky into the Garden of Eden and used it to materialise in front of Eve. When Wolfram von Eschenbach spoke of the *lapsit exillas* – the exiled stone, the stone from heaven – this was what he was talking about.

The stone was indestructible. It was taken to Atlantis where it survived the island's annihilation, but it vanished from history for millennia, until the Templars found a document during their excavations of Solomon's Temple saying that the stone was in Scotland, at the location on which Rosslyn Chapel was eventually built.

The Templars retrieved it and brought it to their main base in the south of France. They gave it to their brothers in the Cathars to inspire them in their struggle against the Catholic Crusaders. After being smuggled out of Montségur, it was hidden in the foundations of a small chapel not far away, on the little hilltop village of Rennes-le-Château. Centuries later, in 1891, it was discovered by a Catholic parish priest when he was renovating his chapel. The priest's name was Bérenger Saunière. When Sinclair's predecessors found out, they went to the priest and paid him a fortune for the stone. They didn't reveal who they were or why they wanted the stone. Overnight, Saunière went from being a poor nobody to an exceedingly wealthy man and a great mystery was born.

After, he became obsessed with understanding what it was he'd chanced upon. He spent the rest of his life trying to solve the mystery, and learned as much as he could about the Cathars and Templars. He rebuilt the chapel in a much grander style, but added several unorthodox features, for which he was condemned by his local bishop. Above the entrance, he placed a Latin inscription: Terribilis est locus iste – *This place is terrible.* On the archway above the gate to the cemetery, he put a Templar-style Death's Head stone carving. Inside the chapel, he erected a realistically coloured statue of a figure that was either the Devil or the demon Asmodeus. According to Judaic legend, Asmodeus was the builder of Solomon's Temple and the custodian of the greatest secret of mankind. There was little doubt Saunière had begun to realise the enormity of what he'd found and of his crime against Catholicism by selling it to the enemies of his faith.

Sinclair said that Hitler then took ownership of the stone when he became Grand Master of the College. It was kept in Nuremberg with the other sacred treasures the Nazis seized from all over Europe.

Sinclair stopped speaking – the grandfather clock at the back of the hall was striking midnight. 'April 30 is here,' he said. '*The world's last day.*'

78

All over Lucy's body, goosebumps erupted. 'What's supposed to happen?' she asked.

'Look at the stone,' Sinclair commanded.

For a moment, nothing happened then the inside of the ball seemed to fill with strange milky clouds. Through the clouds, Lucy noticed a tiny light, rapidly growing brighter. It was unlike anything she'd ever seen: beautiful, tranquil, reassuring. It filled her with a sense of well being she'd never experienced in her life. Her fear vanished, her loneliness, all the hurt in her life. She felt loved, unconditionally, overpoweringly, as though her own parents were inside that light. Then the light began to write, in fiery letters. Lucy gasped when she saw what was being spelt out – *her own name.* As soon it was completed, it vanished, taking the light with it.

'What did you see?' Sinclair asked.

'My name – then it disappeared.'

'That stone is made from no ordinary material. Lucifer himself created it. It contains a glimpse of heaven, and gives the names of those who are ready to make the journey to paradise.'

Sinclair smiled. 'I'll answer something that always puzzled you – why some of the mercenaries fighting for the Cathars at Montségur agreed to convert to Catharism hours before the castle surrendered to the Crusaders, knowing they'd die at the stake. It was because they took part in a sacred ceremony that the Cathars performed in the early hours of 30 April. During that ceremony, they saw their names written on the Lucifer Stone, just as you did. They signed their own death warrants because they knew they'd go straight to paradise.'

'When Section 5 interrogated the Nazi officials in Nuremberg on April 30, 1945, exactly the same thing happened. The Nazis showed the Lucifer Stone to the American officers. Half saw nothing and the other half saw their names written on it. They converted to Gnosticism and killed their non-Gnostic colleagues to stop them discovering the Gnostic conspiracy.

'They took the Lucifer Stone back to the States with them. The Invisible College contacted them and instructed them on how they should proceed. For the last sixty-seven years, we've been meticulously planning this operation. That's why Morson and his men are here now.'

'And what about you? Why are *you* here?'

'My name is a corruption of the French name *St Clair*. My ancestors were Normans who settled in Scotland. St Clair comes from the Latin words *Sanctus Clarus* – *sacred* and *clear*. The purpose of my family, our eternal purpose, was to clear the path to the world of the sacred. My family has had the greatest involvement of any in the long mission to right the ancient wrongs. We are the pathfinders, the predestined Grail seekers.'

He stared at Raphael's mural. 'It's time to tell you precisely why you're here, Lucy. Even though I've prepared you as well as I can, I have no idea how you'll react when you hear exactly what you must do.'

'What are you saying?'

'I'm saying that if there's such a thing as an inconceivable, unimaginable act – *this is it*.'

79

Sinclair led Lucy over to the mural. 'This shows that our mission began before the human race even existed. Isn't that incredible?'

'How can that be?'

'Use your intuition, Lucy. You know this mural better than anyone.'

Lucy closed her eyes. At some level, she understood it perfectly. Far from being complicated, it was simple. It told the story of God and his two leading angels, Lucifer and Satanael, the latter coming to be known as Satan. Absurdly, Lucifer and Satan came to be thought of as the same person when they were the precise opposites. Lucifer, the Angel of Light, was God's most loyal angel, his favourite. Satanael, the angel who stood on God's left side, was jealous of Lucifer and, above all, of God. Satanael had the gift of intelligence. He was ferociously, diabolically clever. Clever enough to think he could challenge God.

The mural was the story of how Satanael tried to overthrow God, only to be defeated in a cataclysmic war of light when the entire universe lit up in every colour: the biggest and brightest lightshow in history. To avenge his defeat, Satanael created the earth, setting himself up as its God. Far from being a simplistic hell of demons torturing and tormenting the wicked, the earth was a laboratory where the most subtle and ingenious psychological warfare was waged against its population. Pleasure and hope were granted as freely as pain and despair. The worst hell, Satanael understood, is the *almost* heaven, a false paradise offering tantalising glimpses of bliss. One day you're in love and you think the world couldn't be better; the following day your lover leaves you, and life, in an instant, is intolerable. When love and hate, pleasure and pain are the closest neighbours, misery is maximised, suffering brought to its apogee.

God gave Lucifer the mission of going to earth to defeat Satanael. But, in his own kingdom, Satanael was much more powerful, forcing Lucifer to seek the help of the inhabitants of Satanael's world. It was essential to make them aware of the predicament they were in, so Lucifer taught them Gnosis – true knowledge. Cain was the first to fully rebel against Satanael's tyranny. His people took up the struggle and war has raged ever since. Raphael's mural showed a coded representation of the struggle, and how it would end, one way or another.

Lucy opened her eyes. 'But how can any of this be real? Science must dismiss this as nonsense.'

'No,' Sinclair answered. 'Have you heard of the God particle?'

Lucy shook her head.

'Its technical name is the Higgs boson. In the 1960s, a Scottish physicist called Peter Higgs predicted the existence of this elementary particle. He said that a field – the Higgs field – permeates the whole of space. Any particles moving through space encounter this field. Many, but not all, particles that interact with it acquire mass.

'Quantum theory says that fields always have particles associated with them. For the electromagnetic field, the particle is the photon. For the Higgs field, it's the Higgs boson. No one has found one yet, but if they do it will demonstrate the existence of the Higgs field and explain where mass comes from.'

'How does this relate to Gnosticism?'

'Gnosticism says there are two universes – one of light and one of matter. The True God rules the former, the False God the latter. The first is heaven, the second hell.'

'I get it,' Lucy said. 'You're saying that Satan created the Higgs field and Higgs bosons. Without these, there would be no mass in the universe.'

'Exactly. Far from being called the God particle, the Higgs boson should be renamed the Satan particle. The whole material world – hell itself – owes its existence to this particle. Without it, there would be no gravity, no relativity theory, no wave-particle duality, no Heisenberg uncertainty principle, no Bell's inequality theorem, no quantum indeterminacy.

'When Satan created mass he also created time. Time, in the universe of light, has no meaning. Pure light doesn't decay. It's eternal. Remove the

Satan particle and nothing would age. There would be no death, no disease, no illness, no misery, no suffering, no pain.'

'But wouldn't we lose everything that makes us human?'

'No, in the universe of the True God where the Satan particle holds no sway, all of our joys are magnified a trillion-fold. It's a timeless, deathless paradise. The souls that inhabit that realm aren't subject to gravity. They can fly, soaring as high as they like, plunging as far as they wish. The restraints imposed by the material universe are removed.

'For humanity, it's impossible to imagine a massless universe. The whole of science is based on the existence of mass. Without it, everything changes. The laws of science are transformed.'

'Why doesn't the True God destroy the material universe?'

'He can't.'

'What do you mean?'

'God is perfect light. He can't interact with the material universe. To do so would make him imperfect and that's impossible.'

'But other things can interact with the material world.'

'That's the paradox. When God creates anything, it must, logically, contain imperfection. If it didn't, it would be perfect too, and therefore indistinguishable from God. That's impossible – there can only be one God. So, all of God's creations are imperfect and it's because of this that they're susceptible to the pull of the material universe, that they can interact with the Higgs field. God is pure light, but all of his creations contain varying degrees of darkness.

'Satan used his dark arts to make his world seductive to all those with a trace of darkness in their souls. Only two people were immune. God himself, and Lucifer, the Angel of Light.'

'But why did God create Satan?'

'Light needs darkness in order to exist. If there were nothing but light, we'd all be blind. The contrast allows us to see. Satan was the Angel of Darkness, the counterbalance to Lucifer.'

'Lucifer and Satan were the two great enemies, light and dark, the right hand of God versus the left, the righteous against the sinister. In the world of the True God, Lucifer shines more brightly than any other created being, while Satan is all-consuming darkness. In Satan's material world, the situation is reversed. Now Satan is the brightest light and Lucifer infinitely dark. For that reason, Satan is able to call Lucifer the Prince of Darkness.'

Lucy pointed at the top panels in the mural. One feature stood out as though it was painted on using a special, glowing pigment. The feature seemed to metamorphose into a physical object protruding from the mural.

'Satan created the Spear of Destiny, didn't he?' she said. 'That's the key to all of this.'

Sinclair smiled. 'Satan could do something with ordinary light that was impossible for God – he could corrupt it, make it heavy, perishable. He could cause it to fold in on itself, to decay. He believed that if he tried hard enough he could actually make it solid. He spent eons experimenting, trying to create mass. Endless attempts failed. Finally, he cracked the puzzle and created the first material object – a weapon. This was the Spear of Destiny itself, and its purpose was the impossible: to allow Satan to kill God.

'If Satan had succeeded, it would have been the first murder in the history of the universe, and the greatest crime of all. The universe would have instantly ceased to exist, or been plunged into a freezing darkness, lasting forever, with Satan commencing a reign of infinite terror.

'But when Satan hurled the spear while God was addressing the Host of angels, it passed straight through God. Satan hadn't understood that God can't interact with material things. The spear flew on and struck Lucifer in the shoulder, wounding him.

'War erupted in heaven between the bright angels loyal to God and Lucifer, and the dark angels who followed Satan. Lucifer's forces, drawing on God's power, triumphed, and Satan and his rebel angels were cast down into the abyss, and Satan's spear fell with him.

'In the abyss, Satan worked long and hard to create the material universe that he alone would control. God had no power over it. The universe was now divided in two, good and evil, light and dark, spirit and matter. God could not harm Satan, and nor could Satan harm God. The Manichean dualist universe was born. The mystery of why the True God seemed to tolerate the existence of evil was no mystery at all. As a being of the purest, transcendent light, a type of light no one on earth can conceive, God simply can't have any relationship with matter, so can't destroy it.

'God did not create evil, Satan did. God *could not* create evil. Evil is a property of darkness, not of light. Every soul was created by God and contains divine light, but all souls also have darkness within them and can exist in the material world. The dilemma facing every soul is to resist the seduction of the material world and embrace the light of God.

'Satan made earth the centre of his material universe. Earth is the domain of the dark lord, hell itself. Satan placed the Spear of Destiny in the centre of the Garden of Eden, knowing it would become the cause of war and violence.

'So it proved. Abel found the Spear and tried to kill Cain with it, but Cain wrestled it from him and killed him instead. Cain, the son of Lucifer and Eve, was Satan's enemy on earth. Satan could have killed Cain at any time, but now he saw the perfect way of spreading discord and conflict forever. Humanity would never be free of strife and suffering. Satan's bloodline, those descended from Adam and Eve, would wage an eternal war against Lucifer's bloodline, those descended from Lucifer and Eve. With the same mother, the two bloodlines would have much in common, which is why it's so difficult to tell them apart.

'Cain and all his descendants were branded by Satan with the Mark of Cain, but it was a sign that appeared only once a year, on the anniversary of

Abel's death at Cain's hands. Also, it appeared only on the forehead of the Cainite holding the weapon Cain used to kill Abel – the Spear of Destiny.

'There's one final thing I haven't told you about the Spear of Destiny, the most significant fact of all. It can't kill the True God, but it *can* kill anyone else in the universe – any human, any angel.'

'Can it kill its Creator?' Lucy asked, and started to shiver. It was terrifyingly obvious now what Sinclair was asking her to do.

The slightest of smiles appeared at the corners of Sinclair's mouth.

'You're asking me to kill God, aren't you?' Lucy hardly believed the words emerging from her mouth. 'That's what this is all about. That's what the mural is depicting. That's what your mission is. That's why the world may be about to end. It all depends on me. The Spear of Destiny is the *only* weapon that can do it.'

'It's not God you must kill,' Sinclair rasped. 'It's Satan. We're asking you to kill the greatest monster who ever lived.'

'I'm not a Gnostic. I was raised as a Catholic.'

'Everyone who isn't a Gnostic is a Devil worshipper. It's as simple as that. You know as well as anyone what a vale of suffering this world is. You can end this hell on earth, you can heal the divided universe. At a stroke, you can bring an end to evil, suffering, and pain. Every soul trapped in this world will be liberated. We'll all return to the true light, we'll all be reunited under the rule of the one True God. This is the most momentous task in history, Lucy, the most sacred task ever given to any human being. Whether you like it or not, you are the Chosen One.'

'But you're talking about killing the Creator. It's impossible.'

'Have you understood nothing? It's impossible to kill *God*, but not *Satan*. He himself is a created being and everything that was created can be destroyed.'

'But how to do it? I mean the actual process.'

'It's right in front of you. The mural shows all the ingredients, everything that must be in place before the deed can be accomplished.'

Lucy gazed at it again. 'Anything designed to strike down God, must, in the end, strike down its maker.'

'Precisely,' Sinclair said. 'It's justice, the completion of the circle, the only way this could ever end. Satan must die by his own weapon. The first weapon must be the last. The eternal conflict will end when Rex Mundi's own evil is turned against him.' He grabbed Lucy by the shoulders. 'How could you be forgiven if you didn't do it? You'd be the biggest criminal in history, the *eternal* criminal, reviled until the end of time.'

Lucy stood there, practically paralysed.

'I understand what you're saying,' she said hesitantly, 'yet, at the same time, I don't. You don't know what you're asking me to do.'

'I'm asking you to end the horror. I'm asking you to fulfil the prophecy. You came into this world for precisely this reason, this one moment in time, this single action. It's your purpose, your fate. You can't refuse.'

'But by killing Jehovah, I kill his Creation too. The world ends. Everyone dies. Six billion people. I can't do it, I just can't.'

'Only Satan dies, and his material world. Darkness will be the only thing left to commemorate their ill-fated existence. As for the rest of us, sure, our physical bodies will perish, but our eternal souls will instantly return to paradise. It will be over in a single flash. No one will suffer. From mortality to immortality, from hell to heaven, in the time it takes for the spear to penetrate Satan's heart.'

'How do I know you're right?'

'You've always known this. Your book is called *The Unholy Grail: The Secret Heresy*. All along, you knew there were two competing religions. This struggle has gone on from the dawn of time. You understood. Not the precise details, but you intuited the big picture. The essence of your book is exactly right: two rival Gods, one of them true, one false. The legend of the Holy Grail has always been one thing and one thing only – a coded reference to the search for the identity of the True God. All those who succeed join God in heaven; all those who fail are condemned to hell, to lifetime after lifetime of despair. A never-ending wheel of human misery. Until now.'

Lucy continued to stare at the depictions of the Spear of Destiny in the mural. They were flashing, glowing with a vivid blue colour. She could almost reach out and touch them.

'Like every Grail Quester, you've always been searching for the truth, Lucy. Place your faith in the one True God. Let his divine light guide you.'

'But I'm not the first to be in this position, am I? Others have been here before me.'

'Not exactly like this, but it's true that Cain's priesthood has assembled this way four times before. The first time was in ancient Atlantis. Their attempt to carry out their sacred mission went disastrously wrong and Atlantis was wiped from the face of the earth.

'The second time was when the great Cathar families of France came together to form the Knights Templar. They went to Jerusalem to discover the ancient treasures and secrets in the Temple of Solomon that would allow Cain's destiny to be fulfilled. The Inquisition stopped them before they could finish their work.

'The third time was when the Freemasons came together to create the United States of America – the Templars' fabled *Merica*, the new Atlantis. But too many secrets had been lost and they were unable to discover the whereabouts of the Grail Hallows.'

'The fourth time was when the Nazis thought they had assembled all of the Grail Hallows. They carried out the ceremony in the ruins of Montségur, but nothing happened. They failed because three of their Grail Hallows, and the Ark of the Covenant, were fake.'

Sinclair explained that the Nazis were completely unaware of Raphael's hidden mural. It was only when he himself became a senior figure in the Vatican that things changed. Rumours circulated that the Pope kept visiting the tomb of Pope Julius II. Sinclair befriended the Pope's most trusted aide and, after years of perseverance, managed to recruit him to the cause of Gnosticism.

'You killed the Pope, didn't you?' Lucy said.

Sinclair nodded. 'The Pope's aide, wearing special gloves, handed the Pope a note impregnated with an untraceable poison. We needed the Vatican to be in crisis. We assassinated the American president for the same reason. Without those two symbols of temporal and spiritual power, the world would be rudderless at the moment of its greatest peril.'

'You've thought of anything, haven't you?'

'There's no room for error. If we don't get it right this time, we'll never get another chance.'

'You haven't told me the most important thing of all.'

'What do you mean?'

'You've told me what the weapon is that can kill Jehovah, but you haven't said how you'll make Jehovah appear. The Spear of Destiny is useless if you can't make that happen.'

'We *have* Jehovah.' Sinclair smirked. 'In a box.'

'What are you talking about?'

'Jehovah's only a mile away, at our final destination.'

'I don't understand.'

Sinclair pointed at Raphael's mural. 'The Ark of the Covenant, Lucy, that's where Jehovah lives. The Ark is waiting for you – at Glastonbury.'

80

'It's time to finish this.' Sinclair ordered his knights to collect the Grail Hallows and the head and bones of Baphomet, and take them to the trucks parked outside. Several soldiers escorted each of the knights. Gresnick and James were pushed forward at gunpoint.

'Burn down the castle,' Sinclair said to Morson. 'We won't be coming back.'

As Morson collected some petrol canisters from a storage area and doused the hall, Lucy wondered why Sinclair was so confident. It seemed ridiculous to say that he had God in a box, as though the Creator were some caged animal. Surely Jehovah could do whatever he liked. This was *his* world. Even Sinclair said so.

'Why hasn't Jehovah killed you?' she asked. 'Why has he let you come this far? If he were as powerful as you say, he wouldn't let you take another step towards him. You would never have been able to trap him.'

'Lucy, everything in this world is part of Jehovah. The law of conservation of mass-energy – the first law of thermodynamics – says that mass-energy can be neither created nor destroyed. When Jehovah created the material universe, he had to use a vast amount of his personal energy to accomplish it. All of the matter, dark matter and dark energy that physicists study is all born of Jehovah, and is imbued with his evil essence. Much energy was also channelled into the Spear of Destiny. The result is that Jehovah is feeble now, with little of the power you'd expect. Shaking the planet with his crude, spiteful earthquakes is the best he can do.

'What the Bible keeps secret is that the Spear of Destiny was always paired with the Ark of the Covenant. The High Priest of Solomon's Temple used the spear to direct Jehovah's energy. Without it, Jehovah's remaining power couldn't be focused. That's why he's now lashing out so wildly and indiscriminately, causing catastrophes all over the world. But without the spear, he's blind. He can't see us, can't target us with his power. While we have his spear, we're invulnerable.'

Sinclair's explanation made some sort of weird sense, yet Lucy remained doubtful. She wasn't even sure Sinclair knew what the right spear was. For her, it was the one she found in the chapel at Cadbury, not the one Hitler took from Vienna.

'Let's go,' Sinclair said as Morson took a candle and set the petrol alight.

Flames instantly engulfed three sides of the castle. They hurried out of the main entrance as the blaze pursued them.

Sinclair clutched the Lucifer Stone. It was an extraordinary object, but Lucy still struggled to accept that it was the real Holy Grail. Oddly, that somehow made it the perfect candidate: unexpected, elusive, enigmatic. Above all – if Sinclair was right – it was an object not of this world. What could be more appropriate as the Holy Grail?

'What about Morson's captain?' she asked as they emerged into the outer courtyard. 'You said there was something special about him.'

'Special?' Sinclair seemed almost amused. 'If my name is special, the captain's is unique.'

'Lucius something,' Lucy said. 'He has the male version of my name.'

'His name is Lucius Ferris, Lucy. When he gazed into the stone, it didn't show his name. For him, the effect when he touched it was entirely different.'

Lucius Ferris. There was something familiar about the name. Lucy felt icy cold, despite the ferocious heat of the burning castle.

'Why are you blocking it?' Sinclair asked. 'You already know the significance of the captain's name.'

Lucy shook her head, but the name was pulsing in her mind like a strobe, burrowing into her unconscious. *Lucius Ferris.* My God, it was so obvious. It was one of the oldest names of all, a name from before time. When the captain held the stone, it didn't show his name for one simple reason. The stone was his. Lucius Ferris – *Lucifer*.

The stone was designed to transform Lucifer into a human. It could do the reverse as well – turn a suitable human into Lucifer. It had changed the captain into an angel, a *dark* angel, the most famous angel of all. All along, that was the presence she'd sensed, first at Tintagel then at Cadbury and finally Cheddar Gorge. Lucifer was walking the earth.

'He's waiting for us at our final destination,' Sinclair said. 'He's at Glastonbury Tor with the Ark of the Covenant.'

Lucifer at Glastonbury? It seemed insane. The early Christian leader Tertullian was famous for saying: *It is certain because it is impossible.* Lucy had always found it a mad statement. Now it seemed the cornerstone of logic.

The two trucks were waiting at the far side of the courtyard. They now had huge Skull and Crossbones emblazoned on their sides: white on a red background, the sign of *No Quarter* to the enemy. Pirate trucks, Lucy thought, making the journey to the end of the world.

As they climbed into the trucks, Lucy caught James's eye, but he turned away and scrambled into the other truck. Gresnick bowed his head and also headed for the other truck. It seemed no one wanted to look at her: not Sinclair, not Morson, nor any of the soldiers or knights. *No one.*

When she took her seat in the back corner, she felt as though she'd been branded an Untouchable. Maybe they were right to avoid her. What Sinclair was proposing was beyond comprehension. As far as she could make out – Sinclair had carefully avoided spelling it out – she was expected to stab the Spear of Destiny into the Ark of the Covenant. Just as it had killed Jesus Christ, the spear would somehow kill God, or, at any rate, what most people called God. To the Gnostics, the god inside the Ark was Satan, but it was impossible for Lucy to shake off the beliefs she was raised with. For her, she was being asked to slaughter *the* God, the one, the only, the *Creator*. It seemed an inconceivable act, yet Sinclair was certain it could be done.

She didn't share his confidence. She suspected it would be a ceremony that ended in failure like all the previous attempts – like her life. Like love? The only person on earth who would never betray her was James, yet he had. The unthinkable, the unimaginable: yet it happened. That was the truth of life. Humanity's Holy Grail was never anything but an unholy Grail.

She couldn't make up her mind. One moment the idea of the world ending at her hands seemed absurd. Even if she could do it, she wouldn't. A moment later, she could imagine nothing better than ending this atrocity exhibition once and for all. Rimbaud said: *Life is the farce which everyone has to perform.* Was it her role to bring down the final curtain on the grand farce?

When the blood ran down her legs at Cheddar Gorge, it was as if her own body had turned against her. Did it understand what she was being asked to do? The material world was full of suffering. Look at all the poverty and pain, the lies, cruelty and violence, the endless wars and madness. It deserved to end. Its greatest benefactor would be the person who put it out of its misery. Did it really fall to one person to end it? *To her*? Was she like one of the leaders in the Cold War with all the apocalyptic nuclear codes in his briefcase, his finger poised over the red button ready to unleash the final destruction?

Those old politicians were prepared to do it. Why not her? But, if she did, she'd be killing billions. She'd be the greatest homicidal maniac in history, the ultimate pariah. Would anyone want that to be their epitaph, even if there was no one left to care?

The trucks motored slowly along the snow-covered roads leading to Glastonbury. Lucy tried to block out what lay ahead. Sinclair, who'd been sitting near the tailgate of the truck, made his way up to the back to sit with her.

'I know it's hard for you to come to terms with all of this,' he said. 'The truth is, everything collides in you, all the forces of history.'

Lucy was astonished by what Sinclair then told her. Her mother was a Jewess who could, he said, trace her bloodline all the way back to Seriah, the last High Priest of Solomon's Temple. That meant she was descended from Aaron, brother of Moses. It was essential for her to belong to that bloodline because the Ark couldn't function properly unless one of Aaron's descendants was present. The Gnostics' attempt at Atlantis had gone catastrophically wrong because no such person was there. The Nazis failed too, and one of the reasons was that they refused to have a Jew amongst them. This time, the Invisible College had ensured everything was done properly.

'Are you saying my father didn't marry my mother for love? It was arranged?'

'As it turned out, your father did love your mother, but he wasn't supposed to. All that was required of him was to have a child with her. Your father can trace his line back to Cain. We have unbroken records dating back ten thousand years, with Cain's name the very first. Your bloodline could not be more illustrious – with Cain on your father's side, and Aaron, the patriarch of the Levite priesthood, on your mother's. You were raised as a Catholic in an attempt to disguise your true heritage.'

Lucy shook her head. No wonder she was at war with herself. Her blood was practically fighting itself. A Catholic, a Jew and a Gnostic all in one. If the legend were true that Lucifer was Cain's real father then she had supernatural elements in her blood, an innate hatred of Jehovah, yet she also had the blood of Aaron, one of the most revered figures of Jehovah's Chosen People. And she was a Catholic, the religion that was the historical enemy of both Jews and Gnostics.

'The final side-panel of Raphael's mural is the summary of this ancient struggle,' Sinclair said.

Lucy pictured it instantly: the one that showed the city of Rome in a mirror with the Vatican displayed upside-down in an egg timer.

'The proper name of Rome is *Roma*,' Sinclair said. 'Roma in a mirror spells *Amor*. Amor is the Cathars' word for love. The Cathars regarded Roma as the symbol of temporal power, of Satan's kingdom. Amor was the antidote, the opposite of everything Roma represented. Amor was spiritual power, the kingdom of light. Roma versus Amor is the eternal war.

'Amor can be split into *a mor* meaning w*ithout death* in the Cathars' language. That's the prize Amor offers – immortality, deathlessness, the final release from Satan's hell. All of us must decide which side we're on: Roma or Amor.'

The truck stopped. 'We're here,' Sinclair said. 'It's time, Lucy.'

The others got out of the truck, leaving Sinclair alone with Lucy. For a second, he held his hand against her cheek and she trembled. Her father used to do that too.

He climbed out of the truck then helped her down, never taking his eyes off her. Was he imagining what he'd do if he were in her position? But he wouldn't hesitate, would he?

They had parked outside Glastonbury's famous *Chalice Well* gardens. Lucy could scarcely believe she was here, just a few hundred yards from her convent. Beginnings and endings – always the same. Scientists said the universe began with a Big Bang. Was that how it would end too? She would pierce the Ark of the Covenant with the Spear of Destiny and it would cause a second Big Bang to reverse the first. With that apocalyptic explosion, hell would end forever.

Let there be light. Perhaps those were the words said before the original Big Bang. Did Satan say them? Jehovah? Allah? God? Yahweh? Christ? Did these names mean anything any longer? Through a dazzling explosion, the material world was born. Through a matching explosion it would die. The eternal symmetry. The perfect circle. As you raced forward, you simply get back faster to where you started.

Morson pushed open the wrought-iron gates of the gardens and everyone went inside. Although the rest of Glastonbury was snowbound, the gardens were untouched by a single flake. As at Carbonek, blue floodlights lit everything.

They walked over a cobbled stone path beneath a living archway of ivy entwined with great oak beams, past two great yews – trees sacred to Druids, Lucy remembered – then past a summer house and a couple of benches overlooked by a sculpture of an angel.

They reached one of Glastonbury's most frequently visited sights – a *Holy Thorn* hawthorn tree. Automatically, Lucy recalled the legend. Joseph of Arimathea, it was said, drove his staff into the earth at Glastonbury, and it miraculously took root and blossomed into a *Holy Thorn* tree. The tree standing here now was a direct descendant of that sacred original and famously flowered at two special times each year – Christmas and Easter. The perfect Christian tree.

They soon arrived at the Chalice Well. Lucy had always found it astonishingly beautiful. She could stand here for hours gazing at it, set in its small sunken stone circle, especially at sunset when it was bathed in a golden-brown glow.

The well's opening was covered by an oak lid, overlaid by an intricate design showing the *vesica piscis* – a sacred geometrical symbol in which the circumference of one circle passed through the centre of a second identical circle – with a 'bleeding lance' going through the middle of both circles. It seemed to represent the task confronting Lucy. She would have to take the spear and destroy the two matching circles: the beginning and the end.

She stared hard at the well, trying to keep her emotions under control. This was where, legend claimed, Joseph originally hid the Holy Grail, the very chalice she'd just retrieved from Carbonek.

Sinclair pulled her away and Morson led the party through the exit, across a road, and onto a snowy track leading towards Glastonbury Tor. They reached a circle of cherry blossom trees, weirdly in full flower and preternaturally pink, at the foot of the Tor.

Lucy stood in the centre. The trees were covered by pristine snow. The sky was changing again, generating an incredible display of fast-moving, coloured streamers, long filaments of glowing light in the darkness.

'The Northern Lights,' Sinclair said. 'The earth's magnetic fields are reorienting.'

The night sky started to flash; huge sheets of rainbow lights, the frequency getting faster and faster, becoming dizzyingly rapid.

'The end is coming,' Sinclair said.

Everyone hurried through the cherry blossom trees towards the Tor. Lucy wondered if apple trees once stood here instead. Glastonbury was reputed to be Avalon, the Isle of Apples, gateway to the Otherworld, where the dying Arthur was taken after the battle of Camlann.

Glastonbury Tor itself was a great 500-feet-high mound shaped like a teardrop. Everything was covered by snow: a spooky white hill surrounded by flat land. On its crest was St Michael's Tower, a roofless remnant of an old church.

Where was Sinclair intending to go? To the top of the Tor? Was the Ark of the Covenant inside St Michael's Tower? Is that where Lucifer was waiting?

'We're going *inside*,' Sinclair said, turning one of the spotlights away from the grove of cherry blossom trees and pointing it at the foot of the Tor. He produced a small remote control and pressed a button. For a moment, nothing happened. Then came a creaking sound. A section of the hillside started to slide to one side.

God Almighty.

A small stone passageway appeared, with a bronze door at the far end, engraved with swastikas. All at once, Lucy realised the truth: Sinclair's organisation had built a secret passage into the hill.

'Come inside,' Sinclair said. 'All the answers are here.'

81

Sinclair went in first to open the bronze door then beckoned Lucy inside. Shuffling along the small stone passageway, she imagined that hell lay in front of her. Above the entrance – the hellgate – was a copper strip bearing two lines from Dante's *Inferno*.

By justice was my heavenly maker moved
I, too, was created by eternal love.

Lucy could accept that hell was created in the name of justice, but it baffled her that anyone might think eternal love was involved. How could a place of never-ending punishment be conjured into existence as an act of love? Was it conceivable that a god of love and forgiveness, as Christ claimed to be, could create a place of limitless pain, of suffering sanctified? It was a contradiction in terms, a category error.

Wouldn't it be an act of eternal justice to destroy hell? Did love demand it? Maybe it would be the ultimate mercy for it to be all over in one flash of light – six billion souls delivered from Satan at a stroke.

Something was welling inside Lucy. Temptation? They would ask her to plunge a spear into a box and, with that simple act, they had promised that everything would end. They said that the stars in the heavens had moved for billions of years to reach an alignment where she would be right here right now to do this thing. Did she have any right to act differently from what was ordained?

The more she thought of the world's suffering, of her own, the more she found the idea of ending it all irresistible. Destruction was what she craved. Euthanasia – a good death – for all of humanity. Over in one cataclysmic, painless instant. No one would know what had happened. Here then gone. If Sinclair were right, she would be killing Satan, destroying once and for all the author of evil. A one-time opportunity to cut out the ultimate malignancy from the universe. No more injustice, cruelty, sin and strife. Wouldn't it be a crime, the worst mortal sin of all, *not* to go ahead?

She went through the door and gasped when she realised that the Tor had been hollowed out. Her eyes practically jumped out of her head. Sinclair's

Gnostics, it seemed, had used all of their wealth – the vanished treasure of King Solomon, the lost treasure of the Knights Templar, the looted treasures of the Nazis – to build the perfect setting for their Doomsday plan.

A perfectly smooth cavern had been hewn out of the rock of the Tor. The rock ceiling was painted to resemble the cloudless blue sky of a perfect day, with an unshielded sun beating down so realistically that the heat was almost palpable. The walls were covered with a cityscape of what was unmistakably ancient Jerusalem. The ground was laid with slabs of golden-brown sandstone. But that was all incidental to the main scene confronting Lucy.

'This is a perfect recreation of King Solomon's Temple,' Sinclair said. 'The original nine Knights Templar found the precise plans for the construction of the Temple during their excavations on Temple Mount.'

In front of Lucy was a long white rectangular building with chambers jutting out on either side, giving it a stepped appearance. Three breathtaking objects stood in the Temple's forecourt. Sinclair explained what they were. The first was a sacrificial altar where animals could be slaughtered and burnt as a ritual offering to Jehovah. The second was an enormous bronze basin supported on the backs of twelve bull sculptures. There, priests were able to wash their hands and feet. The water in the basin represented the Red Sea, and the bulls the Twelve Tribes of Israel.

Directly in front of the Temple were more bronze basins, five on either side, mounted on wheeled carts, and bearing ornamental carvings of lions and palm trees. Any residual blood from the sacrifices was washed off here.

Two bronze pillars guarded the entrance to the Temple, representing, so Sinclair said, King Solomon and his father King David. The pillars were referred to as Boaz and Jachin and they played a pivotal role in the rituals of Freemasonry. Legend said that the originals were hollow and contained the sacred writings of the ancient Hebrews.

'Who did all this?' Lucy asked.

'We've been working on it since the end of the Second World War. We used our influence to get the Government to agree to the secret construction of a top security nuclear command bunker inside the Tor. When the Cold War ended, the military complex was dismantled and we bought the site outright. We created what you see now, using the finest craftsmen in the world. Everything is based on an idea over eight hundred years old. Ralph de Sudeley was the man who dreamt up all this.'

'Who?'

Sinclair gave a rueful smile. 'Isn't it odd how so many of the greatest figures in history are so little known? Ralph de Sudeley was the man who discovered the real Ark of the Covenant.'

Lucy listened in amazement as Sinclair revealed the extraordinary story of the English Templar who found the hidden Ark in 1188 CE. Ralph de Sudeley was the commander of a small Templar garrison stationed in the ruined desert city of Petra, with the job of protecting the lucrative trading route through the Shara Mountains.

Lucy had always wanted to visit Petra thanks to one of the *Raiders of the Lost Ark* movies. In it, Indiana Jones discovered the Holy Grail in an extraordinary temple known as the *Treasury*, hewn out of a sheer cliff-face. Appropriately enough, the ghost of a Templar guarded the Grail. Now, it seemed, the movie had missed a trick. It wasn't the Holy Grail that once lay hidden in the secret caves of Petra, but the Ark of the Covenant.

'In 1188, Ralph de Sudeley was a Templar with no personal wealth,' Sinclair said. 'When he returned to England the following year he was one of the wealthiest men in the world. He made several attempts to start excavation work at Glastonbury Tor, but the technology didn't exist to do the job he wanted, so he wrote down detailed plans of what he was proposing. De Sudeley had French ancestry and it transpired he knew Chrétien de Troyes. In fact, de Troyes helped him draw up his scheme.

'With the approval of the Gnostic College, de Sudeley and de Troyes were responsible for the plan to bury the Grail Hallows in sites associated with the Arthurian legends in southwest England. It was on the basis of this plan that, centuries later, Pope Julius II, Grand Master of the College, commissioned Raphael to paint the mural so the secret locations would be preserved for all time in a safe place.'

'But what about the Ark of the Covenant?' Lucy asked.

'Ever since 1189, the Ark has been here in Glastonbury,' Sinclair answered. 'De Sudeley wasn't able to hollow out the Tor, but he did dig a small underground chamber in which the Ark was stored, awaiting the day when his plan could be put into effect.'

'I don't understand,' Lucy said. 'De Sudeley came along decades after the original Templars. Didn't they find the Ark in the hidden passages of Solomon's Temple?'

Sinclair shook his head. 'The Ark was removed from the Temple of Solomon by the Hebrew prophet Jeremiah in 597 BCE before the Temple was plundered by the invading Babylonians. In 586 BCE, the Temple and the entire city of Jerusalem were razed to the ground as punishment for a Hebrew uprising, but the Ark had long since been removed to safety.

'In the second book of Maccabees, it says: *He came forth to the mountain where Moses went up and saw the inheritance of God. And when Jeremiah came thither he found a hollow cave and he carried in thither the Tabernacle, the Ark of the Covenant and the Altar of Incense, and so stopped the door.*

'That means the Ark was hidden in either the mountain where Moses was shown the Promised Land, or the mountain where Moses spent forty days and nights communing with Jehovah, being shown what the future held for the Jews if they kept their sacred Covenant with Jehovah. De Sudeley decided the latter was more likely.'

'So, Ralph de Sudeley thought Jeremiah took the Ark to Mount Sinai in 597 BCE, and that's where it stayed for the next eighteen hundred years, is that what you're saying?'

'Exactly. It lay hidden for all those centuries until de Sudeley uncovered it – the first man to look upon it since Jeremiah. The reason no one could find it was, amazingly, that no one was sure where Mount Sinai was. It didn't exist on any map, and only the ancient Israelites ever called it by that name. De Sudeley, in his Templar fortress guarding the mountain passes around Petra, became obsessed with solving the mystery. After long study of the Books of Exodus, Leviticus, Numbers and Deuteronomy describing the wanderings of the Jews after their escape from Egypt, he worked out that Mount Sinai must in fact be Jebel Al-Madhbah – the Mountain of the Altar. This was the very mountain into which the *Treasury* at Petra was cut. The Ark and the other items, he soon discovered, were concealed in a secret chamber beneath the *Treasury*, exactly where Jeremiah left them all those centuries before.'

'Jeremiah hid the Ark there because that was where it was made in the first place. It was Jehovah's Holy Mountain, and it was from here that it was taken to Jerusalem. When it had to be removed from the Temple for safekeeping, there was nothing more logical than to take it back to exactly where it came from. It wasn't hidden in any secret passages under the Temple, it wasn't taken to Ethiopia, Babylon, Rome, Southern France, Ireland or anywhere else. It simply retraced its original journey, but in the opposite direction.

'De Sudeley shipped the Ark back to England – to Glastonbury, mythical Avalon. It was the most scared location he could think of in England. Since the Ark was taken from Mount Sinai to Temple Mount, he thought it right that it should be taken to another sacred mountain: Glastonbury Tor. He would never have been allowed to recreate Solomon's Temple on the crest of the Tor, so the next obvious step was to put it *under* the mountain rather than on it. Doing it this way served a second purpose – it demonstrated that Jehovah was a subterranean being, a shameful creature lurking in the dark.'

'But why would Gnostics recreate the temple of the god they hated?'

'Isn't it obvious? – *to destroy him*. Jehovah appears only in specific conditions. He gave Moses precise instructions for the construction of the Ark, and gave Solomon detailed plans for the construction of the Temple to house the Ark. If any of the rules are transgressed, he won't appear. That's the reason why the previous attempts to kill Jehovah failed. This time there will be no mistakes. We've built Jerusalem in England's green and pleasant land, just as it says in William Blake's poem. Jehovah appeared before the High Priests in Solomon's Temple in Jerusalem, and now he will appear before you, the last descendant of the last High Priest, in this exact replica of Solomon's Temple in this New Jerusalem.'

Lucy turned away. The plan seemed both brilliant and insane. Now, she understood, it wasn't a question of poking a spear into a box. They were actually intending to conjure up Jehovah. It would then be her task to pierce him, just as Longinus pierced Christ.

The others had spread out and were gazing reverentially at everything around them. Gresnick and James stood on opposite sides of the bronze basin, staring into the shimmering water.

Lucy wondered what James was thinking. There was such a chasm between them now and it broke her heart. Before this was all over, she wanted a chance to be alone with him, to give him a big hug maybe, or even just hold his hand, if only for a moment. Even though he'd betrayed her, she would forgive him.

The figure that appeared without warning in the corner of her vision took her completely by surprise. No one else had noticed him, sneaking out from a recess under the sacrificial altar. Unlike everyone else, the man's face was contorted with hatred. It took her a moment to realise that his uniform was both familiar and wrong. *That* face. It was Kruger's brother. He must have tracked them all the way from Cadbury, and crept in behind them while they were distracted by the wondrous sights.

'Behold the Antichrist,' he shrieked at Lucy. 'Your name is Abaddon, Azreal, Apollyon.'

There was an object in his hand. He threw it and it rolled over the sandstone towards her feet.

A hand grenade, without its pin.

82

A moment. A lifetime. Lucy watched the grenade bobbling towards her. With each turn, it seemed to move slower and slower. The world had dissolved into slow motion, moving frame by frame. She stared at the faces around her, each showing their awareness that as soon as the grenade exploded they would all die. The Big Bang they had planned so elaborately had shrunk to a small bang here and now.

Sinclair looked deathly pale. Morson's mouth was open, Gresnick wide-eyed. As for James, he was doing what no one else was...he was diving towards the grenade.

She caught a glimpse of his face. There was so much regret in his eyes, self-disgust, sorrow. But there was love there too, love like she'd never seen before. All consuming, indestructible, *aching*.

James succeeded in covering the grenade with his body. Words tried to come out of Lucy's mouth, but nothing emerged, as if they'd collided and destroyed each other before they could escape: *Don't, James. I love you. I forgive you. I can't live without you.*

Then James seemed to glow, his midriff becoming almost transparent with the intensity of the light. He was like some angel, so much brighter than everyone around him. But then the light faded and he seemed to start fragmenting, tiny stars shooting from him. No sound. Nothing at all.

Time accelerated again, dreamtime giving way to real time. Now sound came, such a shattering noise, carrying so much destruction. Smashing bones, tearing flesh, rupturing blood vessels. Bits of James' body flew outwards over the sandstone, beneath the blue-painted Judean sky.

Lucy smelled charred flesh. Wisps of smoke drifted up from James' body. Little sputters of red were everywhere, his lifeblood draining away. Lucy tried to move, but her legs resisted. She wanted to be with James, to kiss him – the last kiss, the kiss to make all future kisses mere shadows.

James twisted round, panting, with his upper body almost separated from the lower. A gaping hole was where his abdomen should have been. Sticky, blasted intestines. Charcoal skin.

Lucy was at last able to move and she crouched over James. He was mouthing something. She put her ear to his mouth, praying he was saying *I love you*, dreading that he might be begging for her forgiveness. She couldn't bear that. Whatever he'd done, she was responsible. She was the guilty one, the one who'd violated love.

In little more than a wheeze, James whispered, 'So much beauty.'

Lucy stared at him, grief-stricken. Life was fleeing from him. She could practically see his memories switching off one by one. With each of those vanishing thoughts, parts of her were dying too. They say we live in the memories of those who know us, but that means we die too when those memories perish.

With one final effort, James reached up and gripped Lucy's shoulder, his lips searching for hers. 'Let the birds sing, Lucy,' he said. 'Let them sing to you of how much I loved you.' He collapsed back, his eyes staring out lifelessly from his pale face.

Lucy wanted to wail, but no sound came. To her right, Kruger's brother had been stabbed by one of the knights and was lying on his back with a sword buried in his chest, blood spreading around his body over the sandstone.

Tears streamed down Lucy's cheeks. She couldn't believe that James was dead. As she took his hand, she felt the warmth of his body dissipating. Soon he was freezing cold. In her mind, blue. *In the blue.* And never getting out again.

83

Sounds. Voices. Faces were gazing down at Lucy. She saw their lips moving, but she couldn't understand anything they were saying.

Sinclair grabbed her shoulders and shook her. She felt her torso surging backwards and forwards. The movement reassured her somehow. She was still capable of feeling. She could channel her anguish into that motion.

Sinclair's voice began to penetrate. 'You can end this vale of suffering,' he was saying. 'Now, more than ever, you can see why this pain must end.'

But superimposed over Sinclair's words, she heard James' dying voice. *So much beauty.* Why did he say that? It made no sense. He said he wanted the birds to sing of his love for her. Why didn't he just say *I love you*?

'Get up,' Sinclair yelled.

Lucy struggled to her feet, trying not to look at James, already trying to forget him. If she didn't, she wouldn't be able to take another step. She'd lie down beside him and simply fade away. Sinclair took her hand and dragged her away. She caught sight of Gresnick. There was a look in his eyes. Pity, regret? It made her feel sick.

They walked up several marble steps, past Boaz and Jachin, the two towering bronze pillars, and stepped into the Temple's porch. The floor was of patterned marble, in black and white squares. A strange coolness spread through the air. And something else was all too palpable – the feeling of an unutterably unworldly presence nearby.

Sinclair kept talking to her and Lucy tried her hardest to concentrate. There was something comforting about the small details he described. They took her mind off James, off the darkness diffusing through her mind like black smoke.

They walked through the porch and into the *Hekal*: the holy place. The walls were lined with cedar wood, bearing beautiful carved cherubim, palm-trees, and flowers, all overlaid with gold. The floor, Sinclair said, was made of fir-wood, again overlaid with gold, making it glint and shine with an almost supernatural radiance. At the far end, gold chains sealed off the next room.

They went past the Tables of the Showbread, six on either side, representing the Twelve Tribes of Israel. These were ornate goldplated tables bearing gold dishes of bread and matching chalices of wine, symbolizing flesh and blood.

Sinclair removed the gold chains and they went up a marble staircase then stopped in front of the gilt-edged, olivewood doors of the *Sanctum Sanctorum* – the Holy of Holies – the last stop on their journey.

Above the doors was a Latin inscription *Et in Arcadia Ego*. Sinclair pointed at it. 'That has nothing to do with the Temple,' he said. 'It's one of Gnosticism's most sacred sayings, which is why we put it there. It translates as *And in Arcadia I*. It means that even in an apparent paradise such as the land of Arcadia, the Evil One is still present. It's also an anagram for *I Tego Arcana Dei*, meaning *Begone! I conceal the secrets of God*. I suppose you could say we enjoyed the irony of putting that message above this shrine to Satan.'

Turning to the others, Sinclair said, 'We've reached the final act, my brothers. The curtain is about to fall and never rise again. I wish we could all see the last performance, but there isn't room for everyone. The knights, Morson and I will accompany Lucy into the Devil's lair. Colonel Gresnick too. It's only fitting that one of *them* should be present to witness the end of all they've mistakenly believed in for so long. He can represent the billions of fools who chose to live their lives believing Satan's lies.

'The rest of you will need to remain on guard out here. If there are any signs of trouble, don't hesitate to come in. Otherwise, let me thank all of you and wish you God's speed. Providence willing, we'll shortly meet again in paradise in the company of the True God, with all of Satan's horrors consigned to history, with evil forever expunged from the universe. Blessed are those who have ended the Devil's reign of terror. This earth was born in evil, from the darkness. With one flash of righteous light, the Sin of Sins will be redeemed, all the jailed souls liberated, the eternal crime expiated.'

The words drifted past Lucy like ghosts. They sounded so grand, so certain, yet maybe this whole enterprise was a stupendous error, itself the work of Satan. She remembered something the philosopher Nietzsche said: *It's not doubt, it's certainty which makes men mad.*

Wouldn't that be the real answer to humanity's suffering? – for everyone to doubt, to admit they weren't sure about anything. Maybe there was a God, maybe there wasn't. Maybe Satan existed, perhaps not. Perhaps nothing was good and nothing evil. Perhaps all of the Commandments were debatable. After all, the Jews preached *Thou Shalt Not Kill*, yet they believed in capital punishment by stoning, they believed in the mass slaughter that accompanied warfare, they believed in ritual sacrifice. To judge them by their actions, they preached nothing *but* killing. Maybe Jesus wasn't the Messiah, maybe the Bible wasn't the Word of God, maybe it didn't matter in the slightest if you didn't keep the Sabbath holy. Perhaps there was no need to slaughter others because they disagreed with you, no need to burn heretics, to cut the heads off infidels, to stone sinners to death, to set up extermination camps, to blithely condemn endless billions to eternal suffering in hell because their beliefs weren't the same as yours. Perhaps people simply had to shrug their shoulders and say, 'Sorry, I just don't know.'

Before they entered, Sinclair opened a gold cabinet and brought out special robes for everyone to wear. They were beautiful vestments of gold, scarlet and purple, embedded with twelve precious stones of different colours, each bearing the name of one of the twelve tribes of Israel. Apparently these were the protective garments that the ancient Hebrew High Priests had to wear whenever they approached the Ark. Sinclair had left nothing to chance.

When everyone was ready, he paused for a moment and then, without a word, pushed open the doors and stepped inside the Holy of Holies, brushing past veils of blue, violet, crimson and gold.

Lucy followed with the others. At first she didn't raise her eyes, resolutely staring at the floor and wainscotting, both made from cedar overlaid with gold. As she lifted her gaze, the walls were the same – cedar covered with gold. The beaten gold sheets were engraved with passages from, Lucy presumed, the Torah.

'Look up,' Sinclair said.

Lucy stood up straight. She was in a room shaped like a perfect cube, every surface gleaming with gold. There were no windows. All the light in the room came from seven five-branched candelabra. There was also one seven-branched candelabrum – the famous Menorah, the emblem of Judaism and badge of the state of Israel. Lucy had no doubt that this was one hundred percent genuine, one of antiquity's most sacred relics.

Guarding the doorway were two giant solid gold cherubim with outspread wings that touched the walls on either side and met in the centre of the room.

At the rear was an extraordinary glimmering curtain made of gold leaf, drawn right across the room. A few feet in front of it, at the precise centre of the Holy of Holies was the gold Ark of the Covenant itself, every bit as wondrous as the legends proclaimed, shining like the sun. She'd seen many representations of it in paintings and movies, but nothing came close to capturing its beauty. It was simply *divine*. It rested on top of a breathtaking crystal altar, transparent yet full of shimmering iridescent lights as though a living rainbow were trapped inside.

Around the altar, a silver pentagram was inscribed on the floor.

'We've placed the Ark inside the most powerful black magic symbol of them all,' Sinclair said. 'Legend says Jehovah has a pentagram on his forehead. We're using his own weapons against him.'

As Lucy studied the pentagram, she realised that the interior lines of this famous symbol formed a very familiar shape – a pentagon. A shiver passed through her. Was it possible that the American military chose the pentagon design for their most famous building because their leaders were secret Gnostics? It was no accident, no coincidence, was it? This was all real. Thousands, tens of thousands, of men and women had conspired over ten millennia so that she could be here at this moment to perform this duty. The child of destiny.

Directly beneath the Ark's altar was an ugly boulder that seemed inappropriate amongst so much beauty, yet it was also magnificent and earthy. She wondered what it was and why it was here.

'So, this is it,' Sinclair said, 'the dwelling-place of the Creator: God, Jehovah, Yahweh. Or, to give him his right titles, the Demiurge, Rex Mundi, the Lord of the Flies, the Prince of Darkness, the Devil, Satan.'

Lucy didn't know what to say. She was overcome with emotion.

'Everything's in place,' Sinclair said. 'In minutes, it will all be over.'

'I never imagined it would be so beautiful,' Lucy said. Tears were filling her eyes. James' voice refused to leave her head. *There's so much beauty*. It was almost as though he'd seen this Holy of Holies before he died, a last vision to take with him on his final journey.

'It transcends beauty, doesn't it?' Sinclair said. 'That's how Satan works. He makes his material world seductive beyond our ability to resist. This is the sparkling net into which so many of us have fallen. Nothing looks as gorgeous, as *tempting*, as Satan's world. Only when the net closes around us do we get the first inkling that we've condemned ourselves. We are the self-damned, those who passed the Last Judgment on ourselves. And only you can redeem our error and save us.'

Lucy pointed at the strange stone under the Ark. 'What's that?'

'It's the Bethel Stone on which Jacob laid his head: the Stone of Destiny upon which the Scottish kings were crowned. We brought it here from its hiding place in Scone in Scotland.'

'But what's its connection with the Ark of the Covenant?'

'In the original Temple of Solomon, the Ark rested on a great flat limestone rock, which still exists on Temple Mount today. The rock is known as *Even ha-Shetiyah*. It's said to be the most significant spot on earth, the exact centre of the world. It was the foundation stone of creation, the first brick of the material world. Standing on that rock, Satan summoned all the rest of his dark creation into existence.

'When he was done, he wrote his secret name on the underside of the stone then joyously took a lump of the rock and threw it into the air. It fell on Bethel, and when Jacob laid his head on it long afterwards, he had a vision of Solomon's Temple, and of the Ark resting on the foundation stone. What could be more appropriate in our recreation of Solomon's Temple than to place the Ark over a block of *Even ha-Shetiyah*? – to undo creation from where it all began.'

He signalled to his knights and four of them, the bearers of the Grail Hallows, stepped forward. They placed the chalice and spear on the left of the Ark, and the dish and sword on the right. Sinclair himself went forward and placed the Lucifer Stone, the true Holy Grail, on top of the Stone of Destiny, to symbolise, he said, Lucifer's triumph over Satan's Creation.

'There's one more thing you need to know about,' Sinclair said. 'Jehovah is *two* entities.'

'What do you mean?'

'There's a thing called the *Shekinah*. Some call it the glory or radiance of Jehovah; others say it's the divine manifestation of Jehovah in the material world, implying that Jehovah doesn't enter fully into material existence. Some say it's the feminine side of Jehovah, or something akin to the Christian Holy Spirit. We say it's the mask Jehovah wears to conceal his true, repulsive nature. When he appeared in ancient times to Moses and the High Priests of the Temple, he used the Shekinah to speak on his behalf.

'But even the best mask slips. The Shekinah will disappear and Jehovah will appear in his true form. Lucifer has said this is the moment when you must strike.' Sinclair pointed at the Grail Hallows. 'The hour of destiny is here. Pick up the Spear of Destiny, Lucy Galahan.'

Lucy went forward and collected the spear. As she raised it up, she realised something wasn't right. She didn't get the same electrifying feeling she'd experienced back at Cadbury Castle, yet the spearhead was glowing, looking every bit a weapon of the supernatural.

'The whole spear should be glowing, not just the spearhead,' Sinclair yelled in sudden panic. 'This won't work.' He turned to the others and they were all equally shocked. 'This is the spear Hitler himself wielded. It *must* be genuine.'

Lucy stood there, dumbfounded. How could something go so wrong at this stage?

'Do something, Lucy,' Sinclair shouted. 'You're the Chosen One.'

Lucy closed her eyes and visualised the spear, trying to absorb its aura, trying to understand what was out of kilter. 'Bring me the other spear,' she said, 'the one I found in the chapel at Cadbury. The Antioch Spear.'

'What?'

'The tip of the Hitler spear is genuine,' she said, 'and so is the shaft of the Antioch Spear. All along, both spears were authentic, at least in part.'

Sinclair barked out orders. Soon the shaft of Hitler's spear was replaced with that from the Antioch Spear. Instantly, the Spear glowed, all of it, shaft and tip.

'It's time.' Sinclair raised his hands, his relief all too obvious. 'Everything is...' He stopped in mid sentence, staring straight at Lucy.

'What is it?' She felt as though she had grown a new head.

Sinclair made the reverse sign of the cross with his left hand.

'What is it?' she repeated.

'Your forehead,' Sinclair said. '*You have the Mark of Cain.*'

84

Lucy held the Spear of Destiny in front of her and stared at the glowing spearhead, at her reflection gazing back at her from the metal surface, a reflection bearing two serpents side by side on her forehead.

So, it was all true: she was a direct descendant of Cain. For a second, the two serpents seemed to shimmer and slither, as though they were alive. In front of her, the Lucifer Stone shone, a vivid, glimmering green.

'What's behind the gold curtain?' Lucy asked, but it was a redundant question. She'd known from the moment she set foot inside here. Every part of her had sensed the strange presence. It was the same feeling she'd experienced several times before, but this time it was so much stronger.

'You know,' Sinclair replied.

'I want to see him.'

'This is not his world. You'd see something grotesque.'

'He's doing something, isn't he? With his mind.'

'You must understand, Lucy. The Ark of the Covenant is right in front of us and inside it is Jehovah himself, the Creator of this world. The Spear of Destiny is here too, his special weapon. On top of it all, *you* are here, a descendant of the last High Priest. Do you know what that means?'

Lucy had a shrewd idea, but she didn't want to say.

'This is Jehovah's final opportunity to save himself. All of his power is directed against you, trying to bend you to his will. If he can make you wield the Spear of Destiny on his behalf, he'll destroy the rest of us.'

'And Lucifer is behind that curtain trying to stop Jehovah getting into my head, is that it?'

'That's it exactly. He's using all his psychic energy to protect you. But he's in the world of his enemy so he's having to expend vast energy to withstand Jehovah's power and put a shield round you. It's producing a devastating effect on him.'

'What do I need to do?' Lucy took a step forward. 'How do we make Jehovah come to us? When he appeared to Moses and the High Priests, everything was on his terms. He summoned *them*, not the other way round.'

'Jehovah thinks of himself as God, but he's just a demon – the most powerful demon of them all, but a demon all the same. The same rules apply to him as to any demon. He must come if you call him by his true name.'

Sinclair gave Lucy a stick of ordinary white chalk. 'Write his name inside the pentagram,' he said.

'His *true* name? But I have no idea know what it is.'

'You *do*. Everyone does. It's the Tetragrammaton.'

'Of course.' T*etragrammatos* was a Greek word meaning *four letters*. The Tetragrammaton was the Hebrew name for God, consisting of the four consonants Y H W H. That was where the name YaHWeH came from, and JeHoVaH as its anglicised version. But there was another factor, one she'd never understood, something about ancient Hebrew not having any written vowels and, consequently, no one being quite sure how to pronounce YHWH.

'Doesn't the language matter?' Lucy asked. 'I mean, don't I have to write this in ancient Hebrew letters instead of Latin letters?'

'Demons know their name in every language. As long as you get the name right in the chosen language, the demon must respond.'

Lucy knelt down inside the pentagram and wrote the letters YHWH then quickly got up and stepped back.

Nothing happened. Not a thing.

Lucy stared at Sinclair.

'This can't be,' Sinclair said. 'The Devil must come to us.'

'He's not the Devil,' Gresnick bellowed. 'He's God, and he'll never do your bidding.'

Sinclair was white-faced, his hands starting to shake. Lucy noticed her father's old ring glinting on his finger. When she was a child, her dad told her the ring had special powers that made him as wise as Solomon, giving him mastery over God himself.

'I know what to do,' she said to Sinclair. 'Give me your ring.'

Sinclair removed it and thrust it at her. She held it in the light of the Lucifer Stone and carefully examined it.

'Don't help them, Lucy,' Gresnick shouted. 'You can stop this madness right now.'

'Wipe those letters away,' Lucy said to Sinclair.

Straight away, the grand Master got onto his knees and, with the edge of his mantle, cleaned the letters 'YHWH' away.

Lucy breathed in hard. She sensed the presence of her soul-line, all the previous lives she'd led in her endless cycles of reincarnation. She sensed too the ancient bloodline on her mother's side, taking her back to the last High Priest who stood in the Holy of Holies of Solomon's Temple before its final destruction. And she felt too the blood of her father coursing through her, the blood of countless generations stretching back to Cain himself. But there was one stage beyond that, wasn't there? Cain's mother was Eve, and his father the Angel of Light himself. Lucy: the offspring of Lucifer. Her ultimate ancestor was standing behind the curtain just a few feet from her, the chief of the seraphim, the highest of the nine choirs of angels of the Angelic Host. 'Seraphim' came from *saraph*, an ancient word for serpent. The seraphim were the serpent angels, hence the serpents branded even now on her forehead.

She knelt down once more with the chalk. Now, she carefully started to write a new set of letters – those inscribed on her father's ring. They formed the words *Shem ha-Mephorash*. They were the magic words, her father had told her, that gave Solomon command over demons and spirits, that allowed him to summon the arch demon Asmodeus to help him build the Temple, and that allowed golems – false men without souls – to be created. They were the very words that Moses pronounced to part the Red Sea. By invoking those words of power, the ring bearer might also glimpse the future.

Lucy's father was keen to tell her one other fact about Solomon, one that now seemed astounding: Solomon had turned his back on Yahweh and become an apostate. How could that be? The very man responsible for the great Temple ended up denying Yahweh and died unreconciled, full of hate for Yahweh. The Temple itself was given over to the worship of Yahweh's enemies. Yet everyone knew that Solomon was the wisest of men. Did that wisdom finally lead him to Gnosticism?

Lucy was halfway through writing the letters when Sinclair told her to stop.

'No,' he snapped, 'that can't be right. *Shem ha-Mephorash* means "the explicit name". It's an epithet for Satan's true name, but it's not the name itself.'

Lucy shook her head. 'You're wrong. This is the name that was written on the underside of the foundation stone.'

Sinclair stared at her, momentarily horrified, but then he started to smile. 'Yes, what else but deception would you expect from the Prime Deceiver? What better way for him to conceal his true name than under the guise of an epithet? Who would ever guess the epithet was the actual name? It's genius.'

Lucy began to write again, but tears clouded her eyes as startlingly vivid memories of her childhood and her father overwhelmed her. Lifting her sleeve, she tried to wipe them away. Noises erupted behind her. Shouts, a scuffle. She heard Gresnick's voice.

'Don't do it, Lucy. You can't let it end like this. You mustn't.'

She twisted round to see what was happening. Gresnick grabbed a sword from one of the knights and ran towards Sinclair, holding the blade double-handed. Morson snatched out his pistol and fired at Gresnick. Two bullets slammed into Gresnick's legs and he sprawled forward, his hands flailing in front of him, his sword clanging onto the floor.

'Shall I kill him?' Morson raised his pistol and took aim again.

'No, I want him to see this,' Sinclair said, 'while he bleeds to death.'

Lucy watched Gresnick's blood spreading over the floor. When it reached her hands, she lifted them up, staring at the blood.

'I can't bear this,' she said.

'Don't destroy us, Lucy.' Gresnick's voice was already growing weaker. 'We bleed, we suffer, but we love too. I beg you, don't kill *love*.'

Lucy hated those words. She'd spent so much time in the last few months trying to avoid feeling anything. Now feelings were crowding in on her from every direction, driving her mad. Lost love, grief, abandonment, loneliness...everything she dreaded.

She thought of her father. Sinclair said he'd committed the greatest of crimes – being in love. Not with the True God, but with the things of this earth. It proved his soul was still seduced by the world's beauty. He wasn't ready for heaven, his name wasn't written in the Lucifer Stone. She'd seen her own name there, but did she want it to be? Wasn't she the same as her father? Life had sickened her often enough, but it could still offer breathtaking moments. Now and again, something transcended the misery, like that lone red rose in the graveyard in the ruined abbey. Its smell, its texture. So infinitely beautiful.

Was that rose really one of the Devil's snares, one of his tricks for keeping souls imprisoned in this world? James, as he died, spoke of beauty. He would have given anything for just one more second to appreciate beauty, wouldn't he? Can one instant of ecstasy redeem a life of despair? Maybe only an artist could live that kind of life. Can beauty exist in heaven where nothing ever changes, where nothing dies or grows old, where there's no cycle of death and rebirth, no seasons of growth and decay? How can there be beauty when everything is beautiful? Maybe beauty, true beauty, exists only when it's perishable, already containing the seeds of ugliness.

'I've changed my mind,' she mumbled. 'I can't do it, I can't.'

'You can't stop now,' Sinclair screamed at her.

'I *won't* kill the human race,' she blurted. 'No one could take that responsibility.'

'Have you understood nothing? You'll be saving us, liberating billions of imprisoned souls. If you don't do this, you'll be the worst traitor of all. Do you want to be the person who damned humanity to hell for eternity?'

The Temple started to shake. The huge gold cherubim swayed, long cracks appearing on their legs and wings. Lucy glanced up. She couldn't get any power into her legs to stand up and get out of the way. The vibrations increased, the cherubim shaking more violently.

'Get out of here, Lucy,' Gresnick croaked. 'The whole place is coming down.'

Lucy remained motionless on her knees, her energy gone. She stared numbly at the Ark, vibrating on its altar. Fragments of the wings of the cherubim were falling around her.

At last she managed to haul herself to her feet. Gresnick was somehow getting to his feet too, despite the blood streaming from his leg wounds. Screaming, he took one step and pushed her out of the way. Both cherubim toppled over. The head of one sheared off and struck Gresnick, its body falling exactly where Lucy had just been.

Lucy crouched down over Gresnick. He didn't seem to be breathing. Her body felt as if every cell were on fire. The pain was intolerable. Leaning over, she kissed him on the forehead, just as she once kissed her father in his coffin. 'Thank you,' she whispered.

Sinclair and the others surrounded her.

'The pain will never end, Lucy,' Sinclair said. 'Can't you see that? Everyone you loved and who loved you is dead. This is a vale of tears. You can end this horror. You can end it now. You have the power. I beg you, release us from this jail, this eternal penal colony. With one blow, you can make hell vanish. You can stop the suffering for all time. No more tragedy, no more pain.' He took her hand and lifted her to her feet. 'End it,' he urged. 'End hell.'

Lucy gazed at the Ark, feeling sick.

'You know what's in there, Lucy,' Sinclair said. 'Jehovah is reaching out, manipulating your mind. You must resist.'

Lucy nodded slowly. It always had to end this way, didn't it? Sinclair was right. There was just too much pain. It wasn't one moment of beauty that redeemed life, it was one moment of suffering that condemned it. For anyone anywhere to be in torment meant the world wasn't worth it.

She returned to the pentagram, crouched down again and completed Solomon's magic word, the word to summon Jehovah.

The whole Temple was trembling now: the floor, the ceiling, the walls. The structure could collapse at any time.

'Look!' Sinclair shouted. 'It's happening.'

Lucy stared at the space directly above the miniature winged golden cherubim on the lid of the Ark – the so-called Mercy Seat where the Shekinah was said to appear. A strange orange glow had appeared, just an intense spot of light initially but rapidly expanding to the size of a tennis ball, then a football, getting bigger all the time, starting to elongate, with new shades of orange swirling into the original colour.

Sinclair's eyes were fixed on the glowing light, his face an odd mixture of hatred and curiosity. Lucy felt as though she should say something, but words seemed futile now. She stood there, rooted, with the Spear of Destiny in her right hand, its blue glow becoming ever more intense. The Lucifer Stone was equally bright, shining like an emerald sun. Was it really happening? Had she truly summoned God?

The gold-leaf curtain behind the Ark rustled and something staggered out from behind it. As the glow over the Mercy Seat became more intense, Lucy gazed at the thing that had emerged – a huge, misshapen figure, infinitely black, with twelve wings, twice the number of an ordinary seraph. Darkness seemed to be issuing from it. It was a grotesque parody of an angel, literally decomposing as it moved, its flesh bubbling and dripping onto the golden floor, feathers of its many wings fluttering around it.

Lucy had never seen anything so repulsive, and its ugliness grew in proportion to the intensity of the orange light above the Ark.

Sinclair grabbed Lucy. 'Don't be fooled. In the kingdom of the True God, he's the most beautiful angel of all.'

She shrugged him off and held the spear above her head, pointing it at the heart of the orange glow. The spear itself now radiated with the same luminous light as the figure taking shape above the Ark. The Lucifer Stone had changed its colour to orange too. Everything in the room was bathed in the same glow. It was as though the ethereal light above the Mercy Seat was absorbing everything, transforming the whole world around it.

'Wait until the Shekinah has fully materialised.' Sinclair's voice was calm and cold now. 'Strike when it's starting to be replaced by the abomination that lurks behind it. You mustn't let the monster materialise fully or he'll destroy you. He's only vulnerable at the point of transition, as he first shimmers into his earthly body. You'll get only one chance. Go straight for the heart. That's what Lucifer instructed.'

Lucy gazed at the wondrous figure flickering into existence in front of her eyes. They had said that the Shekinah was the beautiful earthly presence of the Creator, but that didn't do it justice. It was majestic beyond words. An impossible dream, a glimmering, shining beacon of infinite hope, beauty in every form.

And suddenly there it was, fully in this world. The Shekinah was not so much female as androgynous, but spectacularly, unfeasibly beautiful. The orange light had become a brilliant, dazzling white. The shining figure opened its eyes and they were blue like a sky in a perfect world. If ever God existed, this was God.

Then two extraordinary things happened at once. The Shekinah started to dissolve, replaced by a new, indescribable light beyond anything Lucy had seen in her life. And a Robin Redbreast bird fluttered into the Holy of Holies, landing on the lid of the Ark, just under the Mercy Seat. It began twittering, oblivious to everything around it.

'Do it now,' Sinclair bellowed. 'Strike. Straight at the heart.'

Lucy raised the spear, but now it felt heavy, unbelievably heavy, so heavy she thought she must surely drop it. Everything seemed to be pressing down on her, like the sky on the shoulders of Atlas. She glanced down at her father's locket round her neck, at his glinting ring she'd put on her finger.

The birdsong reached into her mind. *Let the birds sing.* She could hear James' dying voice. *Let them sing of how much I loved you.* The Robin Redbreast took off again and flew in a circle around her head.

'Now!' Sinclair shrieked. 'There's no time left.'

Lucy knew exactly what her father would do, what James would do, what love, *life* demanded. Suddenly the spear felt weightless. It knew exactly what was in her mind, where she wanted to throw the spear.

Hurling it with all her might, it flew forward at fantastic speed and instantly struck its target straight in the heart.

'No!' Sinclair screamed. He staggered forward, staring in disbelief at the spear embedded in the chest of the towering black figure behind the Ark. Lucifer reeled backwards, his huge wings coming apart. He tore down the gold curtain as he collapsed to the ground, letting out a hideous gasp.

Lucy went behind the Ark and watched Lucifer crawling forward, making a pitiful wheezing sound. He managed to get as far as the altar bearing the Ark, and reach out towards the Lucifer Stone sitting on top of the Stone of Destiny. He rolled onto his back and looked up, clutching the Lucifer Stone to his chest. For a second, his body shimmered. The blackness was replaced by a light so bright it was as though the whole world, the whole universe, had lit up.

The dying figure was transformed into a supernaturally radiant angel with brilliant golden eyes, so handsome it made Lucy feel winded, dizzy, sick. He was made of an ethereal, shimmering substance, with twelve perfect wings glistening with living gold. Then he was gone, taking the Lucifer Stone with him, leaving nothing but a pile of ash and a cloud of black dust behind the Ark. A gust of cold wind dispersed the ashes.

'What have you done?' Sinclair screeched. 'Lucifer, Son of the Morning, the Shining One, the Brilliant One, Helel Bel Shaar, Angel of the Morning, Son of the Dawn. *You've destroyed him.*'

Crazed with fury, he took his sword and ran towards the Ark. He swiped at the new figure taking shape above the Ark, but the sword went right through it.

The figure, rapidly becoming less hazy, its features growing more defined with each passing second, sent out filaments of multicoloured light that grasped the Spear of Destiny where it lay on the floor and raised it up. Clutching the spear in its left hand, it pointed towards Sinclair with its right, then, palm-upwards, slowly raised its translucent hand. Screaming, Sinclair was lifted off the ground by an invisible force. He hung suspended in mid-air, cursing madly. The figure clenched its fist then released. Sinclair was hurled backwards through the air and slammed against the far wall. The impact was so violent, his head shattered. Blood, brains and fragments of skull slid down the wall.

Lucy looked away, appalled. She knelt down, closing her eyes. It was too painful to look. Putting her hands over her ears, she tried to shut out the sounds, but it was impossible to block out the screams of the others. It seemed that, one by one, the figure was turning on each of Cain's priesthood, destroying them with fiery beams from its eyes and from the tip of the Spear of Destiny. She heard Morson yelling and firing his pistol, each shot booming like a cannon. Then came a grotesque scream.

The Temple shook more violently than ever. Lucy tried to block the thoughts running through her head. She kept her eyes closed. *I'm going to faint.* She wanted to be oblivious to everything around her. Even through her closed eyelids, she could see brilliant lights. The gold curtain had caught fire. The smell of smoke was overpowering. In her mind, Raphael's mural flashed up. It was burning. Everything was burning. Her heart, her soul. The whole world was on fire. Burn it, burn it all. Incinerate the whole of Creation.

Her eyes sprang open again. The figure above the Ark had fully materialised and was staring straight at her. Slumping forward, she threw up, then slid into her own vomit. The figure was laughing, the sound growing louder and louder until the Holy of Holies shook with the noise.

There was only one thought in Lucy's mind.

God of Mercy – what have I done?

85

One Month Later

The paramedics helped Gresnick down from the back of the ambulance. They had allowed him just one hour for his visit. His doctor told him he shouldn't be leaving hospital at all, but Gresnick felt he must come here to find out what finally happened.

They handed him his walking stick, and he struggled towards the convent's entrance doors. It gave him such a strange feeling to be back in Glastonbury. In hospital in Bristol, he'd thought of nothing else than that night in Glastonbury Tor. He was told he was knocked out by one of the falling statues. Blood loss caused by his leg wounds left him close to death. Another hour and it would have all been over, one doctor said.

It seemed that the nuns in the convent that fateful night saw the whole of Glastonbury Tor lighting up from inside and thought they were witnessing the Second Coming. As soon as dawn came up, on the most beautiful day they'd ever seen, the nuns went to the Tor. What they found was Lucy, wearing beautiful vestments and standing in the centre of a circle of cherry blossom trees. The trees had shed all of their beautiful pink blossom, but instead of falling to the ground, it was swirling all around Lucy, forming strange patterns, almost like great fingers caressing her. One nun said it was as though the Hand of God were holding her. Thousands of Robin Redbreasts were in the trees, singing to her. White butterflies fluttered around her head like a living halo. A rainbow of the most vibrant colours curved over the grove.

Yet the nuns said Lucy was in the worse state of shock they'd ever seen. She looked, they claimed, as though she'd just emerged from hell. Over and over, she repeated one thing: *Forgive me.*

The nuns soon discovered the entrance to the hidden Temple. They went inside and encountered a nightmarish scene. Everyone was dead apart from Gresnick, and he had only the faintest of pulses. They carried him out and drove Lucy and him to a military hospital in Bristol. Lucy was quickly discharged back into their care when it was confirmed she had no physical injuries.

Gresnick shook his head. *No physical injuries.* Lucy was hurt worse than anyone. Mental wounds went so much deeper.

Limping heavily, he tried to negotiate his way through the convent's front doors. Two nuns came out to help him: Sisters Mary and Bernadette, the ones who had carried him out of the Temple. He felt grateful and yet somehow ashamed to see them. He poured out his thanks once again, but was anxious to get away.

Commander Harrington, Gary Caldwell and Dr Wells from MI5 had agreed to meet him here. They'd been in the Glastonbury area for the last week, attempting to piece together what happened, to prepare a detailed report for the Director General and the PM, and to respond to questions raised by religious leaders. Gresnick was eager to discover if the commander had managed to make any sense of those final hours in the early morning of 30 April.

The nuns escorted him to the small chapel where Harrington and his staff had set up their office.

'Good to see you.' Harrington extended his hand and gave Gresnick a firm handshake. 'I hear your wounds are healing satisfactorily.'

That was one way of putting it. Too slowly for Gresnick. Harrington had visited him twice in hospital, but he couldn't remember a single thing about what they discussed. He suspected he'd been incoherent, what with the pain and the drugs. Caldwell had stopped by too, but Gresnick recalled that the young agent didn't seem interested in getting his story from him. Maybe it was understandable. After so many catastrophes, people were preoccupied with getting their own lives back on track.

'Sit down, colonel,' Harrington said. 'I'll bring you up to date with what's been going on. I guess there's a lot you want to know. Here, let's get you a coffee first. Strong and black, right?'

Caldwell was despatched to get the coffees and soon returned with a tray of espressos. They sat looking at the altar as they sipped their drinks. Gresnick wondered if Lucy had once sat here too, transfixed by the gold crucifix in the centre of the altar.

'You know,' Harrington said, 'scientists are claiming the earth is now more stable than at any time in history. *Catastrophic Realignment Theory* – that's what they're calling it. Apparently, the world reaches a point of massive instability where everything starts happening at once – fault lines moving, massive earthquakes, volcanoes erupting, tsunamis, hurricanes, magnetic storms, you name it. It's as though someone has turned a valve to release a huge pressure that's been building for millions of years. Now the pressure's gone and they're saying we can look forward to a thousand years of unprecedentedly benign weather all across the globe. The earth sparkles now, as though it's been cleaned and polished. They're not expecting any more natural disasters for a long, long time. We'll be able to rebuild in peace.'

Despite the optimistic things he was saying, he sounded weary. 'They reckon four billion died, two thirds of the world's population, but it should be a golden age for the rest of us if we can successfully reconstruct our old way of life.'

Gresnick was bemused. Already, the dead were being forgotten. Civilisation in South America, Africa and Asia had practically ceased to exist. Most of North America was in ruins too. Boston, where his parents lived, was the only major American city to survive intact. Huge swathes of territory would be uninhabitable for centuries to come. Only Australia and mainland Europe escaped the worst, but millions died in England when the asteroid exploded over the centre of the country, and hundreds of thousands of others perished when the crisis was at its height.

Even so, everything was getting back to normal with surprising speed. The London Stock Exchange was up and running again and was actually surging ahead – a million new investment opportunities. Capitalism could never be defeated, it seemed.

Harrington said a new Pope had been elected – the first-ever black Pope. It was being hailed as a wonderful sign from God, ushering in a new age of tolerance and racial harmony. Already, talks were well underway between the Vatican, the Anglican Church and the Eastern Orthodox Church about reuniting the main strands of Christianity. Even many of the anti-Catholic Protestant leaders were beginning to make conciliatory noises. Some optimistic commentators were claiming that there was a one-time opportunity to unite all of the different religions and produce a single world faith.

Dr Wells came into the chapel, wearing a smart linen suit, and looking remarkably more comfortable than when Gresnick last saw him in Thames House. Bizarrely, he was eating fish and chips wrapped in old newspaper.

'Good to see you, colonel,' Wells said. 'I was delighted when I heard you were still alive. It's tragic James didn't make it. He was a good friend.'

Gresnick said nothing. He didn't want to think about Vernon.

'What on earth have you got there?' Harrington asked, gesturing at Wells's lunch.

'The fish and chip shop on the high street has reopened. You can't believe how much I've been looking forward to this. They even had brown sauce.' He held out the bag towards Harrington. 'Want a chip? The fish is haddock. No cod. First delivery of fish arrived this morning. A miracle, really, given the state of the oceans a few weeks ago.'

Harrington peered at the fish and shook his head.

'Colonel?' Wells turned to Gresnick. 'You must admit – the smell is amazing.'

It was true. The smell of vinegar from the food was almost overpowering. But Gresnick was concentrating on something else. 'The newspaper,' he said, pointing at the wrapper for the fish and chips.

Wells peered at it then gave an embarrassed shrug.

'I'm sorry, I didn't realise.'

'Let me look at it.'

Wells reluctantly handed over the old sheet of newspaper. 'This was printed at the height of the crisis,' he explained. 'No one understood what was happening back then. Scientists hadn't formulated Catastrophic Realignment Theory.'

Gresnick stared, horrified, at the colour photograph on the newspaper.

Humanity's last hope? the headline above the picture said. Underneath the photo was a single word – *Messiah*.

'God Almighty,' Gresnick said. 'How did Lucy's picture end up in a newspaper?'

'I guess the whole world went a bit crazy,' Wells said. 'It was the Vatican that said humanity should pray for Lucy, that she was the only thing standing between the human race and Armageddon. Everyone wanted to believe it was true.'

'What are you talking about?' Gresnick continued to stare disbelievingly at the picture. All the time he was with Lucy, she was dishevelled, without a trace of make-up, yet, despite that, she had a tremendous natural beauty. Here, her raven hair was neatly combed, her blue eyes shining, her face smothered with expensive cosmetics. Some sort of publicity shot. She looked simply stunning.

'Psychologists concluded that mass hysteria erupted during the week of catastrophes,' Wells said. 'The realisation that the world really could be ending cracked everyone's minds. That's why most of us were ready to believe in a Messiah. We would have believed anything that allowed us to think there was still a chance. But, I mean, how could a woman from an asylum possibly save the world? One leading psychiatrist said the sanctification of a lunatic was symptomatic of the craziness that enveloped everyone. End of story.'

End of story? Gresnick could scarcely believe what he was hearing. 'Doctor, you swore one of our prisoners turned into an angel. Were *you* temporarily insane?'

'I'm not proud of myself. I wasn't immune from the hysteria. I admit it.'

'But you weren't the only one to see the angel. I did too. Others as well, but they're all dead now.'

'Was it really an angel you saw?' Harrington asked. 'Maybe it was just a collective hallucination, like the psychologists said.'

'The angel was there right at the end, in the Temple. It wasn't any old angel. It was the Dark Lord himself.'

'Listen to yourself, colonel. I know I'm never going to write a report saying there was a supernatural being in our interrogation cells in Thames House. I certainly won't be saying the Devil paid us a visit. If you know what's good for you, you'll keep quiet too.'

'But I was in the Temple. I saw what happened. Someone has to bear witness.'

'As far as we know, you were unconscious at the end,' Wells said. 'You were badly wounded and losing a lot of blood. At times like that, the mind plays all kinds of tricks. You might have been dreaming for all we know. The bottom line is that only two people survived whatever went on in the Temple. One is a patient in this asylum, and the other wasn't in a position to clearly see what happened. Isn't it better just to leave it at that? What could possibly be gained from probing any further?'

'The *truth*,' Gresnick snapped.

'What is truth?' Harrington asked.

'That's exactly what Pontius Pilate said.'

'Well, sometimes it's best to wash your own hands of the things you can't control. If you want to resume your career – maybe get yourself a promotion – then you'd be well advised to do the same.'

'What about the Temple?'

'Structural engineers had a look at it. They said it could collapse at any time. After the bodies were removed, we concreted over the entrance.'

'What?'

'Two thirds of the world's population are dead, colonel. The planet faces the biggest rebuilding job in its history. We're satisfied now that whatever happened in the Temple had no bearing on world events. I mean, how could it? We have more important things to do than waste our time on wild goose chases. The crime scene has been preserved, so maybe years from now we'll be able to go back and make some final sense of what happened in there.'

'This is insane.' Gresnick was practically shouting. 'The Ark of the Covenant is in there, and the Spear of Destiny. *Jesus Christ*...the Holy Grail.'

'So you say, colonel. We don't deny there were several spectacular objects in there, but we don't know if they're authentic, and frankly, we're not overly concerned right now. You claim you encountered the supernatural, but in London we were confronting plain old human panic. We didn't see any of what you witnessed. Like I said, we now have a world to reconstruct. In this country alone, five million people died. Do you think the survivors care about myths and legends? They just want to get their old lives back.'

Gresnick shook his head. 'I don't believe this. You're burying the truth. You're trying to airbrush Lucy out of history.'

'She's insane, Colonel Gresnick.'

'God Almighty, she saved the world. I don't care what anyone says, she *did*. We owe her everything. There should be a statue of her in every town.'

'Believe me, colonel,' Harrington stated, 'Lucy Galahan will never feature in the history books. There's not a shred of proof that she accomplished anything. She became the focus of hysteria, a kind of latter-day Joan of Arc. She's not the first and I'm sure she won't be the last.'

'The truth is inside Glastonbury Tor, commander. The people have to know what happened, what Lucy did for us.'

'As I've said, the contents of the Temple aren't a priority right now. I suspect it will be years before anyone gets round to studying them.'

'What about Morson's men?'

'Their uniforms were found lying on the floor with some black powder inside them. Who knows what happened to them? All over the world, people died in horrific and bizarre ways. We can't investigate every suspicious death.'

Gresnick felt numb. Jesus, they were really going through with this. They were prepared to pretend the most momentous event in human history never happened. God had actually appeared on the earth, and Gnostic fanatics led by Sinclair and Morson tried to assassinate him, and only Lucy's heroic decision to hurl the Spear of Destiny at Lucifer instead of God saved the whole of Creation from instant annihilation.

It was impossible not to contrast the religious fanaticism of Sinclair and the others with the casual secularism of Harrington and Wells. If those two were to be believed, nothing supernatural had happened: God and the Devil had played no part in the events of April.

'I need some air before I see Lucy,' Gresnick said.

'Sure. There's a side-door just down the corridor. Shall I come with you?'

'No, I'd like to be by myself.'

Gresnick hobbled out of the chapel and made his way along the corridor. He felt sick. Lucy deserved everything but was getting nothing. She was an embarrassment to the authorities. The Vatican now claimed it was the prayers of good Catholics everywhere that had saved the world. Lucy, it said, was a troubled young woman whose significance was mistakenly exaggerated. Incredibly, they emphasised instead that Cardinal Sinclair died a hero's death, giving his own life to save Lucy from the hands of sinister anti-Catholic forces. They were talking about making him a saint. Gresnick had heard it all now.

As he went out into the car park, he gazed at the beautiful orange sun and the sky that had never seemed so blue. Ever since April 30, all across the world, the weather was perfect. All the dust and dirt particles that were thrown into the sky during the crisis, threatening to block out the sun and bring a lethal permanent winter, had miraculously vanished. Scientists blithely said they'd discovered self-regulating and self-cleansing mechanisms in nature, which, they asserted, rapidly reversed the ill effects of all the disasters. What did *they* know? Just mindless hypothesising. It was God who made everything right, who healed the wounds he'd chosen to inflict on the world because of man's sinfulness.

Gresnick couldn't help thinking about ROMA AMOR. Everything was back to front in this new world. Already, it was off to the worst possible start, founding itself on lies. No one seemed to understand that the reason the earth was so stable now, the weather so benign and beautiful, was that God had made it that way to reward the human race for Lucy's refusal to go through with the Gnostics' insane plan. Lucy, Gresnick knew, could never have killed God since that was impossible by definition, but if she'd thrown the Spear of Destiny at God, it would have been the final proof that humanity was irredeemably lost. Instantly, God would have eliminated the human race once and for all. Only Lucy had stood between humanity and extermination.

He wondered what would happen when the Temple was eventually reopened years from now. What would be done with the Ark and the Grail Hallows? Should they be destroyed to make sure none of this ever happened again? He feared they'd be turned into a tourist attraction in due course and millions would flock to see them, and not understand a single thing of their true significance. Not for one moment would they imagine that these ancient relics concealed the deadliest secret of all.

Gresnick noticed another old newspaper blowing past him in the cool breeze. He stopped the paper with his walking stick. It was dated 10 May and again showed Lucy's picture on the front cover with a headline: *Remember Her? – The False Messiah*, and underneath; *See Page 5 for ten other fake Messiahs*.

So, it hadn't taken the media long to get back up and running, and they'd reverted to their bad old ways without skipping a beat. The world had learned nothing. The human race was as nasty as ever.

Gresnick felt tears welling in his eyes. Of all the people in the world who didn't deserve this, Lucy was that person. She never asked for any of it. Not once did she make any claims for herself. She was always humble and meek. He'd never met anyone so gentle and kind, so concerned for others. Yet the world wanted to mock her. If they could, they would sit her on the back of a donkey and parade her along the streets of every town in the country so that people could throw rotten fruit at her. She'd become the world's scapegoat. She was the ideal person for the role – she couldn't defend herself.

The truth was that the whole world had gone mad with fear for a week. Rather than confront that, reality it was so much easier to say Lucy was the only mad person. Now that she was safely locked up, she had taken everyone else's craziness with her.

The world felt ashamed of how it behaved in that week of horror, how it went to pieces. It didn't like what it saw in the mirror. Now people just wanted to forget. Lucy, sadly, reminded them of everything they wanted to bury.

Gresnick didn't like to admit it to himself, but he'd fallen in love with Lucy. The reason he tried to avoid thinking about it was that he knew he wasn't worthy of her. No one was. If anyone truly was a Messiah, she was. She was far too good, too full of heart and kindness, too sensitive, to be a normal member of the human race. She lacked that savagery that everyone else thrives on.

He limped back inside. His insides were churning. There was no future for him in the military anymore. Not just because he wasn't fit for active service any longer. He simply didn't have the stomach for it now.

His grandfather's theories were right in practically every regard. There *had* been a ten-thousand-year-old deadly conspiracy to kill God, dating all the way back to Cain. The Gnostics, the Cathars, the Knights Templar, the Alchemists, the Freemasons and the Nazis were all involved. It was over now, thanks to Lucy. Was the danger gone forever? That was another question. Out there, there would be new Gnostics, and they might rediscover the secrets of those who went before them. Maybe, one day, they'd try again, and maybe, on that occasion, there would be no Lucy to stop them.

When he got back to the convent, he found Dr Wells finishing his fish and chips. Gary Caldwell was hunched in front of a computer, while Harrington gazed at the sunlight as it shone through the small stained glass walls, laying tiles of different colours on the chapel's cool stone floor.

'Such lovely weather we're having now,' Harrington said.

Gresnick sat down again. He gazed at the figure of Christ on the gold cross on the altar. For a moment, he imagined Lucy up there on that cross. The media had crucified her for absolutely no reason.

'What do you think you'll do now?' Harrington asked.

Gresnick bowed his head. He had no idea what the future held for him. Maybe he'd go back and stay with his parents for a while.

'I wouldn't write your memoirs,' Harrington said. 'I don't think the DIA would appreciate it. Besides, no one would believe you. We certainly wouldn't corroborate any of your material. As far as we're concerned, the world suffered a series of unpredictable natural disasters, that's it. There were no supernatural forces at play. As we assumed all along, the theft of religious artefacts had no connection with the catastrophes. Nothing bizarre happened. No gods or devils came to the earth.'

He smiled in a way that made Gresnick nauseous.

'If you want to have a bright future, or indeed any kind of healthy future, colonel, I seriously advise you to stick to that script.'

Gresnick turned and looked the commander in the eye. 'Forget the official script. What do you *really* believe?'

Harrington gave a half-smile. 'I honestly don't know. If you're asking me if Lucy was some sort of Chosen One who saved the world, I'd deny it utterly. Look at her now – deranged. She's painting crazy pictures again. They're even more disturbed than before.'

'I was there, commander. You weren't.'

'We've been through this before. You were probably unconscious. Maybe you bumped your head. Maybe you were hallucinating. What did you really see? When I first spoke to you in hospital, you were rambling. At one point, you said God materialised above the Ark of the Covenant. I mean, how can anyone take that seriously?'

'I know what went on, I *know*. Lucy saved us all, and this is how we repay her, putting her back here in this madhouse. There must be something we can do. She needs help from someone who understands what she went through.'

'From *you*? You love her, don't you?'

'I...' Gresnick's voice tailed off. He turned away in embarrassment.

'I'm afraid I have to mention some of the odd things that have been happening to her lately,' Harrington said.

'Odd things?'

'She's become a fully-fledged stigmatic, manifesting all five of the wounds of Jesus. She has wounds on her ankles and wrists matching those where Christ was nailed to the Cross, as well as a wound on her side, exactly where the Spear of Destiny pierced Jesus. She's heavily bandaged because her blood won't clot. The wounds stay fresh, but they don't become infected and her blood seems to continually replenish itself so that she doesn't need a transfusion. Her blood gives off a strange, perfumed odour. She's in extreme pain all the time.'

'My God, I had no idea.'

'You should have been here a few days ago. Bleeding welts appeared on her back as though she'd been scourged, and hundreds of bloody marks were visible on her forehead, as though someone had ripped a crown of thorns from her head. Thankfully, those marks all disappeared within twenty-four hours, leaving just the stigmata. The media said her wounds were self-inflicted. Doctors say her disturbed mind is producing these weird effects.'

'What about the nuns? What do they say?'

'Oh, they're certain it's all genuine. They think Lucy is a saint. They've started calling her things like *Holy Lucy* and *Blessed Lucy*. They never throw out any of her old bandages. Everything is kept. I think they're going to build a shrine to her.'

'Jesus, this is some kind of nightmare.'

'Come on, there's no point in putting it off any longer. I'll take you to her.'

Afterwards, Gresnick couldn't remember anything about the short journey he made along the narrow corridors leading from the chapel to Lucy's small room. The closer he got to Lucy, the more his mind tormented him. He couldn't bear to think of the suffering she was enduring.

'Here's Lucy's room,' Harrington said when they arrived outside her tiny cell. Her name was written on a small whiteboard on the door, with a silver crucifix beneath it. 'She's gone somewhere in her head,' Harrington remarked, 'and I don't think she's ever coming back.'

'Let me see her.'

Harrington knocked on the door, and it edged open. A nun peered out.

'Colonel Gresnick is here to see Lucy,' Harrington said and the nun nodded. The room behind her was dark, lit only by candles. Slowly, she opened the door and beckoned Gresnick in.

As he stepped inside, Gresnick felt his stomach churning. Every hair on his body stood on end. Lucy was standing in the corner in black pyjamas with her back turned to him, mumbling to herself.

'*Lucy*,' he said quietly.

She didn't move, but stopped muttering.

The nun went up to her and put her hand lightly on her shoulder.

'Lucy, a friend has come to see you. An American soldier. You'd like to see Colonel Gresnick, wouldn't you?'

At first, Lucy didn't react and then, painfully slowly, she started to turn. More and more of her features appeared in the dim candlelight.

When she turned round completely, Gresnick wished he had never come here. She looked ghastly, almost supernaturally pale, her hair horribly dishevelled, her hands and feet tightly wrapped in white bandages, with blood seeping through them.

Her eyes briefly focused on him. Instantly, she burst into tears, grabbed the pillow from her bed and buried her face in it.

Gresnick twisted away in revulsion, but it wasn't Lucy's reaction that then made every part of him turn cold. He thrust his hand over his mouth, trying not to vomit. 'No one told me,' he screamed, pushing past the nun to get out of the room.

Harrington was standing outside, hands in pockets. 'Maybe you understand now, colonel. That's why this has to end here.'

Gresnick grabbed him by the lapels. 'You bastard, you should have warned me.'

'You needed to see for yourself.'

Gresnick turned away, his heart pounding. This wasn't possible. It couldn't have happened that way. 'My God,' he said, 'what have we done?'

The image in his mind would never be erased. As Lucy turned to grab her pillow, he'd taken his eyes off her for the first time and looked at the rest of the room. It was covered with scores of paintings, every one of them showing a single figure against a blue background, just like those in Lucy's cell when this whole thing first started. But now the figure had changed. Under each was scrawled a message, the despairing words of Kafka: *Infinite hope, but not for us.*

Gresnick started walking away, practically stabbing his walking stick against the tiled floor to allow him to go faster. He longed to run, but his legs wouldn't let him. Excruciating pains shot through them. Glancing down, he reeled as he saw fresh blood staining his trousers.

'Gresnick?' Harrington shouted after him. 'Where are you going?'

Gresnick's legs were in agony, but it didn't match the pain in his head. *Dear God.* The figure in Lucy's paintings was no longer a woman with dark hair and a blank face. Now it was a masculine figure, with a face as recognisable as any you could ever imagine. The figure had other features, like those of no one on earth. The scaly skin, the tail. Above all, the two horns, familiar from a million terrifying medieval depictions. Now he knew beyond doubt what Lucy saw in the Temple of Solomon. There was no question this was the figure she saw seen hovering above the Ark of the Covenant. As long as he lived, he wouldn't be able to escape it. It would haunt his every step, torment him with every breath he took.

The *God* Lucy saw was the one no good person would ever want to encounter. One name resounded in Gresnick's head, an inescapable name. He was branded with it as though it were the Mark of Cain itself. It represented the destruction of all his hopes, the end of every dream.

'I know what she saw,' he screamed into the corridor, to himself, to Harrington, to anyone who could hear. He was hoping, praying someone would grant him absolution. But there was no forgiveness for this. His words echoed in the corridor, becoming horribly amplified, rebounding off every surface as though they were determined to pursue him, to haunt him, to taunt him, for the rest of his life, and for all eternity in the hell that surely now awaited him.

'Not God, not God,' he screamed. '*Satan.*'

'Don't be alarmed, colonel.' The nun had followed him and was now gazing down at him. 'Lucy met the Devil, triumphed over him and saved us all. It's only natural that she should paint these pictures.'

Gresnick lay there in shock, struggling to regain his composure, to convince himself he hadn't gone insane. 'Does she ever speak?' He fought to stop his voice shaking. Pains more excruciating than ever were shooting through his legs.

'Not a word since she came back to her room. She's a conduit for God now. All of her communication is saved for him alone.'

Gresnick tried desperately to find anything he could cling to, the tiniest hope, a single particle of consolation, to stop him going under just like Lucy. There must be a chance of redemption. It couldn't end like this, it just couldn't. Some sort of good had to survive.

'Colonel, your legs...we'll need to take you to our medical centre.'

'No,' he snapped. 'I'm OK.' He gazed back towards Lucy's room. 'Can I be alone with her?' He shielded his face to hide the tears welling in his eyes. If nothing was salvageable, there was no point in going on.

The nun glanced at Harrington and he nodded his assent. 'Well, just for a few minutes.'

Gresnick struggled back to his feet. He dragged himself back to Lucy's cell, ignoring Harrington. He went inside and closed the door behind him. Gently, he removed the pillow that Lucy was still pressing to her face. 'It's not all over,' he said softly. 'We can fight this, Lucy.'

There was no response. She didn't utter a sound. Her eyes had become glassy, refusing to focus.

'I was too scared to tell you this,' he whispered, tidying away stray hairs that had fallen over her eyes. 'I love you.'

There wasn't a flicker from Lucy. Lifeless eyes...her spirit, her energy all gone.

Holding back his tears, Gresnick turned towards the paintings. He detested them more than anything on earth. They'd stolen Lucy from him. In a frenzy, he tore them down, every last one, ripping them to shreds with all the strength he possessed.

'I don't care what you saw, Lucy. I don't care about any of it. I just want us to be together. We need each other to get through this. We can help each other. I'll take care of you until you're better. You'll be well again, I promise.'

He hugged her, but her body was limp. No reaction at all. She was gone, and never coming back. He turned away, desolate, struggling to breathe.

As he reached the door, he heard a sound. He froze. Lucy's voice?

'What?' He spun round. She was looking straight at him, her eyes bright with tears. In an instant, he had crossed the space between them, throwing his arms round her and hugging her for dear life, almost crushing her against his chest. 'Speak to me again, Lucy, I beg you.'

Then it happened. Her voice was unable to rise above the faintest whisper, but he heard every word with perfect clarity. As he felt her hand squeezing his, he started laughing and crying at the same time.

'That's right, Lucy, that's right,' he said, overwhelmed by joy. 'There's infinite hope, infinite hope, all the hope in the world.

Even for us.'

CONSUMMATUM EST

Printed in Great Britain
by Amazon.co.uk, Ltd.,
Marston Gate.